CROSSING OVER

INTO THE LIGHT

DANIEL FRANK

Published by: CT3 Publishing
Printed in the United States of America
First Printing, 2020

ISBN Numbers
(paperback) 978-1-7347099-0-2
(eBook) 978-1-7347099-1-9

Social Media
Instagram: @danielfrankwriting
Facebook: Daniel Frank Writing
Email: ct3publishing@gmail.com

Credits
Developmental Editor: Brad Fruhaff, The Pen & Pint
Copy Editor: Anna Vera, Writerverse Editing
Proofreader: Ashley Swanson
Book Cover Design: Molly Phipps, We Got You Covered Book Design
Book Cover Concept Development: Aaron Holliday
Formatting: Nada Qamber, Qamber Designs & Media

First Edition, Volume I

DEDICATIONS

MOM:

We lost you March 2, 2013 and I can still hear your boisterous laugh. I hear your voice guiding me whenever a gentle breeze hits my windchimes. Clarke and I know you are near whenever we see a yellow swallowtail.

CLARKE ADDISON:

Stay true to yourself and never apologize for following your dreams, no matter how big. Be kind to others and yourself. If it's challenging, it's probably worth seeing through. BelievE.

TRIPP JACKSON:

Make your own rules, but do so in a humble manner. Be respectful, but never let anyone define who you are. BelievE.

TIM, BILL, & KELLY:

In the time since Mom passed away, we have never been closer—and for that, I am grateful. Mom would be proud of what we've become.

FORWARD

Years later, I still remember getting that call. It was 2012. My phone rang. My mom's nervous voice on the other end. She was never the excitable type, and I knew right away something was wrong.

"My kidneys are failing again."

A genetic degenerative kidney disease with no cure. She already had a transplant thirteen years prior. Her kidney function hit a point where she needed to go on the transplant list again, and she was nervous she wouldn't find a donor in time. I called her hospital and put my name on the donor list. I got my blood drawn. A little while later, I received the news we were a match.

Stubborn as she was, she wouldn't move forward with the transplant.

"What if you get in a car accident and it's on the side where you only have one kidney?"

I told her we could think of a hundred scenarios of why we shouldn't go through with it—but she was going to die if we didn't. She finally agreed, after some helpful coercing from my siblings. I started planning. I told my boss I may have to miss some time at work. I drew a tattoo that I planned to get on my side to cover the scar. I was ready.

I received another phone call. Mom was in the hospital. In a coma. She was a nurse and craved the action of the ER floor. She knew the risks. It was well known that people with organ transplants have compromised immune systems, and working in the ER was no place for her . . . I'd begged her to take the training job that was open, but she loved the action, fueled by her stubborn compassion for helping others.

"I got into nursing to help people. I can't help anyone behind a training desk."

A rare viral infection of the brain. Encephalopathy was the final diagnosis— although the doctors never found exactly what caused it. She never made the transplant list, and I was never able to donate my kidney. She passed ten months later on March 2, 2013.

I experienced two different dreams on consecutive nights just before her passing. Dreams so vivid they've stayed with me to this day. Dreams about the afterlife. I wrestle with the purpose and timing of the dreams. The logical part of me says these dreams were just stress. The spiritual side says they were a gift sent to make me comfortable with the idea of where my mom was going.

I wrote the dreams down. Something told me to keep going. Keep writing. Editing. Writing. Tearing it apart and rewriting. Piece by piece. It took me a while, but here it is. Seven years later.

Crossing Over: Into the Light . . . The story of the two dreams that have stayed with me since 2012.

I couldn't save your life . . . but I can tell this story. This is for you, Mom.

ACT I

PART ONE
PETE STANTON
THE CAR CRASH

PETE WAS REALLY CRUISING—HE'D LONG since left the speed limit behind. He was trying to make a meeting, of course, and of course he'd likely be late.

"Slow down—you're going to be late anyway!" he told himself over the sports radio analysis of the Eagles' chances of making it back to the Super Bowl. He had to admit, the fans were tough here in Philadelphia.

But he was making really good time, and a part of him believed he was actually going to make it.

His Audi A8 screamed down the road when he suddenly felt something vibrating against his chest. A quick glance at the car touchscreen showed his phone hadn't connected to Bluetooth. He fished around in the inside breast pocket of his suit coat and located his phone.

Jessica. He had left before she awoke, so he was happy to hear from her now.

He cursed his Bluetooth as he tried putting her on speakerphone while keeping his eyes on the streak of road his Audi ravenously ate up.

"Hello? Jess?"

"Pete? Are you there?" came Jess's voice over the tiny speakers.

"Hi! You're on speaker . . . I can hear you," said Pete. "I'm so glad to hear your voice before I get to work. I can't stop thinking about how great the weekend was."

"Mmmmm. Me too," said Jess. "Mondays always sneak up on us, don't they?"

Pete smiled at the sound of her voice. He could tell she was just rolling out of bed.

"They sure do. Maybe we can extend one of our trips an extra day or two, sometime. Give us more time together."

More time. He never had enough time with her.

"I like the sound of that," she said, but maybe she emphasized *sound* a

1

little. "But there's my research, you know. I'm so *close*, Pete. I can feel it. I need to be here. Close to it. A couple days away is great for a break, but I'd start to get antsy after that."

"Yeah, yeah, I understand," he said, and he did, though it disappointed him.

"But—when I have this breakthrough, when I get this case study figured out—then we can take, like, a whole month together. How does that sound?"

He straightened up in his seat. It sounded pretty good.

"I think I'd be motivated to make that work," he said. "I have some big client meetings coming up these next few days, but hopefully I can make my client work coincide with your research. Hell, I could bring some work along if I had to."

"Santorini for a week or two, and Rome after that?" He could hear the smile on her lips. "Maybe we'll just move to Riomaggiore and never come back."

"Shall I book the flight today?" he offered with a chuckle.

"I *wish*."

He had to slow down a tad to navigate the traffic crossing the bridge. He could just see out of the corner of his eye that the sun was still coming up—it flamed down the river in gold and red.

"Jess," he said suddenly. "I just want to say I am madly in love with you. Since the first day I saw you, eight years ago . . . I'm still hooked—"

The asphalt on the bridge was wet. He hadn't realized until he felt his tires skidding.

His rear-end swerved as his tires failed to grip the road. He was careening out of control but remained too focused on talking with Jessica to have seen it. *The bump.* The sound of his undercarriage scraping the asphalt signaled his car had just bottomed out. Trying to control the wheel, he fumbled his phone; it bounced off the center console and clattered down between it and the seat.

Without thinking, his head followed the fall, and before he could look up he heard the bellow of a tractor trailer. He was drifting into oncoming traffic, where his Audi was about to lose a lopsided fight with a Peterbilt.

Swearing, he pulled the wheel to the right—much too hard for the speed he was going—and nearly sideswiped a bright red Prius. Pete managed to right himself just in time, but he'd scared half the cars on the road, not to mention himself. A cacophony of car horns faded behind him as he sped away from the scene of his own carelessness.

Cursing again, he fished around for his phone—now in a space where he could feel the edge of it with his fingertips, but couldn't quite grasp it.

"Pete," he could barely hear Jess saying, "you forgot your lunch. Pete, are you there?"

He guessed she hadn't heard any of the near-accident, nor was she acknowledging his spontaneous outburst of affection—but that was Jess. Ever the task master. More concerned about his lunch sitting on the counter than Pete's words of endearment. Add it all up and the morning had taken a rather embarrassing turn.

"Don't hang up! I have to tell you something!" Pete yelled, continuing to fish around, the tip of his finger feeling for the touchscreen but unable to find it.

He must have somehow activated the Bluetooth, because Jessica's voice suddenly came over the car speakers.

"Pete, are you there? What happened?"

"Jessica . . ." he said in relief. "I'm okay."

Except that he wasn't. His head was racing, his breath short and labored. He should have slowed down after that near miss. He should have pulled over. He should have forgotten about the phone. *He should have. He should have.*

His drive took him on a road that ran along a hill just above a large, forested park. It was a pleasant kind of park to look at when you could steal a view while winding up and down the hill.

But he hadn't been looking. He hadn't hardly been *thinking* at all. Not until he looked up in time to see a particularly sharp, difficult turn. He knew immediately that he wouldn't make it.

Pete was a lawyer, not a stunt car driver. What did he know about high-stakes driving? Not much beyond what a child knows: push down hard on the gas and see how fast you can go. Well, he was going fast—too fast for the brakes to have time to slow him down enough to hold the curve.

He stood on the pedal anyway, and he pulled at the wheel, and he could hear someone yelling as though in a battle cry. Wheels screeched. The other cars were honking helplessly. The Audi slammed through the guardrail and leapt off the road.

He careened down the small ravine, bracing himself for impact. He tried to control the steering wheel, but it jolted him with every bump.

That's when he saw the tree.

His senses suddenly heightened, as if his brain was trying to give him every tool possible to survive. His eyesight became crisp and clear, a level of sharpness to his vision he hadn't quite seen before. Time seemed to slow down, as if to delay his death just a few more moments.

Objects floated around casually inside the car, the way they might in an orbiting space shuttle: a car charger drifted by, its attached cord twisting and writhing like a coiled snake; loose change spun end over end; a yellow piece of candy twirled in front of him like a tiny sun; a paper coffee cup exploded, its creamy-brown contents spreading upward and outward like a fluid fungus, individual droplets suspended in midair.

No, he wasn't dying. He wasn't here in a floating car. *He was with Jess.* They were still at the Plaza New York. They were getting massages. No, they were having lunch with Jess's mom. She was going on again about their overworked, overplayed lifestyle.

"I don't know how you two do it. If your father were alive, he would have something to say about the schedule you two keep," she was saying. It was almost nice how she would say it, sipping a glass of wine.

"Ma, we've had this conversation before. Pete and I have careers," Jess was saying.

"Yeah, well your career isn't going to replace the emptiness you'll feel when you realize you're too old to have children and you look back and wish you would've had them."

That's right. Children. They were talking about children before their New York trip. No, it was when they were celebrating their engagement with Jess's family.

It wasn't *now*—it was *years* ago.

"When are you going to have children?" Betty was saying, and Jess was rolling her eyes and saying, "Ma, please."

He wanted children. He could easily take Betty's side. Gang up and convince Jess that now was the time. But he loved Jess unconditionally, and while he felt a warm tingling inside—*Now is the time! Tell her how you feel! Tell her you want to start a family!*—he knew it wasn't and it would only alienate Jess further.

"Betty!" he said placing an arm around his feisty mother-in-law. "Have I mentioned yet how beautiful you look this evening?" He shot a wink toward Jess.

"Oh, Peter, you're corny, but you're still charming," said Betty.

No, it was six months ago when Pete had asked her if she had thought about having kids like so many of their friends had. A little boy to take fishing.

Teach him how to throw a baseball. All he wanted was that little boy. The urge coupled with the inevitability of time . . .

"I don't want to be forty-five and have a newborn," he had told her one night.

And Jessica's typical reply: their lifestyle wasn't for everyone, but it worked for *them*. But this time was different. Normally, that was where they might end the discussion. But this time, she followed up with, "I think I'm on the verge of a major breakthrough in my research. I just need a little while longer, Pete. Once I'm finished with this project, then *maybe* we can start a family."

Smiling, Pete pulled her in close and kissed the top of her head. The sweet aroma of her cucumber and green tea shampoo filled his nostrils as he thought about how stubborn of a woman she could be—the stubborn tenacity that made her a successful researcher.

"It's not for everyone, but it works for us," Pete repeated that night, comforting Jessica as she fell asleep—reassuring himself as much as her.

"I wouldn't have it any other way," she murmured into her pillow.

Yes, that was now, or then, and the kids . . . The kids would come later. Unless he was dead, then never. But he wasn't dying now, he was only going to die someday. *Later.*

The tree. Pointed, spiked leaves of a sugar maple. A common tree for eastern Pennsylvania. It was close enough that he could see the rigid bark encasing the tree stump. Such a common, ordinary tree. He never noticed the bark on a sugar maple before. Almost a *crunchy* texture to it.

The tree. It was drawing closer, as if the tree picked up its roots and was coming for him.

"Pete? Pete, honey?"

Jessica. The universe sped up again. A total loss of control. Momentum speeding away. Numb. Floating with the momentum of the car. *Jessica.* Someone yelling. *He* was the one yelling. A violent jolt. *Jessica.* A sudden stop. Ears ringing for a half a second. Then black. Everything black. A dark abyss of nothingness.

The common, ordinary sugar maple that was growing harmlessly off the road, where it should not have been a threat to anyone. The car hugged the tree so tightly that the Fire Department would have to cut it away with a torch. Piece by broken piece.

THE AFTERMATH

PETE BURST THROUGH THE WINDSHIELD, miraculously landing upright. Disoriented, looking himself over. Turning his hands over to inspect them. A crash like that, and no signs of even the slightest injury.

"No blood! No blood? I don't think I have a scratch on me! How is that possible?" he said to himself.

He felt no pain, saw no signs of cuts—not even a single bruise.

Clenching his fists, he threw his hands in the air.

"Yeah! What a rush!" he yelled. "Better than any roller coaster I've ever been on," he said to himself.

He turned toward his car wrapped around the seemingly harmless maple tree.

"I must've been thrown half a football field! How did I get so far from the car?" Pete paused, brows furrowing. "Wow. My car looks like a crumpled soda can."

He felt his heart sink as he traveled closer to the scene.

He inspected the wreckage. The accident scene was horrific. The tree had almost split his Audi in half—pieces of the car were strewn several hundred feet. A tire had flown off and rolled into a nearby parking lot. Broken glass sparkled in the morning sun.

"Jess is going to kill me," he muttered to himself.

He had no idea how he survived that crash. He certainly shouldn't have felt as good as he did. The car engine was still running, and a puff of smoke billowed from the overtaxed engine.

"I need to find my phone and call Jess back—let her know I'm okay."

He approached the car with caution until he heard her voice.

"Pete! Pete! Is everything okay? What was that noise? Pete! Please answer me!" Her voice sounded brittle, cracking as she spoke.

He rushed toward her voice. Somehow his phone was still connected to his Bluetooth. He had to let her know he was safe. "Jess! Don't hang up! I was in a car crash, but I'm okay!"

"Pete? Pete? Please, baby! Talk to me!" A panicked vulnerability rang through her voice.

He made it to the crumpled car and leaned through the broken passenger-side window.

"Jess! I'm here! I'm—" He suddenly froze.

A lifeless body—still strapped into the driver seat. Its right leg was dismembered just above the knee, the tree having cut its way into the backseat. His right arm was bent back above his head in a twisted, hyperextended position—a sure sign of a broken and dislocated shoulder. The left leg had somehow been pulled from under the steering wheel and now rested on the dashboard. Aside from the leg injuries, there did not appear to be much external bleeding.

Pete could only guess what the inside of that body looked like. Broken ribs likely pierced the lungs, the spleen was most definitely ruptured, and arteries probably ripped away from the heart due to the g-forces created by the sudden stop. One thing was for sure: the body strapped in that seatbelt had experienced a sudden death.

"Pete! Are you okay?"

Jessica.

Pete's gaze found the body's face.

That was when he realized the body was his.

THE GATEKEEPER

"PETE? PLEASE SAY SOMETHING!" JESSICA'S voice faded to a distant muffle as he examined the distorted flesh that wore his face.

"Pete! Please! Answer me!" Jessica's flustered voice continued over the speakers.

Pete snapped out of his trance. "Jessica! I'm here! Don't hang up!"

"Pete! Are you there?" said Jessica.

"Jessica!" He frantically circled the car. "Jess! Can you hear me?" He tried to project his voice across the car speakers. "Jessica!" he yelled over and over.

"Pete? Are you there? I can hear something in the background."

The sounds she heard were emergency sirens that erupted in the distance. The truck driver Pete had missed probably called the authorities.

"Jessica!" he tried one last time, but it was no use. "She can't hear me." His voice wobbled with defeat. "I can't believe it. She can't hear me."

The line went dead.

"Jessica?" he said with renewed vigor, the fright of abandonment persuading him. "No! Please no! Jessica!" No response. *Jessica!*

That's when it dawned on him: He was *alone*.

Alone with the carnage of the wreck. Alone with his disheveled body— still sitting there in the driver's seat. Lifeless. Mangled. He traveled a slow, cautious trek around to the driver's side, pausing before peering through broken glass. He jumped back quickly, as though afraid the body might suddenly come to life. He gazed back, seeing his corpse sitting there. Silent. A feeling of remorse came over him. "What have I done to you?" he whispered. "What have I done?"

The guilt faded, replaced with a wave of anger.

"No. This can't be. I have a big client meeting this morning. I planned to meet Jess for dinner later. *Jess.* What is she going to do without me? We have so much to do together. We're supposed to start a *family*. A family! We just talked about slowing down our lives so we can spend more time together! All I ever wanted was to have a baby boy! This can't be happening. *This can't be happening.* This isn't real. Wake *up*, Pete. Wake up . . . Jessica . . . We are supposed to have *children*. Jessica!"

"This is all your fault!" he yelled at his body. No response came. "You've driven this road countless times. Don't you know that turn is a hazard?" He paused. "Now look at you. Look what you've done to yourself."

Another pause.

"And Jessica—she didn't get to hear me when I told her I loved her earlier. Now she can't hear me and it's *all your fault*!" he screamed, feeling betrayed by the shell sitting motionless in the front seat.

He traveled backwards to compose himself. He tried to cry, but his vocalization came out as more of a wailing sound, and tears never came—the pent-up feeling remained. "I can't cry. I want to, but I can't. What's wrong with me?"

He was so focused on collecting himself that he didn't realize someone had walked up behind him.

"Hello, Pete."

The voice startled him, even though it had soothing undertones. He was almost embarrassed by his reaction.

"I, uh . . . I'm sorry . . . I'm just . . . I didn't see you standing there," said Pete.

He turned to see a man of African descent. He looked to be of medium build, sharply dressed in business attire, and he had on a long, tan spring jacket. His white beard was neatly trimmed.

His teeth sparkled as he greeted Pete with a warm smile. "You're blinking."

"I'd say I've been doing a lot of staring, rather."

"Not your eyes," said the man. "*You.*"

Pete looked at his hands and noticed a bright, glowing aura surrounding him. The aura was flashing rapidly, seemingly connected to his erratic emotional state.

"Don't be alarmed," said the man. "It's a common reaction. You've experienced trauma."

"Am I . . . ?"

The man nodded. "Why don't we move away from the scene? The authorities will be here shortly, and this area will be very busy as they tend to your vehicle."

"You mean they are going to pull my body out of that car, and you don't want me to see it," Pete replied.

"Seeing that could cause a triggering response. This has already been a highly emotional experience for you."

Pete looked at the him awkwardly. He glanced toward his car. The first responders were beginning to arrive.

"Come. Let us talk," the man said in a gentle tone.

Pete hesitated at first, but traveled over to the man. They moved together away from the wreck. The man finally spoke when they made it over a ravine, where they were out of sight of the car and barely within earshot of the first responder activity.

"My name is Lagos. I was named after the city where I was born in Nigeria," said the man. The rapid pace of Pete's blinking aura slowed as he listened to the man's soothing tone. "I'm here to help you transition into the afterlife. In a few moments, I will open a portal. From there, I will help you enter and guide you along the way."

"Where does it lead? This portal. Once it opens, what happens?" asked Pete, his aura flashing more rapidly now.

"I'm not at liberty to discuss such matters other than to offer you passage," he said.

"Why not? Seems like a fair question."

While Lagos had a steady resolve that calmed him, Pete's aura's flashing told the story of a sharp bitterness growing inside him. Suddenly snatched from his life with Jessica, his career, and now this Lagos character shows up and expects him just to enter some hole in the ground?

No. He wasn't ready. There was still too much to do here.

"I am here to open a portal and offer you passage. It is your choice to enter. Any resemblance of persuasion would be looked upon unfavorably by my leadership."

"Seems strange. You would go through all that effort to greet me and open a portal if you didn't want me to enter? Yet, you cannot tell me where it leads? I'm just supposed to *follow* you into this thing?" said Pete.

"Your background as an attorney has trained you well. It is not helping you here. My advice: Do not try to investigate everything. Lean into this. Allow yourself to approach things with flexibility, or it may not end well for you," he said.

Pete thought for a moment. "But what about Jessica? Will I be able to see Jessica?"

"I'm sure your wife will be able to meet you there one day, assuming that is the direction she chooses to go," said Lagos.

"What does that mean?"

"It means everyone has a choice," said Lagos.

"So there's no guarantee that Jessica ends up meeting me wherever we are going?" asked Pete.

"I'm afraid I cannot predict such things," he said.

Pete looked at Lagos, unassured.

"I'm sorry to have to speak in such generalities, Pete. Everything will become clear once you enter the portal. Are you ready?" he said.

Pete quietly nodded. While skepticism remained, what option did he have? He was dead. *This must be what people are supposed to do when they die,* he thought. Something still didn't seem right. What would happen if he entered the tunnel? Where did it lead? Would he be able to talk to Jessica? The crushing weight of uncertainty was enough to throw his aura into hyperdrive.

He looked on with caution as Lagos flipped his hand palm-side up, making a waving motion. He clenched his fist, opened his hand, and a small sphere appeared. The sphere started as the size of a large coin and grew to the size of a melon. He placed the sphere at ground level and stepped back. With a sudden burst, the sphere exploded to the size of a large tunnel. The inside roared like a hollow wind. An electrical storm rumbled. The energy within this opening looked like it could power cities.

"How did you do that?" barked Pete. Lagos motioned him to move closer, but he found he couldn't move a muscle. "How did you do that? How did you *do* that? What happens next?"

"We get in, of course," said Lagos.

If the visual of the portal itself was not frightening alone, the thought of not seeing Jessica again was overwhelming.

"I can't do it," said Pete over the roar of the wind shear.

"Ah, but Peter, you are so close!" said Lagos.

"I can't get in there. I can't go. I have too many things left to accomplish here. Jessica. We're starting a family. What about my career?" He stopped himself—a rush of anguish coming over him. Remorse set in. Strong enough to dampen the tone of his aura a few shades. "We were supposed to have children. It's all I ever wanted . . . to have a baby boy."

A solemn tone came over Lagos—changing from the friendly, soothing voice Pete had become accustomed to. "Pete, I'm afraid we're at a crossroads.

I can only offer just this last chance. You must make a decision."

"I'm sorry. I can't go. I have too much left here to do," said Pete.

Lagos walked to the tunnel base and turned toward him. Pete stood for a moment, engulfed by the light—his features now becoming that of a shadowy figure.

"I was talking to Jessica—right before the crash. I told her how much I loved her, but she didn't hear me. I have to stay. Maybe that sounds silly, but I have to tell her I love her, just one more time! She has to know," he yelled.

Pete was an attorney. Everything he did was by absolutes. He only took cases he could win. There was only one thing he'd ever done in his adult life that did not have a predictable outcome and that was marrying Jessica. He did that because he loved her, and now there was no guarantee he would ever see her again if he entered this portal. In fact, he calculated a low likelihood of seeing her again if he entered the tunnel. On top of that, he had no assurance of where he was going. He was not one to relinquish this kind of control.

"I'm sorry. I just can't."

"Very well. Just know that it may be a long time before another portal becomes available. You will still be judged on your actions," said Lagos.

Pete nodded in confirmation, but in his mind he couldn't help but question his decision to stay. Was he making the right choice? He had to choose, and he chose Jessica.

"Remember! Lean into it, Pete!" Lagos said as he entered the portal.

A second later, the portal closed and he was gone.

Pete was alone.

AFTER THE CRASH

THERE WAS ENOUGH ACTIVITY BUILDING at the crash scene to keep him distracted. The police and first responders had shown up, and his aura flashed as he watched them free his lifeless body from the wreckage. He watched as a coroner showed up, the first responders stepping aside to allow him to examine the body. It took him all of thirty seconds to pronounce him dead before they were allowed to load the gurney into the ambulance.

Lagos told me not to watch—I should've listened to him, he thought, feeling something like nausea in the place his stomach used to be.

Workers cut his car from the pole and placed it on a flatbed; it was in no condition to even tow.

As the ambulance pulled away, its lights dark, Pete felt a sudden surge of anxiety.

"Wait! I can't stay out here all alone! Where are you taking my body?" he yelled. He burst into an orb and shot toward the ambulance, surprised at the speed at which he traveled. "Wait! How did I just do that?" He completely overshot the ambulance, tearing through nearby trees as he tried desperately to master this new form of being. Eventually, he steadied his course enough to follow the ambulance, his orb traveling above it.

It was an eerie feeling, knowing his corpse was resting in a black bag inside that ambulance.

"What are you going to do, Pete?" he said to himself.

The ambulance stopped and he heard the scurry of the emergency medical technicians.

"Got another one for ya, Jerry," said a burly EMT as he opened the ambulance doors. He and his partner pulled the crumpled body bag out and placed it on a gurney for transport.

"Wait!" said Pete, rushing to stay with the bag. "Where are you taking my body?"

He stopped as an old man opened the doors to the mortuary and greeted them with a charismatic yell.

"What do you have for me, boys?" he said, shuffling over to the gurney.

"Hi, Jerry. We got a fresh one for you. Real mangled type. Just how you like them," said a portly EMT as his skinnier partner looked on.

"Oh yeah, Rodney?" he said with the fervor of a wolf eyeing a prized lamb. "How'd he go?"

"Car accident. The poor bastard wrapped his car around a tree. Fire department is still over there cleaning up the scene. Took them a couple hours to free that car."

"Well, boys, you know what they say about car wrecks, don't ya?" said Jerry as he scooted closer to the gurney.

The two EMTs stood there, waiting for Jerry to drop a punchline. Nothing came as they watched the old man grab ahold of the body bag.

"Jerry?" the burly EMT finally prompted.

The old man paused, peering at them over his glasses. He seemed annoyed they were interrupting his inspection.

"Yeah, Rodney?" The old mortician looked at the EMT but didn't really give him a chance to respond. "Well? Out with it!" he barked.

The EMTs shot each other an awkward look.

"The thing they say about car wrecks?" said Rodney.

"What the hell are you talking about?" Jerry scoffed as he stared at them.

The EMTs looked at each other again.

"I've been a mortician for—"

Rodney cut Jerry off. "Yeah, yeah, yeah, we've heard it before. You've been a mortician for over fifty years. I tell you what, Jerry. We'll leave you alone so you can do your work. Just sign the chain of custody so we can be on our way."

Jerry stopped and smiled. "Boys!" he said. His voice turned into a sinister whisper. "Let's have a look, shall we?"

"What?" said Steve—Rodney's helper, by the look of it. Pete guessed he was the new guy.

"I'm thinking he's a particularly mangled one. We don't get those very often." Jerry was still whispering. He grabbed the bag and unzipped it before they could reply. "Let's see what we got."

Pete watched the EMTs as they cautiously leaned forward, the temptation of seeing the body again too great. They acted as if it might suddenly come alive and grab them.

"We'll take another look." They positioned themselves next to the gurney, shifting their weight as Jerry opened the bag.

"Wait!" Pete's aura started flashing. "What are you doing?"

Jerry unzipped the bag and opened the flaps. The three of them peeked in. Rodney was first to jump back. Steve following. Jerry stood over the bag, admiring his new project—a thin smile cracking his normally pursed lips. His chiseled face came alive as he peered into the contents of the bag.

"Alright. Zip it back up, Jerry!" said Rodney just as Steve cried, "*Come on*, Jerry!"

"Yeah! Zip it back up!" yelled Pete.

"Come on, boys, where's your sense of craft? This is every mortician's dream. I get to take this poor twisted body and make it into something magnificent." Jerry glanced over his glasses to the EMTs. "What do we know about him? Any family? Wife? Children?"

"We know he has a wife—Jessica, or something like that," said Rodney. "She's been notified and is coming up here soon to identify the body."

"Well, then I have work to do," said Jerry. "I need to get this poor wretched heap ready for her to see."

A call came over the EMTs' radios.

"We got another one," said Rodney. "We'll let you be. Good luck with this one, Jerry."

"Bring me back something nice, boys!" he cackled as he waved Rodney off and danced his way down the hall, singing a made-up song, laboriously pulling the gurney behind him.

"You're one warped old man, Jerry," barked Rodney as they left.

"Yeah, man, I ain't never met no one like that crazy old man," said Steve.

Pete looked on as the old man turned his attention to the heaping pile of extremities on his gurney table. "Let's see now, fella. We need to make you presentable so your bride can come up here and see you! We wouldn't want her to spy you in such bad shape."

Pete leaned over, taking a cautious peek into the bag. The body was so lifeless and cold looking. It was bruised everywhere—skin appearing fake and plastic-like. His facial features stuck in a contorted, swollen grimace. Heavy bags under his eyes. Messy hair out of place. His saggy cheeks hanging off his face. He sprang back—a cocktail of emotions sending his aura ablaze in a startled, blinking mess.

"I can't look any longer. I just can't," he cried out, placing his arms over his face shielding the view.

The corpse was still mangled, but he had to admit—it was an improvement compared to before—given he might have set a new record as far as damaged corpses were concerned. He didn't want Jess to remember him this way. Hopefully Jerry could put him together so Jess wouldn't be devastated at the sight of it all.

After a few disturbing moments, Pete saw the old man working—fixing his body so Jessica wouldn't see it in this condition, and he became grateful.

"Thank you," said Pete. "You're really fixing it up. Thank you for doing this."

Jerry stopped. "Well, now! I didn't think you were ever going to speak! Standing there all quiet like." He continued his work, gently lifting and repositioning extremities. Pete continued on his business, traveling closer to the body to take a look. "You're welcome."

Pete looked up from the body to see that Jerry was staring right at him. "Are you talking to me? Can you actually *hear* me?"

"Of course I can hear you. . . . I can see you too!" Jerry cackled. "Most get into the portals like *you* should've! But others . . . Well, some stubborn ones like you come here to my mortuary after dying—the bodies—*always* following their bodies. I see them. Every last one of ya who come here . . . following your body."

He saw the old man's head tilt slightly to the left, a curious expression falling upon his face. "You're flashing!" Jerry exclaimed.

"It happens when I get excited."

"Or sad, I presume," said Jerry.

"Yes. Happens when I'm excited, sad, angry—you name it. I flash. Not sure why."

"Your aura is connected to your emotional state. Instead of crying when you're sad, your aura dims. Happy? It brightens. Now, yours has a nice glowing hue to it, and you should aim to keep it that way."

"Why does it matter?"

"Bah, you all ask that. I'll get to it, but listen son, I need to ask you a serious question." Pete's aura pulsated softly as he waited in anticipation. "What do you plan on doing with yourself?"

"I don't know. I hadn't thought that far ahead," Pete confessed.

"Those who end up at my mortuary rarely do." Jerry looked at him for a long while before adding, "But I can tell things—just by *looking* at the spirits who come here. And I can tell that you're one who's gonna make it.

Not all do."

"What does that mean, not all make it? What does that mean?" asked Pete.

"A death as violent as yours can be a very traumatic experience for a spirit. I've seen it play out over and over again. In my line of work you see a lot of things," he said.

"How does one *make it?* What do you mean by that?" said Pete.

"That's up to you to decide, but I'd start by avoiding anything that could be triggering or traumatic. To start, I wouldn't be here when she comes to identify your body," Jerry suggested, patting the leg of Pete's mangled corpse.

"Why not?" asked Pete.

"You just passed away. Right now, you are in the most fragile state you'll ever be in—at least in your spirit form, of course. You need to take time to get used to being a spirit before you experience anymore trauma or you could become sick," said Jerry.

"Sick? Like, *ill?* But I don't even have a body. Am I even capable of becoming sick?" said Pete.

Jerry walked over to Pete. "I've said too much already. If they're listening, you're putting me at great risk just by having this conversation."

"*Great risk?* Who's listening?" said Pete, looking wildly around the room.

"Why, *The Others*, of course. The most vile characters I've ever come across. Someone like me could be of great service to them. In fact, I don't know how they've never discovered me all these years," said Jerry.

Pete paused to collect himself, alarmed by the state of his aura.

"There you go flashing again. Don't get too excited," Jerry noted. His voice grew softer. "Son, you have a lot to learn about the new world you've just entered. Here's a tip: get used to the idea of your new state of being. If you feel like it, go attend your funeral. For some, it brings closure. If you feel like the funeral will be too traumatic, then stay here an extra day."

"What do I do after the funeral?" asked Pete.

"Well, that all depends. What is your *reason?*"

Pete balked. "My *reason?*"

"Every spirit has a *reason.* Their reason why they stayed behind, why they didn't enter the afterlife. What's yours?"

"I didn't get to tell Jessica I loved her before I died. I just want to tell her one last time," said Pete.

"Right. I'm afraid I've run out of compassion for you forlorn lovers. You don't know what's good for you," said Jerry bluntly.

Pete could tell something weighed heavily on him. "Did I say something wrong?"

Jerry turned and walked toward the body to resume his work.

"Jerry?" said Pete.

Jerry spun around. "You should've entered that damn portal! I don't know why you all think your silly little lives are bigger than the universe!"

"I couldn't do it. I just wanted to say goodbye," said Pete.

"And how do you expect you'll do that?" said Jerry. "She can't hear you. You cannot communicate with the living. Your bride *is* one of the living."

"I didn't think that far ahead," said Pete. "I just reacted."

"That's right! You did not *think*," he scolded.

"Well, what do I do now?" Pete's aura flashed wildly at the thought of having made the wrong choice.

Pete noticed an empathetic change come over Jerry as he took a deep breath and let out a sigh. He spoke softly. "I just remembered something. I've heard in rare instances, spirits have successfully been able to communicate with the living. Move objects. That sort of thing."

"Really?" Pete said perking up at the possibility that he could somehow signal Jessica.

"Well, who do you think has garnered reputation of mean spirits *haunting* the living? It's my understanding the spirits doing the haunting—knocking on objects late at night, scaring the giblets out of poor innocent people just trying to get a good night's rest—are those who have learned to move objects."

"Remarkable," said Pete, gazing in wonder.

"I don't know if it's true or not," scoffed Jerry, shaking his head. "Could be just a made up ghost lore. You know how these things go."

"I suppose I could try?" said Pete.

"Go home. Go to Jessica. *Try* to communicate with her. Never stop trying. What do you have to lose? But Pete—make no mistake about it. This is a dangerous world you've entered. You must at all costs take care of yourself. Under no condition should you let your spirit become sick."

Pete was silent, wondering why Jerry wasn't telling him to try and take the next portal out of here.

"Now, your wife is gonna be strolling through those doors any moment to come have a look at our friend, here." Jerry shook the body bag, prompting a dead arm to flop around. Pete wished he wouldn't have done that.

"If you want my advice, I'd be gone from here when she stops in. It can be an emotional time. Wouldn't want you to become triggered and have a response. I've seen that happen before. Not something I ever want to see again."

"Where should I go?" said Pete.

"You're welcome to stay here to collect yourself. If you travel through those walls, there is a waiting room. I double-insulated and soundproofed it years ago. I have candles lit and calm music playing to help you relax. Stay there until I come get you. That's when you'll know when she's gone—and you won't have to see her sad state."

"Thank you for being so kind," said Pete.

"It's my job. Now, if you'll leave me be—I need to tend to your body and make it presentable," said Jerry as he shook the body bag again, trying to get a rise from Pete.

"*Stop that!*" Pete acted purely on impulse, reaching out and placing his hand atop Jerry's—releasing an energy powerful enough to stop the old man from shaking the bag.

"How did you do that!?" questioned Jerry with wild eyes.

"I don't know, it just happened!" said Pete.

"Do it again," commanded Jerry.

"I can't—I don't know how!"

Jerry's eyes narrowed with untamed curiosity. "I've heard that spirits like you are out there, but I've never met one."

"What does that mean? Spirits like *me*?"

"Telekinesis, of course. I've heard some can become so powerful they can move larger objects."

"What does that mean for me?" asked Pete.

"There may be hope for you yet! Or, maybe not. You'll see. What you choose to do with it is up to you. Now, if you'll excuse me, I have work to do. Just keep it down, after hours. I'm a light sleeper."

PETE'S FUNERAL

IT WAS A LONG COUPLE of days at the morgue. Pete couldn't physically sleep—after all, the dead didn't sleep, so he kept pacing around the morgue in the lonely darkness after Jerry turned in, his aura flashing excitedly whenever he thought of Jessica. Thankfully, Jerry only slept two to three hours a night. Pete wasn't sure he'd make it through that first night if it wasn't for Jerry's company—but Jerry was the type that, as soon as he roused from his slumber, Pete immediately wanted to him to go *back* to sleep. There was no in between.

Several bodies were brought in. He expected maybe to see a spirit like him come along with a body, but none never showed.

Each time, Jerry would snap a comment over to Pete. "No hanger-on with this one. Smart move. They must have gone in that portal. . . ."

The quiet, empty nights. Back and forth. Back and forth. The unknowns tormenting him. The festering over simple mechanical things, like: "*When should I go home to Jess? Somehow I need to let her know I'm okay!*" Which gradually became more complex: "*Did I make the right decision? Should I have entered the portal with Lagos?*"

Jerry's constant bantering created an unhealthy whiplash affect.

"*If I wanted to contact Lagos to open up a new portal, how would I do that?*"

No matter the question, he always came back to Jessica.

"*Would she be okay? I can't leave her.*"

The mortuary was a quiet place. Eventually he noticed his aura was brightening and was flashing less frequently, settling into a steady hue.

"Well, someone is looking better now!" said Jerry one morning. "How are you feeling?"

"Coming to grips with everything, I suppose," Pete responded.

"Better steady your aura and do it fast, before you enter the *real* world. You're in a safe place here, but once you get out *there*—you'll want to be sure you've righted yourself," he advised as he scooted a gurney down the hall.

They came to get his body on the third day. Jerry had dressed it in Pete's favorite suit, which Jess had brought in.

"It still doesn't look like me," Pete said.

"Would you prefer if I left your leg wrapped around your head?" Jerry cackled.

"It finally looks at peace . . . my body," said Pete, ignoring Jerry's quirks.

"I'll take that as a compliment." Jerry chortled, peering over his thick frames. "Pete, the funeral is tomorrow."

"I know," said Pete, his aura's flashing giving away the uneasiness that crept over him.

"You are going, I presume?"

"I decided it would be best if I went."

"Very good. I think it will be good for you, but you must remember to guard yourself . . . guard your aura. There will be a lot of people there . . . sad people. Your aura will be in a vulnerable state. You must guard it at all costs and prevent yourself from becoming sick."

Looking on as Jerry made some final adjustments, Pete couldn't help but think it didn't have to be like this. It seemed so cruel—being *taken* before his time was up. He had so much more to do. His career. His life with Jessica. *Children.* There had to be another way. . . .

"You know, I've been thinking about something. Why can't I just jump back *into* the body? Bring it back to life?"

"Son, those people showing up tomorrow? They're expecting a *funeral.* Can you imagine what they'd do if you just strutted down the aisle? Do you really want to scare the knickers off poor Jessica? Besides, it doesn't work like that anyhow."

"I'm sure it would frighten her at first, but she'd come around. I know Jess."

"Even if you could—which you *can't*—this body is in no shape to be brought back to life. I got it put back in place, but look here—arm is busted." He lifted a leg that bent at ninety degrees at the thigh. "Broken leg." He shuffled alongside Pete's corpse and placed two hands on the abdomen. "Lumpy. I can feel organs all out of place. That crash ripped your insides to shreds. Pulled a few g-forces with that sudden stop, I suppose. Shall I continue?"

"I got it . . . but can't I at least try?"

Jerry stood erect; as upright as possible, given his hunch. He pulled his glasses off, holding them in two outstretched hands to analyze their clarity before returning them to his normal position resting on his nose. "Be my guest," he scoffed.

Pete nodded as he readied himself. "Okay. I'm gonna do it."

"Get on with it then," Jerry dismissed, visibly miffed.

With that, Pete leapt into the air, aiming for the center of the corpse. Time seemed to stand still as he came cruising down toward the body.

He was really doing it.

Target the midsection, you won't miss, he thought to himself closing his eyes as he readied to slam into his chest. But when he opened them, he saw two scrawny legs dressed in brown leisure pants with a crease down the front.

Jerry. He had landed underneath the gurney.

"It's ALIVE! It's ALIVE!" Jerry cackled.

"Oh, come on!" shouted Pete as he raised. "Frankenstein? Is that really necessary?"

"You gonna just stand in the middle of your own corpse?"

Pete looked down and realized he was, indeed, standing upright through the abdomen of his dead body. His aura flashed rapidly as he hurried away from the gurney. A chill would've surely shot down the base of his spine if he still had one. "I just wanted it to work! I just want to go back to how things were. Is that so hard?"

Jerry's tone turned solemn. "I'm sorry, Pete. I know how difficult this must be. I can't help you. It's now how it's supposed to be. . . . Go to the funeral. Get closure. It will help you accept your current existence." The old man shuffled away to his quarters, shutting the door behind him.

The next morning, the funeral director banged on the door, rousing Jerry—ushering him reluctantly to collect the body. Pete and Jerry went outside, watching the workers struggle as they loaded the heavy casket into a hearse.

"Time for you to go, isn't it?" said Jerry.

Pete nodded.

"I wish you well on your journey," said Jerry.

"Thank you for everything," said Pete.

At first, Jerry didn't say anything. He turned and began to walk back inside his mortuary, shoulders drooping, head hanging low. "You all come visit me and then, just like that, you're gone," he said solemnly.

He slowly turned to Pete; the old man seemed vulnerable. Wire frame glasses. Big bushy eyebrows. Hunched back.

Pete wished he would have been more tolerant of the old man.

"You leave me just like The Others. But don't worry! Just as sure as the sky is blue and the sun will come up, there will be more of you!" he said, pausing to stand tall and size Pete up one last time. He gulped before speaking. "Good luck, Pete. Don't ever give up on your *reason*. After all, that's why you stayed here."

Pete was amazed at how such a bitter old man could sometimes be so gentle.

He listened to Jerry mutter a few things to himself before going inside.

There was a scurry of activity that surrounded the hearse. They were leaving to drive to the funeral service. Pete traveled over and entered the clunky vehicle. The driver lit a cigarette, rolled down the window, and blasted a rap song.

"Hey, pal. Don't you think it's a little inappropriate to play music this loud while driving my body to the funeral service?" said Pete.

The driver didn't respond. Luckily it was a short trip, and the driver tossed his cigarette and turned down the music before pulling into the parking lot.

Pete watched all the people file in.

"Mr. Pannazzo! You made it!" Jessica's stepfather had traveled in from New York. He paid Pete no attention as he hurried into the building.

His coworkers, friends, and family members all shuffled in. He tried to greet every one of them.

I'm flashing again, he realized, looking down at his hands.

When he looked up, he saw her.

Jessica.

Her car pulled in—her sister was driving. Pete burst over to them.

"Jessica!" he said.

She exited the car, catching her purse on the door handle. He watched her rip and pull at her purse, causing the purse to break—contents spilling on the ground. He traveled over and tried to help her pick her things up, his hand passing through a set of keys he tried to pick up for her.

"Jess, it's okay. I'm here," he said.

A black veil covered her face, but he could tell she had been crying.

Jessica's sister, Penny, bent down to help. "Come on, Jess—let's get you inside, sweetie."

Pete always liked Penny. He was glad she was here. He watched them as Penny scooped up the remainder of Jessica's items and placed them in her purse. She gingerly helped Jessica to her feet. They made their way into the building, leaving him standing in the parking lot alone.

"I just wish there was some way I could comfort her," he said to himself. He heard music inside the building playing. The service had begun. "I better get inside."

He was in no hurry to join the service, so he slowly approached and entered the building—moving through the closed doors. The music had stopped, and he was surprised to see his brother Kevin at the microphone.

"People ask me about Pete and I. He was my big brother. My best friend growing up. It's crazy how life can become so complicated. He chose to pursue his career, and I chose to build a family. I always wanted to be an uncle. I wanted my kids to have cousins. So I always had a chip on my shoulder when Pete—" He paused. "Excuse me for a second."

Pete watched Kevin stop his speech to take a sip of water and regain his composure.

Pete moved to the center of the aisle.

"Kevin! It's okay, Kevin!" he said.

He saw Kevin set the glass down on the podium and continue his speech.

"I always had a chip on my shoulder about Pete's lifestyle. I didn't understand it. But here is the thing—I now realize that how my brother chose to live his life has nothing to do with me. If he were sitting here today, I'd tell him I'm proud of him. I still look up to him. He's still my hero. Just some advice for all those little brothers out there: don't do what I did. If you have jealousy toward your big brother, it's natural. Let it go. Don't let it be a barrier to your relationship. I want you to walk out of this service today, call your big brothers, and tell them you love them. You should do that because I'll never get to say it to my brother again—and that is a regret that I will take to my grave. Call your brother. Tell him you love him."

"Kevin! I heard you, Kevin. I'm here!" said Pete.

He watched Kevin walk off the stage. All he wanted to do was bring comfort and reassurance to his little brother.

Pete watched the rest of the service. The officiant said a few nice words, they played a song over the speakers, and then it was over. He watched people shuffle out of the procession—many of them crying.

"I'm sorry I've made you all sad." His aura flashed with the heavy guilt he carried.

He rode in the hearse on the way to the burial. He couldn't bring himself to ride with Jessica and Penny, the guilt too great.

He watched his brother Kevin and the other pallbearers wrestle with his casket and walk it up to his gravesite.

"I'm proud of you for being my pallbearer, Kevin," he said as he traveled next to his brother. "The speech—uh, the speech you said at the ceremony. I never knew you felt that way." He paused to collect his thoughts. "I know we lost touch over the years, but it's not too late. I'm here."

Watching the pallbearers place the casket on the grave stand seemed to signal the finality: the shiny, closed casket with an impressive ring of flowers placed on top. He knew his body was in there, but he just couldn't bring himself to accept it would actually happen until now. Crowd members all took their seats except Kevin, who stood with his head bowed, one hand placed on the casket. Upon closer observation, Pete realized his brother was sobbing. Kevin's wife, Maggie, rushed to his side and offered comforting words, escorting them to their seats, passing Jessica along the way—Maggie giving her a sympathetic look as she and Kevin walked by.

"Jessica!" Pete had been so distracted by the proceedings he hadn't tended to her like he wished he would. A feeling of shame washed over him as his aura dimmed slightly. Standing behind her in support seemed like an appropriate place as he watched the officiant place his hand on the casket.

The man cleared his throat as he readied to speak. *"Eh-hmm.* Gather round. The family has requested we hold hands around the casket," he directed, pausing a moment to allow the crowd to shuffle into position. "Let's begin."

"We lock hands in formation around Peter Robert Stanton, representing the circle of life. A popular Buddhist saying goes, 'What the caterpillar perceives as the end, to the butterfly is just the beginning.' We know that all that life has its beginnings and its ends. Life exists in the time between birth and death, and life's significance lies in the experiences and satisfactions we achieve in that lifespan. Many of you feel Pete has left us before his time was up—"

"I agree with that!" yelled Pete.

"—we know that many of you think it's not fair that Peter was taken from us—"

"You're damn right!" he grumbled.

"—but know that when our time is called, that is the right time. There is no such thing as being taken too early. That's why we should all live life to the fullest."

"You got a lot of nerve to say that!" Pete scoffed.

"Pete lived life to the fullest. He loved his wife Jessica with everything he had."

Pete was silent. He could hear Jessica sobbing. It bothered him to hear her sniffling and be unable to comfort her.

The officiant paused for a moment before lowering Pete's casket into the ground. He directed everyone to take a rose. Pete watched as, one by one, each sad face gently tossed their rose onto his casket.

One by one, until it was just Jessica. She asked everyone for a moment alone with Pete.

Pete remained with her as she stood alone over his burial site, her veil blowing in the gentle wind. She stood for a while, clutching the rose in her hand. Silent. Motionless.

Pete became uncomfortable with her silence.

"Jess. Don't be sad," he said gently. He tried to put a hand on her shoulder, but it passed through her.

After a while, she finally spoke. "We talked about all the vacations we planned to take after my work was done. All the time we would spend together when I finally crack the code to my research . . . and I . . . I know how badly you wanted children. . . . I'm sorry, Pete."

While he wanted desperately to comfort her, he didn't say anything.

"I'm so close to finding the missing link, Pete. If I can just find that one combination, my work would be finished. You would be so proud of me," she said.

"I *am* proud of you, Jess. You have no idea how proud I am," he choked out.

"I'm sorry. I know you always wanted to spend more time with me." Pete noticed her gripping the rose with so much force that her knuckles were turning white. "Time. Time is such a delicate thing don't you think? I wish we had more time." Her voice cracked and she took a moment to compose herself before continuing. "I know I put work before us. I just always thought you'd be here—and when I completed my case study at the lab, then we could've been together. I'm sorry, Pete. I'll never forgive myself for not being available to you."

"Jess—don't put this on yourself. This is *not* your fault." His attempts to console her were no use, Jerry's warnings regarding his inability to communicate with the living inspiring a new and dangerous fear in him. *What if Jerry was right? What if staying behind was pointless?*

"You left me, Pete. You left me. I'll never be the same." She put the rosebud to her nose and gave it a sniff before lowering her arm and gently releasing the flower onto the top of the casket.

"I didn't *leave you*, Jess! I'm right here!" Pete exclaimed. The gulf between them was torturous, and suddenly all he could think was, *You've made a huge mistake. You should've left. She can't hear you, she never will.*

His aura's flashing was enough of a distraction from the burial that he raised his hands to look at them. The sight of it dimming and changing colors so rapidly made him nervous, Jerry's words ringing loudly in his mind: *"Under no condition should you allow your aura to become sick."*

Jessica. He watched her sitting there, black veil draped over her beautiful face, her eyes filled with bewilderment. He traced her black dress and looked at the rose she was clutching. There was something about that rose. So vivid and full of life despite having been snipped and removed from its roots. In that moment, looking at that plump red rose, hope returned to him. "Jerry saw me use *telekinesis*, which means I could be one of those rare spirits capable of it—and if that's true, I can talk to Jessica."

His aura brightened as his *reason* unveiled itself.

"I'm going to live with Jessica, and I don't care how long it takes. I will signal her and let her know I'm with her. *That's it!* I'll signal Jessica that I'm here and to wait for me . . . and when she passes away, we'll enter *her* portal *together*."

GOING HOME

PETE HAD TO ADMIT, LIVING in their house together—his being there, but Jessica remaining completely unaware of his presence—felt a bit awkward for him. Especially the guilt that fell upon him when Jessica didn't get out of bed for three days straight.

"I never meant to cause you such grief," he said one night, watching her while she slept. "Don't worry, Jess. I have a plan." His resolve to learn how to move objects and signal her became stronger. It became his *reason.*

He had never been more grateful to have Jessica's sister, Penny, in her life than now. She came and stayed with Jessica for a while following the funeral.

Having Penny around helped Pete put some distance between he and Jessica during this fragile phase, allowing him to focus on stabilizing his aura. He might have become sick had he not recovered from his erratic flashing at the funeral. It was certainly a traumatic experience, one he was glad to be over with.

Coming back home was an emotional thing. He couldn't follow Jessica and Penny inside, at first. It made him feel like an outsider in his own home. Like the brick walls were watching him, forbidding him from entering.

He tried distracting himself by making a catalog of his new abilities.

"I can pass through objects." Pete swept his hand through a wall, feeling nothing. "My aura flashes when I get excited, and when I get really excited, it starts to change color. Jerry told me to avoid letting my aura become dark at all costs. Plus, it's *terrifying* when that happens," he added with a shudder.

He turned his hand over. His aura was a bright glowing white, as if he had just changed a light bulb.

"Jerry said something about me having telekinesis, but how? How can I unlock it? I must figure it out. My entire plan hinges on me being able to signal Jess," he thought out loud, eyeing a small screwdriver on his workbench.

He carelessly tried to shove the screwdriver, but his hand passed right through.

"Come on!" He charged, his patience getting the better of him as he tried swinging at the screwdriver. Nothing. "Why won't you move!?" The screwdriver sat on the workbench. *Motionless*. As though taunting him.

He tried over and over, concentrating greatly until he gave up. No matter what, it wasn't working. He'd need the emotional vigor he had when he told Jerry to stop touching his body—but he was still too numb from his funeral.

When he finally decided to enter the house, he took a cautious step through the wall. "I don't know if I'll ever get used to this *walking through walls* thing," he said.

He could hear Penny and Jess gently talking upstairs. He couldn't make out the words, but could tell Jessica was upset. He felt like an intruder to their conversation, so he stayed at the base of the stairwell, listening to Jessica sobbing—waiting for Penny to leave Jess's room and go into her own.

"What am I even going to say to her?" His aura flashed as he approached the bedroom door. He didn't dare enter until he was certain Jess was asleep; he couldn't bear the sight of her crying at his expense. "She's mad at me. She said I *left her*," he scoffed, pacing the halls, traveling back and forth. Back and forth. "I never *left*. I'm right here! I just need to make her *see me*." His aura flashed more wildly as he pestered himself with guilt.

"I didn't leave her! I was taken from her!" he growled. He looked down at his hands and noticed his flashing aura. A sudden calming voice came over him: *"Whatever you do, never stop trying, Pete. After all, she's the* reason *you stayed behind."*

"Jerry!" said Pete. Somehow the words of the eccentric mortician calmed him. "He's right. I need to do this. She's the *reason* I stayed."

He built up enough courage and plunged through the walls into Jessica's room.

As soon as he located Jessica, he knew this would be difficult. He was saddened at the sight of Jess lying facedown on their bed. She still had her shoes on.

"How could you leave me, Pete?" she was muttering. "How could you leave me like this?"

Pete approached slowly.

"Jess," he said softly, "I didn't leave you. I'm here."

A heavy sorrow came over him. She continued mourning him into the night, and all night he responded.

"I'm here Jess."

"I'm here and I'll never leave you."

"I'm sorry Jess. I'm so sorry."

"I wish there was a way I could just let you know I'm here."

"I'm never leaving you again."

"I will find a way Jess. I promise you I will find a way to let you know I'm with you."

"I promise."

JESSICA'S PRESENTATION

DAYS, WEEKS, AND MONTHS PASSED—AND Pete began adjusting to his new life as a spirit.

He devoted his time to learning how to communicate with Jess, to letting her know that he was with her became his sole purpose.

Pete kept a structured regimen. He rode with Jess to work and stayed at her lab, trying to learn how to move objects. The lab was the perfect place to keep his busy mind preoccupied. When he wanted to take a break, he'd attend one of Jessica's meetings to see how her research was coming along. It was in one meeting that he learned just how close she was to a major breakthrough.

He walked into a conference room where Jessica was presenting her work at her annual company investor meeting. As soon as he entered the room, he could tell something was off. She always twirled her pen in her hand when she was nervous. No one in the room but Pete seemed to notice.

"It's okay, Jess. You'll do great. Just relax," he tried reassuring her as she set up for the meeting.

He could tell the stakes were high as she took the podium.

"We have asked industry leads and government officials to be present today to report on our findings related to our organ transplant initiative. Every day in the United States, twenty people die waiting for an organ transplant. Last year, there were over 33,000 successful organ transplants, but with only 16,000 organ donors and close to 115,000 people needing organ transplants, the situation is dire. This is just in the United States alone.

"Of the approximately 115,000 people in the U.S. waiting on organs, an estimated 100,000 are waiting on kidneys. As you know, our objective is to use 3-D printing and stem cell technology to create and grow kidneys. Through stem cell and 3-D printing technology, we are able to cultivate new kidneys, and hopefully end the organ crisis worldwide!"

The room erupted in applause.

"Yeah! Go, Jess!" Pete cheered.

The group settled as she continued. "We are so close." She paused as she heard some grumbling in the room. "We are so close to producing a sustainable kidney, and through this research we will save lives and put an end to the archaic organ transplant list."

She smiled as the room applauded.

"At this time, I'd like to open it up for questions," she said.

"I'm proud of you, Jess. You nailed it!" said Pete.

He noticed a single arm shoot in the air. His attention leapt to Jessica as she fielded the question.

"Yes, David?" she said.

"Thank you, Jessica. For other folks in the room, my name is David Rendorf representing BTA—sorry—*BioTech Automation*. Jessica, as you know, we are one of the primary investors in this technology, and while we believe in your work, you are significantly over budget. You mentioned you are close to growing a fully operational kidney. Excuse me for being blunt, but—*how close?*"

Pete noticed Jessica's body language change. She clasped her hands together and became more tense.

"I don't like that guy," said Pete. "There's something about him." He watched Jessica shift on her feet as she prepared a response. "Come on, Jess," he said softly.

"We have run successful clinicals on pigs, which are the closest related animal to humans when it comes to kidney size and function—"

"Excuse me!" David charged. "I don't mean to interrupt, but when you say successful *clinicals*, what exactly do you mean?"

"Would you stop interrupting her?" scoffed Pete.

"Latest tests showed an increase in kidney longevity by two hundred percent in test subjects." Her voice cracked.

"Yeah! Get him, Jess!" Pete exclaimed, but his celebration was cut short.

"What does that mean, exactly?" questioned David.

Pete watched Jess. She was stoic in her body language. "Come on, Jess."

"Our latest results demonstrated an increased kidney longevity by two hundred percent—which means our average test subject lived 146 days, which is up from 73 days just two years ago," she said.

The room filled with chatter. Pete wasn't sure what to make of it. He saw David's hand shoot up again.

"Yes, David?" she said.

"So our firm has invested eighty million dollars in this technology and all we have received is 146 days from a test subject—that is not even human?" he said.

"Hey! Don't talk to her like that!" said Pete. His aura began to flash.

Pete watched Jessica try to talk over the loud side conversations that were taking place. It was no use. She had lost the room.

Jessica's supervisor got up in front of the room. Everyone was silent.

"We'd like to thank you for taking time out of your busy schedules to attend our annual report, and I'd like to commend Dr. Stanton and her team on the marvelous work. This concludes the portion of our scheduled programming. There are refreshments down the hall," he said.

Pete glared at David as he closed his files and abruptly left the room.

"I should sue you for slander!" yelled Pete as David left the room. He followed David down the hall. "Hey! I'm talking to you buddy!" No reply from David. He stopped at a closet and pulled out his beige trench coat. "You have no right to act like that!"

David put on his trench coat and walked toward the exit. Pete followed him outside the hospital and watched as he hailed a cab. He decided not to follow him any farther.

PETE MEETS THE LAB MANAGER

JESSICA WAS IN MEETINGS WITH her superiors when Pete finally tracked her down.

"My aura is really flashing," he said as he examined himself.

Suddenly, Jerry's voice rang once again in his mind: *Under no condition can you allow your spirit to become sick.*

He peered into the office where Jess and her team were meeting. He decided he couldn't do anything to help her, and listening to whatever her bosses were telling her would only agitate him further. He found an empty research room in the laboratory to hide out.

The lab room was lit only by the light from kidney specimens that were growing in some sort of solution. The aerators circulated the solution around the tank, and the sound of percolating bubbles filling the room.

He began pacing back and forth. "What is she going to do if her funding gets pulled? They could shut down her entire project. Then what would she do?" He paced around the room faster. "She's put her *life* into this work!"

His tone grew darker as he thought a previously unspoken, dark thought. "Maybe I'd still be alive if it wasn't for all this."

His aura dimmed.

He stopped at one of the incubators where a kidney was growing.

"She was so dedicated to her work. I wanted to spend more time with her. We would've stayed another day in New York City if she didn't have to get back to her beloved research, and I'd still be alive."

He stared at the kidney, listening to the bubbling solution keeping it alive.

"Well, now! What do we have here?" a baritone voice said, startling Pete. He wheeled around, surprised to see another spirit moving toward him. His vibrant aura brightened the room.

"I haven't seen a spirit flashing like you in quite some time!" the spirit continued. "You better get that under control, son—otherwise The Others are going to show up. Neither of us want that."

Pete traveled backwards as the spirit came closer.

"What's wrong? Never seen a ghost before?" chuckled the spirit.

He was of stocky nature. His brown skin only accentuated his bright aura. He wore a short fade and a neatly trimmed beard. His lab coat was open, revealing a modern looking black turtleneck shirt.

"I couldn't help but overhear. Are you, um . . . You're Pete Stanton, correct?" said the spirit gently.

"Who's asking?" Pete snapped.

The spirit stopped moving toward Pete, seemingly taken aback by Pete's sharp response.

"My name is Jerome. I used to be the lab manager here," he said. "Listen, we were all sad to hear the news. I worked with Jessica for a lot of years. I was sad for her—and well, I was sad for you, too, even though we had never met." He looked Pete over for a moment, as if surveying him for signs of bodily injury or scars from his crash. "Car accident. Such a shame. You and Jessica had so good many years ahead of you." Jerome's aura dimmed slightly as he shook his head.

Pete made no response, but surely Jerome noticed the erratic flashing of his aura. He hated thinking about the car accident, much less talking about it.

Jerome held his hand up. "I'm sorry. I didn't mean to make you upset. I have a family, too. I know what it's like to be taken before your time."

"How did you know I passed away if you were—"

"Dead?" chuckled Jerome. "I live here at the lab. News traveled pretty fast when Jessica didn't come into work for a while. I get to sit in on any meeting or conversation I want. Perks of the spirit life, I suppose."

"How long have you lived at the lab?" asked Pete.

"I died two years ago. I've lived here ever since," said Jerome. "I'm surprised Jess never mentioned me. We were close colleagues—working on this project together."

Pete traveled over to get a look at the kidney sample that was growing in the bubbly solution. "Quite amazing that such a lumpy mass of tissue could be the key to saving thousands of lives, but you know what? This will be Jessica's legacy if she pulls it off . . . and yours too, I suppose, since you were her partner."

"You know, we talked about that all the time when we worked together."

"There was a meeting today and the investors threatened to pull her funding. How close do you think she is?" said Pete.

35

"To growing a kidney?"

Pete looked at him and nodded.

"Oh, we are there. She just doesn't know it yet." Pete gave Jerome a perplexed look and Jerome said, "Come with me."

They traveled through a couple walls and entered a small room with filing cabinets, a desk, and a couple chairs.

"This was my office," he said. "No one has occupied it since my death. I suppose they think it's bad luck or something."

"Maybe they're scared you'd haunt them," Pete snickered.

"A strong possibility." Jerome let out one of those belly laughs that made Pete imagine his midsection jiggling, had he been alive. "Locked inside that desk is the recipe for a solution that will keep the kidneys alive. I found out that if grown in this solution with an electrolyte mix, the kidney longevity increased upwards of three years. We think we could extend the longevity if the patient were to take an electrolyte injection once a month."

"But Jessica said they could only keep a pig alive for 146 days," said Pete.

"Yes. Using her current solution, that is correct," said Jerome.

"Why didn't she use *your* solution? I thought you were partners."

"I never shared it with her. The solution I developed added potassium to the solution." Pete noticed a defiant look overcome Jerome's face. "I got the feeling that someone was following me. I didn't want Jessica exposed. I planned to tell her when I felt we were safe, but I never got the chance."

Was Jessica in danger? Pete's flashing gave away his nervous intuition.

"Pete," Jerome said earnestly. "I believe I was murdered."

THE MYSTERY UNRAVELS

"MURDERED?" PETE GASPED. SUDDENLY, HIS own death felt petty. His fixation. The constant pacing. He had been fixating on his own death like picking at a scab. It was like a scratch that he couldn't itch. Sure, he was taken before his time—but *murdered?* That was something different entirely.

"Yes." Jerome took on a somber tone. "Someone wants to steal our research, but I don't know who."

"How did it happen? That is, if you don't mind me asking," said Pete.

"No, I don't mind. Oddly, I don't quite know. My death was more gradual. I hadn't been feeling well for some time. I had seen doctors and specialists. None of them knew what was wrong with me. Then one day, I buckled over—vomiting violently. I remember it hit me like a ton of bricks. I fell into convulsions, passed out, and never woke up."

"Sounds to me like maybe you were poisoned," said Pete.

"My thoughts exactly," said Jerome. "Whoever did it took my laptop from my office. They didn't realize I had printed files inside my desk—I have an idea what they were looking for."

"The recipe for the solution and injection to keep those kidneys alive!" said Pete.

"You're pretty good at this," said Jerome.

"Well, I wasn't an investigative attorney all those years for nothing," Pete snickered. "So what now?"

"I've been watching over the lab to try and find clues surrounding my death. More importantly, to make sure none of the other physicians are in danger," said Jerome.

Pete paused for a moment. His aura flashing was a dead giveaway to his thoughts.

"Jessica?" he asked. Jerome nodded silently. "Is she in danger?"

"She could be if she finds a cure—which my guess is she is getting close," said Jerome.

"I think I might have an idea on who did it," said Pete.

"Do tell!" Jerome exclaimed sarcastically.

"I've seen scenarios like this before. I tried a case where a large hospital attempted to sabotage patients because a corporation wanted to privatize their research," said Pete. "A cancer drug that they didn't want to make public so they could rake in profits."

"What does a cancer drug have to do with this case?" asked Jerome.

"Well, let me ask you, Jerome. If you had a million dollars in the bank, and you learned your wife got sick—how much of that money are you going to spend to save her?"

"All of it. I'd give every last penny to save my wife," said Jerome.

"So would I," said Pete.

"So you're saying someone wants to steal the research so they can privatize our work and sell the organs for big money?"

"Now, we just need to find out who," said Pete.

Jerome was quiet for a moment. Pete watched as Jerome looked at the floor, his aura seemed to dim as he was in deep thought. Maybe he was thinking about where he'd be right now if he were still alive. He surmised Jerome would probably be having dinner with his wife . . . maybe a couple of boys. It made Pete realize he wasn't the only one with problems.

"Everything okay?" asked Pete.

Jerome shook his head at first. "You know, this goes against everything that we ever wanted in this project. Our goal was to end the organ crisis worldwide, not make it so only the wealthy could afford an organ transplant. We put our heart and souls into this research—and I was *murdered* for it."

They both paused for a moment, looking at the kidneys bubbling in the solution.

"Pete." Jerome was growing serious, even defiant. "When have you ever known Jessica to stop?"

"Ha! Those two words don't belong in the same sentence," Pete scoffed.

"Eventually, Jessica is going to find a solution to keep these kidneys alive—with or without my work. And when she does . . . Well, she could suffer the same fate as me."

"So you're telling me Jessica really *is* in danger?" Jerome nodded his head, so Pete added, "Today, during her presentation—there was a man there from a biotech company. He said he was a major investor."

"David Rendorff. From BTA—BioTech Automation," said Jerome.

There was a slight hint of anger in his voice, and his aura began to flash with a subtle hue.

"Know him?" asked Pete.

"Do I know him? He's one of the prime suspects," said Jerome. "He's been trying to shut us down for a couple years."

"Today, Jessica presented her findings during an investor meeting. He was there," said Pete. "He challenged her work in front of everyone."

"We need to keep an eye on him," said Jerome.

"What should we do?" said Pete.

"Right now? Nothing. You're too newly hatched to be caught up in all this."

"But I can't let Jessica be in harm's way."

"Look at your aura," said Jerome. "It's flashing wildly just from talking about this mess. You're not ready for something like this."

"What does my aura have to do with this?" scoffed Pete.

"I need you to listen to me. You need to learn how to control yourself. It takes some spirits *years* to master. One thing goes wrong, and it's enough to send you in a spiral that you cannot recover from. Your aura turns black, you become sick, and then . . . they come."

"Who comes?" said Pete.

"The Others," said Jerome.

"Who are these Others everyone keeps talking about?" Pete asked.

"Hey! Keep it down! You don't want them to hear you. They are always listening," said Jerome.

"Who is listening? Who are The Others?"

"I've said too much," said Jerome. "Pete, I need you to go home with Jessica. Settle into a routine, but keep an eye on her. If you see her experiencing any sick symptoms—pain in her side, vomiting, lethargic—anything that says she's not herself. Let me know."

"Can't I come back to the lab? I like it here," said Pete.

"If the lab becomes part of your routine with Jessica, then go. But you must form a routine to keep your aura regular. That's the first step. I enjoyed our conversation, Pete," said Jerome.

PETE'S ROUTINE

HIS AURA FULL, STRONG, AND luminous, Pete partially attributed his *recovery* due to adjusting. Settling into a routine. A visit here and there to see Jerome helped on lonely nights, but he mostly stuck to his routine.

There was another reason his aura had stabilized—*Jessica*. It did him a lot of good looking after her. Gave him a purpose for being—his *reason*. She hadn't left the house (aside from work and typical errands) since his death. He liked that she was always around, even though he knew it wasn't exactly healthy for Jess to keep an empty social calendar.

"Go home, Pete. Establish a routine." He heard Jerome's voice ringing . . . and that's exactly what he did.

Sitting down for dinner with her in the evenings brought him great happiness.

"Jess, you remember that time we spent in Paris together? I think of all the trips we took, that was my favorite. The cafés, the food, and oh man—the wine was just delicious."

He rode with her on the way to work, even though being in a car was not the most comfortable experience for him. She was cautious and would often drive five miles-per-hour below the speed limit, but each intersection and sharp curve made him anxious.

"Jess, you better slow down. You don't want to crash."

He would attend meetings with her at work.

"Good point you made there, Jess."

He rarely left her side.

But the lonely times came at night. After he watched over her until she fell asleep, he would aimlessly wander the house. That is when he'd do his thinking. The pacing. The boredom. The *constant* pacing. Back and forth. Back and forth.

"How can I help Jessica advance her research? This is all she's ever wanted. Her and Jerome were so close to their discovery. I have to help her."

It was on one of these lonely nights that Jerry the mortician's voice returned to him: *Never stop trying. After all, she's the reason you stayed behind.*

"I know, Jerry! I know! I'm trying. I travel with her every day to work. I have dinner with her every evening. I sit with her while she reads. I'm with her when she goes to bed, and stay with her until she falls asleep. What *more* can I do?"

Then it happened. The sound.

It was so subtle that Pete could've easily missed it if the house weren't so quiet, or if he were a less alert person.

His sight shot in the direction of the kitchen counter. Jessica left a highlighter out after doing her nightly research. It had rolled ever so slightly, and was now rocking back and forth quickly before coming to a rest.

He caught just enough subtle movement to warrant a closer look.

"How . . . ?"

He checked the windows; they were shut.

"Wasn't the breeze," he said. "If it was a small tremor, the plates and glassware would've clanked and made sounds, but it was only this highlighter that moved."

He edged closer. Right on top of the highlighter now.

"I did that, didn't I? I moved you."

He cautiously tried to touch it. His hand went through, disappearing into the countertop.

He tried again. And again. Over and over he tried to move the marker, and over and over again it did not move. Cursing at the highlighter didn't help. Yelling at the highlighter didn't move it. He was so focused on trying that he didn't hear Jessica get ready for work.

She scampered down the stairs, fully dressed, looking the part of "mad scientist" in her lab coat.

"Jess! Check this out! I moved an object!" he yelled. She walked by him and grabbed her lunch out of the refrigerator. "Jess! Over there—on the counter. Last night, I *moved* that highlighter!"

She walked briskly toward him.

"Jess! Stop! Stop!" He held his hands up trying to stop her, but she paid Pete no attention and walked right through him on the way to the garage. "Wait for me!" he said, following her out the door.

She stopped for a moment. Pete thought maybe he had her attention.

He watched as she patted her lab coat.

"Shoot. I forgot my highlighter," she said as she ran back in and snatched it off the countertop, and then leapt straight into her car and sped off.

"Jess, slow down. You're going too fast. Listen, I made a breakthrough last night. I *moved an object!* Do you realize what this means? If I'm able to move an object, then I can signal you! I can let you know I'm here! I can tell you one last time that I love you! Then I can go get somebody to open up one of those portal things and wait for you! It's the perfect plan," he said.

Jessica weaved her car into a parking spot, bounced out of the car, and scampered into the lab. He sat there in the car for a bit pondering his next move.

THE REVEALING

HE BECAME OBSESSED WITH SIGNALING her, but dutifully kept to his routine.

Day after day, he continued riding with Jessica to and from work, and sitting with her while she ate dinner. This perhaps was the most enjoyable part of his day, as it made him feel alive again.

"So, how was your day at the lab, Jess?"

"How's your research coming along?"

"I was talking to some guys at my law firm and they think the Phillies are going to make a run for it this year."

Of course, she couldn't hear him, but having these conversations made him feel like his old self—which he wanted back so desperately. So much so that it became an obsession. He paid no attention to the fact that Jessica's lack of social calendar wasn't healthy. She'd stopped working out. She was eating things she wouldn't have touched when he was alive.

"Pizza again tonight, Jess?"

All the same to him. In fact, he liked that she was gaining weight. Not wearing makeup. Everything was fitting into his plan. He stays with her until she passes away, then they enter the afterlife together.

His after-dinner routine was set. He would stay with her while she watched TV or did some research before going to bed. Once Jess fell asleep, he would retreat to the main floor where he would work tirelessly at moving objects.

A phone, a pencil, an empty plate—whatever small objects Jess had left out that night, Pete would try and move. It was monotonous and tedious, but it kept his mind from wandering. His endless pacing came to an end.

He'd set his sight on an object and sit there for hours trying to move it.

Night after night, he tried. Night after night, he failed.

Three years passed.

As a former attorney, Pete was meticulous with details. Between time he put in at the lab and working while Jess was asleep, he counted the thousands of hours dedicated to moving objects. It became a mission for him.

Then, one night, Pete was logging his hours when it happened. He moved an object. He was concentrating so vigorously that he didn't know how he moved it—he just *did it.* Not only did he move an object, but it accelerated beyond his control.

A dinner plate Jess had cleaned but left out on the counter before she retired for the evening.

He went through this same scenario countless nights before, only tonight was different. After spending the evening at the table together, Pete would watch Jess clean and wash her plate in the sink. She placed the plate on the counter and retreated to her room to do some work before falling asleep. This was her routine. Every night.

He would stay with her until her eyes became heavy and she drifted off to sleep, then he'd travel back downstairs to try and move the dinner plate.

This night was different. The frustration of three years of failure was getting to him. He considered quitting altogether, and told himself this would be the last time he tried. He had said that many nights before, but tonight he thought he meant it.

The anger. Frustration. Pent up aggression. His aura flashed as vivid thoughts of his car wreck flooded his mind. He thought about the Gatekeeper shutting his portal. The loneliness.

"They left me. Trapped. Stuck here."

He thought about the first night he came home to see Jess after he passed away.

How could you leave me like this, Pete? Her voice rang in his mind. *How could you leave me like this, Pete? How could you leave me like this? How could you leave me? How could you—*

He screamed and the dinner plate flew across the room, smashing into the wall and breaking into a hundred pieces.

Then he celebrated. He yelled. He danced. He screamed. "I did it! I really did it!"

His celebration was cut short when Jessica flew down the stairs—baseball bat in hand.

"Who's there?" Jess commanded.

She coughed. Pete could tell something wasn't quite right with her, but it didn't stop his excitement.

"I did it! I finally did it!" yelled Pete. "Jess! I broke the plate!"

She searched the house and tested all the doors but found no signs of a break in.

"Jess! Look! Over in the corner!" Pete was trying to direct her. He was blinded by excitement, unable to see how nervous she was. "Jess, I did it! I really did it!"

"I'm calling the police!" she announced. "I have a gun and it's loaded!"

"Wait, Jess. You don't have a gun. Don't call the police. There's no one here. It's me. It's *me*, Jess!" he said.

He watched her move cautiously around the house and grab a poker by the fireplace, holding it up as a means to protect herself should an intruder make an advance. "The police are on their way," she said.

"Jess. Put the poker away. There's no one here. It's only me. I moved a plate. Jess!" he said.

She moved toward where the noise had came and finally found the broken dinner plate.

"That's strange . . ." she said as she inspected a couple broken pieces.

Her cat came up and rubbed his body on her leg.

"Did you do this, you bad boy?" she said as she picked up the cat and carried it upstairs. "I'll clean it up in the morning."

"No! No! It was me! It was me—not the stupid cat!" Pete cried.

He spent the entire night in Jess's room trying to convince her that it wasn't that cat. "Jess, please wake up. Wake up, Jess. Jess—it was me. *I* broke the plate." He traveled back and forth, pacing as she slept. He tried moving a few objects in her room. It was no use.

Suddenly, Jessica jumped out of bed and rushed to the bathroom and vomited.

Oh, no, Pete thought. *It's starting.*

THE MYSTERY CONTINUES

"I MOVED AN OBJECT, AND Jessica's starting to get sick!" Pete yelled as he passed through the laboratory door.

"Calm down—you're flashing again," said Jerome in a skeptical tone.

"You don't understand. *I moved something!*"

"I understand plenty. I've been trying to solve the mystery of who's after our research, while you're running around spending your time on something that is *impossible!*" scoffed Jerome.

"Hey! You told me to start a routine!" rebuffed Pete.

"I did . . . but moving objects? Come on. None of us spirit types can actually do that. That's old folklore," said Jerome.

"It was no small object this time. It was a dinner plate," said Pete.

"To hell with your dinner plate," Jerome snorted.

"You're flashing," said Pete, concerned. "I've never seen you flash before."

"Sometimes you need to *listen*," said Jerome. "I think I've made a discovery. I think I can prove who did it."

"Proof? You have proof?" said Pete.

"While you've been pursuing magic, I've been monitoring Jessica. She's a busy lady, but she never misses lunch. She orders a buffalo chicken wrap—hold the blue cheese, but add ranch dressing. Everyday. Just like clockwork," said Jerome.

"Sounds like Jessica," said Pete.

"Like I said, I've been monitoring the cooks. I think they were the ones who poisoned me. Now you come in here telling me, among other things, that Jessica is getting sick. Well, there's one guy who I've been watching. He started acting suspicious anytime Jessica came through the line. He always makes an extra effort to make her order. The guys in the kitchen would make fun of him because they thought he had a crush on her."

"That's interesting," said Pete. "Not sure what to make of that. She is pretty. Maybe he does have a thing for her."

"Well, I thought the same thing until yesterday when I followed him outside," said Jerome.

"Outside? Like, to have a smoke or something?" said Pete.

Jerome chuckled. "Nah, Pete. He didn't go outside to have a smoke."

"Well, what did he go outside for?"

"To collect a payment," said Jerome.

"Payment?"

"David met the cook behind the hospital. He gave him two envelopes. The one he peeked into right away contained money. The other he didn't open till he got home—I decided to tail him—it contained a vile of dimethylmercury," said Jerome.

"Dimethyl—*what*?" said Pete.

"It's a chemical. In some cases, one or two drops given over the course of a month can kill you. Usually those who are exposed die within a few months—even at low doses. In my case, I started feeling sick. I saw a couple doctors. None of them could figure it out. By the time I realized something was really wrong, it was too late. I fell down on one of my shifts and never woke up. They ruled it a heart attack," said Jerome.

"So they got away with it," said Pete.

"That's right, and they are still out there," said Jerome. "Now targeting Jessica."

"How long has this piece of shit been giving this chemical to Jess?" said Pete.

"If he already went through one of those vials, then it could be two or three weeks, I'd guess," said Jerome.

Pete turned into an orb and shot toward the cafeteria.

THE COOK

"WHICH ONE IS HE?" SAID Pete, taking his human form again. Jerome had followed close behind and also reformed.

"Your aura. It's changing color," said Jerome.

"I asked you a question. Which one is he? Who is the son of a bitch who is trying to murder my wife?" commanded Pete.

"If you don't calm down, you're going to become sick. Is that what you want?" said Jerome.

"Fine," said Pete. His guard came down, and he brought his aura under control.

"Pete, I don't know if there's much we can do." Jerome spoke in a somber tone. "Even if I told you which cook is poisoning Jessica, what can we do about it? I've thought long and hard about how we might bring these guys to justice. I don't have an answer."

"There has to be a way," said Pete.

"What are we going to do? Walk into a police station and notify the cops? They can't hear us."

"Jerome, I moved an object last night."

"Yeah, yeah, *yeah*. There's bigger things at work than you *shaking markers*, Pete. It's a nice accomplishment, but let's stay with the task at hand," Jerome replied.

"You don't believe me, do you?"

"I just want to figure out a way to bring David to justice."

"Wouldn't it help if I could move things?"

"Go ahead, Pete. Move an object. Let's see you do it," said Jerome.

Pete glanced around. "Here? In the cafeteria?"

"Yes. Here. Pick up a candy bar off the rack over there."

Pete traveled toward a rack full of candy and small bags of potato chips.

"If I pick up a candy bar, will you tell me which of these cafeteria workers is poisoning Jessica?" said Pete.

"Sure, Pete. Anything you want. If you pick up a candy bar, I'll tell you

48

who did it, and do the chicken dance on top of it," said Jerome.

"Chicken dance? Now I gotta see that. A big guy like you?" said Pete.

He arrived at the candy rack.

"Ok. I'm going to try," said Pete.

"Go on," said Jerome.

He reached deep within himself to try and find the same energy he used to move the dinner plate. He went for it. His hand passed right through the candy bars. He tried again. He tried swiping, pushing, pulling, punching, and gripping. Nothing worked.

"You can't do it," Jerome chuckled.

"I can! I moved a dinner plate just last night," said Pete, still swiping at the candy.

"Then do it, Pete. Pick up a candy bar. Do it!" said Jerome.

Pete began nervously flashing as his excitement grew.

"I *can*!" said Pete.

"Then DO IT! Pick up a candy bar, Pete!" yelled Jerome.

"I'm trying!" said Pete, as he continued swiping.

"Pete, if you don't figure out how to move an object, JESSICA IS GOING TO DIE!" yelled Jerome.

"AHHHHHH!" Pete struck the rack with such force that chocolate bars, bags of candy, and potato chips flew through the air. The rack tipped over with such ferocity that it startled nearby cafeteria patrons.

"You did it! PETE, YOU SON OF A BITCH, YOU DID IT!" Jerome's voice cracked as he yelled. Pete watched as he broke into a celebratory dance.

"Is *that* the chicken dance?" asked Pete.

Pete watched as all activity in the cafeteria came to a halt. Patrons and cafeteria workers came to inspect the rack.

"How did that happen? I didn't see anyone around," said a cashier.

Even the cooks came to get a closer look. Pete examined each one of them for clues. His eyes fell on a particular one who had a suspicious gait to him. He had a neck tattoo and a shimmering gold tooth. He cracked jokes and laughed as he inspected the racks.

"You pegged him, Pete. That's the one," said Jerome solemnly. "Ex-con, by my guess. That's the guy who's poisoning Jessica."

"What do we do from here?" asked Pete.

"Nothing right now. Let's get to the lab and figure out how you can channel those new powers of yours," said Jerome.

MOVING OBJECTS

"CAN YOU DO IT ON command? Move objects like that?" quizzed Jerome.

"It's taken me hours of practice. I can't just move *anything* I want. I wish it were that simple," said Pete.

"Well, what happened when you moved the racks?" said Jerome. "Did you feel anything?"

"Not necessarily. It's like there's this build-up and a release of energy. Nothing I could feel, per se. More of a large emotional dump," said Pete.

"Fascinating."

"How do I do it again?"

"I used to practice martial arts."

"You practiced martial arts?" said Pete skeptically.

"Pete, if we were alive, I'd show you firsthand with a comment like that," scoffed Jerome.

"Sorry. . . . It's just that . . ."

"It was a long time ago, and I certainly didn't look like *this*," said Jerome. "Anyway, focus Pete. There is something even the most seasoned martial artists strive to find."

"What's that?" said Pete.

"Your Chi," said Jerome.

"My Chi?"

"I think you've found it. Somewhere deep within yourself, you've discovered how to build and release kinetic energy. Simply *amazing*, Pete. You don't have to call it your Chi if that makes you feel uncomfortable. It really doesn't matter what we call it; what matters is you *found it,*" said Jerome.

"'Chi' works. Sort of makes me feel like a kung fu master," said Pete and Jerome rolled his eyes. "This *Chi* . . . How do the martial artists find it?"

"Most never do. It takes years of practice and meditation," said Jerome.

"I don't know if I have that much time," said Pete.

"Well, you've done it a few times now, which means it's not a fluke. You have it. Let's try it out," he said. "The pen on the desk over there—can you pick it up?"

"I've moved three objects now, but each one was different."

"Why don't you try?" said Jerome.

Pete swiped at the pen with little effort.

"Damn it, Pete, *concentrate!*" barked Jerome.

"I don't really know how I do it, it just happens!"

"If you want to save Jessica's life, I'm afraid you'll need to figure it out—and fast," said Jerome.

"Let's say I figure out how to move something. What next?" said Pete.

"You leave that to me," Jerome said with a booming authority, signaling to Pete that he had crossed into an area he shouldn't have. "I'm planning our next steps. You just practice."

THE LABORATORY

BEING ALONE IN THE LAB, swiping at objects, was tedious work.

Pete found himself staying busy by selecting different objects to move—a pencil, a solitary piece of notebook paper sitting on a countertop, a trinket left out on a desk. But as time progressed, it started to feel as though he'd never move an object again.

He thought often about just giving up completely. "It's no use, I'll never move an object again. I don't know how I'm going to save Jessica," he said, making a shoving motion toward a chair and moving to rest his hand on a desktop—only for it to float through. He swore under his breath. "It's no use. We're running out of time."

Pete surveyed the room, noticing a stack of papers sitting on a lab bench.

"Concentrate," he told himself while winding up and swiping at the papers. But as always, his hand was weightless—traveling straight through the papers and the countertop.

"Not having much luck, I see," said Jerome.

"Woah! I didn't see you standing there!" said Pete.

"I came back to check on you," said Jerome, floating into the room while chewing nonchalantly on a fingernail. Pete wondered exactly *how* long ago he'd decided to *check up* on him—and how long he'd been secretly watching.

"It's no use. I can't move anything," said Pete, discouraged.

"That doesn't sound like the Pete Stanton I know. Where's that determination you had? Your commitment to the hours of practice you put in to finally move an object?"

"Before, I didn't have as much at stake. I mean, I was focused on moving objects just so I could signal to Jess that I was here in some way. Now, I have to figure out how to stop her from being murdered? This is all too much. I can't concentrate," said Pete, his dimming aura indicating his anxiety.

"No, Pete. You aren't stopping her from being murdered. You're *saving her life*. You're also saving her research so that it doesn't fall into the wrong hands. Not only are you saving Jessica's life, you're saving *thousands* of people in need of an organ transplant," said Jerome.

"When you put it that way . . ."

"Don't worry, Pete. You get to right a lot of wrongs if we can pull this off."

"Pull *what* off?"

Jerome looked at him with wild eyes. "I have a plan."

Pete waited eagerly in anticipation. "Well, what is it?"

"Don't worry about it. Go home with Jessica. Keep practicing," said Jerome.

"Great. That's all? You have a plan, and you want me to *go home*? Meanwhile, Jessica is going to be dead in a couple weeks if I can't figure out how to move an object? Sure. No pressure," said Pete with a scoff.

"We don't need you around here losing your cool and somehow regaining your magical powers and scaring our cook away. In order for this to work, we need to set a trap. It's probably best you're not at the lab until we lock our plan down," said Jerome.

"Our plan? Sounds like it's *your* plan, and I'm just a pawn in it," said Pete.

"You want to get this guy or not?" said Jerome.

Pete hesitated.

"You got a better idea to save Jess?" Jerome barked.

"No," said Pete.

"Good. Then meet me back here in a week."

"A week!? Jess could be dead by then," Pete scoffed.

"After I started feeling ill, it took another three to four weeks for the poison to kill me," said Jerome. "My guess is Jessica has about two to three weeks. If we intercept him, she should be in the clear."

"That doesn't give us much room for error," said Pete.

"No, Pete. It doesn't," Jerome said, and Pete nodded in response. "Keep an eye on her. The cook might not be the only out there after her."

HOME AGAIN

THE ROUTINE.

Tonight was different. Pete's morning unfolded the same way it always had with Jessica: After a long night of pacing and fixating on David Rendorff's potential misdeeds, mixed in with practicing moving objects, Pete would hear Jessica's alarm go off. Usually, he would prepare himself to greet Jessica and join her for a quick breakfast before she hurried off to work—leaving him alone to further ruminate on David and practice some more. It was just like any other morning until he heard a commotion coming from Jess's room.

"Jess! Are you alright?" he yelled. No answer.

He traveled into the hall and saw a light on in one of the bathrooms.

He entered slowly. There was no sign of her at first until he poked his head through the shower curtain. There she was, sitting in the tub with her nightgown on, with remnants of vomit on her chin. It was happening. She was getting sick again. The dimethylmercury the cook had given her was destroying her from the inside.

He heard Jerome's voice: *Once I started getting sick, I only lasted a few weeks.*

He burst through the wall, his aura ablaze at the sight of Jessica lying slouched over in the tub.

"Something's not right," Pete heard her say.

"Jess, we need to call an ambulance. Quickly. You're being poisoned. David—he's paying a cook at the lab to put something in your food," said Pete.

Her lack of response only further agitated him as he paced back and forth in furious thought.

"I have to do something. I have to *do something*!"

Bursting into an orb, he tore out of the house. He headed to see the only person he could think of who may be able to help.

HELP FROM THE MORTICIAN

"WHAT IN BLUE BLAZES ARE you doing here this time of night?" scolded Jerry.

Pete watched the old mortician sit up in bed and reach for his glasses, their thick black frames making him appear gentler than his true, gruff self.

"I wouldn't be here if it wasn't an emergency," said Pete.

"Do you know what you're asking me to do? No. You do not. Because if you knew the consequences of your proposal, you would most certainly not be asking," said Jerry, his furrowed brow confirming his displeasure.

"They are *killing* her," said Pete, watching Jerry get out of bed and shuffle over to the nightstand to take a sip of water from the glass sitting there.

"What you're asking is for me to change the course of action. To intervene. To go against Freewill. Defy laws of the universe! There are very strict rules about these things," said Jerry.

"Aren't there rules against *not* stepping in and helping someone when they're dying? No, correction—when they're being *murdered?*"

"Step aside, will you?" growled Jerry as he moved—hunched over, grumbling, and chewing his cheek—his slippers bouncing with each choppy step.

"Boo!" came a small, cheerful voice.

"What was that?" asked Pete.

"Nothing," said Jerry, visibly growing more agitated.

"It sounded like a . . . young girl," said Pete.

"Pay no attention to that!" yelled Jerry. He was angry. Pete had known Jerry to be grumpy, but he'd never seen him mad like this.

"Boo!"

This time, Pete saw her. A young spirit popped out of the walls and jumped back in. A little girl with blonde pig tails. She had on grey leggings and a black shirt with white polka dots. She couldn't have been older than five years old. He, again, caught her peering around the corner—as if she was playing a game with him.

"Addison, you get back in that room!" growled Jerry, a hint of panic piercing through his gruff command.

The young girl looked up at Jerry with a disappointed frown—her aura flashing, prompting him to scurry over to her and try comforting her. "There, there. I didn't mean to yell," he told her gently. Jerry must have sensed Pete hovering behind him. "She came in last week."

Pete tried to process this grumpy old man showing such concern for a little girl.

"You think *you're* confused by all this? Imagine being a five-year-old little girl trying to navigate the afterlife, like little Addison here," said Jerry.

"What are you going to do with her?" asked Pete.

"I don't quite know."

Pete watched him lean over and ask her gently to go back in the room. She seemed so small. Petite. Too young. Far too young to be in this world. It didn't seem fair.

There was something endearing about Jerry—the way he was caring for her, even in spite of his quirks and generally salty nature. "One thing is for sure," whispered Jerry after Addison went back into her room. "Every minute she's here increases the chances that The Others will find me."

"You keep talking about these Others. Who in the world are they?" said Pete.

"The most vile things that have ever existed. Merely talking about them puts me at great risk," said Jerry.

"Is that why you won't help me rescue Jessica?" said Pete.

"Partially." His voice changed, becoming softer. "You see, a person with my gift has the ability to change the future. Change the course of an individual's Freewill. If I were to intervene, it would cause much chaos in the order of things."

"I don't understand," said Pete.

"You don't have to. You just have to believe," said Jerry.

"Believe?"

"There's nothing in the rules that I know of that says a spirit cannot contact the living—so long as they don't try to intentionally frighten or harm them. That will earn you some bad marks," said Jerry.

"But what do you mean, 'believe'?" Pete repeated.

Jerry walked over to him, taking off his glasses to clean them. Pete noticed the old man's hands trembling slightly as he put them back on. "Believe in yourself, Pete. If you want to save Jessica, you must believe in *yourself*."

"Myself?" said Pete.

"You can do this, son," said Jerry.

"Thanks a lot," said Pete.

"Boo!" Little Addison emerged from her room again.

"Now, if you'll excuse me, I have a little one to tend to. She keeps me up at all hours of the night wanting to play. In a strange way, it makes me feel young again. It . . . feels *good* to be wanted," said Jerry, his sagging cheeks raising slightly as a rare grin emerged.

Pete watched the old man scurry over to the little girl, picking up a small toy and playing with her. He seemed to have a new life about him. His voice was gentle when he said, "Which one do you want to be, darling?" He held out a choice of two dolls for her selection, before pausing a moment looking up toward him.

"You can do it. Believe in yourself," whispered Jerry, and Pete wondered if maybe, just *maybe*, he could do just that.

"Believe in myself," he said feeling a jolt—like a surge of confidence growing just by repeating the old man's words. "Okay, Jerry . . . I'll do it your way. If it means saving Jessica, I'll do it. I believe."

THE PLAN

THE RIDE TO THE LAB was much different this time. Pete looked on in silence, abandoning his usual talk of the past as Jessica drove in anguish. He remembered her being carsick from time to time, but this was different. She was being *poisoned*.

"We don't have much time!" Pete said as Jerome's spirit entered the lab room.

"How is she?"

"She's sick. She had to pull the car over twice to throw up on the way to the lab this morning," Pete said in a panicked tone. He was flashing.

"Alright, man. Stay calm. You won't be any use to her if you go getting sick and having The Others show up," said Jerome.

Pete brushed past Jerome, ignoring the comment. "I went to see Jerry last night."

"Oh, yeah? What did that old coot have to say? He gonna help us?"

"No. He said something about it upsetting Freewill if he were to intervene."

"Yeah, I kinda figured that," said Jerome.

"But I don't understand. She's being *murdered*, and he can't step in?"

"He's a Bridge. There's only a few like him that ever existed," said Jerome. The term was so unfamiliar to Pete, he couldn't help but pause for thought. *What would that have to do with anything?*

"They say Hitler was a Bridge," Jerome added.

"Hitler? Adolf Hitler!?" said Pete.

"They say The Others found out he was a Bridge and manipulated him to try and end humanity. Almost pulled it off, too. Imagine if Hitler got his hands on one of those A-bombs first? *Checkmate.* We probably wouldn't even be standing here right now. Probably never would have existed at all," said Jerome solemnly.

Pete was silent as he tried to process the next steps.

"That's why Jerry won't help us. He's scared of The Others—and for good reason," said Jerome.

"So what do we do now?" said Pete.

"We move forward with the plan," said Jerome.

"What plan?" said Pete.

"We scare this fool into confessing." Pete had never seen this serious side of Jerome. His determination inspired confidence and trust.

"Just how do we do that?" said Pete.

"Come on over here. I'll show you," said Jerome.

THE CAFETERIA

THEY STAKED OUT THE COOK, watching his every movement as he went into the locker room.

They peered around a large column—as if they could be spotted. Old habits die hard, even in the spirit world.

"What's next?" Pete whispered.

"What?"

"*What* do we do?"

Jerome grew impatient. "What the hell we whispering for? He can't hear us."

"Well, I suppose we can step out from behind this column then," snapped Pete.

"Yeah, I suppose so. His ass can't see us *any-damn-way*," said Jerome.

"Are you getting street on me?" asked Pete.

"I may have been a Lab Manager, but I know a thing or two about the streets," said Jerome.

Pete wasn't buying it. Even with his martial arts and his Chi, Jerome was about the gentlest thing since warm milk. "I'm going to do all the dirty work here, aren't I?"

"Yeah, I'm the mastermind." Jerome shrugged.

"Thought so," said Pete.

"Alright. Focus," said Jerome. "The cook is opening his locker. When he puts on his uniform he transfers the dimethylmercury from his coat to his shirt pocket."

Sure enough, the cook changed into his uniform, looked around to make sure no one was watching, and quickly swiped something from his coat and placed it in his pocket.

"Was that it?" said Pete.

"Yeah. It's a small bottle, but it doesn't take much," said Jerome.

They watched the cook slither his way back to the line where he waited to set his trap.

"There's Jess!" said Jerome as they peered out into the cafeteria. "And the cook—he's watching her closely."

"She's placing her order. She doesn't look good," said Pete.

"The soup today," said Jerome. "If we didn't know she was feeling sick before . . ."

They watched as the cashier placed the order. The cook nonchalantly maneuvered himself into position behind the counter.

"I got this one," he said as he took the order slip. They watched him look at Jess and flash a smile. "Let me guess: buffalo chicken wrap?"

Pete watched Jess smile through the anguish she was in. "Am I that predictable? But thank you. Really. I'm not having the best day—it's sweet of you to know my order."

"My pleasure, ma'am. You make it easy on us here at the cafeteria. You get the same thing every—what's this? *Soup* today?" said the cook in a charming voice.

"Yeah, like I said—not having a great day."

"I'll take care of you, ma'am." The cook smiled again.

"He's playing her! I'm gonna kill him!" said Pete as he moved toward the cook.

"Pete! No!" barked Jerome and Pete stopped, despite himself. "Get your flashing under control. If you blow this, so help me—I'll *never* speak to you again! This is our chance to get him. Get your act together!"

The sharp tone got to Pete. He focused on controlling his aura.

"Good job," said Jerome. "Listen, I want this guy as bad as you do. And we are going to get him. Are you ready to do your thing?"

"I think so," said Pete.

"Ok, then. Concentrate," said Jerome.

They watched the cook take the order slip into the kitchen and begin preparing Jessica's lunch. He held a bowl in one hand, then ladled the brothy soup into it. He then subtly took the vial of dimethylmercury out of his pocket and added two drops to the soup.

"I can't watch this," said Pete.

"I know it's hard, but this is the only way," said Jerome.

They watched the cook slip the vial back into his pocket and walk the bowl out to Jessica.

"One order of our Soup of the Day. Hope you feel better," he told her.

"Thanks so much," she said.

Time seemed to slow down for Pete as he watched Jessica walk over to a table and take her seat in the lunchroom. "I have to do something."

"Pete! Don't you blow this!" said Jerome.

Pete turned into an orb and shot toward Jessica. He unfolded just as she was bringing the first spoonful to her mouth.

Tim Sampson, one of the lab technicians, walked by and began chatting with Jessica.

Pete saw his chance. He focused deep within himself. He thought of the car crash; he thought of seeing his dead body for the first time; he thought of Lagos, and the confusion he'd had since he didn't enter the portal; he thought of the frustration he'd experienced with not being able to communicate with Jessica, and he thought of the cook slipping a vial out of his pocket and poisoning Jessica's soup. All of these thoughts built a tremendous energy within him.

When Pete released his energy, the force caused Tim the Lab Tech to stumble into Jessica, knocking her bowl to the floor.

"Oh no! I am so sorry," said Tim as he placed his tray on a table and began throwing napkins onto the mess.

"It's okay," said Jessica.

"No, really. I'm so sorry. I don't know what got into me. I'm so clumsy."

"Tim—it's okay. Really," said Jessica.

Pete looked on as Tim the Lab Tech picked up the bowl and returned it to her tray.

"I'll get you some more," he said to Jessica.

"No, really. It's fine. I haven't been feeling well. I was probably only going to have a little bit, anyway," said Jessica.

"Not feeling well?" said Tim.

"No. It's the strangest thing. It's like I have the flu, but I don't have a fever. I'm not sick, but I just *feel awful*," said Jessica.

"You been hittin' the bottle?" Tim asked with a chuckle.

"No, but it is like a perpetual hangover!" said Jessica.

"Sounds like something's off. Stop by my lab today, and I'll draw some blood and have it analyzed," said Tim.

"Really? Thank you. I just might do that. I am getting desperate," said Jessica.

"Desperate, but not too desperate to go to the doctor?" challenged Tim.

Pete watched as Jessica blushed. "Yeah, well, you know me," she said.

"Seriously, Jessica. Stop by and we'll draw the blood and get it looked at. If you don't come by 2 p.m., I'll send my people after you."

"Your people?" said Jessica.

"Yeah. My people. Big, tall, burly guys in lab coats that I keep around just in case one of my crew isn't taking care of themselves so I can snatch them up and force them to get some blood work. *Those* people," said Tim.

Pete watched as Jessica chuckled. She held her ribs. "Sorry, I'm just a little sore."

"Okay. I'm really gonna send my people if you don't show," said Tim.

"I'll be there. Make it 2:30?"

"If it's 2:31, my people are coming!" joked Tim.

"Thank you, Tim," said Jessica.

"Anything for Jessica Stanton! Now, if you'll excuse me, my people are waiting on me to eat lunch with them," he said.

"Nice work," said Jerome. "That couldn't have worked out any better."

"Yeah, well sometimes you get lucky, I suppose," said Pete.

"You did that all by yourself. On command. It was controlled. You seemed to release just enough force to make him trip on his own. You've come a long way since smashing dinner plates against the wall," said Jerome.

"I'm still a bit rusty, but I'm getting it down," said Pete.

"Are you able to pick up any objects?"

"No, it's mostly just a release of energy where I'm able to move something laterally. Picking things up is a whole different thing entirely," said Pete.

"Well, let's see if you can channel your powers again," said Jerome. "Let's get him tomorrow."

THE LOCKER ROOM HAUNTING

THEY STALKED THE COOK AS though they were lions waiting to pounce on a baby gazelle.

"Javier Romero," said Jerome. "He's worked at this cafeteria longer than I can remember. Strange, he served me lunch every day, and I never knew his name until after I died."

"You mean after he *murdered* you," scoffed Pete.

"True, but I had an epiphany after I died. I've been eating at this cafeteria daily, and these people working behind the counter served me food. Yet, I never knew any of their names. I guess we just go through life hurrying from one meeting to the next, never taking time out of our busy schedules to slow down and live in the present. Here's a kitchen full of people making hot lunches to feed a bunch of people who they'll never know their names. When you think about it that way, the whole system just seems unnatural."

"Feed you, or kill you."

"I suppose. . . . In this case, you're right, but you're missing my point."

"This isn't exactly the time for a philosophy lesson—"

"*I'm going to take a break,*" they heard the cook say.

"Now he'll head to the locker room to put the vial away," said Jerome. "He does this every day around the same time."

They followed the cook as he left the cafeteria and entered a small dark room. Metal lockers lined one wall, and toilets and urinals lined the other. Flakes of paint peeling from the ceiling and sounds of water dripping from pipes made a frightening symphonic melody.

"This room is like we stepped back in time," said Pete.

"Definitely hasn't been kept up like the rest of the hospital," said Jerome.

They watched as Javier grabbed something from his pocket and placed it in his locker.

"There!" said Jerome. "He put the vial of poison back into his locker."

"I'll take it from here," said Pete.

He walked over to the light switch, and his inner thoughts channeled and built up energy.

"Careful, Pete. You're aura is flashing pretty good," said Jerome.

Pete paid no attention. He thought about Javier poisoning Jessica. Charming her unsuspectingly while making her lunch. Smiling through a gold tooth while ladling a bowl of soup. Tattoo on his neck poking just above his white smock. Greasy hair shining through a hairnet. Hoping she *"felt better."* Meanwhile, *he* was the one making her sick.

He released his energy on the light switch—the room became dark.

"You did it!" yelled Jerome.

"Watch this," said Pete.

"Who's there?" Javier cried out. No answer. The room dark. Still. The only noise that of a dripping faucet. "Turn the lights back on! I can't see!"

SLAM!

Pete closed an empty locker door and the metal-on-metal clang echoed through the room.

"Who did that?" Javier's voice cracked despite his obvious attempt at sounding tough. "Jimmy? Is that you?"

No answer.

"Yo! This ain't funny, guys!"

SLAM!

Pete closed another locker door—this time in close proximity to the cook, who wheeled around and began punching the dark, empty air.

"You're getting to him, Pete," shouted Jerome. "Keep it up!"

SLAM! SLAM! SLAM!

"Okay, pause for a minute. Get your flashing under control," said Jerome.

In all the excitement, Pete hadn't realized his aura was blinking erratically. He wanted savage revenge. Javier had killed his friend, Jerome. Poisoned his wife. Tried to sabotage her research. *Her research*—the very thing that had kept him and Jessica from starting a family! Jessica's *legacy*. Pete would be damned if he let Javier steal her research.

They watched Javier feel his way around in the dark. Hands outstretched, trying to find his way out, banging his knee on a bench—cursing random co-workers he'd begun accusing as he went.

"Okay, don't let him get out of the room," said Jerome.

SLAM!

Pete shut a locker right in front of Javier's face.

"ARRRRG!" he turned to run back toward his locker—where he tripped over a bench and landed awkwardly, lying prone on the cold wet floor, gasping for air.

"He landed weird on the corner of that bench. I think he broke some ribs," said Jerome.

"Jimmy, I swear, if this is you, I'm gonna *kill you*," said the cook in between gasps.

Pete and Jerome heard sobbing.

"He's starting to crack," said Jerome.

"I think he realizes this isn't Jimmy," said Pete.

"Please, leave me alone!" cried the cook. "I'm hurt! Please! I'll do anything! Just leave me *alone*."

"It's working," said Jerome.

"Please! Is that you? Jerome? Is it . . . is it really you?"

SLAM!

"I'm sorry! Please, leave me alone. I'm sorry I poisoned you!" cried the cook.

SLAM! SLAM! SLAM!

"It's you! It's really you!" yelled Javier helplessly, curled up in a corner. "Please, don't hurt me, Jerome! Please! I'll do anything! I'm sorry! Just don't hurt me, Jerome!"

All of a sudden, a door burst open and a light flipped on. A scream filled the room as two men—a cafeteria manager and a security guard—rushed to search the locker room, finding Javier stuffed in a locker, screaming in absolute terror. They tried to coax him out, but Javier wouldn't budge, trembling with fear and fighting off their attempts to remove him.

"What's he saying?" asked the cafeteria manager.

"Sounds like he's saying, *'He's here. You have to help me,'*" said the security manager.

"Javier, we searched the locker room. There's no one in here. Come on out."

"He's here!" he yelled, pointing across the room.

Each of the sinks were turned on, scalding hot water covering the mirrors with a hazy fog. There, a message written on a steamy mirror:

MURDERER

"Javier, what's going on here?" yelled the café manager.

Javier stared past them, arms wrapped around his knees rocking back and forth. "Don't hurt me, Jerome! I'm sorry! I'm *sorry*, Jerome!"

"Jerome?" said the security guard. "What are you talking about? What about *Jerome?*"

"You gotta help me," Javier said, eyes wild with fear, clutching onto the guard's shirt and pulling him close. "It's Jerome—he's trying to hurt me. He's here. Jerome, I'm sorry! Don't hurt me!"

"Jerome is dead," the cafeteria manager said. "Happened a couple years ago, collapsed right here in this very cafeteria and died. We chalked it up to a heart attack."

The security guard turned back toward Javier. "Listen, Javier," he said in a calming tone. "I'm not going to let anyone hurt you, but you have to tell me—why would Jerome want to do you harm?"

"Because I killed him! He's trying to get me back! You have to help me!"

"I think we better search his locker," said the cafeteria manager.

JESSICA RECOVERS

"THAT WAS A CLOSE ONE," said Dr. Williams. "You nearly died."

Besides arresting Javier after he'd confessed to everything, administrators at the hospital immediately dispatched an ambulance to Jessica's home as they soon learned she hadn't reported to work that day. Emergency medical technicians responding to the call found Jessica lying passed out in her bathtub with the shower running. The IV they gave her to flush her system and the quick stomach pump on the way to the hospital revived her just enough for her to make it before a flock of doctors swarmed to her aid upon her arrival. Pete and Jerome were there, standing by as they eagerly listened to the prognosis.

"You mean I was nearly *murdered*, don't you?" she snapped.

"What's the treatment plan, Doc?" asked Pete, a nervous flashing consuming his aura.

"I'm sorry. He can't hear ya, Pete," said Jerome sympathetically.

"What's the treatment plan?" asked Jessica, prompting a rebellious snicker from Pete.

"We've given you a transfusion. Changed out some of your tainted blood and replaced it with new. Should get most of that mercury out of your system," said Dr. Williams.

"I already feel better," she said. "I'm still weak, but I don't feel so nauseous."

"You're not out of the woods yet. We are referring you to a nutritionist to put you on a diet to clean up any remnants in your blood. There's also your organs. The mercury . . . it's stored in your kidneys. There's some serious damage to your kidney function; we'll need to keep you here for monitoring. We have you on a temporary dialysis to flush the remaining mercury out and increase your kidney function to an acceptable level," said Dr. Williams.

"*Diet*? What kind of diet?" Jessica bristled, apparently ignoring the part about dialysis.

"That will be up to the nutritionist, but my guess is it will be full of antioxidants. Boost your immunity and purge the remaining impurities from your system," said Dr. Williams.

"Can't you just give me some meds and call it a day?" she scoffed.

"Listen, your internal organs have been through the ringer. You, of all people, should know the importance of kidney function. A dose of meds will be rough on those kidneys—so why don't we try the natural route first?" said Dr. Williams. "I'm releasing you today if you promise bedrest for three days."

Pete watched as Jessica slid her arm to the side of the bed, out of sight of the doctor.

"I promise," she said.

"She's crossing her fingers! Look!" said Pete.

"You got a feisty one on your hands, Pete. She has no intention of staying in bed," said Jerome with one of his belly laughs.

"I'm gonna go with her. I'll see you back at the lab?" said Pete.

"See you there, buddy," said Jerome.

WINDS OF CHANGE

IT WASN'T LONG BEFORE PETE noticed a change in Jessica. It was like something sparked inside her. Her new "you only live once" mentality was a big change from sitting on the couch watching her nightly shows. For Pete, it was almost too much to handle. Up until now, the mercury poisoning aside, his plan had worked almost flawlessly. This was different. There was something about her. As if the death of her husband compounded by being on the brink of death herself erupted something inside her. The late nights out. Keeping very little food in the house. Not eating at all. She had lost weight, and not good weight. Not having food in the refrigerator didn't bother Pete any—he merely saw it as a symptom of her change.

"Hopefully it's just a phase she's working through," he'd say to himself alone after she came home in a drunken stupor, falling asleep in her clothes again. He had stopped going with her—he couldn't bear to watch her drive intoxicated anymore. After a while, he couldn't even be around her.

"You're here late," Jerome said one night when he was on a stroll after hours through the lonely lab hallways. "I thought you'd be home with Jess by now. Working on something?"

"I'm still working on a plan to signal Jess so she knows I'm with her."

"You've been working on that plan for some time now. Seems you have an easier time catching murderers than you do signaling Jess," said Jerome.

"Yeah. I suppose so," said Pete, his aura dimming.

"I mean, why don't you just steam up the bathroom mirror and write a message like we did to you-know-who?" Jerome chuckled.

"I thought about that. Believe me . . . I've thought a lot about doing that," said Pete.

"Well?" asked Jerome. "Seems like the logical thing to do. You can just heat up the old mirror and write her a message. Think about it. Every night before she goes to bed, you could leave a new message: '*Dear Jess, I love you so much,*'" he added in a cheesy sing-song voice.

"You're not helping things," scoffed Pete.

"Sorry, buddy, I just hate seeing you down like this," said Jerome.

"Listen—you saw the reaction of the cook, right?" asked Pete.

"I sure did! We scared the dickens out of him!" Jerome gave one of his signature belly laughs.

Pete crossed his arms in defiance, showing his lack of tolerance at Jerome's belligerence. "The cook was terrified. I've never seen someone so frightened. What if . . . Jess . . . What if I leave her a note on that mirror and she reacts the same way?"

"Ah, I see what's going on here," acknowledged Jerome. "You're afraid to message her because you think you'll scare her off."

"I'm only going to get one shot at this! If I scare her, she'll want nothing to do with me. Who knows, maybe I scare her so badly she sells the house. What if she moves? What then? Do I follow her around the rest of her life and keep leaving her messages?"

"Okay, *okay*. Just calm down now. Your aura is flashing pretty wildly. We don't need you to get sick," said Jerome. "Let's come up with a plan."

"Plan?"

"We figured out how to get Javier, didn't we? Surely we can figure out how to message Jess."

"It's just that she's going through a phase. I don't know what's wrong with her," said Pete.

"I'll tell you what's wrong with her. Her husband *died*," Jerome grumbled.

"Me?"

"Yeah, you. On top of it, she almost died thanks to Javier the cook. That kind of thing does something to a person."

"I get it. It's just that she's getting after it pretty hard. Hanging out at O'Malley's about every night after work."

"I see. She's probably working through some things. I'd imagine losing you and being targeted for murder might have triggered something in her."

"That's what I'm afraid of," said Pete.

"Who's she hanging out with?" asked Jerome.

"Remember that Lab Tech who I pushed in the cafeteria the other day? The one who bumped into Jess and spilled her soup?"

"Sampson. Tim Sampson," said Jerome with a low growl.

"That's the guy," said Pete.

"A bunch of people from the lab hang out there. Sampson is the ring leader," said Jerome. "That group parties pretty hard."

"It's not like her," said Pete. "Plus, she's recovering from mercury poisoning. She's not even supposed to be drinking!"

"I got an idea that might take your mind off things," said Jerome. "Could be our way of messaging her too."

"Yeah?"

"Remember that secret file I had in my office for the recipe for the kidney solution? Now that Rendorff is in jail, I think it's time I share my secret file with Jess. She'll know what to do with it. Maybe discovering the file will get her to refocus on her work again. Plus, I have to think she'll wonder about these little *miracles* like my files just mysteriously showing up on her desk."

"It could be my way of signaling her!"

"Precisely," acknowledged Jerome.

"Let's go," said Pete bursting through the lab room wall. Walls ended up in hallways. More walls ended up in lab rooms. More hallways. More lab rooms before making it to Jerome's office.

"Just as I remember it. Hasn't really been touched except for the guys who ransacked my office looking for my documents," said Jerome.

"They haven't moved anyone in here," said Pete.

"Would *you* want to sit in a dead guy's office?" scoffed Jerome.

"I suppose not," said Pete.

"The documents are in this file cabinet . . . second drawer down. Underneath the false bottom," said Jerome.

"False bottom?"

"I made a false bottom for the drawer when I realized someone was after me. They never did find the documents," said Jerome with a smirk. "Go ahead. Open it. Take a look."

Pete concentrated and released just enough energy to pull the cabinet door open.

"Move those files around," barked Jerome.

"*You* want to do this?" Pete scoffed.

He gently moved the files away just enough so he could peer into the drawer. There, underneath a thin metal piece, was a file.

"Go ahead. Pull the file out," said Jerome, hovering over him, keeping a careful watch. Pete complied, pulling out a file that was stuffed full of papers. "What do you have in here? A sack of rocks?"

"This is what they were after. This is what I was murdered for."

"What now?" asked Pete, noticing Jerome's aura had dimmed.

"We wait. Wait for Jessica to come in tomorrow—then, we transfer it to her briefcase."

"But there's going to be people all over the lab tomorrow when she gets in. A file just floating down the hallway? Yeah. Likely to scare people to death," said Pete. "You haven't thought this through, have you?"

"As a matter of fact, I have. We can't just leave the file sitting in plain sight. Someone would likely come along and swipe it! Then what?"

"I suppose you're right. Maybe we should wait until she gets in tomorrow . . . but we need to be covert about this. No one can see the file floating around. I'm not ready to signal Jess and let her know I'm here," said Pete.

"Deal," said Jerome.

And so it was set. The duo paced back and forth all night refining the details of their plan. They'd slide the file under doors, move it down the hallway, slip it under a table where Jess was having a meeting—and *voilà*! They would place it in her bag that sat at her feet.

If only it went that smoothly.

Pete was so nervous, he forgot the file couldn't pass through a door like he could. As he made his way into the hallway, he passed right through the door, only for the file to get stuck as it made contact with the wood and come crashing down—papers strewn everywhere in the lab room.

"Now you've done it!" yelled Jerome. "Quick! Pick up the papers!"

Pete was panicking. "Aren't you going to help me?"

"You're the one who can move objects!"

Both their auras began flashing wildly. Pete scurried around the room, picking up loose papers and cramming them into the file folder. "She's going to have to figure out the order of my notes now!"

"Jess is a smart girl. She'll figure it out," said Pete. "Okay. Let's go."

And so they did. This time, Pete slid the file under the door only to pick it up after he passed through—their original plan. Only it didn't take long before they were spotted.

"Stop!" yelled Jerome.

Pete froze. The file lay on the floor next to him.

"One of the janitorial folks is coming," said Jerome.

"We need to move," said Pete.

"Okay! On the count of three. One, two—"

"That's odd. A file . . . just laying here?" The janitor's name tag read:

Randy. He was toting a mop bucket.

"Pete, you gotta do something! *Quick*," said Jerome.

Pete grabbed the mop and tossed it. Randy stood looking at the mop for a moment. When he turned back around, the file was gone. They didn't stick around long enough to hear Randy try and come to grips with the unexplained.

They finally made it—after much bantering, bickering, and overall gallivanting.

"Okay, open up her briefcase," said Jerome hunkering under the table. "Her briefcase has a buckle on it I can't quite figure out."

Suddenly, Jessica's hand appeared. She felt around her briefcase for a moment before her hand stopped on the buckle, releasing it.

"Now!" yelled Jerome.

Pete plunged the file into her briefcase before she closed it.

"Yes!" Jerome yelled. He stood through the tables and broke into the chicken dance. Pete wished Jessica could see them now.

It was perhaps the next event that would change the trajectory of Pete's destiny forever.

THE PLAN FALLS SHORT

HE HAD BEEN PACING AROUND the house for a few days now, monitoring Jessica's every move. Waiting for her to open her briefcase and make the discovery.

It was no use. Tonight, she was watching her favorite show about puppies. He sat on the couch with her, watching TV, glad to feel like things were back to normal. Maybe it was a rebellious time for Jess and this phase was over. . . .

Then, the phone rang and Jessica hastily picked it up.

"That's unusual. Jess never talks on the phone," said Pete.

He watched her fumble around and finally gain control of her phone. "Sure, Saturday night at seven. It's a date!" she said as she hung up.

Pete looked up. His aura flashed like a strobe light. "Date? What do you mean *date?*"

Jess picked up the remote and resumed watching TV. She started humming a song, which is what she did when she was happy.

The days leading to the weekend were torture. Pete spent the next couple days at home. He didn't go to the lab with Jess—which was an unusual break in his routine. He had not missed a day of work with her since he'd died.

Instead, he spent the next few days pacing throughout the house in a tormented dance of denial.

"Date?"

"It's a date."

"It's probably not a real *date."*

"No way Jess could've met someone with the type of schedule she keeps."

He eventually settled down for a short while and convinced himself that she was probably meeting one of her girlfriends out for drinks, but that didn't last long. Then, the negotiating came. He'd follow her around pleading for her to reconsider.

"What about our plan, Jess? I'm here! I've always been here! I'm living with you until you pass away and then we'll enter your portal together . . . Live togeth-

75

er forever! Don't you see? We can't enter the portal together if you find someone else. Think about it, Jess!"

Then it came. *Saturday*. He knew because Jess took a break from her normal routine of going to the grocery store and running errands. "She never goes to the mall," said Pete as they pulled up. "Probably just meeting her girlfriends out for drinks," he repeated over and over, holding onto a thin piece of hope.

What sealed it was when she went and got a manicure and a blow-out. "This is the first time in two years I've seen you put on makeup," he said as she readied herself. "You look beautiful, Jess. You really do. I just wish I was there in person to tell you." His aura brightened at the sight of her, but he sensed it wouldn't stay bright for long as he glared at her briefcase—shut and locked, sitting in the corner of the room, untouched since her meeting.

"Jess, you *really* need to open up your briefcase. Jerome and I left you a surprise in there. You're going to want to see it. Why don't you just stay home tonight and look in your briefcase? Some important discovery about your work is in there," he said, moving to the corner and tipping the briefcase over. It made a loud thud as it hit the floor.

He watched as Jessica's attention snapped to her briefcase lying on the floor. "That's odd," she said, walking over timidly and picking it up, pausing to inspect it.

"Go ahead, Jess! Look inside!" he shouted before quieting, watching her holding the briefcase, looking at it with fervor.

"Ah, work. If I open this thing, I'm just going to get sucked in. I have a fun night planned and I'm *not* going to think about work," she said, setting the briefcase down before snatching the keys off the dresser and heading hurriedly to the garage—Pete following in tow.

"Jess, please—just wait. Open the briefcase!"

JESS'S DATE

"I LIKED IT BETTER WHEN Jess was drinking," Pete said to himself as he passed through the restaurant doors.

Parc in Rittenhouse Square. It had an outdoor patio wrapping around the corner. The front faced Locust Street, and the tables ran along the side of the restaurant—18th to Mozart Place. The inside had modern décor—unique lighting mixed with classic art prints. They had celebrated birthdays there. Anniversaries. It was their neighborhood place when they wanted to grab a quick catch up. Now it was no longer he and Jess's spot.

Pete was almost relieved when he saw him walk into the restaurant. It had been a tumultuous few days of suspense and anticipation leading up to now, and it almost felt good that he didn't have to carry the burden around any longer. Now, he knew for sure. But relief quickly changed to a blend of sadness and panic—which he'd been told wasn't healthy for a spirit, especially one who could move things.

He recognized him immediately. *Sampson.* The lab technician she worked with. Tim Sampson. The funny, life of the party at O'Malley's. It had to be him. Given his current state, Pete could easily turn into a sick spirit if he wasn't careful.

"You brought him *here*, Jess? Of all places, you brought him *here!?* This is supposed to be our place!"

He watched her rise from her seat, straighten her dress, and smile as she greeted him. His aura dimmed to a dark grey as he watched them embrace. Her beautiful smile as her date kissed her cheek. She hadn't smiled like that in months—no, *years.*

"How could I have missed this?" said Pete. "I'm at that lab every frickin' day."

All the time he'd spent isolated at Jess's lab working on moving objects caused him to overlook her budding relationship with Tim. Maybe if he would've spent more time at O'Malley's with them, he would've seen the spark.

"I would've signaled her earlier if I had known! I was just waiting for the perfect time. I wanted it to be special."

He watched them take their seats. They ordered drinks. Tim took her hand in his. They talked. Smiled. Never even gave the menu a glance.

"You look beautiful," Pete heard him say as he gently caressed her hand.

"Thank you. It's been a long time since anyone has said that to me." She blushed.

"I say it to you every night before you fall asleep! I told you that you looked beautiful today while you were getting ready!" Pete growled. An occasional bolt of light flashed through his darkening aura.

Pete watched a waiter approach. Hip-looking. Neatly trimmed beard. Black framed glasses. He had bulging, tattooed arms that stretched his short-sleeved, button-up shirt. Over it, he wore a three-button black vest. He hurriedly passed by, carrying a tray full of plates of food and drinks. Pete angrily hit the tray out of the waiter's hands—dumping food over Jessica and Tim's table. Plates and glasses crashed to the ground, breaking upon impact.

The new couple swiftly stood up, reacting to spilled food and drink all over their table. Pete was thrilled to see Tim covered in a cocktail of sugary drinks, salads, and paninis. A hamburger patty had somehow landed on his chest. Jess was largely unscathed.

"That will teach him," said Pete, eyes narrowing to a mischievous squint—but guilt eventually overcame him as he watched the waiter try and redeem himself.

An angry restaurant manager arrived on the scene—along with an army of waitstaff promptly cleaning the area—*firing the waiter on the spot.*

"That's not really necessary. It wasn't his fault!" said Pete as the manager, now covered in food himself, tried frantically cleaning Tim's shirt.

"It's okay, sir. . . . Really. It's just a shirt," said Tim.

"Why do you have to be such a gentleman?" said Pete. "That should ruin your date. Go home and clean yourself up. Report to work embarrassed on Monday. Never see Jessica again."

He watched Tim and Jessica exchange eye contact. Instead of Tim rushing out of the restaurant in an embarrassed heap, he stared deeply into Jessica's eyes, more confident than ever. They broke out in laughter.

"You're all wet!" she chuckled, pointing at Tim's shirt.

She walked over to him and took his hand. They left the restaurant together. It left Pete wishing he hadn't tipped that tray. He stood over the scene he created: the manager commanding an army of busboys, rushing to cleaning up; a waiter who just lost his job; an embarrassed restaurant manager; and a giant mess.

And to top it all off, Pete's interference seemed to drive Jessica and her date even closer together.

JESS MOVES ON

THE RIDE HOME WITH THEM was torture. Pete was expecting Tim would have gone his own separate way after being covered in drinks and burgers, but this was not the case.

"Let's get you cleaned up," Jess told him. "I don't live far from here. My husband was about your size. I still have several of his shirts."

"You're giving him one of my shirts?" said Pete.

"You sure you don't mind?" asked Tim.

"Listen—I haven't been on a date in years. You're crazy if you think I'm going to let some spilled spaghetti ruin our night together. Besides, you look good covered in red sauce. It brings out your eyes."

They laughed.

Pete watched as she took his hand in hers.

They were at a stoplight, Pete watching as Jess leaned in and planted a kiss on Tim's lips—such a long kiss that the car behind them honked when the light turned green.

"Well, okay then," said Tim. "You sold me."

Jess drove the car into the garage after a short drive, leaning in and kissing Tim again before the garage door was even down, sending Pete's aura into overdrive.

It was a passionate kiss, and Pete heard some heavy breathing and a subtle whine from Jessica before she pushed her date back, fixing her smeared lipstick with her finger.

"Okay, you need to go upstairs and shower and get changed. You smell like you've been stomping tomatoes," she said.

The car doors slammed, and Pete heard some flirty giggles from Jess as he watched them enter his house. He stayed in the backseat as they left the car and went inside. His aura kept flashing. He was unsure of what to do. The car offered only a temporary sanctuary.

"He's going to take a shower. Get cleaned up. Then he's probably going

80

to leave. That's right, he'll be leaving any minute now. . . ."

Pete wasn't sure how much time had passed before he finally exited the car. *He had to know.*

He walked through the garage door and stood outside in his driveway. He looked up at his impressive three-story brick home. The top window on the third floor lit up.

His bedroom.

"I was so proud of us when we bought this house, Jess. . . . We started out in a studio apartment in downtown Philly with nothing. I had just graduated from law school, and you had another year to go before graduation. We barely had a penny to our name, but we had each other. That's the only thing that mattered to us. *Each other.*"

He looked around the quiet street, the street lamps lighting a path as if to say, *Pete, no need to go inside. Come this way*, prompting an anger in him. No, he had to know.

"This is *our* house, Jess," he growled. He looked up at the big house. Everything they worked for. "We were going to start a family." His aura dimmed even more; he hung his head. "I have to know, Jess. I have to know if you've moved on."

He formed into an orb and shot into the house, unfolding outside the bedroom door, where he listened to the steady sound of the shower in their master bathroom. He stood there, weighing his options. Wondering if there was another way. *Listen to the street lamps*, a part of him cried. *Leave the house for the night. Just forget this all happened and go back to the normal routine tomorrow.*

No.

He had to know.

He slowly passed through the door, locating Jess. She was sitting at her vanity desk, playing with her hair and drinking a glass of wine. The sound of the water turned off, and Jess sat silently, looking at herself in the mirror. Pete could hear Tim fumbling around in the bathroom.

The bathroom door opened and Tim Sampson was standing in the doorway with nothing on but a towel. "Um, this is a little embarrassing, but were you going to bring me a change of clothes? Mine are completely ruined."

Pete watched her stand up and go over to Tim. She rubbed his chest and kissed him. She began removing her dress.

Pete needed to stop what was about to happen. He flipped the light switch off and the room went dark.

"Hey!" he heard Jess say. She was mumbling. He could tell she was buzzed from the wine she drank.

"Did you turn the light off?" asked Tim.

"No. Did you?"

Pete flipped the light back on.

"Weird. Must be something going on with the lights," she said. She resumed kissing Tim.

"Don't do it, Jess! Don't do it!" he yelled.

Pete flipped the lights off again. This time, he flipped them on and off in a continuous manner, like a strobe light.

"Okay, this is weird," she said. She started putting her dress back on.

"What's going on?" said Tim.

"I don't know. Maybe someone else is in the house," she said, visibly unnerved. They stood motionless together for a moment, listening for any sign of an intruder.

"Boo!" said Jess as she playfully poked Tim.

He almost jumped out of his skin. They exchanged a laugh before kissing again. This time, Pete let them go longer. He had to know. He watched them get under the sheets. *It was going to happen*. He knew he was torturing himself, and yet he couldn't look away.

"I could've gone to the afterlife—but no, I'm stuck here waiting for you!" he hissed, traveling to Jessica's desk where a large crystal vase sat. He'd bought it her for as an anniversary gift. Using every drop of energy he had, he lifted the vase into the air.

Apparently Tim and Jessica were too preoccupied to notice a floating vase in the middle of the room, because they didn't respond. *But they would soon.*

Pete flipped the vase over and looked at the bottom, reading the inscription he had written her.

To Jess, the love of my life. To our first of many years together.

He thought back to when he bought the vase. He and Jessica had walked by a shop that sold crystals, and she had fallen in love with it. At the time, he didn't have money for the vase, but he bought it anyway because he wanted to make her happy.

"You don't deserve this!" He smashed the vase on the ground into thousands of pieces.

The loud noise startled the couple. While they tried to figure out what happened, Pete picked up the bottom of the vase and placed it on her desk—

the inscription facing up so she would know he had been there.

He traveled out of the room. As he made it downstairs, he paused as he heard a shrill scream from Jessica. *She knew it was him.*

He gave a final glance at Jessica's briefcase sitting there, untouched, in the corner. Someday, she'd find Jerome's papers stuffed inside, but he wouldn't be here when she did.

Pete burst into an orb, tearing through the walls of his house, and shot into the dark summer night—his aura burning as blue as the sunless sky.

PART TWO
JOE MORTON
GRANDPA JOE

"PRETTY DAY, HUH, DAD?" SAID Bill.

Joe Morton grumbled at the comment. He wasn't much for conversation these days. Besides, the radiation sapped his strength and the thought of participating in small talk only weakened him further.

They sat quietly, listening to the songbirds in the trees. Joe always loved watching the birds. Gold Finches were his favorite. He loved the way they hung upside down, voraciously attacking the bird feeder—a small distraction from the nausea he felt almost constantly these days.

"Hi, boys. How about some iced tea?"

He nodded as his daughter-in-law, Sarah, poured a glass from a pitcher of fresh-made iced tea. He hated the way she looked at him—with doe-like eyes, full of pity. But he knew she meant well, and truly was thankful the two of them were taking care of him—although he wasn't about to tell them that. No, that would be giving them too much credit.

"I'll leave you two be," she said as she scampered inside.

He took a sip, noticing the way the ice clinked against the glass. The cool, refreshing feeling that soothed his throat. It was the little things these days that he tended to. Things he never quite appreciated before.

"Son?" he said laboriously, with a hand waving, motioning Bill to move closer. Mustering up the mere word caused him a shortness of breath.

"Dad, you don't need to speak. Just take it easy and rest," said Bill, who hadn't touched his iced tea or a single thing from the food tray Sarah had left on the table dividing them.

Joe waved him off, repositioning himself in his chair before continuing—trying to get comfortable enough to have a heart-to-heart with his son. Though comfort always felt out of reach these days, he never complained. No, that wasn't in his nature. He'd rather sit quietly than complain.

"Son—I've lived a long and full life."

"I know you have, Dad," Bill replied.

He held his hand in the air, motioning for Bill to let him finish. "My one regret in life will be if I don't get to meet my grandson."

He watched Bill mimic him—shifting in his own chair, although he imagined his son's shifting was due to nervousness and not discomfort. He paused as Sarah came back outside, clutching a glass of tea.

"It's too nice out here for me to sit inside, all alone. . . . Mind if I join ya?" Sarah pulled up a chair and sat with them, placing a hand on her full belly, where Joe's unborn grandson rested.

"Oh, I'm sorry," Sarah added hastily, sensing tension. "Am I interrupting?"

Joe nodded with a scowl, but Bill said, "No, no, honey. Please, stay. Dad—if it's okay with you, I'd like Sarah to hear your concerns. She may have some ideas."

Sarah seemed confused and a little out of place, but to Joe's chagrin, she stayed.

"So, Dad was just saying he feels sad because he may not get to see the baby—if, uh . . ."

"If I don't make it," Joe snapped.

Joe watched as Sarah calmly put her tea on the table, her glass making a sharp thud. She placed her hand on Bill's leg and patted it twice before leaning forward, taking Joe's hand in hers.

It was his instinct to jerk his hand away, but he let her hold it. It's not like he could get away anyway, as he was bound to his wheelchair. The tension of his bony fingers eventually gave away to the soothing grip of her soft hand.

"*Dad,*" she began, voice firm, as though she'd rehearsed this very moment. "You have fought really hard to see your grandson. Bill and I—we would love nothing more than for you to see our baby. The reality is you're very sick, and it may be time to start thinking about what might happen if you don't make it."

"Sarah!" Bill scolded.

"Wait—*wait,*" she demanded.

She placed her other hand on top of Joe's, rubbing his. Joe felt comforted by her touch, even though he scowled at her.

"Have you ever considered *writing* the baby—you know, just in case? I read a story where someone in your situation wrote eighteen letters to their unborn grandchild, one for every birthday until they were eighteen years old," she calmly stated.

"Hey, Dad, that's a great idea," Bill blurted.

Joe watched Sarah snap a look at Bill, signaling him to sit back in his seat. She continued rubbing Joe's hand. He took his glass of tea with his other hand and drank from it.

It was a good idea, even if he hated to admit writing the letters officially meant there was a possibility he wouldn't get to meet his grandson, almost accepting that he was *giving up*—a theme he forbid himself to acknowledge until now. He took another sip and placed the glass back on the table, and nodded.

"Yeah?" she gleefully replied. "You'll do it?"

Joe nodded again, feeling tears pooling behind his eyes. He choked them back.

"Dad, it would be an honor to have you write these letters," Bill announced proudly, as though the idea were his.

Sarah went inside and returned with a blank notebook and a pen, gently setting them on the table. "I'll just leave these here and you can do whatever you want with them." Then, looking to her husband, she said, "Bill, honey—why don't we give your father some space?"

"Oh, right." He awkwardly began scooting his chair backwards.

"No, Bill. I mean, why don't you *come inside* and let your father be so he can write his letters?" she reiterated with a scoff, even though she held a welcoming smile.

"Oh yeah. Okay. Uh . . . I'll come check on ya in a little while, Dad," he muttered.

And so Joe began writing. When he was done with his first letter, he wrote the second. Then the third. He was determined not to stop until he had all eighteen letters written.

> *Dear Grandson,*
>
> *Today you turn fourteen. As you know, I passed away shortly before you were born. I wanted nothing more in this world than to see your smile. God knows I would have given anything just to hold you once. Being there the day you were born would've been the happiest day of my life, besides the day your dad was born. I still*

remember that day like it was yesterday. I rushed your grandma to the hospital, and I thought she was going to have your dad in the backseat! Scared the daylights out of me. I didn't think my old '69 Chevy station wagon could move that fast.

As I sit here writing this letter, your mom and dad recently found out they are having a boy. I was overjoyed when I heard the news. It means all the Morton traditions will be intact—like going to opening day of the Cubs at Wrigley.

Your parents haven't picked a name, but I think they are leaning toward Josh. I really like that name, and I hope they stick with it. You know by now that I wrote you a letter every year for your birthday up until you turn eighteen.

This year, you turn fourteen. You are quickly becoming a young man. You probably don't like your parents—I certainly didn't think much of mine when I was your age. Once I got a little bit older, I realized just how foolish that was, so you really should listen to them. You only turn fourteen once, so make the best of it.

I remember when your dad was fourteen years old. Every year, we went to the Chicago Cubs game on opening day. Rain or shine. I wish I could be there when you go to your first game with your father. Be sure he takes you. Remember—it's a Morton tradition.

Just know that I'm proud of you.

I love you, and I'm always with you.

—Love, Grandpa Joe

Tired. That's how Joe Morton felt. The calm breeze he felt as he sat on Bill and Sarah's back deck felt cool against his bruised skin. He took a break from writing to watch the gold finches on his bird feeder and listened as the windchimes softly rang. They helped him relax and took his mind off the nauseating side-effects from his recent chemo treatment.

He'd learned of his cancer diagnosis six months ago. Bill and Sarah told him the tremendous news that they were expecting their first child just two weeks ago—and here he was, clinging to life so he could meet his grandson.

Pancreatic cancer. The doctor had given him three months.

He had waited *years* for a grandchild. He couldn't wait to become a grandfather. It wasn't fair, but he was a fighter. It was now his mission to cling to life so he could meet the baby.

It took a lot of emotional energy from him, but he decided to spend his last month writing these letters to Josh. To Joe, simply writing the letters was the equivalent of acknowledging he was giving up, but he figured it would feel good to have left something behind.

And he was right. Two days after he had handed over his final letter to Sarah, he passed away in his hospital room, right as dawn heralded a bright new day he'd never get to personally witness.

He had heard a flurry of activity as machines he was hooked up to alarmed and beeped. The sounds attracted frantic nurses rushing to his aid.

While watching their rushed response, he'd realized something. "I'm standing!" he'd exclaimed. "I haven't been upright in a long time. No more wheelchair. No more bed. No more pain!"

But his celebration had been as short-lived—he became saddened as he listened to a nurse contact his family and ask them to come see the body before they took it away.

"You're not supposed to listen to that," a voice came from behind. He whipped around to see a man wearing a suit and an African Dashiki.

"Where did *you* come from?" gasped Joe.

The man's beaming smile and Nigerian accent calmed him.

"Where did I come from? How long have I been here? Different people but the same questions, time and time again!" the man exclaimed through a toothy grin. "Come. Let us get away from here so we can talk. This noisy room isn't a healthy environment for you to be in right now."

"This room isn't healthy for me to be in?" scoffed Joe.

"You're blinking," the man replied.

"Blinking?" Joe exclaiming in disbelief as he glanced at his body. "I'm blinking! Wait, *how* am I blinking?"

"Come, let us leave this room and I will explain," said the man.

As this man seemed to be in charge, Joe followed him. They roamed the halls, talking for some time.

"My name is Lagos," he said." I am a Gatekeeper sent to open a portal to the afterlife."

"Portal to the afterlife? What afterlife?" questioned Joe.

"There are many things I'd like to tell you, but I am under the strict regulations of our treaty with The Others," said Lagos.

"Who are The Others?" Joe prodded.

"I'm afraid I've already said too much. In a few moments, I'll open a portal. It is then up to you as to whether or not you enter," explained Lagos.

"This afterlife . . . is my wife, Kathy, there?" asked Joe.

"I cannot divulge such information. I can only open the portal and offer you entry," said Lagos.

"If I enter, can I come back and see my grandson when he is born?"

"There is no returning once you enter, but there is a possibility he may join you one day in the afterlife," said Lagos.

"Well, that doesn't seem like a guarantee that I'll see him," Joe barked.

"I realize there is much ambiguity in your situation. Ultimately, it will be up to your grandson whether he enters the afterlife. Everyone has a choice. Much like you do now."

"Seems you've made my choice for me," Joe scoffed.

"Sorry," said Lagos, his smile never faltering. "I do not follow."

"Portal or no portal, I'm seeing my grandson," Joe exclaimed.

"Joe, you must calm yourself. You're flashing is becoming erratic," Lagos pleaded.

"I'm not entering a portal. Not for you. Not for anyone. Not unless I'm able to see my grandson."

"Please. Let me at least *open* the portal. Once you see the amazing power, it could perhaps change your mind."

"Save yourself the trouble," Joe growled before passing through a wall and putting some distance between he and the Gatekeeper. Soon enough, he was outside. "Guess I'll head on over to Bill and Sarah's. I have a grandson to meet," he announced before turning into an orb and bursting toward their house.

THE BOREDOM

ATTENDING HIS OWN FUNERAL HAD almost been too much to bear. Only a handful of people were present at the service, which disappointed him because he'd always imagined people would've shown up in droves to send him off. He told himself it was because he'd outlived most of his friends, but a small part of him wondered if it had actually been his cranky nature that had alienated him. "I thought at least Schoonover would be here," he'd muttered while surveying the group.

He'd walked up to the open casket and peered in, seeing his cold, lifeless body. Hair combed neatly, dressed in a black turtle neck with a sport coat. Just how he would've wanted it to be. "Burying me in my best blazer. Good choice," he'd approved, noticing his bright white aura slightly dimming at the sight—and it had stayed that way ever since, even as he watched the birth of his grandson, Joshua Morton.

The birth of his *reason*.

The days after bringing Josh home from the hospital were filled with a flurry of activity as Bill and Sarah learned how to care for their newborn. Joe found it difficult to watch them blunder through their first week, and he often found himself lashing out in frustration.

"You don't hold the bottle that way! Aren't you going to burp him?"

"Put a blanket on that baby!"

"He's hungry! You should have a bottle ready to go for him!"

Joe's initial excitement of seeing baby Josh slowly eroded to a feeling of disdain. He didn't feel needed. An outsider in his own family. *Dead.* The more he realized he couldn't communicate with Josh, the more his frustration built.

"This is what I stayed behind for? *This?*" he'd said one lonely night after retreating to the attic of Bill and Sarah's home—he'd been staying there, seeing as his house was due to be sold and he wasn't interested in sharing it with strangers. Pacing. Back and forth. Back and forth.

He would often come down from the attic after Bill and Sarah went to bed, watching over baby Josh while he slept. Only Josh *wouldn't sleep*. Figuring he was just colicky, Joe reasoned that his grandson was only going through a phase—even as the baby cried nearly hourly. After a few nights, Joe noticed the exhaustion catching up to Bill and Sarah. That's when the schedules started.

"We have to put Josh on a more consistent schedule. That's how we'll get him to sleep," he overheard Sarah say with a hint of hopeful desperation in her voice.

Feeding schedules. Pumping schedules. Nap schedules. Sleep-training schedules. She had it all mapped out. Bill looked on in a worried astonishment.

Joe's boredom in the attic grew. The pacing. The loneliness. He came down from the attic one day to socialize, only to become angry again. The constant rigor they were putting in place to get baby Josh on a regular routine annoyed him.

"You're being too rigid. Let the boy live, for Christ's sake. He'll tell you when he's hungry. What are you going to do next? Tell him when to go to the bathroom?" Joe complained.

He traveled by the living room on his way back up to the attic, noticing Bill had left the TV on a local sports channel. His aura brightened as he watched the analysis of the Chicago Cubs game the night before. It was a real treat to watch TV. He hadn't watched a Cubs game in quite some time, so to get a glimpse of the highlights was refreshing. For the first time since his death, he was able to focus on something that didn't make him feel *dead*. Watching a young Kris Bryant hit a homerun made him feel alive again.

Just as Joe was settling into the highlights, Bill came in and turned the TV off and went upstairs.

"Hey, I was watching that!" yelled Joe. Almost in a panic, Joe reached for the remote, trying to turn the TV on himself—but as always, his hand passed right through it.

"*No*," he yelled, swiping at the remote.

He tried gripping. Tried pushing the power button. *Nothing.*

He stood, motionless, staring at the blank TV screen and wishing the game would turn back on. Defeated, he retreated to the solitude of the attic. It was the only place he wasn't constantly reminded that he was dead.

Nights were especially long. Standing guard over baby Josh was becoming his purpose, but even that would get boring. He started playing games to keep his attention. His newfound skill—passing through walls—became a source of amusement. "Look at me! I don't need a door!"

He'd begun counting walls he traveled through. He was up to 246.

He devoted many an hour to trying to move inanimate objects. He started by trying to open or close doors, later moving on to lightweight objects—an empty soda can left out on the counter, a pencil, a key.

"Forget it," he said losing interest after just a few attempts—thinking every spirit probably tries to move objects, probably looking as foolish as he did. "I wonder what little Josh is up to."

One morning, he noticed Bill had woke up and dressed much earlier than he had in prior weeks. It was time for Bill to go back to work, and it struck Joe that this would be a big change. It would be just Sarah and Josh at home for a while. And then, Sarah would be going back to work too—which meant no one would be home during the day.

"When Sarah goes back to work, Josh will go to daycare. They'll resume their busy lives. Get up, go to work. Come home, have dinner, watch an hour of TV before rushing off to bed. I'll be alone here. I'll only see them a couple hours a day," Joe said to himself.

The thought sent his aura into overdrive. It was flashing rapidly and even changing colors from white to grey. It was hours after Bill left for work before he brought it back under control. He stayed in the attic for three days.

"This isn't what I expected. I could be spending *eternity* with Kathy," he said out loud as he paced. Not being able to communicate with Josh gnawed at him like a festering wound. "This is nonsense. I should've never stayed. I need to go find another portal to enter. Kathy, darling, I'm going to find a way to come be with you."

It was then that he started thinking of an exit strategy.

He often sat in the nursery's rocking chair, watching over Josh while he slept. Thinking. Pondering. Wondering how he could get out of this mess. Days were spent in the attic, nights were spent sitting in Josh's room. All the while, Joe thought about how he might open another portal.

Joe was startled one morning when Sarah burst into the room and rushed to wake baby Josh and get him dressed. "Today is a big day, baby boy. It's time for your six-month photo shoot." He giggled as she tickled his belly.

"Six months, already!" Joe tried to insert himself into the conversation, if for no other reason than to keep his sanity. "Don't mind if I tag along! I've been cooped up in that godforsaken attic for too long."

The ride to the studio was uneventful. He barked at Sarah a few times for putting Josh in the car seat roughly and driving fast when she had a child in the backseat.

"I'm here for the six-month photo shoot," said Sarah pleasantly as she checked in.

She was glowing when the attendant behind the counter said Josh looked just like his mom, but Joe didn't agree. "On the contrary! He looks just like his grandpa!"

The photographer greeted them and escorted the group to the studio. Joe watched as she positioned the lighting and gently placed Josh into a decorative basket.

"Careful with him!" Joe mumbled. "That's precious cargo you're holding there!"

The photographer assumed her position behind the camera and used props to try and coax Josh into smiling. Joe noticed her frustration after a few attempts.

He watched Sarah eagerly join in. "Come on, baby boy! Smile for me, buddy! Peekaboo!"

Joe couldn't take this inane display, and without thinking, he took a position beside the camera, grumbling, "Let me do it!"

"Okay, buddy," he said gently, leaning toward his grandson. "You gotta smile for the camera for me."

Baby Josh's leg began kicking wildly with excitement.

"There he goes!" yelled Sarah gleefully.

The photographer seized the opportunity and began aggressively using props, which Joe could tell was irritating Josh.

"Okay, buddy. Block all of them out. Look at me!" His hands covered his face. "Boo!" Joe popped his head up and smiled at Josh.

"Ooooooo!" Josh erupted with excitement.

The photographer started snapping pictures while Sarah waved toys around, but something was dawning on Joe.

"Wait? Can you see me?" said Joe. He waved his hands left and right, and sure enough Josh's face followed them back and forth. "Can't be . . ."

The car ride home was awkward for Joe.

"He can't really *see me*. There's no way possible. Nope. Not possible."

He rushed to the attic as soon as they arrived home.

JOE TESTS THE WATERS

IT HAD BEEN A WEEK since Joe hid out in the attic. He kept himself busy by continuing to experiment with his newfound abilities. He tried opening a door, but his hand passed through the door knob. He tried pushing on the door, but his hand went through.

"It's no use," he said.

The anticipation and wonder of Josh seeing him began to bother him.

"If this is true, it should be a *good* thing—but it could cause some problems for the boy. What happens when he goes to school one day and tells his teachers about me? He'll be the laughingstock of the entire class! And what about when he turns sixteen? Is he really going to be able to get a girlfriend with his dead grandpa hanging around?"

He calmed himself down and brought his flashing under control. "I suppose I'm getting ahead of myself. I don't truly know if he can *actually* see me." He paused in deep thought. "I need to find out."

Joe was cautiously determined as he finally emerged from the attic. He paused outside the nursery and listened intently to baby Josh stirring in his crib. He finally entered the room, passing through the door. His aura brightened at the sight of his small grandson swaddled in a blanket.

"This right here," he said joyfully. "*This* is why I stayed behind. You hear that, grandson? I stayed for you. You are perfect in every way." He noticed the shadows on the wall become surrounded by brilliant illumination as his aura brightened. "I wish so badly I could hold you."

Baby Josh lay there, kicking his feet—seemingly looking back at him, smiling.

"Could it be?"

Baby Josh cooed and gurgled before drifting off to sleep.

No. Not possible. This was proof. If the baby could see him, his presence would have kept the baby awake.

Joe left the room, passing through a couple walls, and traveling downstairs. "482 walls," he said out loud as he went. 482 disappointing walls.

Downstairs, Joe began to plan his next move. Maybe, just *maybe* he might be able to talk to Josh someday, and if he could, that would change everything. And he wasn't sure yet whether it'd change everything in a *good* way, or a *bad* way.

Tomorrow, he was going out—some time away would do him some good.

NIGHT IN THE PARK

WINNEMAC PARK IN THE HEART of Lincoln Square was normally teeming with families. A popular hangout for coffee-sipping moms, and a few dads watching their kids play during the day. It was a popular neighborhood for family gatherings—a place to watch Little League baseball games during the evenings and weekends. Make no mistake about it, in Lincoln Square, the baseball diamonds were the place to be. The stands were filled with cheering parents who were there not only to watch their kids' games, but to socialize with neighborhood families. Social events were planned and business deals got finalized in those stands.

It was well after midnight, though, when Joe arrived, and the only evidence of people having been there was the occasional hot dog wrapper he spotted blowing across the baseball diamond. As he wandered through the park, staring at the moon, he thought fondly of his deceased wife, Kathy.

"I wish you were here," he said, staring into the stars as he passed over a small wooden bridge arched over a babbling creek flowing below. "You'd know what to do." The creek's soft trickling was relaxing. And for a rare moment, he felt calm—but that was before he noticed two bright reflections in the water.

"What is that?" he said aloud, moving closer to gain a better look. One of the reflections was that of the moon—a beautiful sight. But then, another reflection appeared. Then another. He figured one was the moon, the other his own aura, but the others?

They resembled his aura, only dimmer.

"That's odd," he pondered out loud.

"Odd? Who you calling odd, bud?" a voice boomed through the quiet night, startling him.

"Yeah, who you callin' odd, bud?" a second voice squeaked.

Joe turned to see two spirits hovering in front of him. One of them was rather large, like he had the brute strength of an ox. The other was shorter and rail thin, suspenders clinging to his oversized pants. Both were dressed in white shirts, and the big one wore a bowler hat.

Joe was startled, having never seen spirits like them before.

"Hey, Cunningham, take a look at this one. I think we got a freshie," chuckled the skinny one.

"Yup, Pinkie, by the looks of that bright aura, I'd say you're right," bellowed Cunningham, prompting a chuckle from his partner.

In all his surprise, Joe backed up, passing through the bridge's guardrail until he hovered over the creek.

"Don't do it! Don't do it!" said Cunningham in mock alarm.

"Oh, the agony! I can't watch! He's going to fall to his death!" Pinkie jeered.

Joe looked down, realizing his predicament. Instinctively, he scrambled to get back to the solid footing of the bridge.

"Look at him! He still thinks he can fall!" Cunningham bucked with laughter.

"He thought he was gonna die . . . *again*!" Pinkie's laugh turned into a squeal.

"That wasn't funny," Joe snapped.

"Hey, buddy, you act like you never seen a ghost before," Pinkie joked.

"Boo!" said Cunningham.

Both spirits exploded with laughter.

Joe was annoyed at first, but came around. There was something compelling about these good-natured brutes. Besides, they seemed normal enough—not like the sad lot of spirits that roamed the halls of Josh's daycare. No, these two had a rapport he had not yet observed in the spirit world, and these were the first spirits he'd really interacted with since his death.

"The name's Cunningham," said the heaping mountain of a man. Joe guessed Cunningham to be about 6' 4" and well over three hundred pounds—*living* weight. "And this one's Pinkie," Cunningham added, nodding at his short, scrawny comrade.

"Yeah, my name's Pinkie," said Pinkie.

"That's a mighty bright aura you got there," Cunningham continued.

"Yeah. That's how we can tell you're a freshie," Pinkie added, snickering.

Both of their auras had a steadily dim, almost grey hue to them.

"What's your name?" asked Cunningham.

"Pinkie," said Pinkie excitedly.

CROSSING OVER

"Not *you*, dummy," barked Cunningham.

"Joe. Uh, Joe Morton."

"Last name's Morton, you say?" questioned Cunningham. "There's some Mortons that live a couple blocks away, right Pink?"

Pinkie didn't say anything. He stared straight ahead, his mouth gaping, tongue dangling in a lackadaisical daze.

"Pink?" prompted Cunningham.

Pinkie seemed to come out of his trance. "Oh, sorry—you talking to me?"

"Never mind, ya nitwit. He does that sometimes," Cunningham scoffed, looking to Joe.

"My son, Bill, and his wife, Sarah, live a couple blocks from here," Joe confirmed.

"That's them!" Cunningham barked. "They just had a baby, right?"

How did they know about baby Josh? Had they discovered his abilities?

Cunningham must've noticed his concern.

"Don't worry—we live in the neighborhood. We know everything about this place. Ain't got nothing much better to do than to keep tabs on people. Oh, and, uh—*congratulations*, by the way," Cunningham exclaimed.

"Yeah! Congratulations! What are we celebrating exactly?" asked Pinkie, coming out of one of his dazes.

"Thanks," said Joe.

"Well, Joe, it's nice to meet you," Cunningham declared.

"Yeah! Nice to meet ya!" Pinkie followed suit.

"Pleasure to meet you as well," said Joe.

"You can stick with us, if ya like, and we can show you the ropes and such," said Cunningham.

"I really should be getting back soon," Joe blurted.

"Back? What, you got a curfew or somethin'?" joked Pinkie.

"Well, I guess not. . . ." said Joe.

"If the Mortons don't know you're living with them, how are they gonna know you're gone?" Cunningham questioned.

"Good point," said Joe.

Joe walked the park with them until sunrise, and suddenly the neighborhood came alive as people woke up and began their daily routines. First came the runners.

"If they knew we was here, I bet they wouldn't be taking a leisurely jog through our turf!" Cunningham mused.

99

Then people walking their dogs came out.

"The lady with the fur coat walking her Corgi comes by here every day at the same time. Just like clockwork," Pinkie chimed in.

"It's gotta be hotter than blazes out, but she wears that heavy fur coat," Cunningham noted. "She comes out early and returns back to her house for the rest of the day. Not really a social butterfly, that one."

It wasn't much longer until the neighborhood seemed to burst with people starting their daily commute.

"So you're probably wondering how it all works," Pinkie smirked.

"How what works?" Joe replied.

"Us. Our world," boomed Cunningham. "You pass through a wall yet?"

"487," said Joe matter-of-factly.

"Oh, wow! You're an expert!" joked Pinkie.

"Try and move an object?" Cunningham prodded.

"Tried for days and days," Joe replied.

"Don't bother. It's no use. We've been trying for *decades*," Pinkie said with a sneer. "So, how'd ya go, huh?"

"Cancer," replied Joe.

"Cancer! That disease is a menace! Back in my day, nobody lived long enough to get cancer," Cunningham jeered.

"Yeah, 'specially not us," Pinkie joked.

Cunningham let out a belly laugh. "Good one, Pink."

"So why'd ya stay behind?" asked Cunningham.

"You mean, why didn't I enter the portal?" clarified Joe.

"Yeah, the portal to the afterlife. Why didn't ya get in?" asked Pinkie.

"I didn't get to see my grandson before I went," Joe stated. He felt like this must sound petty to guys who had gone decades without another chance at a portal.

"Look what ya did, ya big oaf. The poor guy is flashing," Pinkie chided.

Cunningham swung at Pinkie, perhaps more for the satisfaction of the swing than for nostalgia at actually making contact.

"You talk too much, Pinkie," he snapped. "I'm sorry, Joe. We didn't mean to upset ya. Truth is, we all have our reasons, and most of 'em start feeling silly when we realize we can't do nothing but watch, anyhow."

Joe brought his aura under control.

They continued talking for many hours. He learned a great deal from them; they were very open, despite just meeting him. How long they had been spirits, what they did in their prior life, and how the neighborhood had changed over the years. They were surprisingly current on modern events considering their old-fashioned dress and mannerisms.

Joe especially loved the stories of their past. They had worked directly for one of the most notorious men of the Chicago gangland era: Dion O'Banion.

They called themselves "blood brothers"—which, by their definition, meant they had died together. Cunningham had owned and managed a warehouse and suffered greatly when the Great Depression hit. Pinkie was his warehouse driver.

When business slowed, Cunningham struck a deal with the O'Banion gang to store and transport alcohol during Prohibition.

"Sold my soul to the devil," Cunningham retorted. "Turned out I sold Pinkie's too."

"The O'Banion cronies were terrible to do business with. They rarely paid what they actually owed me—so I started looking around for other suppliers."

"That didn't sit well with ol' Dion," Cunningham recalled. "When I realized they had found me out, it was too late. I tried to get Pinkie out of there. I sent him to Milwaukee for a pick up—even though there was nothing to be picked up there."

"They nabbed me in Skokie," Pinkie blurted.

"When I showed up at the warehouse the next day, Pinkie was sitting there, tied to a chair. He had been beaten badly," Cunningham revealed.

"Yeah, but I got a few good pokes in, though," Pinkie gloated as he started flailing and wildly swinging his fists in the air.

Cunningham paid him no attention.

"We were done for," Cunningham continued. "Never got to say goodbye to the family."

"Yeah, the cowards never let me say goodbye to my daughter," Pinkie jeered.

Both of their auras dimmed as they told the story. Joe could almost feel their sorrow. No one said anything for a few moments.

"Hey, the sun is coming up. Let's go get some breakfast," Cunningham boomed.

"Breakfast!? But—" Joe started to question how they would be able to eat, but decided not to.

"Yay! Breakfast!" Pinkie cheered.

They walked over to a local coffee shop called Perfect Cup on Damen that was just opening its doors. Joe had frequented Perfect Cup many times in the past. It was a small boutique coffee shop, and the place looked like it was oozing coffee bean aromas that he wished he could smell just once more.

It was here Joe learned Cunningham and Pinkie's definition of "breakfast."

"We like to sit out here and just watch the people. It's a lot of fun. We get here before the rush," Pinkie explained.

Buses and cars crowded the streets as people began their morning commute. Droves of people walked to the Brown Line to catch the train—many stopping by Perfect Cup to grab a cup of coffee and a pastry. It wasn't long before the place was bustling with commuters.

"Every morning, just like clockwork," Cunningham boasted. "Well, at least during the workweek. Saturday and Sunday slows down a bit. People don't get going until mid-morning on the weekends."

"Yeah, people are always in such a rush!" Pinkie chimed in.

They sat watching the commuters for a while, but the excitement eventually wore off.

"Hey, if we want to get out of the rat race, Pink and I know a house where the guy leaves his TV on all day," Cunningham claimed.

Over the next few weeks, Joe spent so much time with Cunningham and Pinkie that he rarely saw his family. Bill was working, Sarah went back to work, and baby Josh was in daycare—which Joe had learned to stay away from at all costs.

When he'd joined Josh and Sarah on their first trip to daycare, he ended up running into several other elderly spirits who had also stayed behind to visit their grandchildren. By the looks of their dim-looking auras, they had been in the spirit world much longer than he, and they were a depressing, pathetic, and eerie lot. They roamed the halls with mouths gaping, staring off into nothing, as if time had forgotten them—barely even acknowledging him as he traveled by, one of them mumbling rubbish he couldn't understand.

Joe had promised himself he would never return, though it meant fewer hours with his grandson. "Whatever that was, I promise myself that I will do what it takes *not* to turn into that," he'd muttered to himself upon reaching the parking lot.

To make up for lost time, he would often sneak into the house at night just to sit in Josh's room—keeping an ever-watchful eye on him.

It was one of these watchful nights that would change Joe's resolve.

He arrived at Bill and Sarah's in the middle of the night. For Joe, there was no such thing as time anymore—only day and night, almost more like weather—so he came and went as he pleased.

He decided to check on Josh before taking his usual roost in the corner chair. Baby Josh exploded with sobs when Joe peeked over the crib. It was a *fearful* cry. He quickly backed away and was bothered when Bill and Sarah stormed into the room, consoling Josh, finally settling their baby back into his crib. He decided to check on Josh again. Joe approached the crib cautiously and slowly peered over the rail.

Josh let out a scream Joe had not heard before. It pierced the house. Joe watched Sarah tumble down the hallway in a sleepy haze and bang into the side of the crib as she rushed to Josh's aid.

Joe decided not to approach the crib for a while after Sarah put Josh back down, guarding his room like a watchful sentry. He hadn't spent much time with Josh lately, and his grandson's behavior was noticeably different. It was likely he was going through a phase, as kids often would.

But still, Joe had to admit Josh's behavior seemed strange—even for a baby. For one thing, he only screamed when Joe looked over the crib. It truly seemed as though Josh was responding to his presence, but—

Nope. Not possible. But what if?

Get it out of your head, Morton. It's not possible.

He had worked himself up so much that he began to pace. Lonely, nervous pacing. He heard a cooing sound, followed by a baby giggling. Joe stopped to listen. Another coo. This time followed by a high-pitched squeal. Joe approached the crib with caution.

More cooing. Josh was definitely awake. He peeked over the crib and tried to make eye contact with Josh. Then he ducked back out of sight.

He's awake!

A laugh came from the crib.

Could it be? Get it out of your head, Morton—there's no way the kid is laughing at you! Joe lifted his head over the crib again. Josh squealed with delight. He quickly dropped back out of sight.

Josh laughed hysterically.

He leaned over again—prompting another giggle.

"Boo!" said Joe.

This time, a sustained laugh came from inside the crib. Josh held out his arms as if asking to be picked up. That was too much for Joe. His aura flashed—its blinking filling the room.

"Ooooooooo!" Josh squealed, right on cue. *It was too coincidental. . . . Or was it?*

Joe sat in his chair. He stood up. Sat back down.

This can't be happening. Is this real? Don't mess with me like this.

The pacing. Nervous pacing. Back and forth. Back and forth.

He brought his aura under control. He cautiously approached the crib—creeping toward the top guardrail. Slow. His head raised slowly over the railing. He peeked in. Baby Josh was fully awake, now kicking and flailing his arms.

"Ahhahahaa! Ooooooo! Ahahahaaa!"

Josh's laughter filled the house. It was so loud, Sarah clumsily stumbled into the room again.

Joe backed off and watched his daughter-in-law come to her baby's aid.

"You kicked your blanket off, didn't ya, little man?" said Sarah as she gently plucked him from the crib. Joe watched Sarah pick up the baby. As she slowly raised Josh, he pointed toward him. Joe's aura flashed.

"Bah, bah, bah!" In his excitement, Josh pointed and reached toward Joe—again with outstretched arms.

"What are you reaching for, baby boy?" Joe heard Sarah say. She turned around to inspect the rocking chair. "There's nothing there, baby."

Josh continued to reach for Joe.

Sarah walked over to the chair, sat down, and began rocking her baby. "There's nothing there but the rocking chair, buddy."

"What if Josh could really see me?" It was too much for him to process. So badly wishing for this to be true, he needed some time to process. "No. Can't be true. Impossible, Morton. Get it out of your head," he grumbled before passing through the wall and going outside.

He paused a moment. In the distance, he heard baby Josh erupt angrily—probably because Joe was leaving. *That's* when he knew for sure.

"All I wanted was to see my Grandson grow for a while and then find a portal to see Kathy. If Josh can see me, maybe he can see other spirits. I'm sorry, Kathy," he said looking at the dark, cloudy sky. "I need to stay with Josh a little while longer."

He made his way to Winnemac Park.

A CURSED BALL GAME

HIDING OUT IN THE PARK for a few days meant he could clear his head. He still had his doubts that Josh could see him—or was he just trying not to get his hopes up? Either way, he felt conflicted.

What would it mean for Josh if he could see me? he thought. *Would he be frightened by me? He's just a baby, so maybe he doesn't know any better. But what about when he gets older? He's not going to like it much when he's trying to go on a date and his dead grandpa is hanging around. What kind of life would he have?*

He pondered a few moments. And then he spoke aloud, "If Josh can see me, can he see other spirits too? We all stayed behind for a reason. So many frustrated, disheartened spirits coping with their unfulfilled desires keeping them from the afterlife. Would other spirits try to take advantage of him? They could turn on Josh like a pack of rabid wolves. That morbid-looking bunch at his daycare . . . They must never know he can see them. Who knows how they would react."

He'd heard other stories of small children able to describe dead relatives. Maybe *all* babies could see spirits, but lose their ability as they become adults?

Guilt kicked in as he thought some more. "If he really can see me, how could the poor boy sleep at night with my aura filling up the room with light? Maybe that's why he's tossing and turning all night whenever I stay in his room."

He mulled over these questions and more before Cunningham and Pinkie came along and roused him. They seemed suspicious, asking where he'd been—why he hadn't met them for "breakfast" the past few days at Perfect Cup. Joe didn't have any good answers, other than he felt like being alone. Revealing Josh's potential secret wasn't an option. As much as he enjoyed their company, he wasn't sure how they'd take the news. Besides, he might've been over thinking it.

While his absence as of late piqued their interest, Cunningham and

Pinkie seemed to have bigger things at stake. They could barely contain their excitement when they invited Joe to a Chicago Cubs game. It was a day game with a 1:20 p.m. first pitch.

"Cubs game? How have I never thought of that?" asked Joe, his aura brightening, almost returning to its original hue.

"Would you look at that! I think he wants to go, Pink!" exclaimed Cunningham.

Pinkie smiled. "Get ya out of the grind for a little while."

"But wait—I don't have a ticket!" said Joe, disappointed.

"Tickets? Ha! We just walk right in like we own the place," said Pinkie.

"Oh, that's right—the whole *walking through walls* thing," Joe said, remembering.

"Well, by the looks of his aura, I'd say we just brightened his day! Get it? *Brightened* his day?" Pinkie joked.

Cunningham rolled his eyes and shook his head.

They made off to Wrigley Field—home of the Chicago Cubs. Joe was excited to go. It kept his mind off Josh, and the idea of going to a ball game almost made him feel alive again.

"When are the Cubs going to win the World Series again?" Joe asked.

"Ha! World Series!" Cunningham growled.

"What the big fella means is *they won't*. They're cursed," Pinkie said.

"Cursed? That's just folklore," said Joe, scoffing. "Made-up legends to entertain fans."

"Uh, no—you don't understand. The Cubs are *really* cursed," said Cunningham. "Why do you think the Cubs haven't won a World Series since 1908?"

"Bad luck?" said Joe. "I mean, they came close a couple times—1969, 1984, and 2003 were good years."

"Don't you think it's strange in each of those years, something happened to prevent them from winning?" Cunningham demanded.

"I always thought that was just made-up stuff to sell tickets," said Joe.

"Remember when the black cat mysteriously showed up during the pivotal Cubs–Mets series in September 1969? Ron Santo was on deck and the cat walked right behind him. The Cubs were atop their division, but after the black cat incident, the team had a terrible September and missed the playoffs!" Cunningham challenged.

"Many Cubs historians say the 1969 team was one of the best in Cubs history and have a difficult time understanding how they missed the playoffs entirely," Joe rebuffed.

"You see?" said Cunningham. "How about the '84 Cubs?"

"What about them?" said Joe.

"The Cubs finally made the playoffs for the first time since 1945. That year, Rick Sutcliffe won the Cy Young award; and Ryne Sandberg won NL MVP. Things were looking up, and after going up 2–0 against the Padres in the NLCS, they seemed like they might finally make it to the World Series," Cunningham recalled.

"Yeah I remember—Steve Garvey pitched a great Game 3, and the Padres tied up the series at 2–2 in Game 4," said Joe.

"Yeah, but then it happened—in Game 5 Leon Durham let a routine ground ball go through his legs. The Padres went on to win the game and the series," said Cunningham.

"The Cubs curse is a real thing," said Pinkie as they walked to the stadium.

"My son, Bill, and I always thought that it was made-up, but look at us. What else is possible? How can a team *not* win a World Series in over 100 years?" said Joe.

"Sianis," scoffed Pinkie.

"Sianis?" said Joe.

"Yep—Sianis. *William* Sianis," Cunningham bellowed.

"The guy who owned Billy Goat Tavern?" asked Joe.

"Exactly!" shouted Pinkie.

"Back in 1945, William Sianis famously tried to bring his goat to the stadium during a World Series game, thinking it would bring the Cubs good fortune. When not allowed entry, he put a curse on the team," said Cunningham.

"That crazy Sianis is a meddler," Pinkie snapped.

"Think of everything that's gone wrong for the Cubs over the years. The black cat of '69. The Alex Gonzales error in '03," said Cunningham.

"Gonzales was a gold glove shortstop—how is he going to botch a ground ball like that?" said Joe.

"Sianis!" Cunningham and Pinkie scoffed in unison.

"No way!" said Joe.

"You'll probably see him today. He'll at least cause one problem for the Cubs. It doesn't always mean they'll lose the game, but they do have to overcome his pranks in order to win," said Cunningham.

They arrived to Wrigley Field early. The players were taking batting practice.

"This is the best part about being dead," said Cunningham as they drifted past the tellers collecting tickets. "I ain't paid for a ball game in years!"

Joe had to admit, the spirit world was starting to have its benefits. An eternity of free Cubs games? He could get used to that. He was grateful his new friends brought him to the game. It took his mind off Josh.

Pinkie walked out onto the field. Cunningham followed. Joe chuckled as he watched them run the bases. They positioned themselves in the bleachers to watch the game. It was 1–0 Cubs against the Dodgers when Joe saw *a goat walk out into right field.*

"Hey! What's that?" he said, pointing to the goat.

"Siannis is here, the rat. That's his goat," grumbled Cunningham.

"Yup! Won't be long now until that slime-ball shows himself," said Pinkie.

The Cubs took the field at the top of the inning. Sure enough, a man with a long coat and a bowler hat drifted into the outfield. The man had a grey aura with occasional subtle flashes that would jolt through his aura like a dim flare. Joe could tell he had a sense of mischief about him.

The crowd erupted. "Boo! Get off the field, ya bum!"

"Hear that? The other guys here hate Siannis as much as we do," said Pinkie.

"Guys?" said Joe.

"Spirits like us. We're the normal ones in the crowd. I mean, look around—all the mouth-breathers inhaling hot dogs and nachos, guzzling beers, and yelling. You don't see any spirits acting like that around here, do ya?"

It hadn't dawned on Joe the possibility that other spirits were in the crowd. He hadn't noticed them—they did a good job blending into the 38,000 fans. But now that he thought to look, they were *everywhere.*

Joe watched Siannis wave his middle finger at the crowd while making his way to the infield and bending down to seemingly inspect the dirt.

"What's he doing?" asked Joe.

"Looking for small rocks in the infield dirt. Pebbles," Cunningham scoffed. "He does this all the time. It's how he plays his little tricks."

Siannis looked as if he was moving something into position. The spirit crowd's roaring insults only seemed to strengthen his resolve.

"He's found a couple small rocks and he's placing them in front of the shortstop," explained Cunningham.

"How do you know?" asked Joe.

"We've seen his tired act too many times. Remember, you were talking about in '03—the Alex Gonzales error, where the ground ball went between his legs?" Pinkie chimed.

"Same with the botched Durham grounder in '84," Cunningham echoed.

"Siannis?" Joe wondered.

"*Siannis!*" both Cunningham and Pinkie yelled.

"How does he move those rocks?" asked Joe, feeling suddenly very intrigued at the possibility of himself being able to move objects.

"You wanna move a rock? You can move a rock," Cunningham snickered.

"Not me. I gave up a long time ago," Pinkie recalled.

"Takes years of practice. You have to get trained by a specialist," Cunningham asserted.

"A rock-moving specialist?" Joe asked.

"No. A person who specializes in telekinesis," Pinkie corrected. "Only a few spirits I've ever come across can do it. I say you either have it or you don't."

"There he goes!" Cunningham bellowed.

Siannis drifted across the outfield playing up his show—wildly agitating the spirit crowd before stopping to watch his work. Sure enough, the next batter came up and hit a slow, routine ground ball to the shortstop. The ball hit the small rocks Siannis had placed, skipping awkwardly away from the shortstop's glove. The runner rounded first and headed to second base as the ball rolled into the outfield.

Boos filled the stadium from the living and the dead alike. The living—unable to see Siannis—scorched the shortstop for botching what should have been an easy out. The spirits—knowing what *really* happened—cursed Siannis and their own helplessness.

Joe hadn't witnessed such savagery at a Cubs game before. The spirits were unruly and steaming-mad at Siannis.

"Can't anyone do anything?" asked Joe.

"We'd love to give him a good beating, but how are we gonna do that? He's already dead!" Cunningham scoffed.

It was a long trip home, as the Cubs lost the game 2–1.

"That *stinking* Siannis! Cubs are never gonna win with him around. We've tried to chase him off for decades. He doesn't care. He knows we can't do anything to him. If this was the old days, I'd give him a piece of my

Tommy Gun," joked Cunningham.

"Yeah! Rat-tat-tat-tat!" Pinkie held his hands up acting like he was firing at Siannis.

Joe noted how his new partners could be such gentle brutes sometimes. As they walked under the arches, welcoming visitors to Lincoln Square, Joe decided he needed to spend the night with his family. He thanked them for a fun day and went his separate way.

"Hey, Joe! Why don't you come to the conference with us tomorrow?" Pinkie suggested as Joe was leaving.

"Think that's a good idea?" Joe heard Cunningham whisper to Pinkie. Cunningham was a loud spirit, and his attempt at a whisper was more like a normal person talking.

Joe wasn't quite sure what to make of the invite to the conference, but he enjoyed Pinkie and Cunningham's company, so he couldn't help but consider it. Besides, a night out sounded much better than hanging around Bill and Sarah's creepy attic.

"Conference? What kind of conference?" he asked.

Pinkie reacted nervously, his aura flashing as he looked to his partner for approval. Joe could tell Pinkie had made a mistake.

"It's an invitation-only event, ya nitwit. Every spirit in town is clamoring to get one of those tickets. . . . Well, it's too late now to take the invitation back," growled Cunningham. "Just invite him already."

"Well?" asked Pinkie. "There'll be thousands of spirits there. You'll learn a lot."

"Okay, I'll be there. Meet tomorrow for breakfast?" Joe asked.

"Deal," Pinkie confirmed.

Joe watched as the odd characters traveled away. Cunningham's size and bowler hat and Pinkie's small stature made them the perfect pair.

Joe turned into an orb and shot toward the Mortons' home.

LADO

JOE STOOD IN FRONT OF Bill and Sarah's home for what was close to an hour in "living time." He didn't want to go inside and wake the entire house up—if, indeed, it was the flashing of his aura that kept Josh awake. If this was true, he was causing sleepless nights for the entire family and therefore even more problems for Bill and Sarah. He pondered leaving altogether so his grandson could maybe have a normal life.

On the other hand, he was still in disbelief that Josh could see him.

Joe decided he'd go inside, but spend the night in the third floor attic. He could enter the house such that there was no chance of Josh seeing him—plus, it would allow him to devise a plan. He needed to find out if Josh could truly see him, but in a way that was not so disruptive to his family.

It was lonely up in that attic. Dark, shadowy nights. Eerie sounds such as the roof creaking. Wind-blown tree branches scraping the outside window made it seem even more desolate. It was like he was waiting for something terrible to happen. Maybe a crazed spirit would jump out of the closet scaring the daylights out of him. Then it dawned on him that *he* was the one "haunting" the attic.

He thought about the Cubs game he attended with Cunningham and Pinkie. They'd have to do more of those. He thought about how Siannis had moved those gravel pieces. *How did he do that?*

He passed the time by trying to move inanimate objects himself, but that got old fast, and he stopped as quickly as he started. Morning came and he headed for the Perfect Cup. When he arrived, they were clambering on about some passerby who had just jogged by.

"You missed her, Joe. She's a real looker, that one," chimed in Pinkie.

"A real dame. Kinda looked like Marion Davies. Hubba hubba!" Cunningham said .

If he didn't act fast, he knew he'd be caught in a debate for hours between the two of them of which prohibition era leading lady was the best looking. He decided an intervention was necessary. "Hey, Cunningham, I've been thinking about that Siannis character," Joe began, testing the waters.

"What about him?" growled Cunningham. "Don't bring him up tonight at the conference. He's revered in the spirit community."

"An outcast!" cried Pinkie. "He could use his telekinesis for da greater good, but he has to be a showboat and constantly mess with our Cubbies."

"I've been trying to move objects up in the attic when I get bored at night. Where can I find a specialist to train me to move rocks like Siannis?" Joe asked boldly.

"We told you—he's obviously dedicated years to practicing and had some help along the way. They're out there, spirits who can move objects. Like I said, very few who cross over can master it—you've either got it or you don't. And besides, you don't see them very often. They aren't the social types. They get tired of us regular types bugging them for favors," Cunningham said with a dismissive wave of his hand.

"Yeah, I'd love it if one could join us over at the Wilson's place when they leave the TV on. Maybe one of those *object movers* could help me flip through the channels when the infomercials come on!" Pinkie snickered.

Joe couldn't help but wonder if there were really "specialists" who actually trained spirits to move objects, or if Cunningham and Pinkie believed in some sort of rumor. It seemed they completely believed in this, but still— Joe couldn't help but think it might be a little far-fetched. Either way, he decided to let it go.

"So what are we up to today?" he asked.

Cunningham seemed nervous. Pinkie was always fidgety, but today, he was more wired than usual.

"Big night tonight," Cunningham mused.

"Yeah. This is the big annual meeting. Our chapter is hosting," Pinkie noted.

"Chapter?" Joe asked.

"*L-A-D-O*," Cunningham growled. "Life After Death Organization."

"Our Chicago chapter meets monthly. The local chapters are more of a social thing. Helps us spirits interact. Do organized activities and such that make us feel human again. They say the more you feel like a person again, the better it is for your aura," said Pinkie. "Tonight is our annual LADO Worldwide conference. Chapter members from all over will be there. Normally, we wouldn't be invited to such an event. Since we serve on the local chapter, we get an invite."

Joe listened intently. After all, by their standards, he was still a newly hatched spirit and was soaking up the new information.

"Yeah, and we get to bring a guest of honor. Looks like you're the lucky guy, Joe! LADO is a big deal for us spirit types. A lot of research goes into trying to help spirits accomplish their *reason* for being here," Cunningham noted.

"Yeah, like Joe—you stayed behind for your grandson, right? But can you really accomplish your goal?" Pinkie said.

"What do you mean?" Joe inquired.

"I mean, you get to see your grandson—but can you hold him, play with him?" Joe knew Pinkie's question was strictly rhetorical—*of course* that's why he'd stayed, and *of course* he couldn't do any of those things. It dawned on Joe that happiness in the spirit world was a strange thing. Joe's *reason* for staying behind was seeing his grandson, which he did. Now, they were talking about holding the baby. Playing with him. The benchmark had changed. He realized now his *reason* was not a singular task such as *seeing the birth of his grandson*, but rather an ever movable target of impossible feats around communicating with the living.

"Can you talk to him? Sing to him?" Cunningham crowed.

Joe paused. He was unsure how to answer, given recent events. And if Josh really *could* see him, he wasn't sure he could trust his new friends just yet with that type of information.

"Well, I can talk *to* him until I'm blue in the face, but you're right, he can't hear me," Joe said, playing along.

"See! That's what we mean. Most of us stayed behind because we wanted to *do* something, but how can you *do* anything in a world that doesn't even know you're there?" Cunningham averted his eyes to the coffee-drinkers of Perfect Cup, resting his chin in his palm as if he longed so badly to talk to one of them.

Joe sympathized with what it must be like for him—a man who's been dead for so long, without making any progress whatsoever. Perhaps he should be so happy Josh could see him?

"That's what they didn't tell us when they opened up that portal thingy," Pinkie added. "You know, a lot of us spirits, we feel we got a raw deal. Think about it: This swirly portal opens up, and this gatekeeper guy who you don't know from Adam asks you if you want to take a little stroll into this giant windy tunnel with bolts of lightning flashing everywhere. He doesn't say where the tunnel leads—he just says, 'After *you*, friend-o.' All the while, I'm staring at my dead body that was alive two minutes ago, and I'm trying to process the fact that my brains have been blown into my lap!"

"Pink! Pink! Get ahold of yourself, for cryin' out loud. You're gonna make yourself sick!" Cunningham bellowed.

"Now we're trapped. It *ain't* fair!" Pinkie continued.

Cunningham put his hand on Pinkie's shoulder. "We thought by staying behind we would be able to fill a void left by our death—see a loved one, take care of unfinished business, do something we'd always wanted to do but never got around to," Cunningham reasoned. "My wife. She died a few years back. She entered the afterlife. I was never able to contact her while she was living to let her know I was with her. Every time I went to see her it reminded me I was dead. Couldn't say hello to her—*nuthin'*. So eventually, I just stopped. I stopped going altogether. You'll eventually fully transition into this world. You'll see, Joe. Won't be easy, but eventually you won't go see your grandson no more. You'll just be here. *Stuck*. Like us."

"And one day . . . that little boy you stayed behind for . . . he's gonna grow up to be a man, and he's gonna forget all about you. That's not even the worst of it. One day, that little baby boy you stayed behind for? He's gonna *get old* like you did, and that little baby boy is gonna *die*. And we'll be here for you when that happens," said Pinkie, his aura flashing wildly.

"It happened to Pink," said Cunningham. "He stayed behind because he wanted to watch his daughter grow into a woman. Well, she did, and she also passed away—not too long ago, I might add. But you stopped going to see her long before that, didn't ya, Pink?"

"Sure did," he sighed. "It was just too much not being able to communicate with her. It was making me sick."

"So now we are trapped here with no real purpose—no *reason*. It's why we are so interested in this LADO conference. We're hoping to find new *reasons*. Keep our aura bright and healthy and the like," said Cunningham.

"Yeah," Pinkie chimed in. "The LADO researchers might be the key to finding a way outta this mess."

"We all are at a point where we just want to get into that portal. I hate to break it to ya—you're too fresh to realize it, but it *will* happen. The boredom. The monotony. Being on a different time table—awake all night while the human world sleeps. There's no such thing as time for us. We're just lost souls floating around waiting for who-knows-what. . . . If we want to keep our wits about us, we have to still go by the "living time." You know, meet at Perfect Cup in the morning. Go to a Cubs day game—but all that is happening on their time. Not ours. It all gets to ya. Once it takes hold, there's no going back. That's how spirits become sick. Many of them lose their wits and just *snap*," Cunningham explained.

Joe couldn't imagine being trapped in this world without his family. He never pondered the idea that he could be trapped here long after they pass away and enter the afterlife. What would he do then?

"I'm sorry, Joe," said Cunningham. "We upset you again."

While bringing his flashing under control was one thing, dealing with the poisonous thoughts stayed with him. *Would he really watch his family die and be stuck here without them?* He was suddenly obsessed with attending the conference and learning more about this new spirit world—especially if it posed any danger to his grandson.

"So, we don't know how to find portals?" asked Joe.

"Listen, Joe. That's a sore subject for many of us spirits. From what we know of these portals, you only get one chance to enter—and you just had yours," snapped Pinkie. "There are spirits around that are a lot older than us that ain't found a second portal."

"Calm down, Pink," said Cunningham. "We're not totally sure that we're trapped here forever. Some spirits disappear sometimes, right? And if we can't find them anywhere, it stands to reason they found another portal and took their shot. That's why the portals are the most important of LADO's research."

"There's other research?" asked Joe.

"A Bridge is a rare case where a human can see and hear us. If we find a Bridge, that person can help us all fulfill our destinies. We could tell them what we want to say to our loved ones, and a Bridge could relay the message," Pinkie continued.

"A lot of effort goes into finding Bridges. They're very rare, but so far, LADO has found a few," Cunningham assured.

"They have? But then why haven't you fulfilled your *reasons*? What happened to those Bridges?" asked Joe.

Pinkie and Cunningham glanced at each other in silence before looking down, shaking their heads. Pinkie was the first to speak. "I'm sure they will give an update on Bridges tonight. There's an entire task force on the case. Best you hear it from them."

Joe looked down at his hands. He couldn't hide the flashing. He was so close to learning about Bridges, and his eagerness to learn how this may impact Josh sent his aura into overdrive. He knew it would be difficult to hide.

"What's wrong, Joe?" Cunningham asked.

"I, uh . . . I guess this is all just new. I'm just excited to hear more about these Bridges," Joe remarked, glancing back down at his hands and saw them rapidly flashing. The thought that Josh could be a Bridge hit him like a tidal wave. *What happened to the other Bridges? And more importantly, what would happen if they discovered Josh?*

LADO - A GHASTLY CONFERENCE

THE LADO ANNUAL MEETING ROTATES every year. This year, the annual meeting was in Chicago—last year, in Buenos Aires; and since Cunningham and Pinkie served on the local Chicago chapter, they were allowed to bring a guest of honor. Chapter presidents attended from all over the world, and local chapter members were allowed to attend in the host city. Joe didn't realize the privilege he had been offered. His aura brightened a few shades at the thought he was being officially indoctrinated as part of their group. He had to admit, it felt good to be a part of something instead of aimlessly hanging around the Mortons' attic.

Unfamiliar with the event, Joe certainly wasn't expecting the turnout that was LADO. He really hadn't prepared himself for the hordes of spirit protesters outside Union Station. They were an intimidating bunch who heckled attendees as they entered. It didn't seem to bother Pinkie, Cunningham, or any of the other attendees as they made their entrance, but Joe was shaken a bit.

"Happens every year. You have the spirits who are against LADO because they think we are trying to alter the future, and then there's the apocalyptic types who want the world to end. Most of them have had their loved ones enter the afterlife and now they don't want to be here any longer. Lastly, you've got the ruffians who come out just because they are bored and want something to do. None of them are of any harm to us. They're just distraught, that's all," Cunningham explained.

Joe couldn't help but wonder what would happen if one of the living were able to see such a collection of downtrodden spirits. If little Josh could see them, then it had to mean he could see other spirits too—and he didn't like the idea of that at all. He couldn't think of a time he was more relieved than when he escaped the moaning and wailing of these trapped souls as they passed through the gate and into the conference.

Thousands of spirits attended the conference at Chicago's Union Square, crawling out of every nook and cranny—each jockeying for better position to see the stage. These were for the spirits of the elite: many former celebrities, leading academics, and former members of high society. They had managed to keep their fame, even in death.

They were met with the sound of roaring guitars as they entered the grand ballroom.

"We get VIP passes because we're with the local chapter," said Pinkie.

"Yeah, we don't have to fight tooth and claw for a good spot like the rest of these bums," added Cunningham.

"Hey! Who you callin' a bum!?" came a voice from the crowd.

"Yeah? What of it?" growled Cunningham, and Joe couldn't help but laugh—the old prohibition era gangster was clearly not backing down from anyone.

"Come on, ya big lug," Pinkie cajoled, motioning for Cunningham to follow until he parted ways with the stranger in the crowd. He turned to Joe, winking. "See, Joe? Ya can't take the big brute anywhere."

Chicago blues musicians—Muddy Waters, Howlin' Wolf, Koko Taylor, and plenty Joe didn't recognize—provided entertainment. The crowd of spirits danced with excitement as Muddy Waters and Howlin' Wolf exchanged guitar solos.

After the fifth song, a female spirit took the stage. Joe could tell she was a woman of stature; she wore a fashionable evening gown that draped behind her, as if she were a Hollywood-type presenting a prestigious award. He noticed the band members paying her respects as she traveled by.

"Good evening!" she started. The excited crowd began to quiet down, but there was still muffled crowd chatter creating white noise. "Excuse me! EXCUSE ME!"

The white noise from the crowd of socializing spirits wound down as they turned their attention toward her.

"My name is Gabriella Rodriguez, and I am a representative from LADO Worldwide headquarters. I'll be your host for this evening." A few scattered cheers came from the crowd. "Let's give it up for the band—weren't they great?"

The crowd erupted and the band members took a bow. She waited for the crowd to quiet and continued.

"Welcome to our annual meeting. Let's thank our Buenos Aires friends for hosting last year!" The crowd cheered. "And let's thank our Chicago hosts for having us this year!" Once again, the crowd erupted. "A lot of work goes into planning such a prestigious event, and we have a power-packed agenda this evening."

The crowd shook with anticipation. Joe noticed a sort of pent-up excitement. Lights danced along the Union Station walls as auras started blinking.

The hostess continued. "Tonight, we will hear from three guest speakers—world renowned researchers and professors, leading experts in their field."

Muddy Waters accented this with a high-pitched tremolo.

The hostess raised her hands, soliciting calm among the crowd.

Joe was hovering among the crowd when something caught his eye. A spirit traveling toward him. Drawing near. Something wasn't right. This spirit was in *agony*, his aura pulsating rapidly between dark grey and black.

"He's sick," Pinkie warned.

"Sick?" Joe was instantly paralyzed at the thought of becoming sick himself. It was every spirit's deepest fear, especially a spirit as newly hatched and susceptible to sickness as Joe.

"Yeah, he don't look so good. Wonder how he even got in here," Cunningham muttered.

They paid no attention to the spirit as he passed, so neither did Joe—even though he was horrified at the sight of the dark, ragged spirit. He was perhaps more relieved to see the sick spirit disappear in the crowd than he was when the haggard, wailing spirits outside were heckling him.

The hostess went on, "Tonight, we will hear about searches for portals. Searches are underway, and Professor Edvard Von Offel—who joins us all the way from Germany—will provide an update on field research he and his team have performed to find portals to the afterlife."

The crowd roared with delight, but Joe hovered motionless. LADO, the protesting spirits outside, the mass of spirits crammed into every nook and cranny . . . The entire experience of it all was overwhelming and a lot to take on.

"Following Professor Van Offel, we will hear from Professor Mimi Tchamba Diallo from Ivory Coast, who will discuss her team's work on Bridges." Aura lights bounced off the walls and ceiling like an active disco ball, signaling the excitement among the spirit community as they roared with delight. "Finally, our last speaker, Professor Dante Canelli, will give an update on his work related to Doomsday."

This time, the entire crowd fell silent in the wake of the word "Dooms-day." The mere mention of the word made Joe shutter. The thought of fires in the streets, crowds fighting for scraps of food and contaminated water—and Bill, Sarah, and baby Josh subjected to it all made him cringe.

"This is a sensitive subject," said Cunningham in his best attempt at a whisper. "We think Doomsday will probably mean a lot of portals for spirits to enter, but we still don't want it to happen."

"Yeah—that's why all those End-the-World-Now types were outside protesting. I mean, when the stuff hits the fan, I'm pretty sure we won't feel anything, but none of us want to see the living suffer through *the end of the world*," Pinkie acknowledged.

"Especially those who have loved ones still among the living," Cunningham proclaimed. "There's a distinct divide among us spirit types. For the first time in our history, those with no living relatives like me and Pink outnumber those like you—with *living* relatives. That's why there's so many of those nitwits outside protesting. They think they have greater influence than newly hatched spirts like you—a bunch of hooligans trying to push us closer to *the end* so they can get their portals."

Joe, again, felt a sudden wave come over him at the entirety of it all as the band broke into a quick instrumental to cheer up the crowd.

"Let's introduce our first guest: Professor Edvard Von Offel. Professor Von Offel was one of the world's leading paleontologists before his death and currently leads an expedition team in the search for portals. His re-search will hopefully lead to the discovery of a portal that we can enter."

The band fired up as the professor took the stage. Joe noticed the profes-sor dressed in field gear, which, though unnecessary for this event, somehow seemed to confer authority upon him.

"Hello. My name is Edvard Von Offel." The crowd went silent as they listened to his pronounced German accent. "My team has been dispatched all over the world in search of the very thing we are all seeking—the evasive portal to the afterlife. This year, we focused on tips in the Africa and Asia sectors."

The crowd erupted with excitement.

The professor continued, "Our worldwide search for a portal yielded valuable information. While we were unable to *find* a portal, we did—through a series of tips—gain a better understanding of how the portals work. We spirits have seen a portal, and we know since the treaty was formed that Gatekeepers are the only ones who can *open* a portal."

A few scattered boos echoed through the halls as the crowd became restless, talking amongst themselves, producing a sea of white noise beginning to drown out the professor as he spoke.

"I could've told you that one!" yelled Cunningham.

"Yes, yes. Well, there's more. We now know there is a powerful spirit who coordinates all the Gatekeepers. His name is Keryx."

This got everyone's attention and the rambunctious crowd settled, hanging on every word the professor said.

"This is the first we've heard of this Keryx character," said Cunningham, prompting a nod of validation from Pinkie.

"We think Keryx holds the key to the portals and if we can summon him, perhaps we can learn from him how we may find another portal or, in the best case scenario, persuade him to open a portal for us."

The crowd became jubilant, and the band spontaneously broke into song.

The professor nodded to the band, and Gabriella waved her hand to cut them off. The crowd calmed as the professor continued. "We also placed a team of domestic researchers in a hospital in Germany. This study involved finding sick patients and waiting in their hospital room until their death. The hypothesis was that if a portal opened up shortly after the patient's death, our researchers would be able to intercept it and/or its Gatekeeper."

This struck Joe as a much more obvious approach than searching the far reaches of Africa.

"In fifty-five cases, we were able to identify fifty-five portals." The crowd cheered but the professor held a hand up, adding, "In all fifty-five cases, we were unable to *intercept* the portal."

The crowd fell silent.

"We identified, in all cases, a sort of barrier surrounding the recently deceased spirit making it impossible for our researchers to communicate or even access the associated Gatekeeper or the portal. Our researchers described it as almost a spherical shape that engulfs the spirit. Our researchers were unable to pass through this barrier. We hypothesize that there is some sort of energy that is emitted from the portal that repels foreign objects—in this case, *us*—from entering.

"We have added leading physicists to our team who will be examining these structures with the hopes we may learn more about them."

The crowd emitted a disappointing silence.

Gabriella addressed the crowd as she retook the stage. "Let's give Professor Von Offel a hand!"

The band played "Sweet Home Chicago" as Professor Von Offel left the stage, but only a few spirits made half-hearted attempts to applaud him.

"Well, that's a letdown. I thought we'd learn a whole lot more," Cunningham scoffed.

Pinkie following suit. "We waited an entire living *year* for this?"

Gabriella motioned to the band who cut off their tune as she approached the stage.

"Before we introduce our next guest of honor, I'd like to mention a few words from our sponsor—Life After Death Organization Worldwide:

"Loneliness. Restlessness. Abandonment. These are natural feelings that we *all* experience. As LADO chapter heads, we are all leaders in our individual communities, and we should be supporting outreach to help spirits in our own communities with these issues. LADO Worldwide offers extensive resources for chapter leaders and their members.

"LADO Worldwide: The Best is Yet to Come!"

A group of LADO staff and representatives in the front rows made some perfunctory noises while Gabriella's huge, tantalizing smile glared at the crowd from the huge screens mounted above her. Joe looked to Cunningham, who only grumbled, "Well, they have to keep a bright outlook for the rest of us, don't they?"

"Without further interruption," Gabriella said, clearing her throat, "I'd like to introduce our next guest—someone for whom I have the utmost admiration. One who stayed behind to continue her research so that we could all benefit. Mimi, why don't you come up here, please?"

The band continued with "Sweet Home Chicago" as a spirit slowly approached the stage. She was short in stature—much shorter than Gabriella. Her hair hung in a single braid down to the small of her back. She wore a brightly colored tunic.

Gabriella continued: "Before her death, Mimi Tchamba Diallo had done extensive research on psychic abilities. While never fully recognized, and relatively unknown, her work revolutionized human communication with those in 'other dimensions.' She found fame among the spirit world for using these skills to identify Bridges. The pursuit of Bridges is a serious endeavor toward which great amounts of resources are committed."

Professor Mimi traveled forward—short and petite in stature, but her command of the room was large.

Joe paid close attention.

"Thank you for the warm welcome, and thank you host city Chicago for having our team, and thank you Miss Gabriella for hosting this event.

"We are all well aware of the importance of Bridges—those in the living world who can communicate with us. It is because they are so important that I need to remind you all to take the utmost care, should you identify a Bridge. Remember, there are so *many* of us and so *few* Bridges. Should we identify a Bridge, we *must* approach them with delicacy and through the proper channels, as we don't want another Ping Zhiruo situation. . . ."

The other spirits seemed to know what this meant. But when Joe looked to Pinkie for answers, he just said, "It's better if you *don't* know."

"Which brings me to my next point," Mimi went on. "We feel we are at a point in our research where we need to appoint a Ministry of Bridges through which spirits may appeal for access. But as with any bureaucracy, it also creates the potential for controversy, dissension, and attempts to circumvent red tape. It also relies on the system working and spirits going through due processes."

The spirit crowd erupted in confused talk, anger, and uncertainty.

"They've hinted at this move before," Pinkie whispered. "But spirits don't want to go through some process that could take years to meet a Bridge. By then, their loved ones could have come and gone."

"*Psh*—and whose numbers you think will be called first?" Cunningham added, jerking his thumb toward the front rows.

They listened intently as the presentation continued.

"My research to date involves three separate case studies, and I am happy to announce that through this work, we were able to identify *three* Bridges."

The crowd roared. Gabriella intervened, helping get the crowd back under control.

"To be perfectly honest, I would temper my excitement," Mimi said. "While we identified the three Bridges, the three case studies tell us that several missteps took place once identified—ultimately making the project unsuccessful to date."

Sighs and moans. Here and there, Joe noticed sick spirits with grey auras breaking into tears.

"You see, each of these Bridges quickly became overwhelmed once identified. Spirits from all over the world came to see the Bridge—asking them to communicate with their loved ones. It wasn't long after the discovery that the Bridges were severely affected.

"In one case study, our Bridge committed suicide. The pressures of us spirits swarming him, asking for his help—the constant badgering that we put him through. In the end, it was too much. He suffered from insomnia because we simply would not give the man a break.

"Our second case study—Abby, a woman in her mid-forties—suffered a similar fate, but instead of killing herself, she checked herself into a mental institution. While spirits are still visiting her, how can she help them if she's locked away and placed on a concoction of medication that renders her essentially speechless?

"Our third case study, Ben, was only a young boy. He was out riding his bike when he was distracted by a spirit begging for his help. I'm afraid he rode in front of a car and was killed instantly." The crowd grumbled with shock and horror, but Mimi carried on. "I'm also afraid that, to date, the spirits of all known Bridges have all chosen to pass through their portals, no doubt wanting to move on due to their experience with lingering spirits."

"That could be Josh one day," Joe whispered to himself silently. For the first time at the conference, his aura began blinking. *Rapidly* blinking. He couldn't control it.

Cunningham and Pinkie noticed and looked at each other suspiciously, but their sympathy for him seemed to take over. Pinkie tried making light of the situation. "Joe, it's okay. I know it's a lot to listen to on your first conference. Especially you being a freshie and all!"

Mimi continued. "There is a fourth case of a Bridge that we all know too well."

An eerie sort of growl erupted from the crowd, taking Joe off guard.

"Adolf Hitler was a Bridge—turned by The Others to do their will. This is a good time to remind everyone just as *we* are seeking Bridges to help us, so are The Others—which is why we need due process and protections for these Bridges."

While Joe was curious about The Others, the shrieks and gasps among the crowd at the mere mentioning of their name told him all he needed to know at the moment.

"We need your help. Chapter leaders—we *must* encourage our members to use constraint when Bridges are identified. Our recommendation through this research is to appoint someone as a primary communicator with the Bridge and to funnel all requests through this contact. Report all Bridges to your local LADO chapter, who will report to LADO Worldwide Headquarters so proper oversight can be administered. I know we are all excited to be able to pass along a message to our loved ones—it is the sole reason we stayed behind. But it is also our responsibility to create sustainability and allow these Bridges to lead a normal, living life.

"I have a second request. We need your help in identifying new Bridges. We will be training chapter heads on Bridge identification techniques. We are requesting that all newborns in your districts be tested with these identification methods. The hope is that we can discover new Bridges who might have previously gone unidentified. Through this program, we will succeed in helping each and every one of you communicate with your loved ones. Thank you. Good night."

The band played Mimi off the stage while Gabriella returned.

Joe missed her introduction because his aura was flashing like he had never seen before. He almost felt embarrassed. Spirits next to him began to check on him—which only made it worse.

The third speaker took the stage.

"Good evening. My name is Professor Dante Canelli, and I am a former member of the Bulletin of the Atomic Scientists. From 2008–2012, I served on the Science and Security Board, which oversees the infamous *Doomsday Clock*."

Everybody's auras wavered with this announcement. Joe wished he could simply be relieved.

"The living created the Doomsday Clock to estimate and warn world leaders how close we were to global annihilation via nuclear war. The idea is that once the hands of the clock struck midnight, life on Earth would be annihilated. The clock has evolved over the years to include other threats to human civilization, like climate change or the threat of a global pandemic.

"The end of the world is a delicate subject for us spirits. While we do not have a Doomsday Clock in the spirit world, rest assured there most certainly is a Doomsday. We believe the world ending would allow us to finally reach our afterlife destiny. However, this comes with a catch, as it would result in tremendous suffering by our loved ones among the living, which none of us wants to see.

"In my years at the Bulletin of the Atomic Scientists, we believed the world would end via nuclear proliferation. My committee now believes that the world will end because of a Great War with The Others. I have been asked by LADO to research spirit demographics and determine where we are at risk of losing large quantities of spirits to The Others, as we must do all we can to prevent them from winning the Great War."

"I've seen them once," said Cunningham. "I never want to see those guys again, that's for sure."

"I spent time in Russia observing spirits who passed away in the battle of Stalingrad," continued Professor Canelli. "Approximately 1.9 million people are thought to have died in possibly the bloodiest theater in history—certainly in the modern era.

"In what is now called Volgograd, I encountered hundreds of thousands of spirits on the battlefields outside the city still fighting what they believe is World War II. What we saw there was a commitment to their cause like no other. We determined approximately fifteen percent of these spirits were in critical danger of becoming sick.

"There are places like this all over the world where war, famine, natural disaster, or catastrophe lead to mass death, and we need to somehow intervene and rescue these spirits before it is too late."

The crowd cheered their support.

Gabriella took the stage and spoke with the professor before she turned to address the crowd.

"Hey—that sick spirit is back!" Cunningham warned.

Joe and Pinkie saw a small commotion as the sick spirit they saw earlier was pacing back and forth. *Ill.* It was the only word Joe could use to describe him. He looked scraggly, rotting from the inside out. Other spirits noticed and were trying to distance themselves from him.

"Help!" the sick spirit cried out.

Gabriella tried to locate the calls for help in the crowd. "Is everyone alright?"

"HELP ME!" the sick spirit moaned.

"We better get outta here," Pinkie asserted.

"Yeah, I got a bad feelin' about this one," Cunningham agreed.

Joe could almost feel the nervous energy as he watched the crowd part around the spirit, and several spirits began to leave.

"Please! Everyone stay put, we haven't concluded the evening's events quite yet," Gabriella announced.

Joe watched her try and cue the band. Muddy Waters became disagreeable, shaking his head and leaving the stage—the rest of the band following.

Joe turned to leave and was immediately swept up in the mass exodus, and thus was separated from Cunningham and Pinkie. He looked back at the stage—even *Gabriella* had left.

This can't be good, he thought, but remained in place—confused, almost stunned, not knowing what to do or where to go.

Panicked spirits darted and dashed everywhere, while some shocked souls collapsed to their knees and wailed in fright. White noise from the crowd filled the ballroom as the spirits dispersed—many passing through the walls exiting the building entirely, while others took safe haven behind objects such as pillars and peered from behind to catch a glimpse at whatever was coming.

Suddenly, a powerful explosion burst above them. The spirits who were sauntering along with the mass now scattered, some turning into orbs and shooting across the lobby in a mass panic. Joe's aura flashed rapidly as he heard screams as spirits buzzed everywhere. He was caught, unsure what was happening, in the crowd as he looked for Cunningham and Pinkie.

Joe saw a dark spherical shape form above the crowd. It looked like it might be a portal—but it was completely black. Hollow inside.

Two beings exited the portal—which remained open—and dropped to the main stage. They were dressed in black, modern-looking suits. Joe was close enough to see one of them had a tattoo on his cheek, just below his eye. The other had a similar tattoo on his neck.

The swiftness with which they moved was unlike anything Joe had ever seen. They morphed into two black orbs and burst across the room. The orbs hovered above the crowd for a moment. When they spotted the sick spirit, they darted towards him and morphed back into their human-like forms. The spirits near them fell apart and instead of simply passing through the building, raced away, shrieking for the exits.

The whole thing had a freezing effect on Joe, who would have had better luck moving if he was chained to a pillar.

A passing spirit stopping abruptly giving him direction: "Get out of here!" he yelled, eyes wild with panic, his aura flashing wildly before settling in an ominous-looking dim—telling a tale of terror falling across his entire being. "It's Mallum and Malitae!"

The dark spirits moved slowly by Joe, a confident menacing look about them as he met their eyes with his. *No! They've seen me!*

But there was no place to go. He was caught in the open, the other spirits either scurrying for hiding places or vacating the building altogether. He attempted to flee, but it made no difference. Something held him in place. It was like he had fallen under a sort of paralyzing trance that was holding him there, powerless.

As they approached, he noticed they looked like brothers. Perhaps twins. One had slicked back hair—dark as night with a sheen as if a bright moon were shining across a lake, while the twin with the tattoo on his cheek wore short spiked hair. Joe caught the sound of a throaty language he didn't understand, as they turned their attention on him.

They're coming this way, he thought while his eyes helplessly searched for someone to come to his aid. They seemed to notice him watching them, peering directly at him through jet-black eyes. Their movement was almost mechanical. Robotic in nature. As if the two of them were somehow connected or intertwined.

One of the twins seemed to revel having an audience. He smiled through jagged fangs as a snake-like tongue rolled out of his mouth. He flicked his tongue two times and slurped it back behind mischievous grinning teeth.

"We know who you are, Joe," the fork-tongued brother proclaimed.

The brother let out a mischievous laugh, seemingly enjoying the torturous spell he had placed Joe under. Joe's aura was frantic. Dimming. Brightening. Dimming. If he still had a heart, he was sure it'd be beating out of his chest.

"We know everything, don't we, Malum?" the brother with the spiked hair went on, following his brother's lead. "We are watching. Has the boredom gotten to you yet? Has the frustration set in? Watching your loved ones live out their lives and unable to do or say anything to them? Where are your spirit friends? They abandoned you. *Left* you here. For what? They don't care about you."

"We can help you—can't we, Malitae?" the brother with slicked hair added before grabbing the sick spirit and pulling him toward the black portal. The sick spirit's eyes were wild with terror.

"Look at this spirit. Look how despicable he has become," Malitae hissed, returning this gaze to where Joe was standing, still frozen. "This is what *your* fate is."

"It doesn't have to be like this, Joe." Malum pointed at the black-hole of a portal, his voice a charming yet terrifying croon. "It's much more fun if you join us on your own volition. Remember, we can *help* you." The pair effortlessly pulled the kicking sick spirit into the portal, which made a fizzing and popping sound as it closed behind them.

The twins were gone as quickly as they had arrived. Joe, hovering in a frozen state, looked around as hundreds of terrified orbs bolted around the room, still fleeing the hideous brothers. He decided he had one choice.

Joe turned into an orb and bolted toward the sanctuary of Bill and Sarah's attic.

AFTER LADO

JOE SPENT SEVERAL WEEKS FOLLOWING the LADO conference retreating to his safe spot in the attic. Sure, it was lonely, but The Others had truly terrified him, and he was disappointed in Pinkie and Cunningham for not preparing him. Leaving him behind, helpless to face the terrifying duo.

He couldn't help but reflect back to the night of the LADO conference, to the things those fork-tongued brothers had hissed: *We can help you . . . They abandoned you . . . Look at this sick spirit! This is your fate!*

Their voices poisoned his mind. *Where were Pinkie and Cunningham when I needed them most? They let me fall under those menacing brothers' spell. They left me—just like everyone else.*

"Clearly the twins were powerful enough to open portals. Maybe they *do* have the ability to help me. Kathy . . . I miss her so much. Maybe they could somehow get me to her," Joe said to himself. "But at what cost?"

Joe pondered many things in the time he spent in the attic. He worried about the "Great War." He wondered about how he might be able to open a portal . . . and about what happened to the spirit the twins pulled into their portal. *We can help you.* A portal. The twins could *open portals.* Maybe they could be the ones to get him out of this mess, reunite him with Kathy once again.

No, he thought to himself the second the thought occurred. *Don't even think about it, Morton!* It was tempting, but he knew it wasn't worth it. *Those twins are nothing but trouble. Wherever their portal leads, it won't take you to Kathy.*

He thought about leaving. His presence alone could be putting baby Josh in danger. *I can steer them away from Josh.* After much debate, Joe decided he would stay. He needed to know if Josh was a Bridge; if he was, it would be up to him to protect him. *But how?* He knew he needed to seek the counsel of his friends, Cunningham and Pinkie, but even then he didn't fully trust them with such sacred information. *I'll stick with Cunningham and Pinkie, but I won't tell them about Josh being a Bridge just yet.*

It was on a night where he finally decided to leave the safe haven of the attic, wandering alone in the park on a hot summer night, considering these matters, when Cunningham and Pinkie sauntered along.

"Hey—look who it is!" said Pinkie.

"We thought you was a goner!" joked Cunningham.

"Why didn't you tell me about them?" Joe snapped.

"We, uh, planned to tell you after the conference. We figured you'd have a lot of questions. You know, Bridges, portals—"

Joe cut Cunningham off. "Supernatural demon spirits who pull sick spirits into *dark portals* didn't seem urgent to you? They put me under some trance! Some spell . . . and you *left* me!"

He watched as Cunningham shifted around, looking at the ground. He tipped his big bowler hat to partially cover his face, but his dimming aura told Joe all he needed to know. The big spirit felt bad. "Joe's right, Pink. We never shoulda left him like that."

"Yeah, I know. I don't know what we was thinkin' leavin' Joe behind like that." Pinkie's scrawny stature sulked in shame as he kicked at the air and fidgeted with his hands.

"We were just as scared as you were, Joe," said Cunningham.

"You? I don't believe that for a second," Joe scoffed.

"You should've seen him! I never seen the big fella squeal like that!" said Pinkie.

The thought of Cunningham lumbering away, *squealing,* was all Joe could take. He burst out laughing—Cunningham even joining in.

"We're sorry, Joe. We shoulda looked out for ya," he said. "You forgive us?"

"Sure, big guy. How could I not? Afterall, what am I gonna do with myself? Spend the rest of my days pacing around the Mortons' attic? Palling around with you guys and watching TV over at the Wilsons' is way more fun. There's just one condition."

"What's that?" barked Pinkie.

"No more sick spirits for a while," said Joe.

"That's it for a while on social events for me," Cunningham conceded. "I never want to see those guys again."

"Yeah, we need to avoid crowds. Bound to be at least one sickie in a crowd!" said Pinkie.

Joe cringed at Pinkie's callousness and hoped he never became that matter-of-fact when it came to sick spirits. From what he knew, it wasn't their fault they were becoming sick. Hang around this world long enough and eventually there'd be no choice.

It actually comforted Joe to see they were as scared as he was. In a moment of weakness, Joe remembered the brothers' offer. *We know everything. We can help you.*

"They spoke to me. They said they could bring me to see Kathy—my wife who passed before me," Joe recalled. "If they can open portals, maybe they can get us out of this mess."

"Joseph, listen to me *very* carefully," cautioned Cunningham. "They will *not* help you. They are manipulating you. Sure, they can open up portals. Perhaps they can even take you to see Kathy, but if you agree to let them help you, they'll *own* you—and being owned by The Others is not a position I'd ever want to be in."

"As long as your aura has a speckle of grey in it, they cannot touch you. That sick spirit we saw at the LADO conference? His aura was dark as night. That's why they were able to nab him. Don't, under any circumstances, let yourself become sick," Pinkie commanded.

"Yeah, I got that part. But how does one become sick?" asked Joe.

"Plenty of ways. Give up. Trauma. Lose faith," Cunningham explained. "Some spirits just snap. The loneliness. Boredom. Monotony. The human world wasn't built for the likes of us, but we have to overcome. Stay in the game, as they say."

"Did you just make that up? Stay in the game. Did you make that up?" Pinkie prodded.

Cunningham scoffed and ignored his scrawny counterpart, going on about his business.

"Somethin' we outta talk to ya about, Joe," grumbled Cunningham, his demeanor becoming more serious. "Me and the wise guy here—we've been asked to be *testers.*"

"A tester?"

"Yeah," shot Pinkie. "Testers! After the conference, them LADO leadership types decided to ramp up a new strategy to find a Bridge . . . Sweeps!"

"Sweeps?" Joe asked.

"Yeah. We are testing newborns for signs of Bridges. Every newborn in our jurisdiction, we gotta test."

What if they find Josh!? He had to think of something. "That's a lot of newborns," he decided on saying, trying unsuccessfully to contain his aura from flashing.

132

"What's wrong, Joe? Why are you flashing?" asked Cunningham.

"Yeah ... somethin' I said?" said Pinkie. "My breath smell or something?" he mimicked checking his underarms for body odor. "I seem to smell alright to me."

"Just seems like a lot of work. I liked catching breakfast at the Perfect Cup," said Joe.

"It's pretty boring work," Pinkie admitted.

"You got that right—none of these snotty kids can see us," Cunningham grunted. "Still, it's not like we don't got time on our hands anymore."

Since they served on the local LADO chapter, Cunningham and Pinkie were trained by "experts" in Bridge identification techniques. They were then asked to test each baby in their assigned area and report back to the LADO Chicago chapter with the findings.

"You wanna help us out, Joe?" asked Pinkie.

"Hey, that's a good idea! We can train him well enough—less work for us, right?" Cunningham agreed.

"Yeah, boss—the sooner we get finished, the sooner we can go back to Wrigley to watch the ball games!" Pinkie prodded.

Joe agreed to some on-the-job training and tagged along with Cunningham and Pinkie on their rounds that evening. He was a fast study and learned they largely used three methods.

Eye contact.

"He looking at you?" said Cunningham.

"Nope," said Pinkie. "Looking right through my chest just like all the others."

Voice recognition.

"Helllllllooooo! Hey kid! Can ya hear me?" said Pinkie.

"I think everyone on the block can hear ya. This kid's failing pretty miserably," said Cunningham.

Eye-Track Test.

"Ok, how many fingers am I holding up, kid?" questioned Pinkie. He slowly moved his hand back and forth in front of the baby's face.

"He can't see you. He's looking off somewhere in the distance," said Cunningham.

"Alright, let's check this one off the list," Pinkie confirmed. He held his thumb to his fingers and pulled them down a few inches in the air in front of him. A kind of tiny newspaper appeared, which Pinkie swiped downwards until he found the headline he wanted. Touching this, another page appeared with a map of the neighborhood and a list of names. He crossed off one Harrison McMaster.

"Is that some kind of smartphone?" Joe asked.

"Not like you mean, but yeah," said Cunningham. "You can do it too. We'll show you."

They went on like this for days. Joe followed along silently—listening to their banter and watching carefully.

"I think I'm ready to take on a section of the neighborhood. If we fan out, we can get done faster," Joe suggested.

"I think he's ready," Pinkie acknowledged.

"Great, I'm going to concentrate on children's daycare centers in the area. Seems like we'll get further that way rather than going house to house," Joe volunteered.

"Why didn't *we* think of that?" Pinkie cried.

"How about I start down in the southeast and work north?" They didn't realize it, but this section of the map included Josh's daycare. He waited a moment—anxious that they may shut down the offer and end up covering Josh's area instead, and if that happened . . .

Pinkie seemed almost a little too excited about the idea. . . . What if Pinkie wanted that route for himself? What then? How would he distract him then?

Joe knew the longer he kept Josh a secret, the wider the gap between them would grow if he was discovered. *What if they find Josh? Surely they would cast me out of their group . . . and what then? I'd just live out my days pacing around Bill and Sarah's attic. Probably become sick with treacherous boredom within a couple years.*

Joe didn't want to think about it. It was a chance he was willing to take to protect Josh. Afterall, he wasn't even sure Josh *was* a Bridge. Better to know for sure before drawing any attention.

"Sounds like a plan, Joe!" bellowed Cunningham. "You take that route, help us finish up our sweeps, and we'll be back at Wrigley watching Cubs games again in no time."

Off he went. He knew exactly where he needed to start.

JOSH'S TEST

JOE DARTED STRAIGHT TO JOSH'S daycare, moving room to room until he saw his grandson.

He did a quick assessment of the room to verify there were no spirits lurking around. He didn't need the surly bunch that hung around here catching on that his grandson may be a Bridge.

There were about twelve children in Josh's room—all taking naps in cribs. Three teachers were assigned the room, sitting and watching movies on their smartphones or tablets while the children napped.

His aura brightened at the sight of his grandson, who seemed peaceful as he was sprawled out across the mattress in his crib. He wished terribly that he could pluck him up and rock little Josh while he slept.

Josh eventually stirred and woke, flashing a look of surprise before a calming smile settled on his face—indicating to Joe that Josh had immediately recognized him, but needed to administer the tests to confirm.

"Josh! Hi buddy!" said Joe gently.

Josh slowly roused, stretched out, and yawned. He smiled at the sound of Joe's voice. *Voice recognition*—one test passed. Joe held a finger up, and Josh followed it as he slowly moved it side to side—two tests passed. Finally, Joe locked eyes with Josh, who held it even when Joe moved his head side to side—three tests passed.

Josh was a Bridge!

Joe pulled his fingers down like he'd learned. His home page looked like the familiar smartphone display. He clicked the app he wanted and pulled up the list of children. He scrolled down to Josh's name and held his finger over it.

Lying to LADO could mean exile from the spirit community, which would put him in danger of falling sick. He closed his eyes and crossed out Josh's name.

ACT II

PART ONE
PETE STANTON
PETE MEETS DEBORAH

FOR THE FIRST TIME SINCE his passing, Pete was on his own. It reminded him of when Jessica had hung up the phone, just before he discovered his still strapped-in corpse. The same uncertainty, only this time it felt more permanent. After all, his *reason* for staying behind was now in the arms of another man, and he was standing out in a dark summer night giving his old house one last look before he moved on. Since his passing, it hadn't provided him shelter so much as the *sense* of home, or at least a sort of routine that approximated what home was to him when he was alive.

That part of him—the part that made him still *feel alive*—was dead now.

He stood and stared at the quiet house so grand and proud. Constructed brick by brick. A house that felt so warm and inviting now dark and cold, as if the walls were now saying *keep out*. A passing stranger could not have guessed the turmoil that he had left Jessica in.

Traveling to the end of the street put greater distance in between him and Jessica. Reaching the end of his neighborhood at 22nd Street and Market began to feel unfamiliar. People he didn't recognize passed by, likely on their way to enjoy an evening out.

He paused at the Schuylkill Boardwalk and looked at the river. He and Jessica had walked this Boardwalk many times, and he wanted to recount a few memories before fully moving on.

"There's a lot of history in this place." He was startled by the voice behind him, though it was soothing.

Turning to see a spirit slowly traveling toward him, he was puzzled by her approach. She wore a large dress—he had seen photos of similar dresses worn by women in the colonial period. Although she had a dimly lit aura, when it was compared to Pete's, hers seemed to light up the night. She paid no mind to a few people riding bikes on the boardwalk.

"People just seem to go on about their lives, don't they?" He watched her eyes briefly fall upon the bicyclists.

Her English accent was so thick that he could barely follow. "If folks truly knew what happened here all those years ago, they might understand. They might slow down and take a little more pause in their actions to appreciate just what went on, and the sacrifices of so many."

They both paused for a moment. She inspected Pete.

"You don't look so well. . . . By the looks of it, you haven't been dead that long either. Something traumatic happened to you. Most spirits in your condition are much older than you."

You don't say? He thought to himself. *I saved my wife from a murderer and this is how she wanted to repay me? Getting under the covers with Tim Sampson? Tim Sampson!*

"Do we know each other?" he asked, miffed.

"Oh, heavens, no. I died a long, long time ago—and I've lived on these river banks ever since—waiting for my husband to return," she explained.

"I'm sorry, you're just, eh—you look different than the other spirits I've met." Pete warmed to her as she spoke with confidence, yet wasn't afraid of showing a vulnerable side.

"Ah, the dress?" she asked, striking an elegant pose.

Pete nodded in confirmation. He had seen women like her in history books and documentaries about the British colonies.

"How long have you been dead?" she asked.

He had to stop and think for a moment. Perhaps he'd been so focused on managing his routine that he completely lost track of time. Then he remembered the anniversaries. He always celebrated his anniversary with her. . . .

"Over four years," Pete shared.

"Only four years!? Why, you're just a baby," she exclaimed.

Pete looked at her, puzzled.

"Sorry, I didn't mean to minimize you," she conceded. "I mean you haven't been dead that long."

Pete examined her dress once more. She had to have passed away well over a century ago. "No, ma'am. I don't suppose I have been dead that long—compared to some."

An awkward silence followed.

"If you don't mind my asking . . ."

"Car wreck," Pete grumbled. "I stayed behind and lived with my wife—who, just this evening, has decided she wants to move on with another man."

"Well now, that's a lot to take in. I had something similar happen once," she recalled. "My first husband—the scoundrel—he spent my dowry and ran off to the West Indies. Never did return. My only hope was that the slave he took with him killed him and made his way to free land. I always hated slavery."

"That's terrible," Pete proclaimed.

"It was different times back then," she acknowledged.

"Well, here I am. I don't know what I'm going to do next, but I do know I can't go back to my home," Pete confessed.

"Well, why not?" she asked.

"I kind of frightened her," Pete admitted.

"Frightened her? But that's impossible. We can't communicate with the living," she stated.

He traveled over to the path, bent down to ground level, and swatted a small stick into the river.

"My heavens," she gasped. "Why, I've met tens of thousands of spirits, and I've never seen one able to do that."

Another awkward silence fell on them as she watched the ripples in the water.

"I stayed behind because of *her*! I even saved her life. Me and Jerome—the coworker at the lab she works with—"

"Jerome? Is he one of the living?"

"No. The same guys who were trying to kill Jessica had killed him for his research."

"Gee, that's terrible."

"Well, Jerome and I found the killer, and came up with a plan. We scared him into confessing," he said.

"You mean you haunted him. You used your ability to move objects to scare the man half to death."

"Right. He's a murderer. What's wrong with that?"

"Nothing, I suppose." Her pursed lips gave away that she wanted to say more, but decided to listen. "So what happened with your wife . . . *Jessica*, was it now?"

"Yes, Jessica," he spoke faster as his excitement grew. "She brought someone home. Just tonight. He's up there right now as we stand here talking.

In my house!"

"Ah . . . I see," she said in a genuine tone. "I'm so sorry, Pete."

"Me too. I should've got in that stupid portal! Now I'm out here wandering around, all alone. I don't know where to go."

"You got mad and broke something, didn't you? When she brought her new lad home. Probably scared that poor woman half to death."

Pete hovered in place, waiting for her to continue; he looked at his hands, noticing his aura flashing erratically.

"Listen, let me tell you something. I've seen spirits that have been dead for centuries whose aura is in better shape than yours. If you don't heal yourself, you are going to be in a lot more trouble than I think you realize. In fact, I'm surprised they haven't come already to snatch you up," she vowed, eyes slipping to that of his aura: a dull, hoary color.

"Who's *they?*" he said.

"Why, The Others, of course. And another thing—you can relate to this one, I suppose—my second husband, whom I loved dearly, had gone over to Britain on a mission and stayed for over ten years. I was lonely waiting for his return. Sadly, I died before he came back. I've been here since the day I died—waiting on him to come back to Philadelphia."

"If you don't mind me asking, who was your husband?" Pete asked.

"I'll give you a little clue," she taunted. "My name is Deborah Reed."

It didn't register with Pete.

"It's disappointing—you youngsters have all but forgotten us," she said. "My husband was Benjamin Franklin."

Pete stood motionless.

"I loved Benjamin dearly. He thought he could further the American cause by living in Britain and influencing Parliament. I suppose he thought the American dream was bigger than our relationship. So, I know how lonely it can be—but enough about Benjamin. I only tell you this story to show you you're not the only one who has experienced the agony of someone moving on . . . but you need to heal yourself, and do it quickly."

"How do I heal myself?" He knew she was right. If he stayed stuck feeling sorry for himself, he would surely be a goner. He needed to do something quick in order to save his aura from becoming sick.

She stopped for a moment, her colonial dress hanging motionless, hiding her feet. He wondered if maybe that was the dress she was married in, but he dared not ask.

"If I were you, I'd use those powers of yours for good instead of scaring the giblets off that beautiful wife of yours." She began traveling away, then she stopped and said, "Remember, Pete—even though she moved on, she still *loves* you."

He watched Deborah gracefully glide through a railing before making it to shore. She disappeared behind the bridge and was gone.

Suddenly, Pete's aura brightened a few shades. Bolts of light flickered around as if trapped in some sort of bottle or container. He seemed to have a new purpose, but he wasn't out of the woods just yet.

PETE MOVES ON

PETE TOOK SPECIAL INTEREST IN something Deborah said: *You should use your newfound powers for good.*

"How could I have been so selfish?" he said out loud.

He didn't consider his ability to move objects as a gift that could *help* the living. He had worked tirelessly for years to obtain these abilities, but only thought of using his tools to contact Jessica. His ability to move objects had helped him save her from David Rendorf, but they also caused him much grief when he used them to announce his presence to her. He could never go back to her. Not now. Not only could he not live a life of torment watching her find new love, but he could not face her after frightening her. The desire to communicate with her would be too strong and he would only alienate her further.

Deborah's words motivated him to set a new course.

He didn't have to look very far to apply his skill set. Humans were no doubt the clumsiest species in the animal kingdom, and being a spirit allowed him to see things while remaining unseen.

An object on the trail caught his attention as it sparkled in the moonlight. A large piece of glass.

This could cause someone injury if they stepped on it, he thought, tossing the piece glass into the river. His mood lightened and his aura seemed to brighten. Even though he scared the cook into confessing, there was still a darkness he felt while doing so. Removing this piece of glass from the trail gave him a bit of a jolt—it reminded him of the temporary joy he felt when he would buy a sandwich for a homeless man who stood outside his office.

While removing a piece of sharp glass from the trail was good, Pete didn't think that was what Deborah had in mind.

In that moment, Pete decided he wanted to do something big to help people. He didn't know what that meant or where to go, but one thing was for sure: He didn't want to stay in Philadelphia. It was too close to Jess. He decided he would head west—would travel onto Walnut Street, which went all the way to Lancaster before turning into Route 30. He would figure out a strategy from there.

He just needed to get out of Philadelphia.

He must've traveled in a westerly direction for at least a couple miles before he determined it would be much faster to get to Lancaster if he hitched a ride. He had ridden in Jess's car plenty of times before but never had he attempted to hitch a ride in a moving car.

He moved into the road as a moving car approached. Instinctively, he braced himself and put his arms up as he prepared himself to be hit by the car. Before Pete realized what happened, the car drove into him and passed through him.

"Woah!" He wasn't sure if he had actually felt something or if it was all in his head, but it was a rush.

He decided to try it again. A tractor trailer rumbled down the road straight for him. The semi-truck must've been going about fifty in a thirty-five zone.

"I haven't seen a semi over here before. He must be lost or something."

He braced himself again as the truck was right on top of him. The bright lights of the semi were blinding. He put his hands up just as the truck passed through him, his eyes closed. The whooshing sound of the semi passing through him was like standing on a fault line during an earthquake.

His eyes still closed, he felt nothing, but over the roaring sound of the engine he could make out the sound of a Waylan Jennings' song. Pete opened his eyes to see himself looking out the windshield of the tractor trailer. From what he could tell, the ride seemed jolting—the driver bouncing in a suspension seat on this bumpy stretch of road. *Somehow, he had been able to latch onto the moving truck!*

"I did it!" he yelled in excitement, his aura flashing wildly.

The slurping sound of a straw trying to suck up the last bit of a carbonated drink prompted him to look in the driver's direction. An older, heavyset man wearing a baseball hat and a flannel shirt was driving the truck. Pete observed him for a moment.

Unexpectedly, the portly man began belting out the chorus:

Mammas, don't let your babies grow up to be cowboys!
Don't let 'em pick guitars and ride in old trucks
Let 'em grow up to be doctors and lawyers and such!

"Hey, buddy!" yelled Pete.

No reply from the driver. He just kept singing right along.

Mammas, don't let your babies grow up to be cowboys!
They never stay home, and they're always alone
Even with someone they love!

He was glad the man couldn't see him, because his sudden appearance probably would have startled the truck driver and caused an accident. The thought seemed to trigger his aura, which now flashed wildly.

"Yup, ain't nobody drive a rig like good ol' Ben Teskar," the driver said to himself.

Ben Teskar. That's his name? Well, one thing was for sure: he looked *like a Ben Teskar.*

On the other hand, Pete looked at poor Ben with sympathy, as it sure seemed like he could use some company, and in that moment he wished he could provide companionship for the man. He wondered what they might talk about. Maybe they had a bit in common. *Broken hearts.* They'd surely talk about the women they loved who had left them. The thoughts seemed to calm Pete's aura.

"Let me tell you about my wife, Jessica, Ben. She left me," he said, giving one look back at the bright city lights. Something inside him told him it would be the last time he would ever see the Philadelphia skyline.

THE BLUE PEN

PETE WAS CONTENT WITH NOT knowing where he was going, exactly, as long as the truck motored westward.

What did it matter anyway?

He had made his decision to leave. He couldn't stand to watch her move on. Would she marry Tim Sampson the lab technician? Maybe she and Tim would have children together—the children Pete always wanted. Stay in the house he and Jessica built. Build the life he always wanted. Watch Tim Sampson live out *his* dream. It couldn't happen. If he'd stayed he surely would have become sick . . . and then what?

He just needed to move on, and maybe search for another portal to enter. But how?

You should use your newfound powers for good.

He was happy he had met Deborah. Her voice seemed to ring in his head and was a reminder that he had a new purpose.

The semi was now outside of Philadelphia, heading west. Pete estimated this was a long-haul truck—probably to the Pennsylvania turnpike, then headed cross country. The further he could get away from Jessica and her new boyfriend, the better.

"You know what?" he said to the driver. No response. "You'll never believe this."

The driver kept on singing. His belly jiggling with every high note.

"My wife, Jessica—she left me tonight. Moved on with another man."

The driver fidgeted with the radio station before settling on a new song.

"You know what? She deserved to move on. Be happy. I don't know how I could have been so foolish. Wait for me? She's in her late thirties. Her prime years. Of course she was going to move on. Did I really expect her to live *alone* for the rest of her life?"

The driver slurped his drink in response. It was one of those long, drawn out slurps followed by a satisfactory belch. *Why didn't I get in that portal?*

147

Why did I stay here? Why?

Boredom set in later into the ride. The driver had listened to a full country western album, and now songs were starting to repeat. The only thing worse was when the driver began to sing along, making Pete almost vacate the vehicle before settling in and thinking more about Jessica. Talking aloud to drown out the driver.

"I should go back," he said, ignoring the singing driver. "I should go back and signal her and let her know I'm here and I mean her no harm. Surely she'd wait for me and we could enter her portal together. There's no *way* I wouldn't scare her, though. You saw her reaction when she found that vase, Pete! If she even senses you being there again, she'll probably freak out . . . sell the house . . . then what are you going to do? *Move* with her? Follow her all around the rest of her life signaling her? That's called *haunting*, Stanton. That's what you'd be doing . . . *haunting* your wife. Is that how you want Jessica to remember you? No. That's not—but moving on is hard. Where do I go?"

A sudden jerk. He didn't feel it so much as notice the subtle disruptions. A stainless steel thermos clanking back and forth in the cup holder. A magazine falling from the dashboard. Minty air fresheners dangling from the rearview mirror swaying back and forth. He took a break from his self-pity to search for a landmark to gauge his whereabouts.

The bitter darkness told him he was well on his way to Lancaster. Another jolt. This time more noticeable. The stainless steel thermos almost bounced out of the cup holder.

"Hey! Take it easy. I don't like being in a vehicle in the first place—" Pete's voice trailed off as his aura went into sudden hyper-flashing. To his surprise, Ben the lively truck driver was hunched over the steering wheel, dead asleep.

"Wake up! We're headed straight for the embankment!" Eager to liberate Ben from his slumber, Pete tried swatting, tugging, and pushing the large man. If the truck hit the embankment, it had a good chance of going through and crossing into oncoming traffic like a heat-seeking missile. He looked out the windshield and froze as a row of cars came traveling the opposite lanes, heading straight eastbound toward Philadelphia.

"Hey! Wake up!" Pete tried, but Ben couldn't hear him.

He became paralyzed with dread as the horror of his own death flashed across his mind. His aura blinked with a frightening thought of another car accident. He wouldn't be able to stand another fatal crash where he'd have to watch spirits figure out they were dead like he'd had to.

The people driving the cars in the oncoming lanes had no idea what was about to hit them. They were probably on their way home from third shift—or traveling to work, their day just starting. Brothers or sisters . . . fathers or mothers . . . wives or husbands. Whoever they were, Pete knew they didn't deserve what was about to become their fate.

"Jump out of the truck!"

The truck barreled toward the embankment, swerving from lane to lane—tires squealing as they hugged the road.

Do something, Stanton! "Hey! Bozo! Wake up! Come on, big guy! Wake up!"

No use. They were going to crash—their fates sealed.

"Get out of here, Stanton!" Terrified to witness another crash, Pete slid his leg through the passenger side door. It was as if in his panic, he resorted to clumsy human behavior, forgetting he could just turn into an orb and shoot right out of there. He stuck his head, leg, and a full arm out of the truck and was looking for a place to jump when Deborah's voice came back to him.

You need to put those powers of yours to good use.

"Dammit," he said, pulling himself back into the cab. He saw a blue pen rolling around on the passenger seat. A plain, unassuming pen.

Instinct took over, and he reacted.

All in one motion, he lunged with his left hand—scooping the pen up and throwing it at the driver. It seemed like slow-motion, and he watched in disbelief as the pen traveled through the air, end over end, finally striking the man's right cheek.

Ben sprang awake, flailing his arms in the air, knocking his curve-billed sweat-stained hat from his head before clutching the steering wheel.

"Woah!"

The embankment. Speeding up. As if it had fired up the engine and began racing toward them. Pete had seen this before. The maple tree. The harmless maple tree with the crunchy looking bark—just before his crash. A feeling of guilt flushed over him as he replayed the thoughts of his own crash. His desire to tell Jessica he loved her that day. What he *really* wanted to say was that he wanted children. Why did he have to tell her *then*—at that time, while he was driving to work and she was probably just getting ready for work? That desire, the want to tell her at that very moment, cost him dearly. He paid for it with his life.

The embankment. Coming for him like a mobile fortress. Pete instinctively held up his hands, as if they offered him protection from the rebel embankment flying toward them.

At the last second, the driver grabbed the wheel and jerked right. *Overcorrecting.* The truck lumbered back over the centerline into the right lane, aiming for a guardrail—the driver jerking the wheel left, then right, then left again. The cab rotated as the trailer lifted off.

"Gonna lose the rig!" yelled Ben, yanking the wheel—first left, then right—until settling the truck at last. Pete felt the driver downshifting. Finally slowing down. Pulling to the shoulder.

"Hey!" yelled Pete. "Do you realize what you could've done?"

Ben hopped out of the cab. Pete did the same and approached him, noticing the driver down on one knee. His hands were shaking.

"Are you okay, buddy?" As Pete traveled over, he realized Ben Teskar, the big, tough-looking semi driver was crying.

Even though his presence didn't necessarily contribute to anything, Pete felt like staying with Ben in this moment was the right thing to do. Pete approached cautiously, finding the mountain of a man collapsed on his knees, breaking down in seemingly a sob of relief. In a strange way, he felt shameful at his earlier annoyance and irritation toward him. His anger for being put in a position where he had to relive his death quickly faded as he watched the burly man take off his hat and wipe his running nose with his sleeve, which was both endearing and disgusting.

Eventually, Ben got to his feet, standing on wobbly knees. Placing his vented hat atop his head, he fished around in his pocket for his phone. "Hey, it's Dad." He paused. "Yes, I know what time it is."

Ben paused again as he listened to the person on the other end speak. Pete was so close he could almost make out the words as the person on the line spoke.

"I'm fine." Another pause. Pete could hear a muffled voice. "I wanted to call and tell you I love you."

Pete's aura flashed as a feeling of regret fell over him. "I wish I would've got to tell Jessica I loved her one last time," he said.

Suddenly, blue and red flashing lights approached as a squad car pulled up. A spotlight shined brightly through him and onto Ben. A young-looking state trooper with blonde hair clipped to a single length exited the squad car. He approached the driver with a confident swagger and a relaxed gait—

shoulders pulled back, chest out. He initiated contact, taking control immediately as he stood over in front of Ben, legs spread wide, claiming his space. Pete followed.

"That was some trick back there. You're lucky to have walked away from that one."

All of the color had left Ben's face. "Good evening, officer."

"I would like to see your Commercial Driver's License, physical card, proof of insurance, and your driver logs."

"Sure thing, officer."

Pete watched the trooper shine a flashlight at the truck driver's shoes. He couldn't help but notice the pile of vomit on the ground—and it was clear the police officer noticed too.

"You got something on your shoes. Have you had anything to drink tonight?" His sharp, direct tone told Pete perhaps the officer had military experience.

"No, sir. I was just scared after almost losing my rig like that."

"Okay, grab your documentation and meet me back here," the officer ordered in a commanding, yet easygoing, manner.

Pete looked on as Ben clumsily entered the cab and felt around for his documents while the officer conducted a physical inspection of the truck—eventually returning to the driver's side, where Ben was waiting for him.

"Sorry—paperwork's a little wrinkled," Ben said sheepishly.

The officer reviewed his documentation and CDL. "Ben Teskar."

"Yes, sir. That's me."

The officer didn't look up, continuing to review the paperwork. "Well, Mr. Teskar, you are over your hours of service for the day. It says here you have not had a break in over fifteen hours. Is that correct?"

Ben looked at the ground. "Yes, sir. I thought I could get through some of the turnpike tonight, and I would pull over and get some sleep before traffic started up again."

"Mr. Teskar, you put your life at risk, and the lives of motorists around you. You're lucky I'm standing here talking to you and not scraping you up off the ground right now."

"Sorry, officer." Instead of making eye contact, Ben looked down at the ground, confirming his shame.

"You are getting an Out-of-Service citation tonight. If I or another officer catch you on the road, you are getting a felony citation. Do you understand?"

"Yes, sir."

"Now, what the hell happened back there?"

"I—I fell asleep at the wheel. I was trying to finish my run early so I could get home and see my family. My daughter has a basketball game at the end of the week."

"Asleep at the wheel, huh? You *sure* you didn't have anything to drink tonight?"

Remorse returned as Pete saw Ben shifting his weight, talking with his hands. His body language coming alive as he defended his position. It seemed Ben was just trying to finish his route so he could get home to his daughter. Sure, Ben did a foolish thing, but so had he—only he was grateful it hadn't cost the big man his life.

"Not a drop, officer. I don't drink. I gave that up a long time ago. The penalties for drinking and driving are steep nowadays."

"Okay, well I don't smell any alcohol, but I did see you vomit when I was pulling up—which is probable cause. Let's do a field sobriety test. If you pass, I will tag you Out-of-Service for being over your hours limit and let you go. You're getting a fine, and you'll have to stay off the road for eight hours, but you won't go to jail. If you fail the sobriety test, the judge in this jurisdiction will throw the book at you, and he'll see to it that you never get behind the wheel of a tractor again."

Pete watched as the officer administered the field sobriety test. He felt the officer was being a little tough on Ben, but then again, Ben *did* just turn his truck into a two ton missile.

"All right, all right—you pass the test for today, Mr. Teskar. You will be able to drive again, but not for at least eight hours. Here is your OoS violation."

Ben took the yellow piece of paper from the officer. He looked defeated and humiliated.

"This is a hefty fine, officer. My boss is going to have my hide."

"It could've been a lot worse, Ben."

"It's hard to argue that, officer. You won't see me on the road before the next eight hours. I am going to climb in the sleeper cab and get some shut eye."

"Mr. Teskar—"

Ben turned around and climbed back down off the semi. "Yes, officer?"

"So, off the record—what happened?"

"Officer?"

"What really happened back there? I've seen enough of these accidents, cleaned up enough crashes to know how lucky you got."

"Well, officer, I don't know when I fell asleep, or how long I was out. It couldn't have been more than thirty seconds to a minute, but with the perfect alignment of these rigs—it could've been longer if the road was straight."

"Do you remember waking up?"

"It was the strangest thing. I was asleep, and someone in my dream was trying to wake me. In fact, whatever it was, the person hit me or slapped me in the face."

Ben squinted and tilted his head away as the officer beamed his flashlight on his face and walked toward him to get a closer look.

"Where did you say the person slapped you? In your dream, I mean?" asked the officer.

"Right here. It's the weirdest thing. I can almost feel it. Funny, my wife doesn't even hit me that hard after I make an inappropriate joke at the dinner table."

Ben began to chuckle at his own joke, but was abruptly stopped by the officer's rigid silence. Neither of them spoke. The close proximity of the officer inspecting his cheek seemed to make him nervous. Finally, the officer broke the silence.

"You say a person in your dream hit you in the face when you were sleeping, huh?"

"Yes, sir. At least I think so, officer—it all happened so fast, and I didn't exactly see anyone hit me in the dream. It was more like I felt someone hit me, so I just assumed I dreamt it."

"And just to be clear, no one is riding with you—no family members or coworkers, anything like that?"

"No, officer. It is just me and my rig. I had a dog that traveled with me for a while, but he died last year. Sad story actually, I had to bury him myself—"

"Mr. Teskar . . ."

"Yes, sir?"

"Only answer my questions, please."

"Sorry, officer, I get to babblin' when I get nervous."

"Mr. Teskar, I want you to answer me truthfully. Did you say no one is with you, you felt someone hit you in the face, and you thought you dreamt it? Is that correct?"

"Yes, sir. That pretty much sums it up."

"And you said you still have a feeling on your cheek as if someone actually hit you in the face."

"Yes, officer."

"Can you point out where you think the person in your dream hit you?"

Ben pointed to his right cheek just below his ear.

Pete traveled over to get a closer look. He could see blue ink on his face, and a red mark that was bleeding slightly.

"Mr. Teskar, can you look into your rearview mirror for me?"

"Sure, officer, but that seems like an odd request. Is this a new form of field test or something?"

"Mr. Teskar, this is a voluntary request. You have something on your face, in the exact spot that you said someone in your dream hit you, and I want you to look at it."

Pete watched Ben clumsily climb his semi, and looked in his rearview mirror. He was struggling to hold onto the door handle and look in the mirror at the same time. The officer walked behind Ben and shined his light in the rearview mirror so Ben could get a better look.

"Woah!" Ben threw his hands back, jumping at the sight of his own face—falling off the steps of his semi. The officer caught the husky man, or at least broke his fall enough to save him from landing on the ground.

"That's what I thought," proclaimed the officer, taking note of Ben's surprise.

"My face is bleeding!"

"Yes, Mr. Teskar. You also have what looks like a blue ink streak on your right cheek next to the laceration. Any idea how that happened?"

Ben suddenly became weak. He was breathing heavily. He couldn't speak. He sat down on the steps of his semi, tears coming to his eyes.

"Mr. Teskar, I don't exactly know what happened here, or how you got a laceration and blue ink on your face at the same spot where you thought you dreamt a man struck you in the face. All I have to say is I can't really explain what happened, but it looks like someone upstairs was watching out for you tonight. I don't know if you are a religious man, Mr. Teskar, but if I were you, I would be saying plenty of prayers tonight."

THE THREE WISE MEN

NOT ONLY HAD PETE SAVED Ben Teskar and likely a dozen other motorists on the road that night, but in doing so, he realized he'd saved himself. After the heartbreak of watching Jessica move on, he'd come dangerously close to becoming a sick spirit—a fatal semi crash, he suspected, would've sealed his fate. But after saving Ben's life, his aura had brightened several shades. He wasn't fully in the clear yet, but he was in much better shape than before he had met Deborah.

Pete watched poor Ben clumsily enter the cab of his truck to retire for the evening—his ride wouldn't be going anywhere for a while. And so he stood on the side of the road, looking at the stars on this cloudless night. He guessed he was somewhere on the outskirts of Lancaster, but he didn't know how far.

As he stood, motionless, staring up at the night sky, thoughts of Jessica entered his mind. He reminisced about the New York trip they took together the weekend before he died. It was there that he thought he'd worked up the courage to tell Jessica he wanted to start a family, but ended up abandoning the idea—only to regain his confidence the morning of his death.

"I would have been a good dad," he said aloud.

The images quickly deteriorated, replaced by visuals of Jessica together with Tim Sampson.

"They'll probably start their own family together, now—the family I always wanted. If only I could have signaled you sooner, Jess. Maybe you and I would still be together."

They were foolish, dark thoughts, and he shook his head as he lifted a small pebble, recalling his newfound purpose. "*Use your powers for good*,' huh, Deborah? All right, I hear ya. I'm going."

Although time didn't matter to him, he estimated it was somewhere between three or four in the morning. The highway was completely empty other than the occasional semi-trucks rumbling by, trying to make it to

Pittsburgh before morning.

He'd had enough of the trucking life for one day and decided to travel alone for a while. He stood outside the truck trailer admiring what was an hour ago his ticket west. "Goodbye, Ben. Thanks for the ride. I hope you make it home in time to see your daughter's game."

Pete reached the town of Atglen sometime around mid-morning. A sign just outside the town said "POPULATION 1,402," —which, by the looks of things, Pete thought might be a stretch. He hadn't heard of Atglen, so he went to the local gas station to see if he could collect some intel on his whereabouts.

As he approached the gas station, three older gentlemen were sitting on a bench. After watching them a while, he deciphered their names were Lenny, Jim, and Stan, and this seemed to be their regular hangout. The old coots were early-birds, likely visiting this bench around sunrise daily so they wouldn't miss the first customer.

"You know what really chaps my ass," said Lenny—apparently the leader, "is those high school kids with those souped-up Hondas racing through town."

"You got that right, Lenny," Jim grumbled. "In my younger years, I might've done something about it."

Pete could tell Jim was a no-nonsense type. He wore a hat that read: *U.S. Navy Korea War Veteran 1950–1953* .

"What would *you* have done, Jim?" said Stan, the instigator. Clearly trying to provoke a hostile reaction from his peer for his own entertainment.

As long as Pete had been there, Stan was poking at the other two—egging them on until they lost their temper. It quickly became a predictable shtick, and Pete suspected Lenny and Jim recognized Stan's jabs, but played into it because they liked complaining.

"Well, I'll tell you what I'd do, you son of a bitch!" said Jim, raising his voice before exaggerating how he would have dealt with the situation.

He noticed they would pause their arguments whenever a customer walked up. Though they argued and yelled at each other, they would become united in their apparent mission to approve or deny entrance for whoever approached. They never denied anyone; they just acted as if they could if they wished.

An African American woman approached the door after filling up the tank of an early 2000's model Toyota Camry. She wore a form-fitting summer dress as she headed inside to pay, spotting the three seniors.

"Morning, boys!" she cheered as she opened the door, posturing her curvy body while intently looking away so the old trio could enjoy a good stare.

"Hi, Bree," they said in unison, while climbing over each other, fighting for any square inch of bench they could claim, and quickly snapping back into position when she'd give a sultry glance their way. Oh, they tried their best to look innocent—hands folded in their lap, looking up at the sky, pretending they hadn't been looking.

His first instinct might've been one of disgust, had Pete seen three other men practically drooling over her, but Pete quickly realized these three were about as harmless as a stingless bee. On top of that, Bree sure seemed to be enjoying the extra attention, suggestively flaunting her body and bending over tying her shoe in front of them, allowing a look down her shirt. Pete shook his head and chuckled to himself as he watched them carry on.

"Hubba hubba." Lenny chortled after she went inside. "You see that, Stan?"

"I was sitting right next to you, wasn't I?"

"She's mine," Jim boasted. "We went on a date the other night."

"Yeah, *right*," Lenny challenged.

"If you went on a date with her, then I'm Frank Sinatra," Stan said.

A squabble followed until the little bell from inside the door sounded an alarm, signaling somebody was coming back out. They quickly resumed their roles as solemn inspectors, watching side-eyed for whoever was coming out that door. It was Bree.

She seemed to sense their eyes on her and turned around to them. "Hey, Jim!"

Pete watched the old man sit up straight. A surly grin formed on his wrinkled face.

"What time am I picking you up Wednesday night for BINGO?" she asked.

"Seven o'clock sharp." Jim smiled. "Better yet, why don't you make it six and I'll take ya out for ice cream? I know a good place over on 12th street."

"You got it, baby," she replied, glowing. She turned and walked away with a brisling shimmy she knew would get everyone's attention.

"She's a provocative one, isn't she boys?" Jim taunted.

Lenny and Stan didn't respond. They sat with their mouths gaping, watching as Bree got into her car.

"Well, boys—that's my cue to head home," boasted Jim. "Landscaper is coming by to clip the grass and I have to be there to make sure he mows in a straight line." Neither Lenny nor Stan responded. "Plus, I need to get home in case Bree decides to come over."

"Oh, come on!" Lenny scoffed, waving him off.

"I'd bet my left leg that she's not coming over. I'd bet my right one, too, but—you know." Stan lifted his right pant leg exposing a metal prosthetic. It made a pinging sound as he tapped it with his cane.

"I've officially seen everything," grumbled Stan as he gripped his walker, preparing to stand. "I gotta go. It's ten o'clock—landscaper will be at my house soon."

"Let's go, ya old bag of bones!" yelled Lenny.

He and Jim started walking off, not realizing the dire situation Stan was in.

Pete had represented a lot of slip and fall related cases back in his attorney days. He knew falls were the leading cause of death of people over sixty-five, resulting in over 27,000 fatal injuries a year.

"Come on, ya old fogie!" barked Jim.

Stan was visibly shaking as he tried to settle his wobbly walker. He over-corrected, and the walker slipped out. He was going down.

Instinctively, Pete leaped toward the walker and held it in place, while at the same time maneuvering Stan so he kept his balance, stabilizing the old man and the walker. He could sense Stan knew he had a close call, but maybe wasn't sure how he recovered himself.

"You okay, Stan?" yelled Lenny, genuinely concerned.

"*Phew*—close one!" Stan admitted. He still maintained a serious facial expression.

Pete watched Jim saunter over and picked up Stan's hat, dusted a few grass clippings off before handing it to him. It had taken a couple of minutes for Jim to waddle over, and by then, Stan seemed to regain his composure.

"Gonna take more than an old rickety walker to take me out, boys!" he chuckled.

"Well, let's get going, ya klutz," Lenny taunted.

"I'm going, I'm going," he replied, shuffling his walker with each step.

Jim walked with him until they caught up with Lenny.

Pete wondered where they were headed, but knew wherever they went adventure would follow.

CHARLIE

PETE WONDERED IF HE SHOULD'VE stayed with Lenny, Stan, and Jim. Not only did they promise a constant source of entertainment, they also looked like a rowdy bunch who could use someone like him watching out for them.

He decided to let them go. After all, he knew where to find them if he changed his mind.

Atglen seemed like a quiet little town where everyone knew each other. A bearded, Amish man on a horse and buggy rolled by. That was something he didn't see every day living in downtown Philadelphia.

He was almost surprised when a late model Mustang pulled up with AC/DC blaring over the speakers. The rusty sports car, the loud music—it clashed with the quiet surroundings.

The driver got out of the car and lit a cigarette before he went inside. He had a shaggy mullet, acid-washed jeans, a grey tank top, and a leather jacket. His tank top looked like it hadn't been washed in a couple days, and his jeans were tattered and dirty. He looked as if he were attempting to grow a beard, or more like he hadn't shaved in four to five days.

Pete moved in to get a closer look. A woman stayed in the car while the driver went inside. She didn't seem very happy, but it was too early to tell why. He glided around the car, getting a good view inside. The back seat was full of empty fast food bags and whatever trash the driver decided to toss back there. Cigarette butts spilled over the ashtray. The deplorable conditions inside the vehicle making Pete thankful he no longer had a sense of smell.

The passenger looked to be in her mid- to late-twenties and far too pretty to be mixed up with a greasy dude with a bad mullet. Makeup ran down her face as if she had been crying. The heavy eyeshadow was accentuated by what looked to be a poor attempt to apply bright red lipstick—probably while riding.

159

She wore tall black boots and a tight mini-skirt that Pete thought was a couple sizes too small. A cheap-looking jean jacket did a poor job of covering up her revealing outfit.

She threw her cigarette out the window when the man came back out of the gas station. He looked like he was in a hurry and paused briefly to tuck what looked to be a pistol into the back of his pants.

"Ready, baby?" his raspy voice sounded over the squeaking door as he got in the car.

Pete could've easily let them go on their way, but he felt compelled to learn more about these two. He phased into the backseat as they were pulling away. He didn't like his choice of ride, but his instincts told him to stay. Besides, they were heading in the direction he wanted to go, even if his investigation turned out to be for nothing.

"You get me a water like I asked?" the woman said. She approached him with a confidence, which told Pete she knew this man, but her body language said otherwise. Her legs crossed away from him, so exaggerated that her entire body was contorted away from him. She held her jacket with both hands tightly, wrapping herself like a cocoon.

"Nah. Sorry, babe. No time."

"Ugh. Stop calling me *babe*. That's the third gas station you've been to in an hour, and you can't get me a water?"

He swiftly grabbed her hand and began twisting, generating a cracking sounds as one of her knuckles popped. Pete watched her grimace in pain.

"Listen, I'll call you *babe* if I want. You got that? As long as I'm paying you, I'll call you whatever I want," he snapped.

She pulled her wrist away. "I'm hungry. What are you doing in these gas stations anyway?" she asked.

"None of your business," he barked, prompting an eye roll from her.

"Fuel light just came on. I gotta stop and get some gas, then we'll hit the road again".

His voice. Pete hated his voice. A scratchy kind of voice that amplified the nastiness of his words and made Pete dislike him even more.

"We just left a gas station. You're not very good at this if you're driving around robbing gas stations on an empty tank of gas," she said, miffed.

"What do *you* know about what I'm doing, Stacy!?" he exploded.

"I wouldn't be very smart if I couldn't pick up on what you're doing. You've gone to three gas stations, haven't bought anything—and you have an *empty* tank of gas?"

"You think you're smart? *You?* You're out here working the streets. Remind me, *babe,* which Ivy League school did you go to?" His belly jiggled as he chuckled, proud he got one over on her, as though he enjoyed taunting her.

"Hey, I went to college for three years. Almost got my Bachelor's in Fine Art," she objected.

"Fine Art? You got pregnant and flunked out of school. That what you had in mind? Sounds like some *fine* art to me." His wheezy laugh made Pete wish the man would choke on his own phlegm.

Pete stewed in the back, his aura burning as dark as the thoughts that clouded his mind. The more the man harassed her, the more helpless Pete felt.

"Don't be an ass, Charlie," she snapped. Pete knew she was trying to be brave. Stand up for herself. But it was a feeble attempt. He could tell by the white knuckled grip she kept on her jacket that she was terrified.

"Charlie. Now I know your name," said Pete, his eyes narrowing and aura pulsing like a beating heart as he looked on.

Charlie clearly favored the back roads as they traveled another twenty twisting and turning miles before they pulled into a gas station on the outskirts of Elizabethtown.

"This guy likes his gas stations. He's probably wanted all over the state," said Pete.

He watched with careful interest as they pulled up to a gas pump, leaving the engine running. Charlie took a long drag off his menthol cigarette, and flicked the ashes out the window—scoping out his target. His long hair bobbed and weaved as he looked around, noticing doors and driveways in and out of the lot.

"Get out and pump," ordered Charlie.

Stacy didn't argue. She got out of the car and began pumping the gas. The driver side door squeaked something awful as Charlie exited, leaving it running with the door open. His cowboy boots clanked against the dry cement as he eagerly scurried inside.

Pete passed through the car and stayed with Stacy. Despite her acquiescence to her asshole partner, he felt sorry for her. She had somehow fallen on hard times, it seemed, and ended up out here hanging around guys like Charlie.

While she was pumping gas, Pete decided to explore the vehicle. He saw an opportunity with Charlie still inside. He traveled through the passenger side door and made his way to the front seat.

Besides a messy car, he didn't see any evidence out in the open that suggested foul play. He tried to open the glove box. After several attempts, the latch released.

The glove box was full of Charlie's junk. He peeled back some loose papers—which was harder than throwing the pen had been—and found a pistol and several knives. There was a bag of white powder, which Pete suspected was some type of drug.

He put back the loose objects and closed the glove box, looking up to observe his companions. Stacy was still outside pumping gas, and Charlie was standing at the gas station counter.

"He'll be back any minute," said Pete.

He decided to open up the center counsel. It only took two attempts; his skills seemed to be getting better.

He rifled through some loose papers and candy wrappers before finding a bag of cash. Probably cash Charlie had robbed from the gas stations. Underneath the bag, he found an envelope that read:

To: MOM.

"That's strange. He's going to write a letter to his mother?" said Pete.

He opened the letter and read it. He could tell right away it was a man's hurried, sloppy handwriting:

> *Dear Mom;*
> *I'm sorry that I let you down. Tell my daughter that I love her.*
> *Please raise her right.*
> *—Stacy*

Stacy didn't write that letter. Besides the handwriting, Stacy didn't seem suicidal, and wouldn't she have mentioned her daughter by name?

Tell my daughter I love her.

"He's going to kill her!" yelled Pete.

His aura began a frustrated flash as he rushed to fold and stuff the letter back into the envelope. Pulling the letter out was much easier than the precision of placing it back in.

"Get in the car! Let's go! Let's go! Let's go!"

He looked up to see Charlie's hair bobbing wildly as he sprinted toward the car. He had his pistol out in one hand and a small bag in the other.

Stacy panicked and dropped the nozzle while trying to put it back in the gas pump.

"Leave it! We gotta go!"

She left it on the ground, gasoline spraying out of it.

Pete quickly closed the center console before Charlie got in the car.

They jumped in and sped off. Pete looked out the back window and saw an angry clerk chase them out of the parking lot. He had a phone to his ear, most likely communicating Charlie's license plate to the police.

Pete needed to act fast, or Stacy was either going to jail as an accomplice or suffer her fate at the hands of Charlie.

CHARLIE'S NEXT MOVE

REMOVE THE PISTOL FROM THE *glove box and blow him away.*
Get a knife from the glove box and plunge it into his chest.
Strangle him with his seatbelt.
Grab the steering wheel and cause a crash.

Pete cycled through his options, but while he wanted to stop Charlie, none of them seemed viable. He could kill Charlie—but no police officer in the world would believe Stacy didn't do it. She'd be convicted and never see her daughter again. Plus, he was not unaware of his darkening aura. He thought of the dire warnings about The Others. He thought of the mysterious words of the Gatekeeper: *You are still being judged on your actions.* Though he could kill without fear of earthly authorities, he wasn't sure what the eternal consequences might be.

"Where exactly are you taking me?" said Stacy, finally breaking the silence. "I don't like robbing gas stations. This isn't part of the deal."

"Listen. I'm a paying customer. You don't ask questions. You hear me?" said Charlie. His raspy voice grated on Pete.

"The cops are probably on our tail," she said.

Charlie kept driving.

"I got one more stop, then we can go back to the hotel. I got us one of those nice rooms with HBO," he said.

"I'm sure it's a regular paradise," she said under her breath.

Pete needed to return the fake suicide note back to the center console before Charlie realized it was missing. Except Charlie was sitting right there, occasionally resting his arm on the console in question.

"Damn it! Get in the envelope!" He was much more successful at moving things by swatting or pushing. Fine motor skills such as holding paper between his finger and thumb and precisely sliding it into the envelope proved difficult.

In his rush, he jammed the letter inside, causing a crumpling sound.

"What the hell was that!?" yelled Charlie, his drug-induced paranoia getting the better of him.

"What?" replied Stacy. "Would you slow down? You're going to get us killed!"

"I heard something in the backseat rustling around. Check it out," he barked. She rolled her eyes and scoffed, but complied.

Pete slid the envelope under the seat. Now wasn't the time for Stacy to discover the letter. With Charlie in a drug-fueled rage screaming down the road, the mere sight of the letter might be enough for him to drive into a tree, and Pete was not prepared to experience another crash.

"There's nothing back there," said Stacy.

"You didn't even look!" said Charlie, his scratchy voice turning into a squeaky pitch, signaling his growing agitation.

"I did so," she said.

Charlie whipped his gun out and held it to her head. "I said look in the backseat! Now *look!*"

"Okay! Don't get your panties in a twist!" Stacy said, though she cowered at the sight of the gun.

"Look! I said LOOK! Damn it!" he snarled.

Pete was ready to pounce, but he didn't want to escalate the situation. Stacy searched the backseat, and Charlie settled down slightly.

"Just a bunch of junk back there. It was probably a family of mice going through your mess."

He put the gun down and let out a sinister laugh.

"He enjoys this. Dominating her like this—he's *enjoying* it," said Pete. It was getting dark, and he was beginning to worry about what would happen if they made it to the hotel.

Stacy's continued hesitation and body language made Pete think she was now being held against her will. They were several hours away from where Charlie had picked her up. It was dark, and Charlie decided to slow down. Pete guessed they would arrive at their hotel soon, and he couldn't help but think about Stacy's fate if they made it there.

Thankfully, Charlie's seemed addicted to robbing gas stations, and soon enough they made a pit stop.

"All right, babe. One more stop, then it's the honeymoon suite for you and I," he said as he exited the car.

Pete saw Stacy subtly clinch her seatbelt. He could tell she was frightened and saw Charlie as a bad person, but she seemed out of options.

"What did you get yourself into?" Pete said to her.

Pete looked inside and saw Charlie flipping through the magazine racks, waiting for a customer to pay and leave.

"Run! Get out of the car and run!"

It was no use. She couldn't hear him.

His frustration took over and his aura wildly flashed.

He floated out of the car to get a closer look. Flying insects fluttered and buzzed as the fluorescent lights above flickered and popped. He could see Charlie inside the gas station taking his sweet time, milling around waiting for the other customers to leave before he made his move.

The bell jingled when the door opened and a customer walked out. It was just Charlie and the attendant now. He watched Charlie rush over to the door and flip the deadbolt, then drew his pistol from the back of his waistband.

The cashier flailed his arms in the air in an apparent panic.

"I can't let this happen." Pete jumped through the cement block walls to get a closer look.

"Let's just calm down now," Charlie growled.

"You get out of my store right now and never come back! You make fun of my heritage and religion—you should leave!" The cashier was defiant.

"This is my country, and if you don't like it, get the hell out," Charlie rasped, and Pete had about enough. So this was Charlie's call sign. He would ridicule and toy with his victim before robbing them. Pete was disgusted, and his aura began to flash.

"You know what? I call the cops." The cashier walked over to the phone and picked it up.

"I wouldn't do that if I were you," Charlie said in a sing-song tone as he waved the revolver. "Give me your money and if you move an inch toward that emergency alarm, the front of your head is going to meet the back of your head."

The cashier reached into the register and pulled out several paper bills and held them up. Charlie snatched them out of his hand looking over his spoils.

"This looks a little light. Come on! All of it! The entire drawer!" barked Charlie.

The cashier slowly lifted the drawer, at a slower pace than Charlie liked.

"Are you stalling for the cops!?" he yelled. He was waving the gun erratically. He reached over the counter and pistol-whipped the innocent cashier, who cowered behind the desk while Charlie ransacked the counter for cartons of cigarettes and bottles of hard alcohol.

"If I don't do something, he's going to kill that man," said Pete as he watched Charlie tear apart the store.

He scoured the aisles for something he could use. He traveled to the supply aisle and stopped at the car products. There were several quarts of motor oil sitting on a shelf. Pete tried to pick up a quart of motor oil. His hand passed right through—he needed to concentrate.

Deborah flashed in his mind. *Use your powers for good.*

He thought of Ben Teskar, the truck driver who was falling asleep and veering off the road.

He thought of poor Stan who might've died from a hard fall had he not settled his walker.

He thought of Jessica. He missed her.

His attention snapped toward Charlie when he heard the undeniable sound of a hammer cocking back. "I said open the safe and give me the rest of the money!"

"I don't have the combination. Besides, there is no money in the safe. We empty the safe every night. You're an hour late. You have everything. Just take it and leave!" replied the cashier.

Pete was flashing wildly. He thought about how he shoved the crystal vase off Jessica's desk. Because of that, he could never go back to their home. If he could shove the vase, he could shove something else here, couldn't he?

He reacted. A full shelf of motor oil went flying—crashing onto the floor. The noise caught Charlie's attention.

He saw Charlie wheel around and point the gun toward the sound. Then he pointed it toward the store entrance, but looked back at the gas station cashier.

"I thought you said you were alone! Who the hell is in here?" he growled.

The cashier kept his arms held above his head. "Nobody. I told you, I work alone on this shift."

Pete pushed another shelf over three aisles down.

"Who's there?" yelled Charlie, waving his gun around the store.

Pete watched him move around to check the aisles. Anger dimmed his aura. By the looks of it, if he didn't do something, Charlie would probably kill the attendant . . . and what about the girl? The note. *Tell my daughter I miss her.* It was only a matter of time before he killed the girl.

"I locked the door. No one else was in here," Charlie growled.

He watched Charlie walk over, peer out of the window, and shiver a jittery twitch. He opened his mouth frequently, as if in some sort of nervous tic. "It's not that bitch I picked up earlier; she's still in the car."

Charlie walked aisle to aisle nervously flailing his gun. He came across the motor supplies Pete had knocked over. There were quarts of spilled motor oil, antifreeze, and cracked open jugs of window cleaner.

"Looks like somebody made a mess over here," said Charlie, picking up a tire gauge and putting it in his pocket before walking toward the cashier. "Did you let somebody in the back when I wasn't looking, you little bastard?"

The cashier kept his hands up.

"You *did,* didn't you! Get back from behind that counter. Get over here!"

Pete opened a cooler door and slammed it shut. He opened another cooler door and knocked all the soda cans out. Some of them rolled toward Charlie.

He could tell he was getting to Charlie. He saw his agitation grow with every noise he created.

"Stop that!" Charlie aimed and fired a round toward the cooler, shattering the glass door. Milk jugs burst and glass sprinkled onto the floor.

He saw the cashier drop to the ground and hide behind the counter.

He opened another cooler and slammed it shut. He opened another. Charlie fired two more rounds, one of which passed through Pete and lodged in a half-gallon of ice cream. He held the door open, more in surprise than with any intention.

"Ha! I must've got the bastard," said Charlie, but his celebration was cut short.

Pete slammed the door shut, then another. Charlie fired several more rounds, bursting glass. Exploding, fizzing beverages and frozen pizzas littered the floor.

Pete heard empty shell casings ringing as they fell to the floor. While Charlie reloaded, Pete mocked him by frantically opening and shutting more doors.

"Who's there? Who's doing that?"

Charlie fumbled his ammo, dropping shells on the ground. He closed his revolver and opened fire again. Glass shattered as the remaining coolers were struck by bullets.

There was a pause as single cooler door swung slowly open. Charlie walked nervously down the aisle to inspect the damage.

Pete slowly rolled a beer can toward Charlie. The aluminum made a gritty sound on the tile floor.

Charlie screamed and fired four rounds. The can exploded and sprayed beer all over the aisle, as well as his face and clothes. "Damn it!"

Pete whipped another beer can against the wall so it exploded beside Charlie's head. Charlie emptied his pistol in a soaked rage.

"When I catch you, I'm gonna treat you *real* nice. Charlie Schmidt ain't no sucker!" he growled reloading again.

Pete watched him start running down aisles in a frantic attempt to find his rival. He tapped Charlie on the shoulder. He wheeled around, flailing his gun about nervously. He tapped Charlie on the other shoulder, and again Charlie flung himself around vigorously only to find no one to attack. Thinking fast, Pete grabbed a bag of chips off the shelf, watching Charlie's expression turn from rage to bewilderment as he saw what looked like a bag of potato chips floating in mid-air. He moved the bag suddenly as Charlie reached for it. He toyed with Charlie—moving the bag side to side again and again, all the while Charlie flailing in his attempts to grab the floating bag.

"What in the hell is going on?" yelled Charlie.

Pete watched him raise his gun and shoot the bag. Potato chips flew out the back.

Charlie chuckled in triumph.

"That will teach them to mess with me!" he said.

Pete raised the bag above Charlie and dumped them over his head. The chips stuck to Charlie's beer-soaked hair and shirt. Charlie screamed, shooting a couple rounds at the bag. Pete crumpled the empty chip bag in Charlie's face, causing him to flinch so wildly that he fell to the floor, convulsing.

Now more scared than enraged, Charlie grabbed the crumpled bag and flung it away from him. He shot another round off blindly, causing a ceiling tile to fall down on him. He army-crawled down the line of coolers, shoving cans and frozen food out of his way, cursing all manner of empty threats to his invisible tormentor. When he finally stood up and tried to compose himself, Pete saw glass stuck in his clothing and hands and florets of blood forming on his elbows and knees.

Pete flipped the lights out. The gas station was completely dark aside from the soft hue of the cooler lights.

"Turn the lights back on! Who did you let in here, you little bastard?" he yelled to the cashier.

There was no reply.

Pete flipped the lights on.

"What the hell is going on?" yelled Charlie.

Pete flipped the lights off. On. Off. On. Off. It was like a strobe light.

"Stop that! STOP!" Charlie was clearly panicking.

Blinded by his rage, Pete turned the lights off. His hatred for Charlie crept over him, ruling his mind. It wasn't fair that a jerk like Charlie was alive and well, running around and robbing gas stations, being a complete *degenerate*—while he, a good, upstanding contributor to society, had been killed in a stupid car wreck.

He threw objects. A can of soup. A box of sodas. He crinkled a bag of chips. All mere distractions in an attempt to scare Charlie out of the building. Save the gas station attendant from his wrath. He'd figure a way to deal with Charlie before he hurt Stacy.

"Who's there? Where are you?" Charlie was yelling in fright as the noises drew nearer.

Then, it got quiet. Pete traveled silently closer to Charlie.

The darkness and the silence put Charlie on edge. A shot rang out as he fired blindly.

Pete slammed a cooler door.

"Let me outta here!" Charlie charged toward the exit like a stampeding rhino.

Pete watched Charlie make for the door. He flipped the light back on, which startled Charlie. He watched him try to change direction, but he had wandered into a concoction of spilled motor oil, milk, and soda—and his feet went right out from under him. He landed with a horrific thud and a crack.

Pete traveled toward Charlie, who lay motionless on the ground. He heard a gurgling sound as the air left Charlie's lungs.

Charlie Schmidt—the self-appointed gas station baron—was dead.

CHARLIE'S SPIRIT

PETE TRAVELED OUTSIDE THE GAS station, watching the commotion. Police officers stormed the building, finding the nervous cashier and dead man.

One of the officers came outside to give a debriefing.

"Chief, looks like we got an attempted robbery turned accidental death. Need the EMTs to carry out the body."

"Anyone still in there?" asked the Chief.

"Sir, we have a gas station attendant who is shaken up, and claims he and the deceased were the only ones inside. Says he hid behind the counter and hit the panic button while the perp went on a rampage. It's a real scene in there. The entire place is trashed."

"He couldn'ta done it?"

"Not without getting oil and soda and whatever else all over his shoes, at least, but he seems to have stayed hidden 'til we showed up."

The Chief took a sip of coffee from a Styrofoam cup before sucking the remnants from his mustache with his lower lip making a slurping sound. "How about the girl? She involved?"

The Sergeant produced a crumpled envelope and handed it to his superior. The Chief took the paper out and unfolded it.

"Wish I could've done it that easy," said Pete.

"Suicide note," the Chief grumbled as he continued reading it. "No way this is hers."

"My thoughts exactly, sir. She was likely not involved. She says he picked her up in Camden. Drove her all the way out here. Held her against her will."

"New Jersey?" grumbled the Chief.

"Just outside Philly. Over the bridge."

"Hm. Something isn't adding up," scoffed the Chief. He looked down at the envelope again, flipping it over. Examining it closely. "Said you found this under her seat?"

"That's right, sir."

A passing officer walked briskly by, attempting to look busy among the sea of law enforcement that had descended on the scene. "Hey, get this to forensics. See if the girl's prints are on it."

"Yes, sir." said the officer, eager to have an assignment.

The Chief turned back to the Sergeant. He seemed to read his mind. "Just a precaution. If she's clean, we'll discharge her."

"Yes, sir." The Sergeant produced a notepad and scribbled something on it.

"ID the perp?"

"Sir, identification was found on the body. Charlie Schmidt—fits the description of the guy who's been robbing all these gas stations and leaving dead prostitutes all over eastern PA. Forensics is on the scene collecting evidence to confirm."

"Surveillance?" the Chief grumbled. "If this is our guy, it's going to escalate to a federal case. We need all our I's crossed and T's dotted on this one."

"We have three different cameras. Tech is onsite viewing copies in their van as we speak."

"Very good. Sounds like you got it covered, Sergeant," the Chief said before getting back to paperwork he had been tending to.

"Sir, there's something you should see."

Pete traveled with them as the Chief and his Sergeant walked briskly to a white van where technicians were watching surveillance footage. A technician poked his head out of the van and spoke with an urgency that left him out of breath. His thin framed bifocals gyrating up and down as he was spewing small beads of spit—yelling about never seeing *anything* like this before.

"Let's see the tape," the Chief commanded.

They watched the scene unfold. Cooler doors seemingly opening and closing on their own. Charlie shooting wildly at targets he couldn't see.

"Something is shoving these cooler doors. Look! They open back up and slam shut on their own! The racks are being flung, but no one nearby!" said the tech.

"Anyone else inside while this was going on?" asked the Chief.

"The only person I've seen on tape so far is the perp and the gas station attendant."

"The girl?" asked the Chief. "Could she be involved somehow?"

The tech flipped on a screen showing a camera footage from outside. "She's sitting in the car the entire time this is going on. You can see her become frightened during the gunshots. We responded to her call. I don't think she was in on it."

"She called in that her date was going crazy and had a gun," the Chief corrected.

The tech clicked back onto the footage from inside. "How are those lights flashing on and off like that?" asked the Sergeant.

"Look at this! A floating bag of potato chips emptied out on the perp's head!" yelled the tech, pausing the tape as they tried to make some sense of what was going on. "Chief, what do you think?"

"Something strange went on here that's for sure," he replied.

"Are you thinking what I'm thinking?" asked the Sergeant.

"I've been in this line for thirty-two years, and I know when something's going on. Someone was behind this. We've got to examine all possibilities," the Chief commanded, pausing for a moment. The eyes from his entire crew were locked on him. "Something happened here that is not explainable. Let's wrap up the crime scene, get a statement from the attendant, and bring the girl down to the station so someone can pick her up. I want those tapes. *No one* says a *word* about this when the FBI shows up to the station."

"Yes, sir," replied the group in unison.

The Chief walked away while the rest of the officers resumed watching the tape in bewilderment.

It was hard for Pete to watch footage of Charlie's death, so he traveled within an earshot of Stacy. One of the officers was standing by supervising, but let her make a phone call.

"Yeah, Mom, it's me. I'm coming home. For real this time. I'm sorry, Mom," she said.

It was an intimate moment, so Pete decided to let her have her privacy. He turned one last time to observe the scene and saw the blue and red police lights of the police cruisers bouncing off the building.

"Who are you?" a raspy voice sounded. The voice familiar, scratchy, irritating—but Pete couldn't quite place it. He contorted around to locate the source and was met with a sight that threw his aura into throbbing shambles.

Standing at the base of the parking lot entrance was *Charlie*.

But *how?* He was no longer covered in potato chips and motor oil, and his head wound had remarkably healed.

"I saw my body in there." Charlie was looking at him through a cold, evil stare. "Am I dead?"

It was the first time Pete had seen a newly hatched spirit. Watching him try and figure out how to navigate his death made Pete remember the panic he felt right after his own car crash.

"You gotta help me. Tell me what's going on!" said Charlie.

"You're a spirit, Charlie. You passed away tonight."

Pete almost overlooked Charlie's aura because the black outline blended into the cold darkness of the night. Charlie was already sick. He remembered what Deborah told him when a spirit becomes sick. *"Use your powers for good."*

"Charlie, you need to listen to me. You need to heal yourself."

Charlie's head tilted to the side as he seemed to examine Pete for a moment. "Are *you* dead?"

"I died a few years ago, but we can talk about that later. Right now, we need to figure out how to heal you."

"It's funny you just happen to milling around this crime scene. And when I think about all those strange things that happened in that gas station before I died."

He knows! His aura began flashing—a dead giveaway.

Charlie cleared his throat, more so out of nervous habit than to clear a blockage. *"You* did this to me, didn't you?"

"Charlie, listen to me very carefully. If you don't heal yourself—"

"You did this to me! I had to see my dead body in there!"

KAABOOOOM!

They were interrupted by a sudden shockwave so deafening it sounded like a freight train hitting a semi-truck.

LEVEL ONE

PETE REALIZED THAT WHILE THEY had been arguing, a black spherical tunnel had been forming in the middle of the parking lot. Then it cracked open with a violent concussion, bolts of energy flashing erratically inside, prompting his own aura to flash in a terrified state.

The tunnel seemed to disappear behind dark clouds of mist or spray that emerged. Before they could react, they were sucked into the black vortex and falling at a blazing speed. This was one time Pete was glad he couldn't feel anything, as the wind shear blew threw him—where it surely would've slammed him into one tunnel wall after another had he been living. He lost visual on Charlie, but he could hear his raspy screams echo.

They didn't feel anything when they landed, but somehow stopped abruptly, as if something was keeping their weightless beings from traveling any further. He noticed Charlie trying desperately but failing to find an escape within the tiny room's pitch-black walls. Some sort of barrier was keeping him here. Oddly, they could see the gas station parking lot where they had traveled from.

"How is this possible?" Pete said.

"How is what possible?" Charlie growled as he continued to search for a way out.

Pete joined Charlie at the wall, peering out into the gas station parking lot and observing law enforcement swarming the scene like a nest of angry bees.

"You're a car guy. How fast do you think we were going in that tunnel?" asked Pete.

"I'd say over four hundred miles an hour."

"That fast? Judging how long we were in that tunnel, traveling at that rate of speed—I'd say we should be much further away from this parking lot."

"What are you, some sort of mathematician? You're *dead*. What does it matter?" replied Charlie.

The sound of a heavy metal door slamming nearly caused them to burst out of the room.

"You hear that?" asked Pete, so frightened that he reflexively appealed to Charlie as an ally.

"Yeah," said Charlie. "Whatever is coming through that door can't be good."

It was a tormenting few moments waiting for what may come down that hall. Some sort of strange beast? A man with an axe? He prepared himself for the worst.

Two men exited the portal. They were dressed in black tailored suits, which were hemmed perfectly to fit their sculpted bodies. They had matching jet-black colored shirts under their suit coat—each rebelliously unbuttoned enough to show their chiseled chests and upper abs. Their shiny black boots shined to perfection. Each had a matching necklace, the band made of a fine leather material. A strange symbol resembling a unique looking star hung just below their neckline. They were exotic looking, *otherworldly* even, with high cheekbones and good bone structure radiating a god-like confidence.

If it weren't for their different hair styles, Pete would've had a hard time telling them apart. They had perfectly groomed beards, which came to a point at their chins. Their hair was cut short, but long enough to style in a fashionable manner. One wore a modern-looking spiked hair style, while the other had a sheeny, slicked-back look.

They portrayed strange mechanical, almost *jerky* movements—yet smoothly, as if they were interconnected somehow. Pete noticed some type of insignia tattooed on each of their foreheads, but he couldn't quite make out the shape. They also had mirroring tattoos below opposite eyes and on the opposite sides of their necks.

To Pete's utmost relief, it seemed these strangers were fixated on Charlie. He couldn't flee. He was stuck in a stationary terror. Their dark, unblinking eyes focused on him as if they were starved wolves ready to slay a baby fawn. Charlie didn't seem to notice—seemed *oblivious,* even—to the danger Pete sensed they were in.

The one with slicked-back hair spoke first. "I'm Malum. This is my brother, Malitae. We are your greeters this evening."

"We have been waiting for you," said Malitae. His awkward gaze made Pete uneasy. He noticed each of the men had a dark outline around them like Charlie.

"We have been watching you, Charlie," said Malum. He flashed a warm smile, showing perfectly white teeth. It was a quick smile, but Pete caught the impression of fangs. He wasn't completely sure. "You have made us very happy."

"Well, I don't know what I did to make you two twin towers happy, but if you're happy, that sure puts me in a good spot," Charlie boasted. "Although, I can't say that sounds good for our friend Pete here."

It was clear Charlie did not have the same impulse to ally himself with a fellow human. Pete felt both contempt and a fearful isolation but tried not to let either show.

The twins looked at each other, raising their perfectly manicured eyebrows. They looked as if they were ready to burst at the seams with laughter, but they held it in. Pete watched them refocus intently upon Charlie. Heads tilted slightly to the side, unblinking dark eyes examining Charlie's slightest movements.

"Welcome to Level One, Charlie. You are the guest of honor tonight," they replied—so perfectly in unison, it almost sounded like a single voice.

"Level One? What is this, some sort of video game?" Charlie chuckled at his own joke.

You idiot! Can't you see they are toying with you?

The twins snapped a ferocious look toward Pete. His aura blinked—telling his frightened tale for him. They slowly contorted their heads back to Charlie's direction.

"Charlie, here at Level One, we introduce you to all the accommodations you will come to know during your stay with us," said Malum.

"Hey, I like accommodations. Sounds fancy," he replied.

Pete kept quiet. While he had a bad feeling Charlie was playing right into their hands, he knew he was powerless. With Charlie lacking the simple awareness to properly assess the situation there was nothing he could do.

Suddenly, the dark, empty room transformed into a grand hall. A long ornately decorated table stretched the length of the room. On top of the table was every comfort food one could imagine. Carving stations with different types of succulent, glistening meats. There was a cornucopia of dishes from all over the world, each looking as if it had been made by the finest chefs in the region.

It almost made Pete *hungry* again. As a spirit, he hadn't felt hunger since his last meal with Jessica in New York City the night before he passed. He thought about that dinner for a moment, but quickly refocused.

"I've never seen this much food! You can barely see the end of that table, there's so much food!" said Charlie.

"Just over three hundred dishes," said Malum.

"Three hundred and *thirty-three* different dishes, to be exact," replied Malitae.

"Huh, that's an odd number," said Charlie.

Pete watched the twins look at each other, smiling only to finish with a sneer.

"Mathematically, you are correct. It's definitely an odd number, Charlie," said Malum.

"Math was my favorite subject in grade school," Charlie chuckled, trying too hard to play along. "Guys, let's talk about these—what did you call them—*accommodations?*"

"What do you want to know?" asked Malitae, apparently trying hard not to appear too eager as Charlie investigated the table.

"Well, this here food isn't gonna eat itself is it? I mean there is enough food here to feast for days," he said.

Pete couldn't help but feel like he was watching an inattentive fly buzzing above a spider's web just before it made its last and fatal mistake.

"Charlie, are you hungry?" asked Malum.

"Come to think of it, no. I'm not," said Charlie.

"Then why do you want to eat if you are not hungry?" said Malitae.

"Look at that food! Who wouldn't want to eat it? I have never seen food like that in my life!" replied Charlie.

Malum presented an offering to Charlie. A silver tray filled with a number of deserts: a delicious looking Key lime pie, a spiraled strawberry cheesecake, a hot fudge sundae sprinkled with plump looking peanuts. In the center of the tray sat a small piece of hard candy in a shiny gold wrapper. You'd almost have to reach through the other deserts to even grasp it—all of which seemed to Pete much more tempting than the boring piece of candy.

"Charlie, in your current state, you cannot enjoy this food. Neither can your friend, Pete," he said.

Don't bring me into this, Pete thought. Both the twins again snapped their attention to Pete. *Fangs! I knew I saw fangs!*

The twins robotically turned their attention back to Charlie before resuming.

"Charlie, in your current state, you cannot enjoy this food. You cannot eat, smell, or taste. You cannot physically feel anything." Malum held the silver tray out further tempting Charlie. It was working.

"We have the ability to unlock your senses. You will be able to taste this food again, hold it in your hand, and feel the texture of the food as it hits your mouth," charmed Malitae.

"Guys, I gotta tell you, this food looks too good to pass up," said Charlie. "I don't want to ruin my appetite with a dessert."

Even Pete, alert as he was, could feel the attraction. It was like a nervous energy pulling him in.

"I can see you are skeptical," said Malum.

"Most who meet us for the first time are," said Malitae. "But it's simple, Charlie. All you have to do is choose a dessert—and the food is yours."

"That's all I gotta do?" asked Charlie, skeptical.

"That's it," said Malum watching Charlie with the anticipation of a crouching lion ready to spring.

Pete saw Charlie contemplating the offer.

"There's no catch? It seems too easy. All I have to do is eat a dessert."

"Just choose a dessert. Take a bite. You don't even have to eat the whole thing if you're worried about ruining your appetite," charmed Malum.

"And I can assure you the rest of the dishes are quite exquisite," said Malitae.

"Okay, give me the small piece of candy," Charlie demanded.

Eyes gleaming, Malum lifted the candy to Charlie, who reached out and was able to grasp it. He paused to unwrap the gold foil and rudely tossed the wrapper on the ground before holding it to his mouth. He suspiciously tasted it with his tongue, as if to test it. "My mom always told me not to eat sweets before dinner. But she ain't here now, is she boys?"

The twins glanced at each other and snickered with delight as he held it to his mouth, pausing before biting down with a loud crunch. "Best damn piece of candy I ever tasted!" proclaimed Charlie. "Hey, I can feel things again. That food smells terrific!"

Pete watched as Charlie walked over to the table to claim his prize. Oddly, he gave a sudden wrench as if he were in severe pain. He folded over and cradled his stomach.

"What's happening to me?" Charlie cried.

"Charlie, how are you doing?" asked Malum.

"I am hungry. I have never been this hungry before. I can barely move, it hurts so badly," said Charlie in a panicked voice.

"We said you would feel hungry again, Charlie," they jeered together. "Well, there's a whole table full of food here."

"Yeah, good idea. I don't know if I can make it to that table. I am so hungry!" he said.

Charlie lurched over to the table in agony, clutching his abdomen with both arms. Breathless, unable to even reach for sustenance. Charlie located a plump, juicy turkey—beautifully bronzed and shiny, as if prepared with a delicious glaze that caramelized the skin. He screamed in agony as he laboriously reached—juices splattering—as he ripped a drumstick from the turkey.

"This ought'a help," he said, desperate to ease the hunger pangs. His eyes wild with primitive hunger, his mouth gaping, preparing for a large bite from the turkey leg. Keeping the turkey leg in one hand, he now grabbed a piece of ham from the table and shoved it in his mouth. He was eating so voraciously, that Pete wondered how he didn't choke.

In between bites, Charlie withered with more and greater hunger pangs. He had eaten almost an entire turkey leg and several hunks of ham, and seemed no less hungry than when he first started eating. He only ate faster and more greedily attempting to sequester his ravenous hunger.

Pete looked away from Charlie, making a mess of himself and the banquet, and turned his attention toward the twins.

What are these guys up to? he thought as he carefully observed them.

He heard a hollow dull sound as he watched Charlie bite into a piece of juicy prime rib. Charlie's teeth clinked together, as if he had completely missed a bite. He looked at the hunk of flesh and was completely perplexed.

"Hey! What is this?" he said, still holding the prime rib.

"You wanted to feel the sense of touch again, you wanted to feel hunger again. We granted you your wishes," said Malum.

"You have all the physical senses of when you were human, but you are dead," said Malitae.

"Why can't I eat this thing then? I am starving!"

All of a sudden, the prime rib slowly start to dissolve into dust.

"Please, I'm so hungry!" Charlie pleaded.

He watched Charlie desperately run back to the table and grab another turkey leg. It dissipated to dust in his hand. He grabbed a knife and vigorously begin slicing another hunk of prime rib. The entire carving station withered to dust. He grabbed a fork and dipped into a large bowl of pasta, which pulverized into a dust pile.

"What is happening to me? I am so *hungry!*" cried Charlie, wrenching his abdomen with both arms across his midsection.

"Charlie, you said you wanted to be hungry again, and we have given you hunger, which you will have for eternity. You also have other senses, which we will help you rediscover," said one of the twins.

Pete watched as Charlie stood crying, forgetting about his hunger for a slight moment—leaning on the table, defeated. The entire table turned to dust and landed at his feet. Balls of dust clumped together as Charlie's tears fell into the pile.

"I don't understand what is happening," said Charlie.

The twins approached Charlie and whispered something in his ear. Charlie looked up and nodded to them, as if he understood what they were saying. He left the room with Malitae. Pete heard the sound of a metal door being opened and closing with a bang.

He heard Charlie's shrill cries soon as the metal door slammed. "Wait! I don't want to go! Please! Help me! I don't want to go! Pete, please! Help!"

"They always do that," said Malitae with a charming smile as he entered the room. They uttered something to each other in a language Pete did not understand. An ancient language composed of short, throaty clucks. After the exchange, they turned their attention to him. His aura was dim, but flashing wildly with different colors. The twins stood in front of him, Malum digging into his jacket pocket and producing another piece of gold foil wrapped candy.

"Where did you take him?" asked Pete.

"He speaks! We were beginning to wonder," said Malitae, cracking a sinister smile.

"We took your friend Charlie to Level Two," replied Malum. "Plenty more fun to keep him busy."

"Let's talk about *you*, Pete," Malum continued. "The spirit who can move objects! You know, we could use someone with your talents around here."

"Or better yet, let's talk about your wife—Jessica, is it?" Malitae added.

A vision of Jessica suddenly appeared. She was working at the laboratory in one of the clean rooms. She was alone. She looked up and started to cry. The vision was so real Pete ran toward her.

"Jessica!" he cried out. He struggled to get through the barrier, but it was no use. "Can she hear me?" he asked the twins. He hastily turned back toward the vision. "Jessica! *Jessica!*"

"You can have her back, you know," said Malum. "You could comfort her. Right now."

"Tell me how. I'll do anything," he said.

"We can change everything—erase your memory. You wouldn't even know you were dead before. You could be reunited *tonight*," responded Malum.

"Together again in a . . . warm bed?" said Malitae.

Pete hesitated, but said, "What do I have to do?"

He watched the twins sneer with delight.

"All you have to do is eat the candy," said Malum.

That's where they made their mistake. If it had been some other thing than the candy, perhaps he would have faltered. "You don't plan on sending me back there—letting me be human again."

"But whatever do you mean?" said Malum.

"Reunited. That's what you said. Jessica and I could be reunited again."

"Yes, Pete. Isn't that what you want?"

"You have no intention of sending me back. If I eat this candy, you're going to have her killed and collect her spirit so we can be *reunited* here. In this place!"

"Malum, it looks like Pete is on to us," Malitae snickered.

"You know, I love a good game. Bravo, Pete. *Bravo*," said Malum with a snarky confidence that told Pete there was something more yet to come.

"But what about your child, Pete? A baby boy. You always wanted a son. We can make that happen for you," Malum charmed.

"Get that candy out of my face. No matter what you do to me, I am not eating that."

"Whoa! We have a feisty one on our hands. We are not here to harm you, Pete. We are simply offering you an option. You have Freewill and can make your own choices. We are offering you a choice to be with your wife again—the chance to have your *family* back," said Malitae.

"And I already told you, I'm not eating that."

"We knew you wouldn't, Pete," said Malum.

"But we thought we would try anyway. After all, it is a rarity we get to play with a spirit like you," said Malitae.

"A spirit like me?"

"Yes, Pete, we aren't able to bring spirits like you here. We were able to capture you because you aided in the death of one of the living," said Malum.

"You've been a very bad boy. You killed your friend, Charlie. That's a big *no-no* in our world," said Malitae.

"But for some reason, your aura didn't turn dark. Must be because your actions saved the lives of those other two," added Malum.

"So we are not allowed to keep you—unless, of course, you choose to stay with Jessica and align yourself with us under your own Freewill," explained Malitae.

"You mean unless you tempt me into staying with your cheap tricks?" replied Pete angrily.

"We simply offered you an option, and you declined," replied Malum.

"But we cannot keep you, or the mighty Keryx would be mad," toyed Malitae.

"Keryx—the mighty one! Ha! We are shaking in our boots!" Malum jeered.

"Who is Keryx?" asked Pete.

The twins snapped to attention.

"Don't say that name here! You'll find out soon enough, you miserable scum!" Malitae snarled.

"You are free to go," said Malum. "Just remember—you're still being judged. You will be held accountable for your actions made when you were living *and dead*, until you enter the afterlife."

"And if you keep killing the living, we'll most likely see you very soon!" Malitae barked.

Suddenly both twins started shaking, and Pete watched their black eyes roll up as their bodies pulsated. Their bodies seemed to painfully rip as they grew in size and changed shape.

He froze as one twin stood over him—in the shape of a bull—a large creature with long, dark, coarse, scraggly hair covering its body. It stood on hind legs and Pete barely came up to the creature's midsection. It had broad, battle-tested shoulders made evident by the scars that ran the course of its rough hide.

Malum's black eyes were gone—turned glowing red. Long pointed horns protruded from the creature's thick skull. It hovered over Pete, drool and mucus spraying as it snorted and pawed the ground with its enormous hoof.

The second twin shifted into a reptilian creature. It was covered with an armor of scaly skin—thin, bony fingers armed with elongated sharp claws, and a mouth full of rows and rows of razor sharp, hooked teeth. Beady red eyes stared upon Pete, flicking its tongue as if it were tasting the air to gather his scent.

The reptile stood on hind legs and snapped a menacing tail. It maneuvered next to the hooved bull, trapping Pete against the wall. Bits of saliva dripped from its mouth with every breath. The bull let out a powerful roar. A sharp hollow sound came from the reptilian creature as it snapped its jaws and let out a snarling hiss. Instinctively, Pete put his arms up, trying to guard against whatever terrible thing the creatures were going to do to him.

The creatures let out a sinister laugh, and in a flash, Pete was standing in the gas station parking lot. His arms were still up in a protective position before he realized the creatures were gone.

The red and blue lights from the police cars still flashed. He saw the Chief loading Stacy into the back of his squad car. It was like no time had passed at all from the time he had been picked up by the twin spirits. The only difference was Charlie's spirit was now gone. Pete caught a glimpse of a white portal and an armored Gatekeeper, who only shook his head sadly and walked away.

"Wait! Please wait!" The Gatekeeper looked at Pete with pity as the portal collapsed, and within a moment, the portal and the Gatekeeper were gone. "You're just going to go and leave me like that? After they took me to their lair? You're just going to leave me!? Abandon me once again? Leave me back here in this place all alone? Maybe the twins were right! Maybe they *can* help me!"

An immediate jolt of terror flushed over him as he thought of Charlie's frightful screams. He didn't dare say another word.

PART TWO
JOE MORTON
THE GUARDIANS

BABY JOSH HELD HIS ARMS out, signaling he wanted to be picked up. Joe tried to place his hand on top of Josh's little chest, but it went through his body—sticking out the other end of the cot. His aura began flashing softly as a slight frustration grew.

All he wanted to do was *comfort* the boy.

"Easy, Morton. Remember, you've been given a gift here," he said to himself, taking consolation in the fact that his grandson could, indeed, *see him*—which meant one day they'd be able to communicate.

All the other spirits he'd met would give anything to have a similar opportunity.

"I know you can hear me. I'm going to make sure nothing bad happens to you. You got that?" he whispered softly.

Josh whimpered and continued reaching to be picked up. His cries attracted the attention of a teacher who came over and obliged.

"I love you, Josh," said Joe. "I promise I'm going to keep you safe. Nothing bad is going to happen. I have to go."

Joe left and headed straight home for the dark, secluded attic, lit dimly only by his aura. He stirred tonight. Pacing. Back and forth. Back and forth. Endless, frustrating pacing. Until it finally came to him. The plan, such as it was, was to create a consistent pattern of behavior that would keep Cunningham and Pinkie away from Bill and Sarah's house. He met them every morning at Perfect Cup, and went with them for the day—always ending their rambles in the evening and traveling back to Bill and Sarah's. This was normal behavior by spirit standards, so they never suspected anything. He decided he would keep his interactions with Josh minimal. As much as it pained him, Joe wouldn't want to establish too close a relationship with the boy, lest the child accidentally blow his cover.

This worked until one evening, when Josh was about three years old. Joe was observing from the attic window while Josh played in the front yard with Bill.

A sudden movement caught his eye. Two spirits were traveling down the street! He had been watching Josh with such intent that he barely saw them until they were virtually on top of Josh and Bill.

"Hi!"

"No, Josh. No! Don't speak to them!" Joe was frozen. It was too late. The damage was done. Josh had engaged with a spirit.

Joe's aura flashed rapidly as the spirits stopped and inspected Josh, who was still waving. They wore expressions of cautious disbelief, pausing to speak to each other before pointing to the little boy. Then the spirits began to approach. They entered Bill's lawn to get a closer look.

Joe surged from the attic to the front lawn, which only seemed to further pique their interest.

"Hi, Josh! Hiya, buddy!" a loud voice came from across the street. It was Mr. Smith taking the trash out.

"My word, Mr. Smith thinks Josh is waving at *him*," Joe muttered under his breath.

The spirits snapped a look across the street. They looked back at Josh, shrugged, then moved on. "He wasn't waving at us you, buffoon! He was waving at his neighbor."

Joe listened to the bickering spirits as they traveled on—one glancing back at the boy with suspicious eyes.

His cover was saved for now, but the damage was done.

"I hear there might be a Bridge around," said Cunningham one morning when they met at Perfect Cup. One of the spirits must have started talking about the strange boy they thought could see them. Legend of this boy was spreading like wildfire amongst the spirit community. It's all any passing spirit talked about. Now Pinkie and Cunningham were starting to buy in—much to Joe's chagrin.

"Yeah, word is that some little boy was playing out front of his house and waved at a spirit. Supposedly happened up here on the northside somewhere," said Pinkie.

"I'm not buying it. You know how those rumors go. Seems like every week there's a new story about someone finding a Bridge," said Cunningham.

They continued their usual banter and the group went on their way. Joe didn't like hiding his secret from Pinkie and Cunningham. They were his only friends in the spirit world, and he cursed the day they would eventually find out he had been hiding Josh from them all this time. Could they trust him any longer if they found out? The idea of losing them made him quiver, but it was a price he was willing to pay to protect his grandson.

For a fraught two weeks, there seemed to be a lot of spirit traffic on Josh's street, but Joe managed to avoid another incident in part by sticking close to whichever adult was with the boy. There was nothing unusual about him being near his grandson, and there was nothing unusual about a toddler interacting with an adult. If a spirit got close, Joe would run interference: "Hey, the Wilson's down the street left their TV on!" He'd then happily watch the spirits excitedly scurry away, and to Joe's relief, it wasn't long before the rumor calmed.

Joe knew now more than ever he had to protect his grandson. It was his *reason*. But he didn't realize how difficult it would be to keep a fledgling Bridge from speaking to spirits. For the next five years, he would work tirelessly to guard Josh's secret—near misses almost a daily occurrence.

Each new milestone in Josh's life meant more risk of discovery. He knew he couldn't keep Josh hidden forever, especially with Josh becoming more independent by the minute. Bill and Sarah enrolled Josh in baseball—Bill hoping Josh would follow in his footsteps and become a professional player.

"That kid's got an arm, I tell ya. With a little coaching, he could go all the way," Bill could often be overheard saying. Joe always thought that was an awful high expectation to set on a child, and he wished he could sit Bill down and provide him some fatherly advice.

Josh played outfield partially because he had one of the strongest arms on the team, and none of the other kids could field a ball. Bill was proud his son was playing left field, but envisioned him as a pitcher one day.

"I need to get him his own personal pitching coach. Tie his right arm behind his back. Make him learn to throw with his left. Pitching is where all the money's at in the bigs."

"Do you ever stop?" Sarah would scoff.

It was on one of those games where Josh was playing left field when it happened. A ball was hit out his way and he made a great throw. He turned around to walk back to his position when he saw her. A little girl walked through the fence and sat down in the outfield.

"Hi," said Josh.

"Hi," the little girl replied.

"I'm Josh."

"I'm Cynthia."

Josh could hear his coach calling to him to get his head in the game. A ball was cracked out to left field. Josh picked a dandelion and walked over to Cynthia and gave it to her. The dandelion fell through her, landing on the ground.

"Thanks anyway," she giggled.

"I have to go," said Josh. He ran to get the ball—but Jared Carpenter, the center fielder, had already come over and picked it up.

"What are you doing?" barked Jared after he threw the ball into the infield. "You gotta get the ball!"

Disappointed parents groaned as the go-ahead run crossed the plate. The coach tried not to act upset. His teammates shook their heads.

"What's that kid doing out there, Morton? *Picking flowers?*" said little Jared Carpenter's parents.

Bill was mortified, but Sarah turned and snapped, "Oh, come on! Like your kid is any better!"

The girl got up and traveled by Josh. "I'm sorry. I ruined your game."

"It's okay," Josh said. "I live up the street if you ever want to hang out."

"Where do you live?" asked Cindy.

"On Sunnyside," Josh replied.

"Okay," Cynthia traveled off the field. Josh looked toward the field and glanced back. She was gone.

Joe got home just in time to hear quite an argument downstairs. Bill was hot.

"You're out in the field picking flowers and talking to invisible friends!? Sometimes I wonder if you even want to play baseball!" Bill scolded.

Joe's aura flashed wildly. *Invisible friends?* He saw Josh catch a glimpse of him, despite his best attempt to hide. He decided to retreat to the safe haven of the attic.

In the meantime, he needed to get in front of this to see if the news had hit the streets. He went out to meet Cunningham and Pinkie. He knew exactly where they'd be—posted up, watching TV at the Wilson's a few blocks away.

The family believed leaving their TV on would make it appear like they were home to would-be intruders. It provided Cunningham and Pinkie endless hours of entertainment as a result. When Joe walked in, they were watching an infomercial about a new vacuum cleaner.

"You're up late!" they joked.

"Couldn't sleep."

They all chuckled at the irony.

Joe stayed with them through the night and most of the next day before retreating back to the attic—news of Josh's interaction with the spirit girl hadn't dropped yet.

It was a couple days before the rumors started swirling.

Pinkie and Cunningham didn't want to let this one rest like they had before.

"They say it happened during a baseball game. Some boy was talking to a little spirit girl," said Pinkie.

"Why don't we go to the park and watch the baseball games. If the kid shows up to play, he'll see us. We'll be able to identify him," Cunningham plotted.

"Sounds like a good idea," Pinkie affirmed.

Joe was hoping Pinkie might talk him out of it.

"Why don't we go see a real game—like another Cubs game?" Joe suggested.

"Finding a Bridge can change a lot of things for us. If only it was easy. Like, what if your grandson were a Bridge? Wouldn't that be great?" Cunningham dreamed.

"You leave my grandson out of this!" Joe snapped.

"Woah! Somebody struck a nerve," Pinkie clucked.

Joe knew he showed a card and tried his best to pivot. "Sorry, this has been a little stressful since I learned of Malum and Malitae. The thought of them somehow finding Josh scares me. I mean, uh—it would scare me if Josh were a Bridge—but he's not, thankfully. I tested him myself."

Joe watched as Cunningham's eyes narrowed—a sure sign he was assessing Joe's story.

"Hey, don't mention it, Joe. I get it. Family is a sensitive subject. I won't mention it again," he grumbled.

He could tell Cunningham wasn't buying it.

Joe knew at this point Josh was in real danger of being discovered. At the very least, the excitement of a Bridge discovery would result in spirits from all over converging on Josh, and any possibility of him having a normal life would be ruined. Worst case, The Others could discover him, and who knew what they were capable of doing to an impressionable young boy.

"Meet me in the Morton's attic tonight," Joe directed.

Cunningham and Pinkie seemed puzzled.

"I have something to show you," he continued.

It was a gamble, but it was a matter of time before a spirit discovered Josh, and Cunningham and Pinkie were the only ones he trusted.

"What do you mean you found a Bridge!?" yelled Pinkie shortly after they had assembled in the Mortons' attic, as Joe requested.

"Keep it down. He can hear us," Joe whispered.

"Wait, you mean the Bridge is *here? In your house?*" Cunningham bellowed.

"*And you kept him a secret for how long?*" yelled Pinkie.

Neither of them lowered their voices. They both started pacing around. To Joe's surprise, they started flashing. Joe hadn't seen this reaction from both of them at once.

"Guys?" Joe checked in.

"Pink—do you know what this means?" Cunningham quizzed.

"Sure do," Pinkie replied.

"*Guys,*" Joe echoed.

"I want to see the boy," demanded Pinkie.

"No, he's sleeping," Joe rebuffed.

"Why not? Just a little peek," Cunningham pleaded.

"This is exactly why not! Because the two of you want a peek and next thing you know, every dead spirit in Chicago would want a peek. Spirits of all types—young, old, and even the *sick* spirits," Joe scoffed.

"Sick spirits! I hadn't thought of that," Pinkie muttered.

"If we let this secret get out, then Josh's life is ruined. Maybe The Others even find him—then what?" Joe continued.

They paused for a moment.

"Do you remember that conference you took me to? The LADO conference?" asked Joe.

"Yeah," Pinkie replied. "What about it?"

"Don't you remember what the guest speaker said about Bridges? The ones they had found?" Joe asked.

"Yeah," Pinkie recalled. "They all went crazy and ended up in the loony bin."

"Or worse," Cunningham barked.

"That's right," Joe confirmed. "This is exactly why I've been protecting him all this time. If our kind where to find out he's a Bridge, his life would never be the same."

"We need to protect him," Cunningham immediately declared.

"Protect him?" Pinkie cried.

"You heard Joe. If this gets out, every spirit would swarm this boy. He needs to be protected until he's old enough." Cunningham clearly didn't mean to sound intimidating, but his booming voice put Joe on alert.

"But what about LADO? If they find out you've been hiding a Bridge, then . . ." Pinkie trailed off.

"LADO ain't what it used to be. It's a bunch of newer generation spirits only looking out for their interests. What about us guys who've been around the block?" Cunningham griped.

"Yeah, but if they forbid interaction with you, that's it. No one will talk to you. *Complete isolation.* You might as well call up The Others and tell 'em what time to pick you up," cried Pinkie.

"Pull yourself together, Pink!" said Cunningham. "Think about where we came from. Joe is our friend. We don't turn our backs on our friends. If Joe needs to protect his grandson, then we protect his grandson."

Just like that, Josh had become Pinkie and Cunningham's *reason.*

If Joe could've cried in that moment, he would've. It was a relief to have them sign on to protect Josh—he need not worry about being banished from their group and have them turn Josh in. A joyful comfort aroused within him as he noticed his aura brightening. But being sentimental didn't last long. They needed to figure out how to protect Josh from LADO and what could be far worse—The Others.

And so their guardianship began. Josh accepted them instantly. He was happy to have the companionship and quickly latched on to them.

Joe worried Cunningham and Pinkie might have a change of heart and tell LADO, or that Pinkie might slip up and inadvertently tell another spirit. Those fears were calmed not long after the introduction. An immediate bond formed between Josh and his new comrades, and Cunningham and Pinkie proved to be loyal and vigilant watchmen. Meanwhile, Joe's aura glowed a brilliant white as he spent more and more time with his grandson.

Josh being a Bridge gave Joe something few spirits got to experience, but they still had a job to do, and protecting Josh from discovery became more challenging the older he grew.

They were on constant guard. If he left the house, the three of them were with him. They walked him to school—distracting any spirits from Josh they encountered along the way. They went with him to baseball practice. They joined him when he played with the neighbor kids. Most importantly, they coached him endlessly on how avoid other spirits and how to defeat the "SWEEPS" the other spirits were doing to identify Bridges. Their tactics worked so well that he was largely unbothered by other spirits.

Joe would never forget hearing about the day Josh was at school when a spirit decided to meander through his classroom.

Pinkie had been on guard that day, which meant it had been his job to become more interesting than any of the living people. From what he'd told Joe, he could instantly tell the spirit was a hokey, almost gullible type and had decided to see if Josh remembered his training before intervening. He'd looked on as the boy kept his eyes on his teacher as the spirit slowly passed.

"Way to go, Josh," Pinkie had whispered to himself. While Josh had flawlessly applied his training skills, he knew another spirit hanging around could only increase the likelihood of Josh being found out. He'd decided to intervene.

"Hey! Beat it! This is my classroom!" Pink had yelled.

"Oh, sorry about that!" the affable spirit said and compliantly moved on from the room.

Near misses like that were common—and if it weren't for Josh's guardians, he would have been discovered years ago.

They took turns walking Josh to school so as not to overwhelm him. Joe relished the fact that he got to spend time alone with Josh when it was his turn.

"Grandpa, tell me again about the time my dad caught that foul ball at the Cubs game," Josh said one day.

"We used to go to opening day every year. It was a Morton family tradition," he recalled.

"I know. Mom reads me letters you wrote me on my birthday. They always say *make sure your dad takes you to opening day—it's a Morton family tradition,*" Josh replied.

"Yeah? Well, it's true! My dad used to take me, and his dad would take him before that," Joe recounted.

"Think I'll get to go with my dad one day?" asked Josh.

"I bet so . . . but, you should ask your dad to go to a game. It would show him you're interested in baseball and you're ready to go. I have to think the day he takes you to your first Cubs game will be one of the happiest days of his life," Joe suggested.

"Okay, I'll ask him," replied Josh.

"You want to know what the actual happiest day of your dad's life was?" asked Joe.

"The day he caught the foul ball?" Josh answered.

"Close," Joe chuckled. "I had never seen your father more happy than the day you were born. I should know—I was there."

"But I thought you had died before I was born?" Josh wondered.

"I did. But I stayed behind to see you. It was the happiest day of your father's life, but it was also the happiest day of my *new* life. I don't expect you to know what that means—but one day you will."

Josh didn't say anything as he pondered what his grandfather meant.

"All I want you to know is how proud your father is of you."

A tear ran slowly down Josh's face and he wiped it as he opened his bag. He pulled out a stack of envelopes. "I keep these with me every day," he said.

"My birthday letters?" Joe exclaimed.

"I keep them hidden and read them when you're not around," Josh said.

"Well, I didn't expect to be around when I wrote those. I was very sick, and I knew I wasn't going to make it to see you. Nothing troubled me more in life than not being able to see my grandson. But things just have a way of working themselves out," said Joe.

"*Hey, Josh!*"

One of his friends was yelling at him as they approached the school grounds.

"Go on ahead. I'll see ya in class. I'll be the old guy in the back of the room," Joe snickered.

"Love you, Grandpa."

"I love you too, Josh. More than you know." Joe smiled.

JOSH MEETS A GIRL

"IT WAS BOUND TO HAPPEN sometime!" Cunningham boomed.

"I just need my grandson to be safe at all costs—but *this*? This presents an entirely different set of circumstances for us," Joe complained.

Pinkie loved giving Josh dating advice. "So, ya really like that one, huh? What ya gotta do is impress her. Invite her to your next game and hit a home run for her."

Cunningham had a different style.

"If ya *really* want to impress the dame, I'd say buy her flowers."

Pinkie didn't like the idea. "He'd get laughed out of school, ya big dope!"

"Chivalry is dead!" cried Cunningham. "Kids today don't know how to treat a lady."

"What do you think, Grandpa?" asked Josh one time when they were alone, his impressionable nature asking for approval.

"She seems nice," said Joe. "Treat Melissa well. Don't take her for granted."

"I won't," he replied. "I think I really like her. . . . How did you and Grandma meet?"

"You never met your grandma, but when I first saw her—I was stunned. I could barely work up the courage to say 'hi.' But when I finally did, I made her laugh. And from that day forward, we laughed every day until the day she passed away. If you make her laugh, you'll win her heart."

"Grandpa? Melissa asked me to the school dance," he said.

"That's great, son!" Joe exclaimed, though his flashing gave away his trepidation.

"So, I need to ask you something," Josh said.

"Shoot," Joe replied.

"I want to go—but I want to go alone . . . without you and Pinkie and Cunningham," he explained.

Grandpa Joe stood and began pacing the room, his aura flashing rapidly. "I'm not so sure that's a good idea," Joe cautioned. "You're only thirteen. Too young."

"But Grandpa—Pinkie and Cunningham will just make jokes the entire time, and I won't have any fun with Melissa," Josh pleaded.

"This is not up for debate," Joe decided. "At least one of us needs to go with you."

"But why? I don't see why just this once I can't go by myself," Josh stated. "Will I ever have any privacy in my life?"

Suddenly the door to Josh's room swung open.

"Who are you talking to?" asked Sarah, standing in the doorway.

"Um, no one," Josh said.

"Mm-hmm. I heard you talking to someone," she insisted.

"I was—uh . . . I was just practicing for a presentation for the science fair."

"Well . . ." She appeared stumped—but a proud, thin smile pierced her pursed lips. "Well, I better leave you alone then."

"She bought it!" said Joe, celebrating at his grandson's new found independence.

"Close one," whispered Josh.

"Yeah, it was," Joe replied.

They both started laughing.

"You know, I suppose just this once we can let you go by yourself," said Joe, proud Josh had handled the situation. *Just like I taught him,* he thought to himself.

"Thank you!" Josh cried.

"SHHHH!" Joe snapped.

"I mean, *thank you,*" whispered Josh.

JOSH IS DISCOVERED

"WHAT ARE YOU WORRIED ABOUT? It's just a dance! Besides, the spirits who live at the school are harmless. I've been dealing with them for years," Josh proclaimed as he tucked in his dress shirt.

"I just want you to be careful. You haven't been out of the house without one of us ever," Joe replied.

"Grandpa, I'm older now. Eventually, I have to learn to stand on my own."

"That's what I'm afraid of, son."

"You've taught me everything I need to know."

"Not everything," Joe murmured under his breath. "I haven't told you about the dark portals."

Josh seemed to pay no attention to his grandfather grumbling and continued getting ready. He looked in the mirror and was fumbling with his tie. Joe took notice.

"All right, son, take the left side and bring it underneath. Then loop it around, put the end through that spot right there . . . and pull the rest of it the way through. Voilá!"

"I did it!"

"Let me look at ya, kid. Stand up straight." Joe looked upon his grandson with vigorous pride, regretting that he was aging so quickly.

You blink and they are all grown. He couldn't help but think maybe he had been too hard on Josh—not letting him out of his guardians' sight for fear he may be discovered. In all the rotation schedules and planning to keep him safe, Joe realized he hadn't *really* been able to enjoy his grandson. Moments like these made him wish he could rewind time and start over. He knew one day Josh would be all grown up, and then he wouldn't need him any longer. He'd just be the strange Grandpa Joe who haunted the attic. He was constantly reminded Josh would eventually pass away, leaving him behind . . . and what then?

He need not poison his mind further and decided to enjoy the moment he was sharing with Josh because there would never be enough moments like these.

"You, sir, are looking like a Morton if I ever saw one." Josh smiled as he helped him make final preparations. "Now you're ready for the big dance," Joe announced.

"Thanks, Grandpa."

The doorbell rang—his friends arriving to take pictures with their dates. "They're here!"

Josh cast a smile Joe's way, but his aura dimmed as a void of emptiness filled him as Josh left the room, leaving him behind.

The attic seemed even more dim and dreary than normal, even though Pinkie and Cunningham were there to keep him company.

"Sooner or later, we're gonna have to let the kid live," Pinkie conceded.

The three of them watched out the attic window as Josh and his friends left for the dance.

"I know this isn't easy for you, Joe. It's not easy for any of us. The three of us have practically raised him since he was a boy," Cunningham grumbled.

"We've taught him a lot—but he's not out of the woods yet. He's still a boy. He's impressionable," Joe stated, remaining at the window even though the car Josh was riding in had pulled away and was well out of sight.

He stayed at the window well after it turned dark.

"You can't do anything for him now," Pinkie coaxed.

"Yeah, Joe, why don't you come away from that window?" asked Cunningham.

"I got a bad feeling about this," Joe stated.

"Think we should make a trip over to the school and check out the dance?" asked Pinkie.

"No," Joe replied. "I don't want him to lose trust in us."

The three were quiet and thought about their next move. They didn't have to wait much longer because a car pulled into the driveway.

Josh burst out of the back seat, rushing into the house. An adult got out of the driver's seat—presumably a teacher or chaperone—and approached the house. Joe watched as Bill and Sarah greeted Josh, only for him to brush them off and hurry to his room. The chaperone returned to her vehicle and drove off. Joe, Cunningham, and Pinkie traveled down to the first floor.

"Wait out here," Joe commanded as he traveled into Josh's room.

Joe tried calming Josh, but was no use. He was in a frenzy.

"Melissa—she's mad at me," Josh kept repeating.

Joe finally brought Josh to a calmed state. "What happened, son?"

"Grandpa—these spirits showed up. I'd never seen anything like them. They were unlike any spirits you've ever shown me. First, there was this spirit who came into the dance. He had an aura like yours—only his was *dark*."

"A sick spirit," Joe muttered to himself.

"He seemed afraid—kept saying someone was after him, so he came into the school. He asked me to help him, Grandpa."

"Did you avoid him like I taught you?"

"I tried. Once he noticed I could see him, he wouldn't leave me alone."

"Oh no, Josh. That's very bad. Did any of the other spirits living at the school see you interacting with him?"

"No. I asked him to leave me alone, and I tried to go back to dancing with Melissa when all of a sudden this, I don't know—it looked like a *tunnel* opened up and two spirits came out of it."

Joe began pacing. "Pinkie and Cunningham! Can you come in here?" he yelled.

"You saw The Others, didn't ya?" said Pinkie.

Cunningham read Joe's narrowed eyes and flashing aura. "Sorry, Joe. We didn't mean to listen in. We just, uh—"

"It doesn't matter! Josh is in real danger. Josh, listen to me very carefully. The two spirits who came out of the portal—what did they do?"

"They grabbed the spirit who was asking me for help. The one with the dark aura."

"These, uh, two guys . . . what did they look like, the ones who came out of the tunnel?" asked Pinkie.

"They were dressed in all black. They wore suits. One had spiked hair, the other had hair slicked back. They both had tattoos—one had a tattoo on his neck, and the other had a tattoo on his cheek, just below his eye."

"Did they say anything to you?" asked Joe.

"I was afraid, Grandpa. When they showed up, it surprised me so much that I just collapsed to the ground. Everyone at the dance—the music stopped—they thought I *fainted*. The two spirits, they must've noticed me. They stood over me and said, 'You can see us, can't you?'"

"Did you respond back to them? Did you look past them and ignore them like we taught you?" asked Cunningham.

"No! I was scared!" Josh's outburst caught the attention of his parents who knocked at the door. "I'll be out in a few!" he said.

"All right, Cunningham and Pink. Let's give him some room. What's done is done. There's no taking it back."

Cunningham, the large brute, grumbled worrisome chatter to himself as he traveled back.

"Grandpa, I was so scared. I didn't say anything to them, but I nodded. They knew I could see them. I shouldn't have nodded to them—that was it."

"It's okay, Josh. Did they say anything?"

"They said, 'We'll see you soon.' It was like they planned to come back and find me." Joe, Pinkie, and Cunningham shot each other concerned glances.

"Okay. What happened next?" asked Joe.

"They spoke in some language I didn't understand. After that they smiled at me. Before they left, they went over to the other spirit—the one with the dark aura. He tried to run from them, but they caught him and dragged him into the tunnel. That's when I left, running out to the parking lot, and a chaperone drove me home."

When Joe huddled with Pinkie and Cunningham, they all agreed the best thing was for Josh to return to the dance and show he was all right.

Josh was reluctant at first. "I can't go back! They all think I'm a freak! Melissa probably hates me now because I left her."

"Just tell Melissa you weren't feeling well," Pinkie prodded.

"Okay, I'll go—as long as you all come with me," replied Josh.

The three guardians could barely keep up as Josh rushed down the stairs. "I forgot something. I'm going back to the dance," he said as he shot through the living room and burst out the door. Bill and Sarah were bewildered but amused.

"*Teenagers*," Joe heard Bill mutter as he sauntered back to the TV.

Bill and Sarah's house was walking distance to the school, and Josh made it back in a lightning pace. Joe watched his grandson try to make it up to his date. He could tell it took some convincing, but eventually Melissa let it go. The rest of his class, however, did not—people were pointing at Josh and rumors started about his "meltdown" at the dance.

"Middle schoolers are so mean," said Joe.

"Ya shoulda seen them back in our day," said Pinkie.

The next few days were hard on Josh and his trio. Josh fought rumors at school, while Joe, Pinkie, and Cunningham tried to figure out how they should confront the new danger of The Others knowing Josh's secret.

Pinkie was the first to come up with the idea of bringing Josh to a

LADO chapter meeting.

"You know, guys—I've been thinking. It's better for Josh if we take him to LADO. They might know how to protect him," he suggested.

"That's crazy!" barked Joe. "We've been protecting Josh from that exact idea for years. They'll destroy him!"

"Be reasonable!" Pinkie pleaded. "The Others have found Josh. Do you know what that means?"

"He's got a point, Joe," Cunningham broke in.

"*I know he's got a point!*"

They gave Joe space for a few moments and let him bring his aura under control. It was Cunningham's contrasting gentle demeanor and imposing size that got Joe to finally calm down.

"Listen, I'm sorry I had the outburst. You both have been good friends to me over the years," Joe conceded.

"That's alright," Pinkie offered. "We all have outbursts from time to time."

"Yeah. Like the old saying goes: If you're frustrated, it's only because you're dead," Cunningham chuckled.

"Yeah, yeah," Pinkie agreed. "Or how about this one: If you're not desperate, you're probably still alive!"

They shared a brief, releasing laugh.

"We're in over our heads," Joe conceded. It was settled. They would bring Joe to the next LADO meeting. Aside from the annual conference he attended a few years back at Union Station, this would be Joe's only interaction with LADO. He had wanted to steer clear of LADO to not put a link between he and Josh. Better to keep a low profile, but now he clearly needed their help.

"Don't expect the LADO folks to be happy we are bringing Josh to them," Cunningham cautioned.

"Yeah—they ain't gonna be happy we've been hiding this from them," Pinkie chimed in.

Two days later, they were standing in front of the LADO chapter presenting their case.

"There's no going back now," Pinkie proclaimed as they traveled in.

They were met with a panel of three LADO members who Joe recognized as Chicago chapter members that Pinkie and Cunningham had introduced him to at the LADO Worldwide event. Back then, he was largely indifferent toward meeting the spirits as he was so new to the spirit world and didn't know what to think of the conference in the first place. Today, standing before them betraying his grandson, he looked upon them as mortal enemies.

"How dare you keep this secret from us? Selfish bastards! We have destinies to fulfill! We have our own reasons for being here. What gives you the right? Give him to us!"

Cunningham silenced the room with his booming voice. "This is why we didn't disclose Josh to LADO! You're behaving the same way we expected you to! This kid wouldn't have had a chance if we told you about him. You're only thinking of yourselves and your *reasons*. What about the boy? What, you just want to use him to help you and then cast him aside like all the other Bridges you've encountered? You should all be ashamed of yourselves and your behavior!"

Joe stood near Josh, feeling enormous gratitude for his friend's loyalty.

Everyone stopped bickering and stood at attention when a new spirit entered the room. Even Pinkie and Cunningham straightened up and awaited her first words.

She traveled over to Josh and Joe.

"How do you do?" she asked.

Joe nodded. A spirit emerged from the group and stood next to her.

"Gentlemen, this is Denise Roberson. She is the President of our local chapter," one of the LADO members announced.

Denise was an older spirit in the group, but not as old as Pinkie and Cunningham. She circled the room for a few moments before commencing. She took her position, listening to Joe's case before presenting her thoughts.

"Yes, these spirits were wrong to hide a Bridge from us." She paused again. "But they are not wrong that LADO has a long, tragic, even *disastrous* history with Bridges. You all know I have long been critical of LADO HQ's methods with Bridges. We have an opportunity here. There is an option—let's call it "the nuclear option"—where we can, in the case of extreme emergency, call upon a certain spirit to help us."

The room was silent. She continued. "This spirit—he is an old spirit. A powerful spirit."

"Which means what?" asked one of the chapter members.

Denise became solemn in her expression. "Long before I became LADO chapter lead, our chapter had summoned Keryx. They were tired of being stuck between worlds, and they wanted a portal—so they called him. In an act of selfishness, they attempted to entrap Keryx with old, dark spells, and they demanded he open a portal and take them to the afterlife. But the magic did not hold, and he broke the spell, and in his anger he banished them all to this world forever."

"What happened to them? Why have we never met them or heard about them?" asked Pinkie.

"It was such a long time ago that none of us really talk about it, but they eventually became sick and were taken by The Others. It was their punishment for their disobedience."

Gasps filled the room.

"Legend has it that Keryx felt so badly about the consequences of the punishment that he summoned the LADO leadership and set forth the conditions under which it would be acceptable to contact him in the future," she continued.

"And what are those?" asked Cunningham. "I'm a chapter member, and I ain't never heard nothin' about no rules for contacting powerful spirits."

"The truth is I never thought in my time as Chapter President that we would ever meet any of the conditions, but one of the stipulations for contacting Keryx is if we find a Bridge."

"And this Keryx will help us? He'll let us fulfill our *reasons*? How do we summon him?" spirits began to say.

Roberson held up her hand to silence them. "According to folklore, Keryx gifted each of the LADO chapters with access to an energy field. Ours is located in what is now the basement of a banquet hall and restaurant called the Chicago Brauhaus. Only a living person can open such an energy field—with special instructions by a spirit," she explained.

"One of the *living* opening the portal would ensure that only a Bridge was opening the energy field!" Pinkie interjected.

"That's correct. Once the energy field is unlocked and opened, it will signal Keryx," she agreed.

"Summoning Keryx sounds like the easy part. Getting Josh away from his girlfriend to the Chicago Brauhaus will be the challenge," Pinkie said.

"Hey! Maybe this works out in his favor. Maybe he can convince Melissa to open the beacon," Cunningham bellowed.

"Have him there tomorrow at 4:30 pm," commanded the Chapter President.

"He'll be there," Joe promised.

THE BRAUHAUS

"JOSH, LISTEN TO ME VERY carefully, son. I cannot protect you any longer. *We* cannot protect you any longer. If The Others have found you, it's only a matter of time."

"Fine," said Josh. "I'll go. But whoever we are meeting must be just as powerful as The Others—or you wouldn't be bringing me to them. I want Melissa to be able to see you so that she'll believe me. That is my condition. If you can do that, I will go," said Josh.

Pinkie, Cunningham, and Joe all looked at each other. Joe—still a relatively new spirit of under fifteen years compared to their hundred—looked to them for advice.

"Do you know what this is like? Do you? To walk through life talking to your dead grandpa? To have dark spirits chase you from your high school dance? To not be able to have a normal conversation with my girlfriend for fear a spirit is going to walk in the room and distract me? I need Melissa to see this—if only for a few seconds—so she can understand. So *someone* can understand."

"Okay." It was Cunningham who spoke. He nodded to Joe and Pinkie as if to say, *Just go along with it, we need to get Josh there then we'll figure it out.*

"We'll make it happen," said Joe. He hated making a commitment to his grandson that he couldn't fully deliver on.

"Fine—where are we going again?" said Josh.

The Chicago Brauhaus is a German banquet hall offering traditional fare including beer steins, Bavarian pretzels, polka music. Open six days a week, except for Tuesdays, the Brauhaus was usually full of people looking for an authentic German restaurant experience. Oktoberfest was a big hit among the locals at this place.

Today wasn't a regular scheduled meeting, but the local LADO chapter assembled at the Brauhaus anyway in anticipation of seeing the energy field opened. It was dark, and the doors screeched and echoed through the large banquet hall as Josh and Melissa entered.

The local chapter members were excited to see Josh—their flashes filled the empty hall like a nightclub.

"Josh . . . Who are we meeting here? We are the only ones," Melissa whispered as she squeezed his hand. "We better leave soon or we are going to get arrested."

"Who is she?" snarled Denise Roberson as she entered the room.

"She is with Josh. They come as a package or not at all," demanded Cunningham.

"You and your friends are on thin ice, Cunningham," barked Denise. "Any more surprises, and you'll be banished from our community. Do you understand?"

The other LADO members gasped at the idea.

"Do you want me to walk out of here right now?" Josh threatened. "I don't go by your rules."

The LADO members excitement could not be contained.

"He *can* see us!"

"It's true! A *real* Bridge!"

Denise held up her hand to command silence among the group.

"The way I see it, you need me more than I need you—so do me a favor and treat my friends with a little respect." Joe's aura brightened as he proudly listened to his grandson.

Denise traveled slowly over to Josh. She circled around him twice before stopping in front of him.

"You remind me of my son. He was around your age when I died," Denise recalled.

"Do I know him? Does he go to my school?" asked Josh.

"Oh heavens no," she chuckled. "My little boy died some time ago. He lived a long life. He was 87 years old when he passed . . . but he was my *reason* for staying behind. If I would have found someone like you, maybe I would've been able to say goodbye to him. I watched him for many torturous years. I cheered him on at baseball games. I was there at his college graduation. I was there when my grandson was born. Do you know what that did to me as a mother? To go through all of those milestones and not be able to communicate with him? That's why we are so glad you are here. You mean a lot to our community," she said.

"Denise—if I may, this might be difficult for my grandson to grasp. He's still a boy," Joe interjected.

She paused and recollected herself.

"There are people in this room who would give anything to have you help them. Back then, if you could've let my boy know that I was with him, it would've caused me great peace," she continued. "This is the gift that you can provide us. Look around us. Look at the spirits in this room and the reaction they have. Their auras are brighter than the day they died. You give them hope. You give us . . . hope."

"I'm not sure what to say," he said. "All I've ever wanted to do is live a normal life."

"Unfortunately, Josh, you'll never be able to live a normal life, but understand you are special. And I don't expect you to understand this—but we need to protect you. There are very bad spirits among us who could use you to do great harm," she said. "Josh, I don't know how to say this other than you are in grave danger. You might be the key to the world as we know it—and definitely the world as you know it."

She went on to explain the possibility of a Great War building. The Others had been stretching the boundaries of the rules for some time. Should they find a Bridge, they could with the right degree of manipulation and coaching—build him into a powerful force that could carry out deeds against humanity.

Should The Others gain control over Josh, they would be able to influence both living and spirits alike. Josh would simply be a pawn to help The Others collect more spirits. And when the Great War should come—then humanity as we know it would be over.

"We need to move swiftly. If The Others find out we're here, they will most certainly show up and interfere. The girl you've brought with you . . . I'm not so sure this is an appropriate place for her to be at the moment."

Josh glanced at Melissa sitting at one of the tables playing on her smartphone.

Denise went on, "We cannot protect him. None of us can. The only chance Josh has is by us contacting Keryx."

One of the chapter members spoke softly.

"Josh, what Denise will tell you in the next few moments might surprise you. You are only one of a few people in history who will be able to do what she asks of you."

"Thank you, Lucas," she said with great poise.

"Is he, uh—*Keryx*—a good spirit?" asked Josh.

"Josh, we've learned the balance between good and evil is a complicated one. Sometimes rules are set in place with good intentions, yet they lead to suffering among the living and equally among our kind. This is not so much a debate about good and evil but the survival of our world," she said.

"I'm not sure I fully understand," said Josh.

"There is much you will learn in your time as a Bridge. I'm afraid you've not even begun to realize your full potential. Your grandfather and his friends have done a masterful job in helping mentor you as a youth, but as you come into adolescence and adulthood, you gain more independence—which means more exposure to the outside world and beyond."

"She means The Others," said Pinkie.

"That's correct," she said.

"Have you thought about the possibility that they return for you?" she asked.

"Who? The Others?" said Joe.

"Yes. The Others."

"I, uh—I try to pretend I'm not afraid, but they were the most horrific thing I've ever seen," Josh replied.

"Would you like us to summon Keryx?" she asked Josh.

"Are you sure my grandson will be protected?" Joe intervened.

"No spirit that we know has ever summoned Keryx. But the way I see it—what choice do you have? What could be worse than The Others following you around the rest of your life trying to manipulate you?"

Joe watched Josh turn to him and give him a nod of approval. "I think we should do it," said Josh.

"I agree. Pinkie, Cunningham, and I—we can't protect you anymore," said Joe.

"Joe's right," acknowledged Cunningham.

"Josh, I just want you to know that I am proud of the man you are becoming. Whatever choice you make will be the right one," said Joe.

"Yeah, kid. We're with ya all the way," said Pinkie.

"Thanks, Grandpa. That means a lot," said Josh, turning to face Denise. "I'm ready. Let's do it."

They made their way to the basement and found the relic. Melissa was scared, and Josh found a quiet corner for her to sit in while he worked with the spirits.

"Hang in here a few more minutes and I promise we'll leave soon," he told her.

"This place gives me the creeps. We need to leave *now*," she said.

"Melissa, I need you to do something—and I promise if you help me, it will make you understand. Just please stay with me," he said.

She nodded. "Okay."

"We found the relic!" yelled Cunningham from the next room.

"Wait!" she said. "Are those, uh . . . *spirits* . . . your grandpa and his friends—are they talking to you right now?"

"Yes."

"That's so cool!" she said.

"You actually believe me?" he said.

"I believe in you, Josh Morton." She took his hand and peered into his eyes.

"Josh! Get in here!" yelled Pinkie. "We have to move fast!"

"Let's go," he said to Melissa.

Josh took Melissa's hand and walked into the room where the spirits were standing around what looked to be an old passage to a tunnel that was capped with some sort of cover.

"Here it is!" boomed Cunningham.

"I have a feeling once we open this, there's no going back," said Pinkie.

"Let's begin," said Denise.

Josh looked at Melissa and nodded.

THE SUMMONS

DENISE PROVIDED JOSH INSTRUCTIONS TO open the energy field, which, to Joe, didn't seem like much. It was an elongated circular column that protruded from the cement basement. It had a stone cap with wooden handles jutting out of the cap. If no one had told him it was an energy field that could summon one of the most powerful spirits in existence, Joe might've thought it was a decorative container that held expensive wine.

"It's a combination of sorts. Turn the cap using the wooden handles. Twelve clicks to the right, seven clicks left, four clicks right—then, according to folklore, the cap should come loose," said Denise.

"What happens after that?" asked Cunningham.

"I suppose we'll find out," she said.

"Why can't *you* open it?" asked Josh.

Lucas—who was Denise's compliant assistant, happily doing every task she commanded—was ordered to perform a demonstration. He attempted to push the cap, failing as his hands passed through the beacon, and confirming that only a Bridge could open it.

"*Duh,*" said Josh. "Why didn't I think of that?"

"Only a member of the living can open the beacon. Only we know the combination. This is a protective safeguard to ensure only a Bridge can open the energy field," said Denise.

"Okay, I guess I'll try it out. Twelve clicks to the right?" said Josh. He leaned up against the gritty wooden handles, pushing and pulling to no avail.

"Come on, boy! Put your back into it!" shouted Cunningham.

The rest of the spirits cheered him on as he grunted and pushed against the handles.

"Josh, what is it that you're doing?" asked Melissa.

"Come here and help! I need to remove this cap. Grab one of the handles and push," said Josh.

"I'm not sure that's a good idea. She's not a Bridge," said Lucas.

"Do you want the summons to happen or not?" asked Pinkie.

Melissa joined Josh and the two of them grabbed hold of a wooden handle.

"I feel like I'm going to get a splinter," she said.

"Just push!" yelled Josh.

They pushed, giving it everything they could—and still nothing.

"I have an idea," said Josh. He gripped the wooden handle. Dust poured off the ancient beacon as the cap lifted slightly off its foundation. "Push now!"

The spirits cheered as the cap made a grinding sound as it slid and fell into a notch.

"That's one click! Do that to the right eleven more times," said Denise.

The cap was heavy to lift, but became much easier to manage when Melissa and Josh figured out how to synchronize their efforts. The spirits looked on cheering, counting, and encouraging them—although Josh was the only one who could hear.

"Okay! That's twelve! Let's go the other way for seven clicks," said Pinkie.

"I need a break!" said Melissa, much to the chagrin of the spirit clan, who shouted different variations of the same message: "Oh, come on! You're so close. Just four more the other way!"

"This thing is *heavy*, Josh. What exactly are we doing?" she said, wiping her brow.

"I just need you to trust me. All we need to do is go four more clicks in the other direction. Then we're done."

"Okay, but I still don't know what we're doing," she said, continuing only to half-heartedly push, as if she was not fully bought in to the task at hand.

The spirits waited in anticipation with every click the cap made as it was laboriously moved into place.

"Four!"

"Three"

"Twooooooooo!"

They were wild with excitement when Josh and Melissa gripped the dusty wooden handles to lift and push the heavy cement cap into place for the last time. The sound of the last notch echoed through the room.

"Okay, last one done," said Melissa as she walked away from the beacon.

"Wait—nothin' is happening," said Pinkie.

Cunningham walked up to the beacon and tried to kick it with his large boot. "What gives?" he growled.

"I don't understand," said Denise. "As acting head of the Chicago LADO chapter, I was told this is how the beacon works."

"Do you think you used the right combination?" asked Lucas.

"I've memorized these numbers for *years*," she said. "Twelve to the right, seven to the left, four to the right."

"Did we do it right?" asked Josh, hands on his knees, panting.

"Let's get outta here," said Cunningham. "We'll have to think of another way to protect Josh from those heathens."

"Josh, I'll meet you back at the house," said Joe.

They grumbled and began to leave—but something happened just as they neared the walls to exit. The cap lifted from the beacon, flooding the room with light.

"Josh! The beacon!" yelled Joe.

"Remove the cap!" said Cunningham.

Josh ran to the beacon and removed the cap. A concentrated blue light shot straight up, penetrating the basement ceiling. Cunningham was first to brave the beacon, walking up and attempting to touch it.

"I've never seen light this color. It's brilliant!" he said.

All eyes turned to Melissa as she moved forward, indicating that even *she* could see the radiant blue light. "Fascinating! I haven't anything so vivid before," she said.

"I wouldn't touch that if I were you," a voice boomed. Suddenly, a shadowy figure appeared in the beacon, sending Cunningham scrambling for cover.

Melissa appeared unphased by the figure as she continued to move forward.

"Melissa, whatever you do, don't touch it!" warned Josh, causing her to jerk her hand back and take a position next to him.

The figure traveled out from the beacon, prompting gasps from the spirits.

"Hello. My name is Keryx."

KERYX

STANDING BEFORE JOSH WAS A spirit of magnificent presence. Joe could feel the energy pulsating from his aura. He saw Josh cover his eyes due to the brilliance, removing his hands only a moment later, as his eyes adjusted.

Keryx wore a purple linen cloak cut perfectly to fit his sculpted shoulders. It was loose-fitting, draped—cropped just above the knees. It was a simple garment—yet dyed a radiant purple—clearly the color of nobility, reflective of his great power. Leather sandals hugged his feet and a series of leather straps wrapped around his lower leg. Josh was particularly interested in a set of scrolls he carried under his arm. He carried no weapon—no battle armor, no sword or shield.

The LADO members gasped at his presence, while Joe stood with Josh admiring the spirit. He had seen photos that looked like Keryx in history books, although there was no photo in any history book that could quite capture the nobility that was this spirit.

"Are you a Roman?" asked Josh, skipping greetings.

"I'm Greek," said Keryx, exuding a sense of pride when he spoke. "I lived in a land called Sparta. I am a warrior. At least I was when I was living—but my people are all gone from there now."

Keryx surveyed the room, seemingly searching for the one who opened the beacon. His eyes settled upon Josh, examining him in great detail—his brow furrowing when he looked upon his jeans, hoodie, and sneakers with perplexity.

"You are the one who can see me. Communicate with me," said Keryx.

"Yes," said Josh.

"The girl, too?" Keryx pointed to Melissa.

"No. She's with me."

"I see." Keryx looked around the room as if trying to locate something. "Are there any others with you? How did you know to open the beacon?"

That was when Josh realized his supporting cast had scattered, leaving him to face whatever was coming out of that energy field alone. "Come on out, guys."

"Josh, what's happening?" whispered Melissa, moving closer to him and clasping her hand around his.

"I'll explain later," he whispered back and gripped her hand tightly.

Joe and the others faded into the background, observing. Denise moved past them assuming her leadership role. "Greetings, Keryx," she said confidently as she introduced herself as the head of the Chicago LADO chapter.

"Salutations," he said, bowing gracefully. "Whom chose to summon me?"

"It was I," said Denise. "We have found a Bridge."

"Yes, we've established that," said Keryx. "Under what conditions have you made the summons?"

"I'm afraid the boy is in real danger. He has been contacted by The Others," said Denise.

His eyes narrowed. His square jaw tightened, chest protruding as he stood straight. "Is this true?" he asked, turning his attention to Josh.

"Yes, sir."

"Malitae and Malum." Josh caught sight of Keryx subtly making a fist as his arm hung at his side. It was the only sign of displeasure that Keryx displayed, but it was enough for Josh to know he was not pleased. "Was this your first encounter with them?"

"Yes."

"Not mine," said Cunningham. "I've seen those two a few times."

"I've also seen them," said Joe. "They threatened me once."

Josh flashed Joe a stare as if to say, *You never told me about that.*

"I'm glad you chose to summon me," said Keryx. "The boy is in real danger if he has been contacted by Malitae and Malum. If they had any doubts you are a Bridge, they don't now. They too are also watching this energy field, and its presence will signal my arrival." He gripped his scroll tightly. "They will not be happy I'm here. It will be looked upon that a Bridge has aligned with our side . . . a sign of escalation."

"Why are they so interested in me?" asked Josh.

"I'm going to tell you all a story. Believe it or not, I've been dead for a thousand years. In that time, I've only met a handful of Bridges. This should tell you how special you really are. But that's not the purpose of my story. I once met a boy around your age. He had not yet been corrupted by the world. I visited the boy from time to time and learned about his abilities. He was a remarkable case. He could see spirits—and even had a grandfather much like your Grandpa Joe who was guiding him. Your first World War had ended a few years before, and the German population of what you call Germany was suffering because of the reparations they had to pay back in the war. There was a belief that a certain group of people living in Germany were more wealthy than others and had become so unjustly."

"The Jews?" said Joe.

"Yes, so they are called that. There was animosity that grew between the Jews and the German population. The people called Germans had just lost a war. Had just entered into great poverty. People all around struggled looking for unity. The Others saw this and exploited it."

"How so?" asked Joe.

"Through the Bridge, of course. They started by befriending him. Attached to his every move. Once they gained his trust, they would whisper exaggerated social agendas to him: *Why should the Jews have all the money? They are not even of German blood. We need to protect ethnic Germans living in other countries. You know what we need to do? Take back the Rhineland. That land belongs to Germany.*

"They radicalized him. Manipulated him to do their bidding—almost succeeded, too, had it not been for a couple miscalculations. They helped him rise to power, and on March 7, 1936, he invaded an area called the Rhineland—beginning your second World War."

"Hitler," said Joe.

"Correct. So, you can see just how damaging Malitae and Malum can be. With your modern weaponry, it would be easy to inflict mass damage should a Bridge fall into the wrong hands."

"I, for one, am glad you're here to help Josh," said Denise, the rest of the spirits grumbling in agreement, yet fearful for what they had heard—for Keryx's implication meant Josh, if manipulated by The Others, could be the key to the Great War.

Doomsday.

"I can't recall a time when tensions have been so high between our two sides," said Keryx. "We must protect Josh at all costs."

"Why do they want to end the world?" asked Pinkie.

"They want to end Freewill," said Keryx.

PART THREE
PETE STANTON
MASTER SERGEANT WAGNER

SHAKEN TO THE CORE, PETE bolted from the gas station and traveled night and day. He rushed in the woods for cover, but he kept moving—afraid the twins would come and catch him again if he stayed still. He could change into an orb and shoot away . . . but, *no*. The twins would surely detect him as an orb . . . Best to stay hidden among the trees.

Had he been living, Pete would've died from fear from what he'd just seen. His mind was a swirl of confused thoughts. He felt as though his stomach had fallen out somewhere in the parking lot.

He traveled far and long until he wasn't quite sure where he was. Dark night in central Pennsylvania was a lonely place.

He avoided roads or public places. His options were travel himself or hop in a car. The thought of hitching a ride in another car or commercial truck was sickening. The experience with Charlie had soured him.

The rolling hills told him he was getting close to Appalachian country. Hills that would have once taken a day to traverse he now scaled easily.

"I guess that's one advantage to being dead," he said out loud.

He stopped when he reached a summit looking down on a small town below. The moonlight bounced off a church steeple like a dim beacon.

"It's beautiful," he proclaimed.

His aura brightened and stopped flashing.

The town was nestled in a valley and settled near an adjacent river. The steeple of a church marked the tallest building in town. A large American flag flew in the town center. Across the river, smoke poured out the stacks of a large factory.

Most of the townspeople were probably fast asleep, with the exception of whatever crew was pulling third shift in the factory.

"If the people down there had any idea what's going on around them . . ."

Moonlight punched through the clouds, and the stars glittered like a lamp covered with a black sheet with thousands of small holes in it. He thought of Jessica, their life together, his career, everything that was taken from him.

Why does it have to be like this? I had a good life. A happy life.

He felt a loneliness burn within him. He had left his only purpose—Jessica—back in Philadelphia.

"What am I supposed to do?" he called. He looked up to the sky for answers. "Give me a sign."

As if on cue, a small beam of red poked through the horizon. Shades of oranges, yellows, and reds followed, filling the eastern horizon, exposing the dense fog that was covering the town in the valley below.

Pete's aura brightened in response.

He heard a rustle in the bushes next to him and a doe burst out. The deer stared at Pete, unsure whether or not to bolt. It stopped and began sniffing the air. It looked at Pete but couldn't get his scent, so it went back to grazing.

"Animals can see me . . . but they aren't threatened by me?"

The deer twitched its ears as if it were intently listening for something. Its fluffy white tail signaled alarm as it shot into the air.

"What are you listening to, girl? There's nothing up here that will harm you."

He walked closer to get a better look.

Bang!

A gunshot rang through the woods directly behind him.

He jumped in terror and his aura flashed with excitement. Instinctively, he dove for cover.

He looked up to see a pair of trail-beaten boots—one missing a shoelace, the other rife with holes. His aura flickered dark red and orange as he looked straight down the barrel of a Kentucky long rifle.

"I take you prisoner of the Army of the Confederacy!" bellowed the man.

Pete stood with his hands raised and examined what he hoped was not a trigger-happy mountain man.

"Sorry! I didn't realize I was trespassing," he said. Then he looked closer as the man's words started to register. *The man was a Confederate soldier!*

He wore a grey uniform with insignia. The uniform was dirty, as if it hadn't been washed in months and had several patched holes. He wore a ragged hat that was cocked slightly to the left.

"You spooked my dinner," the man growled through gaping yellow teeth. He noticed one of his front teeth was badly chipped, perhaps broken off. He was met with beady eyes—the cold, inflexible kind, and framed by greasy, trail-dusted hair that looked unwashed. The knees of his pants looked patched over twice, and loose stitching and missing buttons in his sun-bleached coat indicated traumatic wear.

But how? Pete thought.

The soldier's aura wasn't quite black, but it was greyer and darker than Pete's, blending perfectly into his uniform.

He's close to being sick, Pete thought.

The Kentucky long rifle pointed at him was a favorite weapon of Confederate soldiers during the civil war, and an accurate weapon for its day. While accurate at a distance, it was easily broken in hand to hand combat. You could fix a bayonet to it, but it could not withstand the rigors of battle. It served a purpose in guerilla warfare, where soldiers could take sniper positions.

"Hands up!" said the soldier.

"I surrender," said Pete.

"You are now a prisoner of war. We will march to find the rest of my unit, where you will then be conscripted into the Confederate army to fight against the blasted Yankees," the soldier commanded.

"Woah," said Pete. "I think we are moving a little fast here. I usually start with names first."

The soldier ignored him and looked him up and down with some consternation. "What kinda uniform is that you're wearing? You some sort of spy? A foreign prince? A dadgum railroad man?"

"It's a business suit," Pete replied.

"Name and rank! If I suspect you is a spy, I have every right to string a rope!" the soldier demanded through his yellow, chipped teeth.

"Sir, I have no rank. I am not a soldier. I am an attorney from Philadelphia. I have a wife, Jessica, who still lives there. She's one of the living, and she's a researcher for a medical technology company."

"Name and rank!" the soldier shouted again.

"Pete Stanton, Philadelphia. No rank, because I am not a soldier," he replied.

"Philadelphia?" said the soldier. "Sounds like you is a Yankee! I bet you can't even Whistle Dixie, can ya, boy? Go on—*try it*. Whistle Dixie and maybe I'll believe you're fighting for the rebel cause."

"Sir, the war is over. I hate to break it to you, but your side lost."

"No," said the soldier. "The war still rages on. I lost my regiment about ten miles ago. We were marching through—moving southwest to meet an entire division. We're going to overrun those blue bloods. My men are starving, so I aim to secure meat and rejoin them."

Everything Pete had read about the Confederate army was that they were an illiterate bunch made up mostly of farmers and landowners. While this soldier had a thick drawl and was difficult to understand, he appeared to be somewhat educated. Pete guessed by the insignia patches the man wore on his shoulder that he was an officer of some kind, which probably meant he could read, write, and communicate fairly well.

"Say," said Pete. "What is the name of that town down below?"

"Lewiston. Full of Yankee sympathizers," barked the soldier.

"That's a beautiful little city down there. I don't get to see these little river towns very often living in Philadelphia. I didn't catch your name, by the way," said Pete.

"Master Sergeant James Wagner. Actually, my full rank is Quartermaster Sergeant."

"Okay, Master Sergeant," said Pete. "Where are you taking me, exactly?"

The soldier kept his rifle trained on Pete. He turned in the direction he had come from.

"I'm part of the eighth South Carolina regiment formerly commanded by Colonel Hengan. We all serve under General Hickman now. We've heard reports of blue bellies in the area, and they asked me to find them and report back for an ambush. I lost my regiment just northwest of here. Never did find any of those Yanks. 'Cept *you*, of course."

"Where do you think the troops are going?" asked Pete. Something told him he should form an orb and burst away from there immediately, but his curiosity overcame him. The idea of seeing a marching band of Civil War era spirits was too much to pass up, and besides—perhaps he could get in good with them and they might protect him from the twins.

The Master Sergeant looked at Pete for some time. He cocked his head sideways and gritted his yellow teeth together, his tongue slipping through the chipped tooth like a snake trying to slither through an opening.

"You really some sort of spy?" commanded Sergeant Wagner. "I already told ya what we do with spies around here." His beady dark eyes squinted with suspicion.

"No. I'm an attorney," said Pete.

Pete watched as Sergeant Wagner's aura flashed slightly and he gripped the stock of his gun tighter. His eyes became wild with fear.

"Gettysburg," said Sergeant Wagner.

WE WANTED TO KEEP FIGHTING

THEY STUCK TO MOUNTAINS AND game trails as they made their way south. All the while, Sergeant Wagner's head pivoted, scanning the countryside for any sign of the enemy.

The cherry trees were out in full bloom along the countryside.

"Keep marching," Sergeant Wagner barked from time to time, showing no interest in trying to wrangle a wild cherry.

And march they did. They marched through several straight nights. They stopped on the third night after they reached a peak and viewed a faint light four or five ridges to the south. They happened to be on one of the higher peaks, and they could see the entire mountain range and valleys below.

"I'll bet those are my men," said Sergeant Wagner.

"How can you tell? That light looks pretty small," said Pete.

"I'd say that's about a good half-a-day's march from here. A light that far away would never be visible at this distance if it were a single fire," said the Sergeant. "That's a camp."

"Still seems pretty dim to me," said Pete. "What if it's some kids messing around, starting a fire or something?"

"It's my men all right," said the Sergeant. "It's either my men, or it's the Federal troops. Either way, I aim to find out."

"Let me guess," said Pete. "Forward march?"

"Stay here," said Sergeant Wagner. He disappeared into the brush as if the entire forest swallowed him whole.

Pete scanned the horizon. *Run, Stanton!* again screamed into his mind. But no—he decided to stay and wait for the soldier. The idea of venturing out alone terrified him for fear he may run into Malitae and Malum. Constellations popped into view and a shooting star darted across the sky.

Jess would love it out here.

"We're staying put!" boomed Wagner.

Pete nearly jumped out of his skin, or whatever was the spirit equivalent.

"Aren't we going to march?"

"No. We found what we're looking for. If those are my troops, I know where they be headed. If they is Federals, well, we shouldn't be in a hurry to go sneakin' up on their camp. Probably get caught by a picket before we even got close. I don't know 'bout you but I don't feel like getting strung from a tree today. We'll wait here until mornin' and see which way they goes. That'll tell me who they is," he said.

"What next?" asked Pete.

"Sit down, take a load off," said the Sergeant as he pulled two coffee cups out of his pack. "I got somethin' that'll put some hair on your chest."

"Aren't you worried I'm a spy?"

"*You*?" The Sergeant looked him over. "I treat everyone like they is a spy initially, but I figured after a short time you wasn't no spy."

Pete watched as the Sergeant pulled out a bottle from his bag. It was empty. The Sergeant held the bottle over each cup in a pouring motion—despite that fact that nothing was pouring out of the bottle. He handed Pete a coffee cup. Pete looked down into the cup. *Empty.*

"Go on now and drink. It's nothin' but a bit of 'shine. Secret family recipe my uncle makes," said Sergeant Wagner as he held the cup to his lips.

Pete raised the cup to his lips and took a drink. He actually *wished* the cup was full of moonshine.

"Ain't that some good stuff?" said Sergeant Wagner through his yellow teeth. His tongue slipping through the gap in his broken tooth.

"Sure is," said Pete. "Best I ever tasted. Should we make a fire or something?"

"If you want the Federals to march through with cannons, horses, and a couple hundred infantry, then sure, by all means, strike a fire," smirked Sergeant Wagner, his tongue poking out of his chiseled tooth.

The dim light coming from a few ridges over made Pete wonder if there really were other spirit soldiers out there, or if Sergeant Wagner was stuck, *alone* like him—thinking he was still fighting for the Confederate Army.

"So," said Sergeant Wagner. "If I might take a liberty, I'd say you look pretty fresh."

"Fresh?" said Pete.

"Yeah. Fresh," said Sergeant Wagner. The Sergeant took a moment to spit and looked back at Pete, who watched him wipe his beard with his shirt sleeve.

"You ain't been dead long, have ya?" said the Sergeant.

"No. I haven't," said Pete.

"I'd say one year, maybe two. Three years, tops. You's just a baby," said the Sergeant.

Pete wasn't impressed.

"How'd you go?"

"I was in a car crash," said Pete, his aura now flashing.

"A car crash!" said the Sergeant, slapping his knee. There was an awkward silence as the Sergeant helped himself to more invisible moonshine. "You don't like to talk about it, do ya boy?"

"No. I don't," Pete scoffed, bringing the metal cup up to his mouth and playing along. It seemed to please the Sergeant.

"How did *you* go?" asked Pete.

"Shot in the back. By my one of my own men. We was in the Battle of Sharpsburg, Maryland back in '62 and all hell broke loose. Was outnumbered close to two to one. Thousands of troops met their demise that day. Bloodiest single day battle in the war they say," Sergeant Wagner recalled. "We fell back to a choke point, and we were giving them blue bellies a run for it. Might've been outnumbered, but we was givin' 'em hell. We put a charge together to take their right flank as they advanced. They hit us just when we started our charge. Soldiers all around me were droppin' like sacks of rocks. Saw a guy next me get hit with a minié ball. Blew his head clean off. I dropped into a hole to take cover and put a new charge together. Here come some blue bellies trying a flanking maneuver and I knew we'd be done fer if they took the high ground. So, I stood up to help secure the flank just as one of my men fired on 'em. Problem was, the soldier who fired that shot was right behind me. I was dead instantly. My body dropped like a sack a' potatoes, but the funny thing was I was still standing there. Seeing all the chaos. Dirt exploding all around me from artillery shells. Dead horses everywhere. The smoke didn't burn my eyes anymore. Bullet zinged right through my body and I didn't feel nothin'. All I could do is stand over my body, lying there in a heap. Then I saw other spirits like me. Ran to 'em. One of 'em drew a sword and we charged . . . We've been fighting them blue bloods ever since."

The Sergeant pointed at a red stain on his uniform and opened his coat to show his wound.

I really do wish this cup was full of real moonshine, Pete thought again.

"Wasn't how I was supposed to go. I was fine with dyin' in battle. Just not like that. Shot in the back like a goldarn traitor. How is my family supposed to remember me? If I died a hero's death, they'd still be talking about how proud they was to this very day. But no, none of them even remember me anymore," said the Sergeant.

"Friendly fire was common in the Civil War?" asked Pete.

"Why do you say that?" the Sergeant grumbled and stirred.

"Stonewall Jackson. Wasn't he accidentally shot by his own men?" *Anyone who's ever read history about the Civil War knows that*, Pete thought.

"Don't you say that name! Stonewall Jackson was the finest General to serve in the war! A darn blasted picket shot him in the arm when he rode through camp! Horrible way to go for such a great man. Some say Confederacy never recovered after he died, but I know it's true!"

"Is Stonewall Jackson leading the soldiers you're here with?" asked Pete.

"Nah, all the Generals left when they had the chance. General Lee died in '70 at his home. Heart failure or somethin'. He had enough—they say he went to the afterlife the first chance he got. Never looked back, I suppose. Lee, Longstreet, Pickett, Jackson—all of 'em. It was like their war was over when they passed. Same with the Yankees. Meade, Hancock, Chamberlain. None of 'em stayed behind. Not like us. All the same, if you ask me. We serve under General Hickman—he's a man who will never abandon the cause."

Pete pondered the moment. They were talking about men he had read about in history books as if they were contemporaries. The Sergeant paused to take a sip before wiping his beard with his uniform sleeve and spitting.

"Like I said, I was killed in Sharpsburg, but many of us spirits stayed with our regiments—fightin' for the cause. Gettysburg. Never saw fighting like that. They had the drop on us, those blue bloods." He stared into the distance, his eyes turning darker than the night. "Had the high ground, they did. They got the high ground first and we was scattered out over a mile. Lee ordered charges and that's what we did. We charged, all right. The first day of real fightin' Longstreet's men charged on the right. Ended up in some godforsaken terrain. Man can't fight and climb rocks at the same blasted time! All of us dead spirits killed in earlier battles stayed to fight with the soldiers. We all tried to warn General Lee. We knew it was a mistake going that way. Problem was we couldn't communicate. '*Push around to the right! It's open! Keep pushing around the right flank, and you'll cut 'em off at the knees!*' we'd yell, but they couldn't hear us. The day the fightin' started, we knew it was gonna be a disaster, but didn't stop us from yelling—tryin' anything we could to signal the General to move right. We sure was a frustrated bunch that day when we saw all our men droppin' like sacks of rocks.

"We tried and tried. But Lee was a stubborn man, rest his soul. He knew we had better men. Better fightin' men . . . and we did. We had been whoopin' up on the Federals for some time even though we was outnumbered, but a man can't fight in terrain like that. No, sir." The Sergeant spat and stuck his tongue through his chipped tooth.

"The Devil's Den," Pete recalled.

"That dadburned Devil's Den. I watched wave after wave of our men—good men, many of whom I fight with still to this very day—die trying to take that hill!"

Pete brought his cup to his mouth. Was that something like liquor he tasted?

"We tried hitting them in the center the next day. Longstreet got fresh troops. Good fightin' men—some a the best in the war, I presume. Not them dumfungled soldiers, like the Union Army. General Pickett's men, mostly. They charged that day right up the center. Marched a thousand yards across the valley straight into them Union soldiers firing from the high ground. Bravest, dumbest thing I'd ever seen. Pickett lost a lot of men that day—his field leadership was almost totally wiped out. You ask me, he was never the same after that. None of 'em were."

Wagner looked off into the night with his black beady eyes, like he was searching for something. When he fixed them back on Pete, it was like he found himself again.

"Once the fighting was over, and the living troops moved on, is when we truly seen the devastation this war caused. Townsfolk dug mass gravesites anywhere they could find open dirt between the bodies. Packs of feral dogs tore the rotten flesh right from the corpses. You know what that would be like for a newly hatched spirit to see his body lyin' bakin' in the hot sun for days—blowing up like a balloon, only to have a rabid dog come along and start feeding? It was hell on those boys, I tell ya. Spirit troops on both sides called a ceasefire until the bodies were buried. Us spirits who died earlier in the war consoled the newly hatched spirits, as seeing their bodies strewn across rocks and fields wasn't a pleasant site for their poor eyes. I remember helping a little boy just after he died. I'd never seen such rage as he watched his pa cry over his dead body. He tore off, and I ain't never seen that boy again.

Prolly got sick or some dang thing. . . ."

Pete was embarrassed as his aura began flashing. The Sergeant seemed to not take notice, but Pete knew he was only being courteous.

"But the ceasefire didn't last long. Once the last body was put in the ground, the cannons fired and we started fightin' again. Right there on the battlefield. Spirits like me on both sides fought . . . and we still fight to this day. It's why we stayed behind." They fell silent for a few moments each bringing their cup to their lips. "We ain't never gonna stop fightin'. This is our destiny, Pete. Our *reason*."

They sat silently for a moment, listening to the breeze whisper through the trees almost singing to the valley below. *If he is still fighting the Union army, where are the rest of his soldiers? Does his gun really fire and kill other spirits? Does he run out of ammo?* It didn't make sense to Pete, but he figured he'd keep his attention on portals—as that sort of information might serve him better. If he could find another portal, maybe he could get out of this jam.

Finally, Pete spoke. "But what about the portals? Why didn't you all go through back in Sharpsburg?"

"What in the Sam Hill is a portal?" replied the Sergeant.

"You know," Pete went on, "the big white tunnel or hole that opens after you die."

"Yeah, that happened, but we didn't call 'em no portals," said the Sergeant.

"Well, what did you call them?" asked Pete.

"We didn't call them anything," said the Sergeant.

"Describe it for me," said Pete.

"Describe it?" said Sergeant Wagner. "All right. Well, this big, uh . . . *hole* opened up, and the Confederate and Union troops alike lined up to enter. There was a person at the entrance of that hole helping people get in. Called himself a Gatekeeper or some dang thing. There were so many dang blasted troops lined up, that they was bound to start fighting each other. The Federal troops called us names like Butternut, Greyback, or Reb, and we would call them Yank, Doodle, or Lincoln Boys. It didn't take long 'fore the troops in line lost tempers and the fighting started. The Confederate spirits banded together and began firing on the Union spirits, who drew their swords and charged us.

"Didn't care none that we were dead. We *wanted* to keep fightin'. The portal closed sometime during the fight, and we've been stuck ever since.

Truth be told, it happened again at Gettysburg. Couldn't stop us from getting into it again. Too much life left in us spirits, *heh*. I reckon there's over thirty thousand of us trapped here. Maybe more. Who knows how many actually died. I'd say much more than's stuck here. But us thirty thousand brave, we're the last of our kind. This battle will rage as long as the good earth spins and the golden sun comes up."

Pete lifted the cup to his lips. He wanted to know if Wagner had ever seen the Twins, but he wasn't sure it was safe to ask. For all he knew, saying their names might summon them.

"So you died in Maryland?" asked Pete.

"Yes, sir," said the Sergeant.

"So, why are you in Pennsylvania?" asked Pete.

"There are no borders for us, Pete. We go where the fighting goes. We usually end up at some of the major battlegrounds—Chickamauga, The Wilderness, and of course, Gettysburg—we'll fight there for a while, and then disperse, go our separate ways for a while. Some of the men go back and tend to their farms or what not, but they eventually come back and fight. We'll fight forever."

They fell silent for a few moments and then heard a noise in the distance.

"*Shhh*, quiet—don't make a sound." The Sergeant's demeanor changed. He sprang for cover and raised his rifle. "Stay here."

Sergeant Wagner drew his sword and disappeared into the trees. Pete could faintly hear the sound of horses braying in the distance.

Run for it, Stanton! If there were any time to get away now would be it. *But where would I go?*

This place was crawling with spirit soldiers. He'd probably be recaptured within a day, perhaps by spirits less honorable than Sergeant Wagner.

He watched small pebbles vibrate and bounce in a dry creek bed as the ground shook from nearby cavalry and troop movements.

All of a sudden, the crackling sounds of gunfire rang out.

"Run, Pete!" Sergeant Wagner's voice rang out. "Run! They's a comin' your way!"

THE CONFEDERATE CAMP

PETE HEARD THE HEAVY BREATHING of a horse closing on him. For centuries, men on horseback have been fighting ground troops in battle. The primal sound of pounding hooves and hot, panting breath were the last thing many an infantryman heard just before falling to a cavalry rider's sword. It was about to be the same for Pete, but he dove into a ravine just as two mangled spirit soldiers on horseback emerged from some trees and slowed down to scan the forest undergrowth. His blinking aura was a dead give-away, and it was only a matter of time until the murderous beasts found him.

Do something quickly! Pete urged himself.

He located a small stone and attempted to clutch it—his hand passed through. He could almost feel the hot breath of the horses drawing closer.

Come on Pete! Pick it up! His nervous hand passed through the stone again. The horses glided through the undergrowth and were nearly on top of him. They'd have him dead to rights in seconds.

Pick it up, Pete! He clutched the stone. *Yes!* He flung it in the opposite direction. The horses brayed, and the spirit riders snapped toward the sound of the rock crashing into the underbrush below.

"Over there!" The riders pulled their sabers and lit off, allowing him to slip away.

Close one, Stanton, he thought to himself as he crouched in the vege-tation. He decided to hide until nightfall, so he found a rock formation to hide his aura behind. It was just after sunset that he heard a faint sound.

All was quiet in the valley. He heard a soft breeze rustle the leaves on trees. Birds sang. Squirrels chattered and traipsed across the forest floor. Suddenly, the silence was broken. A gunshot crackled through the under-brush. Then another, piercing the quiet mountainside like a runaway train.

He didn't dare move from his hiding spot, although he worried about Sergeant Wagner. He needed to find him, and quickly—for fear one of those haggard looking riders find him first. He listened, and listened some more, his ears ringing from straining so hard.

But there was no sound of horses or Sergeant Wagner.

He waited until he thought it was safe and ventured toward the direction of the gunshots. Whoever had fired those rounds was likely long gone, but maybe Sergeant Wagner would still be in the area—probably scouting for sign. He traveled through the trees, the forest floor laden with fallen branches, pine needles, and small saplings. He moved to the place where he was sure the gunshots came from. No sign of anyone.

A flicker. Something caught his eye. He glanced at the direction. It happened again. A glimmer—something shiny laying in the grass. He moved closer to inspect, and was startled at what he found.

Sergeant Wagner's rifle!

His aura flashed with worry as his mind filled with thoughts regarding the Sergeant's fate. He looked for signs that he'd been shot—discovering that two rounds had been fired earlier, based off shells littering the grass.

Maybe the riders shot him. Maybe they captured him.

He stayed there for a long while, hoping the Sergeant would make his way back. It was when he heard a horse bray nearby that he knew he needed to leave. The riders were probably still canvasing the area for him.

But what about Sergeant Wagner? And where would he go?

He decided there was only one place he could go. The Confederate's camp. If he showed up with Sergeant Wagner's rifle, perhaps Wagner himself would show up to camp to claim it. It was either that, or venture out on his own and face the Union cavalry riders. . . .

Or worse, the twins. It was sometime in the middle of the night when Pete made it to the camp.

The faint sound of music and laughter filled the valley. The light of campfires dimly lit the encampment, and he could see shadowy spirits moving about.

Pete's white aura and business attire caused immediate alarm. The pickets sounded the alarm and hundreds of growling spirits descended upon him.

"Yankee!"

"Shoot 'em!"

"String a rope!"

The rabid bunch closed in, displaying a violent bloodlust full of gaping teeth and tobacco-stained beards.

He held Sergeant Wagner's rifle up as two cavalry riders moved through the spirits to engage him, each with sabers drawn.

"Name and rank," yelled one of the riders as they approached.

"Pete Stanton, Attorney—Philadelphia," he said.

"Yankee!" one of them yelled.

The other cavalry rider raised his hand and the crowd fell silent. He had a cavernous wound to the midsection and was missing a leg. The horse he rode was missing a front leg all the way up to the shoulder.

Must've been hit by artillery. Horse and all. What a horrible way to go, thought Pete.

"That's Master Sergeant Wagner's long rifle. Where did you get it?" demanded the rider.

"I was with Sergeant Wagner and we were ambushed by Union cavalry. I brought this rifle to camp hoping he would make it here to claim it," said Pete.

"Kill him! Hang him!" The mob went wild. Horrified, Pete realized that it made no difference that Sergeant Wagner was his friend—*they were out for blood.*

The rider again held his hand up and silenced the crowd.

"I'd like to speak with your commanding officer," said Pete. "I have information that would be valuable to him."

The second soldier on horseback rode up to Pete and collected Sergeant Wagner's rifle. "Come with us."

The legless rider wheeled his horse around. "You men all have work to do to break camp! We ride out in the morning!"

Disappointed grumbles followed as the battle-starved crowd began to dissipate.

"Looks like you're a fresh one," said the rider.

"Everyone keeps reminding me of that." Pete's aura flashed wildly as they approached camp. He had not been around this many spirits before—certainly not such a savage lot like this.

Many of them looked to be starving and unkempt; some with mangled or missing extremities, others with open head wounds, and very few others fully intact but with paper thin uniforms draping off their malnourished bodies.

Pete surmised that the men with scraggly beards and straw hats were likely farmers, men who had joined the cause because they believed in preserving their way of life. The soldiers wearing sharp looking grey uniforms were likely officers who had seceded from the Union army—many who had formal military training.

Pete followed the riders deep into camp. Soldiers strummed banjos, played fiddles, and sang around a fire. Some men were cooking while others fought over a bottle. The Confederate flag was raised atop almost every tent. Pete estimated there were about five thousand men encamped here.

"Prisoner!" a rider yelled to a guard as they approached a cabin. A plume of white smoke poured out of the chimney. "Take him to see General Hickman," commanded a rider—a high-ranking officer.

"Aye, sir." A guard saluted.

The guards watched him with a certain impertinence.

I'm never going to make it out of here . . . but what option do I have? It's either face these spirits and hope Wagner returns to collect his rifle, or set off alone again—and risk getting caught by the twins? I'll take my chances here. There is no chance whatsoever this camp measures up to the dread of the twins' lair.

"The General will see you now," said one of the guards. He looked as if he wanted to run his bayonet right through Pete, but something was holding him back.

The rundown cabin looked as if it had once been used as a hunting or fishing lodge where folks stayed when they visited the countryside. The interior was set up as a war room. Maps hung in rows along the cabin walls and a battle station set up on a long table. Several high-ranking officers and a few assistants stood in a circle around the General's desk.

General Hickman looked like any Civil War era General Pete had seen in history books. He was a larger-than-life character and commanded instant respect from his troops. His presence radiated confidence as he gracefully glided through the room, taking roost in an old rocking chair. He lit a cigar and dismissed his aides who were circling like a group of hungry vultures.

Pete wondered if General Hickman might be the highest ranking Confederate officer in the spirit world.

"So, this is the spirit who showed up mysteriously with Sergeant Wagner's rifle?" he pondered. "I'd ask your name and rank, but by the looks of it, you've never donned a uniform."

"That's right. My name is Pete Stanton and I'm from Philadelphia. I died five years ago," he said.

"Pete Stanton from Philadelphia, huh? Well, Mr. Stanton which side are you on?"

"I beg your pardon?" asked Pete.

The General rocked silently, waiting for an answer. He didn't seem like the type to repeat himself.

"Well—um, I'm . . . on *your* side, of course," said Pete.

"That's comforting," said the General. "I'm sure you'll be eager to do your part, then."

"Um . . ."

"Sergeant!" yelled the General.

A soldier appeared.

"Yes, sir!" The Sergeant clicked his boots and stood at attention.

"Look around and see if you can find Pete here a spare uniform," commanded the General.

"Yes, sir," said the Sergeant.

"So, tell me, Mr. Stanton—how did you come into possession of Sergeant Wagner's rifle?" asked the General.

"Sir, me and the Sergeant were traveling together. He found me just north of here and he was bringing me to this camp, when we were ambushed by Union soldiers," said Pete.

"Ambushed, huh? You sure that's what happened?" said the General.

Pete looked at the General for a moment, sensing suspicion.

"Yes, sir," said Pete. "I'm sure of it."

"And how many of these Union troops were there, Mr. Stanton?" said the General.

"Two cavalry and three infantry," said Pete. Technically, that was true. They had been ambushed by Union troops before Pete shot Wagner.

"Two cavalry and three infantry!" said General Hickman. "Sergeant!"

Another Sergeant appeared, gleefully clicking his boots to attention. Ready to serve.

"Yes, sir!"

"Take a party north of here and find these troops and dispatch them," said the General.

"Yes, sir!" The Sergeant left the cabin.

"If there's troops where you say they was, he'll find them," said the General. "And he'll also find out if they killed Wagner. Something's odd about your story. Sergeant Wagner is a decorated officer. He's been fighting these battles for 150 years and never once been captured or killed by roaming

Union troops. You see, that is not his destiny."

Pete stood silent as the General examined his flashing aura. *It's a dead giveaway.*

"Sergeant!" bellowed General Hickman.

A bearded Sergeant appeared—clearly eager to do the General's bidding.

"Take this man. He is a prisoner of war. He is to be contained and put on trial for the death of Sergeant Wagner," said General Hickman.

"What!?" said Pete.

"Come with me," said the Sergeant. The Sergeant and several guards began ushering Pete out.

"Wait!" yelled Pete. They shoved him toward the door—rifles trained on him. "I said, *wait!*"

The General had his back to him signaling the meeting was over.

"Wait! I have information you need to know," said Pete.

"Go on," boomed the General as he inquisitively looked over Pete's attire.

"General, when you died on the battlefield, a portal opened up—and there was someone there to help you gain entry into this portal, correct?" said Pete.

"That's correct, but none of my men entered. We chose to stay behind and fight," said the General.

An applause of battle cries filled the room. The General raised his hand and silenced them.

"Well, I've seen another portal—a different type. A *dark* portal," said Pete.

"Malitae and Malum," the General grumbled.

"You know them?" said Pete.

"They pick off my men when they become sick," said General Hickman. "I imagine they are among the lowest creatures that ever set foot on this green earth."

"And do you know where the sick spirits go? Once they are taken to this portal?" said Pete.

"No one knows that," said the General.

"I do," said Pete.

Gasps filled the room.

"They picked me up with another spirit. They took me to a place so terrible that I cannot put it into words," said Pete.

"What happened to the other spirit? Did you kill him too? You must've done something terrible for them to have captured you," said the General.

"Charlie was alive when I killed him," said Pete.

More gasps and murmurs.

"And just *how* did you kill one of the living?"

Pete could tell the General was skeptical, so he leaned down and picked up a small rock and whipped it against the cabin wall.

"By gracious!" gasped the General. "He can move objects!"

The entire room burst with surprise.

Pete continued, lest he lose his momentum. "They pulled us into the dark portal. Took us to a horrific place. They had to set me free because I wasn't sick—but they kept Charlie."

The General eyed Pete suspiciously. He seemed suddenly unsure if Pete was an asset or a curse.

"You should not have come here. If they captured you before, rest assured they have their sights set on you. Probably want to use your ability to move objects for some treacherous purpose," said the General. He paused and walked up to one of his maps. "They've been picking my men off for years. Do you have any thoughts on how to destroy them?"

"Destroy them? You can't destroy them. By the looks of your auras, you're all dangerously close to becoming sick. If that happens, they'll be back—and they'll take you and your men with them!" said Pete.

"That'll be all. Take this spirit to the prisoner quarters until we figure out what to do with him!" ordered the General.

The "prisoner quarters" were nothing but an empty tent, but at least it provided a barrier against the Confederate troops, who were frothing at the mouth to kill anything that didn't wear grey.

Pete could hear scurrying outside as the army broke camp. An occasional spirit passed through Pete's tent and harassed him, but they were quickly summoned back to work by their superior officer, which he was thankful for.

Sometime during the night, Pete was visited by one of General Hickman's assistants.

"That was quite a story you told earlier," said the soldier. He was a husky fella. More well-fed than most—even the Generals. He had a slash across his neck that held Pete's attention even though he knew he shouldn't look. His long curly hair seemed to bounce with every movement.

"I'm Jerald," the solider went on. "One of General Hickman's assistants." He puffed his chest out, proud to be working directly for the General. Pete knew the type. Conniving sort. Would sell his soul to the devil himself for a piece of information that would further his own position. "That was some story you told back there."

"It was only the truth," said Pete.

"No one doubts it was," said Jerald.

"Then why am I being held as a prisoner?" said Pete.

"Because you are valuable. You've certainly frightened the General. I've never seen him like this. After you left, he scolded his staff for a good thirty minutes. He's not the yelling type."

"It wasn't my intent to upset him," said Pete.

"You'll be marching with us tomorrow. The General wants to bring you along. He thinks you may be able to help us if The Others show up."

Pete nodded, intrigued at the possibility of seeing a Civil War era march and possibly being part of something. It made him feel more purposeful—like he had *meaning*—a feeling of purpose returning for the first time since he had left that gas station.

A feeling a lot like a *reason*.

Jerald looked him over as if he were wondering what sort of information he might extract from him.

"The General is a brilliant man. Trust him," said Jerald. "If you need anything—just ask for me."

All night, Pete heard commotion around the campsite. There was the clanking of a saber as soldiers passed; the braying of a horse and pounding hooves as the cavalry assembled; the squeaking sound of a rusty truss as a wagon passed; the grunting and hooves slipping as a horse pulled a cannon. Men yelled and cracked whips encouraging the horses to pull. Pete didn't dare peek outside. Officers barked orders to the infantry. At daybreak, he could still hear the sounds, but they seemed distant. He was actually relieved when Jerald popped into his tent.

"Be ready to march in two hours," he commanded.

"Where are we going?" asked Pete.

"The General ordered the entire regiment to mobilize. Joining up with another troop regiment to make us over ten thousand troops strong."

"Where's that?" said Pete.

"The General thinks we must be somewhere near Carlisle. He thinks there's another regiment south of here stationed outside Chambersburg."

"Chambersburg?" said Pete. "Didn't the Confederate army burn Chambersburg to the ground during the war?"

"That's correct," said Jerald. "I can imagine if there are any spirits in Chambersburg, they likely won't bother us. They'll be afraid and hide when we march through."

"Maybe I should just go my own way," said Pete. "I don't belong here."

"You of all people belong here. You just don't know it yet. See you in the morning."

Just before dawn, Pete was ordered from his tent. He saw quite a different camp when he emerged. The entire unit was broken down and gone. It was like no spirits had ever been there. No footprints, no wagon trails, no horse tracks. Even the campfires were completely gone.

An officer with a booming voice gave the order to march and the entire regiment lurched forward, slithering through the forest. The regiment lined up, four abreast. Grumbling could be heard as this was considered a heavy-march, where soldiers were required to carry their own heavy packs. During the war, these would be sixty to seventy pound packs, and malnourished troops lacking water marching with a heavy pack often succumbed to the heat of the day—some straggling behind the regiment and others getting left behind entirely.

Some of those men don't even have boots on, Pete thought. It shouldn't have even mattered, except it seemed to matter to them.

The coordinated march of five thousand soldiers under heavy packs appeared methodic in its entirety, but Pete began to notice how benign the march could become. Quartermasters riding on both sides of infantry spurned soldiers along. The march was highly organized as soldiers were in step for the first mile, when Pete noticed the pace slowed.

"Fall in line, soldier!" a Quartermaster would bellow as an infantryman fell behind. Some infantry broke off from the march entirely looking for water or walking the creek beds in search of food.

"Marches always start out grand and end up paltry," said Jerald. He seemed disheartened as he watched the men fall out of line. "Habits. These men are running on pure instinct and habits," he said.

He took off his hat and cursed at the sky.

"Don't you men know you're dead? You don't need to fill up your blasted canteens!"

Jerald tore off after the soldiers aiding the Quartermasters in patching the infantry lines back together.

Pete took his place in formation in the rear next to a wagon train.

Despite the indiscriminate infantry, the regiment pitched a light camp outside of Chambersburg after just a two day march.

Pete was ordered to stay with General Hickman who didn't acknowledge his presence. This didn't bother Pete, who tried his best to stay out of the way. The General's tent was constantly buzzing with aids, Lieutenants, and Sergeants. Everywhere he turned, Pete was in danger of being trampled by a horse or in the way of infantry.

He was relieved when Jerald rode up.

"Get ready. We're breaking camp," he said.

"Already? We just got here," said Pete.

"General sent scouts ahead. They must've found something," said Jerald.

The regiment had made their way around Chambersburg with no incident and would camp on the southern outskirts. In the morning, General Hickman would send scouts to the area where he thought a second Confederate regiment was stationed.

"Word is we are joining a Confederate regiment commanded by a General P.F. Ward. They're over 4,800 strong mostly made up of 1st Texas Infantry and volunteer regiments from Georgia are joining. Texans and Georgians—good fighting men. 4,800 in total, which would put our troop total close to ten thousand if combined. We'll be marching again soon. Around Chambersburg of course—there may be Union loyalists there. We don't want them to alert their troops," said Jerald.

THE SPIRIT TROOPS ASSEMBLE

THERE WAS SOMETHING PRIMAL ABOUT the battle cries that erupted when the two armies converged. It would've been enough to send chills shooting through his living body.

"The General will meet General Ward and his leadership to discuss chain of command," Jerald was saying. He seemed to think he and Pete were some kind of friends, or else he just got bored talking to the same old people for over a century. "There's a lot of details to work out when merging like this. Even though we are on the same side logistics and planning must be detailed. You see, armies of this magnitude rarely happen. Our troops aren't used to fighting alongside theirs. It can be a recipe for disaster when you introduce new troops to soldiers used to fighting with each other. Soldiers who have bled together want to fight together. The merging of these armies must be handled delicately."

They watched the Generals meet in a clearing.

Whooping and hollering from celebratory soldiers on both sides filled the mountainside. Jerald leaned in toward Pete.

"General Hickman is the commander of the Northern Virginia Army—a designation that long ago belonged to Robert E. Lee. It was a sad day for the south when we learned General Lee chose to pass through the great tunnel. We sure could've used him in a time like this—but General Hickman and General Ward are highly capable," said Jerald. "I'm assuming our General will assume full control of the armies. At least I hope so for our men's sake."

Pete thought for a moment about his place.

"Jerald, can I ask you something?" said Pete.

"Sure," Jerald seemed overly enthusiastic at the possibility he was going to learn new information. Pete surmised spying for the General was how Jerald was able to gain such good fortune of a horse and three to five hearty meals a day. He'd observed how soldiers clammed up when Jerald was around.

"The cause. Aren't you fighting over slavery?" asked Pete.

"Depends on who you ask, Pete. It's true. Some of these men owned slaves, but many did not. Folks who owned slaves were mostly landholders. The average farmer or tradesman—many who are fighting this war—wouldn't have owned slaves. But the cause is about the U.S. government tellin' us states what to do. We believe the states should be free to have they own rules and govern they selves."

"One of those rules the government was pushing was making slavery illegal in southern states. Is it not? So isn't that truly what the cause is about?"

For the first time since Pete met him, Jerald was lost for words.

"I don't see any black soldiers in all of these soldiers marching . . . didn't the South have black soldiers with them?" Pete continued.

Jerald bowed his head a moment.

"We did a horrible thing, Pete. Even the General would tell you. Putting another man in chains is a terrible blemish we all shamefully carry around. We are here 150 years after the war ended, still fighting for the South. The South we still believe in, but slavery is one piece of our history many of us wish didn't happen," he said solemnly.

"But what about the soldiers? I don't see any black soldiers. I'm sure you brought some with you during the battles," said Pete.

"Aye, many a black soldier fought and died bravely in the war. I wish I could say they was fighting for our cause voluntarily, but I can't. You don't see any black soldiers here because none of them stayed behind. They fought and died on the battlefield just like me and the rest of this army, but their cause wasn't the same as ours. Every last one of them entered the portal to the afterlife when they were given the chance—or lit off on they own—and who could blame 'em?" Jerald scoffed. "I wish I could say I never owned a slave. It torments me to this day. Now, there's many a troop mixed in here who don't share that same sentiment—but I bet if you asked around most of these folk are ashamed at what they did."

They paused to share the solemn moment. Pete thought about his friend Jerome and the heavy burden of slavery he likely carried around even now—150 years after slavery was abolished. The mark on history some of these men caused was horrific, and while he was here voluntarily, his need for protection kept him there at least momentarily, but still, he felt as out of place as one could be.

"Maybe I shouldn't be here," he said.

"Sometimes we don't realize our destiny until it's revealed to us. But one thing I've learned after all these years is to press into it. You're here with us because that is where you are supposed to be at this very moment. Release your need to resist and things will become more clear," said Jerald.

General Hickman was mighty as he rode back from his meeting with General Ward. Pete could tell Jerald wanted to be the first to know any new plans. It gave him something to gossip about.

Jerald took position in the rear with the General. They spoke for a few moments before the General issued his commands. Jerald seemed to squeal with delight as he learned the new strategy.

"Forward march!" the General's voice thundered.

It didn't take long before Pete heard whispers among the spirit soldiers in the ranks that they would be marching through the night to Gettysburg—a sign Jerald was purging information like an old rusty faucet.

AWAY DOWN SOUTH IN DIXIE!

HALFWAY THROUGH THE NIGHT, JERALD rode next to Pete and confirmed his greatest fears.

"Gettysburg?" yelled Pete. "I can't go to Gettysburg to fight the Union army. I've never even shot a gun! What makes you think I can fight a war with no military training?"

Snarls and grumbles ripped through the spirit soldier ranks.

"Quiet down, Pete. We don't need you causing dissent in the ranks. The men are edgy enough as it is," commanded Jerald.

Pete's wild flashing couldn't hide his tumultuous feelings. He turned away from Jerald and watched the marching army. The regiment snarled and snaked through the trees moving as if it were a single being. General Hickman's army had doubled in size, and with well-trained soldiers under what was formerly General Lee's Northern Virginia Army, they were now poised to take on the Union troops stationed at Gettysburg.

This wasn't the first time these soldiers had fought in a lopsided battle. Fredericksburg saw over 77,000 Confederates take on 122,000 Union soldiers in a decisive victory. The battle of Antietam—a decisive Confederate victory and one of the bloodiest campaigns in U.S. history—saw just 38,000 Confederates up against 87,000 Union soldiers. The Confederates had well-trained soldiers, used an attacking style, and their soldiers were radicalized believing in their cause. Many Union soldiers were enlisted via the draft, or even worse—brought to the front straight from foreign enlistment—making communication in training, and on the battlefield, a challenge.

The actual battle of Gettysburg happened on July 1–3 in the year 1863. The union army was commanded by General George G. Meade and General John F. Reynolds, who combined led a total of 93,321 troops. Robert E. Lee led the Confederate army totaling 71,699 troops. The actual battle saw the Union troops in defensive positions using the rugged landscape and high ground in defensive positions with the Confederates using their signature "rebel charge"—sending waves of attacks from the northern and western flanking positions.

Outnumbered and on the offensive, the Confederate spirit troops now faced similar conditions.

After what must have been hours of rhythmic marching, General Hickman ordered a halt and sent scouts ahead.

Pete saw an opportunity to speak with the General now that the regiment had halted.

"General, may I have a word?" he asked.

"Make it quick."

"Sir, I don't belong here. Maybe I should just excuse myself?"

The General looked at him perplexed. "Fall in line soldier."

"But I'm *not* a soldier—"

"Everyone is a soldier of something. They just don't know it until they find it inside. Now fall in line," he barked.

The scouts returned with a dire message. There were over twenty thousand troops stationed at Gettysburg—all Union. They were, once again, grossly outnumbered.

Pete listened to General Hickman probing the scouts.

"Any idea who's leading them?"

"Sir, it appears General Arlington is in command."

"Arlington. Just as I suspected."

Pete didn't know it but General Hickman and General Arlington had been adversaries for over a century. Time and time again, they had clashed in a duel of spirit troops.

"We've been outnumbered before, but our men just want it more," he said. "The Union army has greater numbers, better equipment, and better training, but Confederate army has something they don't—bravery and resolve. I'll take bravery and resolve over equipment and training any day."

Night fell on the camp and Pete fell into a trance as he watched the flames dance around burning logs.

"What you thinkin' about?" The voice jolted him from his daze. *Jerald.*

"Nothing," said Pete.

"A man starin' into the flames like you was has somethin' on his mind," said Jerald.

"I was thinking about my wife, Jessica," said Pete.

"How'd she die?" asked Jerald.

"Die? She's still alive. She lives in Philadelphia," said Pete.

"Oh, sorry about that. Habit I guess. All of our wives have long been gone. Rare to talk to a man who has a living relative let alone a living wife," said Jerald.

Pete stood and shook his head, as if cleansing himself from his thoughts of Jessica.

"That's right. Shake it off. Cuz you gonna need a clear head tomorrow," said Jerald.

"Why's that?" said Pete.

"See that road over there? We gonna march up that road. Four men by four men. One step at a time. We gonna march. General Ward wants to go to the right. Keep pushing past. Attack quick and hit 'em hard, but move fast to capture Washington. Says it's the key to victory. Hickman says his job is to catch the Federals and draw 'em into the open. He wants a fight."

Jerald stood, entering his own trance. Pete watched the flames dance in the reflections of his eyes.

"Gonna be a lot of men dead tomorrow," said Jerald as his dark beady eyes stared into the fire.

Nearby a band flared up. Banjos. Fiddles. A snare drum tapped but slightly off rhythm. A soldier produced a bottle and passed it around.

"Think they have any idea?" asked Pete.

"In some ways, we all know we're going to fight. When them cannons roar and the bullets start zinging by, none of us think we're gonna die. If you do, you shouldn't be on that battlefield. The second you think you's gonna die is the second you's gonna die. Make any sense?"

"I suppose," said Pete.

"I mean, I seen it time and time again. The moment a man gives up is the moment when he goes out. It's the fearless, most savage ones who live through battle. The ones who run into the fire."

"A lot has been written about the momentum of battle," said Pete.

"Momentum? I don't know . . . it's a simple as you kill more troops then they kill of yours. In our case, we have to kill twice as many because we're outnumbered . . . and our boys—our shoeless, starving, outnumbered boys— put a whoopin' on those Federal troops through the entire war," said Jerald.

"That's the goal tomorrow?" asked Pete.

"It's always the goal, but I don't know if we'll achieve it if'n we get to the bottom of that hill and Hickman sends us into that godforsaken Devil's Den."

Jerald turned to mount his horse.

"Guess we'll know tomorrow," he said.

The burly man mounted the horse that never could have carried him were he alive.

"I'd tell ya to get some sleep, but . . . Well, you know," said Jerald.

"I know," said Pete.

"Take care of yourself, Pete. Come find me in the morning. I don't want you to get caught up in the march. The middle of a march is no place for a newly hatched spirit."

Pete couldn't help but feel himself warming to the jolly man as he trotted away.

MARCH INTO GETTYSBURG

"MOVE 'EM OUT!" BARKED THE General.

The line of soldiers snaked through the trees for miles. Pete looked ahead and saw a sea of grey uniforms twisting around land formations. They were about an hour into the march when he noticed something just as Jerald rode up.

"What's going on with the men?" asked Pete.

"Dixiephobia," said Jerald.

"Dixiephobia?" asked Pete. *Did he just make that up?*

Spirits were flashing wildly in anticipation of battle. They trembled in terror and their auras dimmed to a dangerous darkness.

"So many troops experience this strange reaction whenever we approach a battle. It's like they can almost feel their bodies lurching from bullet holes," said Jerald.

"Dixiephobia, you call it?" asked Pete.

"Heh, yeah," Jerald chuckled through crooked, yellow teeth. "Some guys started callin' it that and it just kinda stuck."

"Dixiephobia. Huh," said Pete.

"This route brings back terrible memories for many troops who fell here," said Jerald. "All these men were killed in battle. I suppose revisiting war does somethin' to a man."

Suddenly, General Hickman appeared and the spirits encircled him.

"The General is about to address the troops. Let's go have a listen," said Jerald.

The General started his speech just as they came within earshot.

"Brave men of the Confederate army, we know the Union has numbers, but we have resolve. We have a mission. We have courage, and we have bravery. I would put these traits up against any defending army the world has ever produced."

The troops erupted into cheers.

The General raised his hand prompting the men to quiet down.

"Many of us may not make it through the battle. We will leave behind loved ones, farms, and other physical possessions. But what these men cannot take from us is our cause. Our cause is an idea, and an ideas don't die with bodies. They live on in spirit," said the General.

The soldiers erupted again, black powder smoke filling the valley as bearded men gleefully fired their guns. Bugles sounded and banjos sprang to life.

"You all have made great sacrifices to be here. Let us honor those sacrifices on the battlefield. Take this time before battle to remember loved ones. Ready weapons—but most of all, prepare your hearts and minds, as this battle will sap every last ounce of courage from your bodies," said General Hickman.

The crowd remained quiet.

"Thank you for your service and your commitment. We attack in four hours," said General Hickman.

A sporadic cough could be heard from the restful crowd.

The General began to sing.

"Oh, I wish I was in the land of cotton, Old times there are not forgotten . . ."

The General paused, and the regiment joined him:.

"Look away, look away, look away Dixie Land!
In Dixie's Land, where I was born in, Early on one frosty mornin'.
Look away, look away, look away Dixie Land!
I wish I was in Dixie, Hooray! Hooray!
In Dixie's Land I'll take my stand, to live and die in Dixie.
Away, away, away down south in Dixie!
Away, away, away down south in Dixie!"

PART FOUR
JOE MORTON
BEGINNING OF THE END

THE BASEMENT OF THE BRAUHAUS—A dark and dreary place—was lit brightly by the beaming blue light from the energy field that had brought Keryx to this place.

Joe watched Keryx—the mighty Spartan warrior—engage with Josh. The thought of Josh being the catalyst to *Doomsday* was almost too much for him to bear.

"Just how do you plan to protect my grandson?" asked Joe. "He's just a boy, and I'm afraid the three of us are no match for Malitae and Malum."

"No way," Pinkie agreed.

"What is it you want for the boy?" asked Keryx.

"I'd like for him to have some sense of a normal life."

"Yeah, I mean we love the kid and all. But think about it from his point of view. His three best friends are ghosts. How's he supposed to live like that? Nobody in the living world understands him," said Cunningham.

"Can we show Melissa? Maybe then she'd understand me!" Josh grew excited as he spoke.

"Show me *what*, exactly?" Melissa asked him.

"I'm asking them to show themselves to you so you can see them," he whispered.

"Really? This is so bizarre," she said.

"If you want him to be able to blend in, he'll need someone to help him. Understand him," said Joe. "Melissa is his friend and would be a good candidate."

"What you're asking . . . I'm afraid I cannot grant her these powers. It could be very dangerous for her. It would put her at risk of being found by The Others," said Keryx.

"We're not asking you to make her a Bridge. Just allow us to show ourselves to her so she believes," said Joe.

They watched Josh tend to Melissa, trying to explain what was happening.

"She's retreating. This is all too much for her to take in," said Joe solemnly. "It is important for Josh to have one of the living understand him in the world he lives. His abilities. That way he doesn't seem like a societal castaway."

"We already see it," boomed Cunningham. "Kids at his school think he's different. We've tried our best to help him along but it's not the same."

"You've done a masterful job mentoring him," said Keryx. "But you're right . . . he needs one of the living to understand him." They looked on as Keryx traveled over to Josh. His presence was mighty. He was powerful, yet carried himself lightly—almost delicate by nature.

"I need her to see," said Josh. "I need someone to see what I see—if only for a minute—a few seconds, even. Long enough so that she can understand me."

They glanced at Melissa, who looked on with discernment.

"Joshua. What you are asking . . . What you are asking has serious implications and could upset the order of things. I sympathize with you, but we must be careful at all costs."

"What do you mean?" asked Josh.

"We have agreements in place with The Others. Just my being here with you could be perceived as manipulation of a Bridge—which in our world, there are strict rules against," explained Keryx.

"I don't understand," said Josh.

"There are rules in our world. These scrolls represent a treaty between us and The Others. Violations of our treaty can result in serious consequences. If I were to grant Melissa this ability, even for a few moments, it could be looked upon as manipulating Freewill. Altering the course of her own destiny."

"I wish I was never born with this curse!" said Josh.

"If you only knew how important your gifts truly are. I am under strict orders not to escalate the situation with The Others any further, but I understand you need someone like Melissa here to understand you."

"The Others have been playing havoc with us spirit types for years!" Cunningham boomed.

"Yes, the escalation occurring on behalf of The Others is calling for drastic measures. It was reported that Malitae and Malum captured a healthy spirit and took him to Level 1—a direct violation of our treaty," said Keryx.

"See?" said Pinkie.

Keryx turned back to Josh towering over him. "Is this what you really want?"

This was all a lot for a boy to take in—even if his grandson had grown up seeing spirits, he'd never seen one quite as impressive as Keryx. He sensed that should Josh have had an aura, it would have been flashing with nervous energy.

"Bring her here . . . And Josh, if I grant this request, I must ask you do something for me. Of course, it is your choice on whether or not to execute the request, but I will ask nonetheless," Keryx said.

"Anything," Josh replied.

"Josh—are you sure? You do not even know what it is that he wants," said Joe.

Cunningham brushed passed them barreling toward Keryx. "No offense, big guy, but we just met ya. Around here we don't just let spirits ask our boy any old favors without vetting it through us first."

"Yeah! You go through us first!" said Pinkie, who then quickly ducked for cover behind Cunningham.

"Come on guys," Josh said as he approached Joe, Pinkie, and Cunningham. Joe looked into his eyes and saw his desperation. "Grandpa, I need this. I need Melissa to see this. I've gone my entire life with no one who understands me. I trust her."

"Grandson." Joe's aura was flashing wildly. The grey area between protecting Josh and sequestering the boy's independence was uncomfortable and his grip on the situation was slipping with every passing second. "We tried our best to protect you and give you a normal life."

"You did, Grandpa. I wouldn't have made it this far without you . . . but I need something more now."

"Whatever happens next . . . whatever Keryx is proposing will likely change your life forever—and we don't even know what it is yet."

"Joe, there was bound to come a time where the kid was ready to fly the coop," said Cunningham gently. "But know that whatever mission this guy's sent ya on kid, we'll be right there with ya!"

"I'm afraid that's not possible," said Keryx.

"What do you mean not possible?" said Joe. "I've been with Josh since he was born. If I don't go, Josh doesn't go."

"I'm afraid it's far too dangerous and I cannot risk putting healthy spirits in harm's way," said Keryx, prompting grumbles from Cunningham and Pinkie.

"All the more reason for us to go!" challenged Pinkie bravely.

"I need Josh to go. His grandfather, I can make an exception for—because the boy will need a guide."

"Where are we going?" demanded Joe.

"Gettysburg," said Keryx.

THE DECISION

"GETTYSBURG?" CUNNINGHAM GROWLED.

"There are thousands of spirit soldiers still fighting what was your Civil War. Young Josh here is going to help convince them to lay down their weapons and enter the afterlife," said Keryx.

"What's so significant about these spirits that you want to collect these soldiers?" asked Joe.

"That information will be revealed in time . . . but right now, Josh is asking for one of the living to see what he sees. If he agrees to take this mission, I will grant him that wish," said Keryx.

"Yeah, we just met him and all of a sudden we are hitching our wagons and headed to Gettysburg? Are we really supposed to trust this guy? No offense, Mr. Keryx," Pinkie said.

"None taken."

Pinkie, Cunningham, and Joe looked at each other with concern.

"I'd feel a lot better if we was there," said Cunningham.

"Well? He's your grandson. What'cha think, Joe?" asked Pinkie.

Joe was still for a moment, pondering his decision. "I think we've taken Josh as far as we're able. It's only a matter of time before he falls into the dangerous hands of The Others if he stays under our protection. I don't see how we have any choice but to align with Keryx."

"Thank you, Grandpa!" Josh exclaimed.

"Something tells me we just made the most important decision of your young life, boy," said Joe.

THE REVEALING

"BRING HER TO ME," KERYX commanded. "We must be very careful. She wasn't born with these gifts like you, and to simply imprint them upon her could cause her great fear and stress."

"I understand," Josh said, frowning slightly.

"But tell me, Josh, does she have any deceased loved ones she was close to?"

"Her grandmother—she calls her Granny."

"Tell her to close her eyes. Tell her to keep them closed until you tell her to open them again."

In the moment, Joe warmed to Melissa. While he was keen on protecting Josh at all costs, he caught sight of the young girl trying her best to support Josh while nervously following Josh's role in all this, even though there was no way should could understand or comprehend.

"Unconditional love. That's the type of love Kathy and I had. Josh is lucky to have her," he said to himself before snapping his attention to Josh as the boy relayed Keryx's instructions.

"Melissa, I need you to trust me," he said. "He's going to let you see what I see. Just for a moment. Don't be afraid."

"You mean, see ghosts?" she asked. Joe noticed a slight tremble in her voice.

"No, not really. You'll see. Close your eyes."

"Okay, but hold my hand," said Melissa swiftly taking Josh's hand in hers.

They looked on as Keryx removed a crystal from his pouch, holding it up to the light—inspecting it before placing it into the beaming blue light of the energy field. The LADO spirit representatives hardly containing themselves, crowding closer, watching as Keryx closed his eyes and concentrated, waving his hands to unlock the pathway. Suddenly, a shadowy figure appeared within the energy field.

"Granny?" said Keryx. "Is that you?"

"Yes?" her voice filling the room. "Whom do I have the pleasure of speaking with?"

"Wait! I recognize that voice," gasped Melissa.

"Keep your eyes closed," said Josh.

"Dorothy Jean Scott? Do you have a Granddaughter named Melissa?" asked Keryx.

"That's correct. What is this about?" she said.

"My name is Keryx."

"I know who you are."

"Ms. Scott, we need your help."

"What kind of help? Who are all these people? I can't make any of them out through this haze," she said.

Keryx nodded to Josh, signaling it was time to show Melissa. "You can open your eyes now," Josh said softly, gently releasing her hand.

They looked on as Melissa's eyes widened. "Grandma? Granny Dorothy—is that you!?"

"Melissa? Darling? Is that you? Come closer so I can see," she said.

Melissa slowly approached the energy field.

"Just a couple rules," Keryx commanded. "Do *not* under any circumstances let her touch the energy field. She can talk to her grandmother, but please, do not try to pass through the energy field."

"Why? What would happen?" Josh asked.

"You don't want to know. It has the potential to disrupt the order of things if one of the living were to enter. It wouldn't be good for Melissa, either. She surely wouldn't live through it."

"Look at you, darling! Look at the woman you've become!" said Dorothy. To the spirits, she remained a blurry figure—hard to make out through the energy field, but they could sense her presence.

"Awe, thanks, Granny," said Melissa. "I think about you all the time."

Joe softened as he saw a pool of watery tears form in her eyes. He looked on and felt some regret as she ran toward her grandmother. While a touching moment it was, he couldn't stop thinking about how this may change Josh's life. *This girl better be the one for him.* It was a lot of pressure to put on such a young couple, which is why he didn't say it aloud.

"I miss you so much, Granny."

"I think about you, too. I wish I could've been around more to watch you grow up—but seeing you here . . . now . . . it's a gift that I will always cherish."

"Me too," said Melissa.

"How is your mother? I miss her."

"She's well. She'd want to see you." Melissa's voice cracked as she answered, prompting an empathetic gasp from other spirits in the room while Joe looked on, wondering what Josh's future looked like now.

"Please tell her I love her and I'm with you both . . . always," she said.

"Josh, I'm afraid time is running out, and we need to ask Melissa to say goodbye to her grandmother," said Keryx.

The goodbyes were emotional for everyone. "I'll always be with you," she said. "You've made me very proud. Goodbye, Melissa. I love you."

"Goodbye, Granny," she said, clutching and squeezing Josh's hand—another tear trickling down her face as she watched her grandmother turn.

With that, they watched as the shadowy figure faded within the energy field. She was gone. The spirits crowded around Josh as he comforted Melissa, who cried on his shoulder.

"Thank you," she exclaimed as more tears trailed down her cheek, one stopping at the bottom of her chin for a moment before falling onto the dusty floor. "Thank you so much!"

THE PLAN

"KERYX, WHAT'S NEXT?" ASKED JOE.

"I need to discuss Josh's mission," said Keryx.

"What kinda mission are we talking about?" said Cunningham.

"Spirit retrieval, of course."

"Spirit retrieval?" scoffed Joe.

"All around your world are pockets of battle trained spirits—those who perished fighting in war. These spirits are of special significance, as they could help us amass a great army in preparation for the Great War. The Others have taken particular advantage of our treaty and have been collecting these soldier spirits—tipping the scale into their favor. Before you summoned me, I was monitoring a dire situation at a place you call Gettysburg, where there are over thirty thousand spirits who are converging on the battlefield. They are spirit soldiers still fighting your Civil War," Keryx explained.

"What does that have to do with my grandson?" snapped Joe.

"For over 150 years, these spirits have been marching the hills of Pennsylvania and have continued to fight your Civil War. It has been their *reason* for staying behind. The situation there is bleak. Many of these spirits are on the verge of becoming sick. We think The Others have positioned themselves there to capture these spirits. That many spirits with battle experience could have significant impact should the Great War occur. We need them on our side. That's where Josh comes in. His job is to help convince these spirits to lay down their weapons and enter the portal."

"Why can't you just march an army down there and stop them?" asked Cunningham.

"I'm under strict orders not to be involved. My mere presence could have serious implications. Any act of aggression toward The Others from me would be a direct violation of the treaty and bring us close to the Great War."

"Speak plainly. What is it that you're asking?" said Pinkie.

"We need Josh to intervene. Convince the spirits to lay down their weapons on their own—and enter our portal. It's the only way we can offer these soldier spirits safe passage."

"I'll do it!" said Josh.

Joe felt his aura dim and his eyes narrow as they met Keryx's fond smile for Josh after he'd accepted the mission without hesitation. For Joe, it was as if any control he had over the path Josh would take to adulthood had vaporized, like trying to hold dry sand in a gust of wind.

"Josh—I will not be able to help. It's strongly against the rules, but don't worry . . . you're going to need a guardian," Joe's aura brightening at the thought he would be the one chosen for guardianship. "I have someone you should meet," Keryx continued.

Suddenly, a bright orb exploded out of the beaming blue light of the beacon, tearing through the room before it finally stopped—hovering in front of the group.

The orb expanded in size radiating a light so brilliant, it would've knocked Joe over had he been alive. It was a good thing Josh was leaning against a support beam. Out of the light, a shadowy figure appeared—the orb disappearing as it took human shape. A large figure stepped out of the light. Upon closer look, Joe saw the figure resembled a medieval knight. He first noticed the bucket helm—a metallic helmet polished to a point where it reflected light. The helmet had been riveted together and had a slit for eyesight. A gold, cross bracing ran the length of the helmet dividing the eye slot. Chain mail armor comprised of small interlocked iron rings hugged the knight's muscular body. A dark brown mantle draped across his chest, hanging just below his waist. A crimson red cross stitched across the mantle sat perfectly across the knight's chest and midsection. A leather sword belt clasped just above his waist and a sheathed longsword hung at his side. Joe could tell it was a single hand sword of medium length. Most likely double-edged tapering to a point that could pierce armor plates he may encounter in battle. He carried a metallic shield bearing a red cross in his off hand and was strapping his shield to his back armor as he stepped out of the portal—making carrying the shield easier in non-battle situations—and also afforded rear protection from projectiles, such as arrows.

"Sorry to startle everyone. Their entrance can be quite dramatic," said Keryx as the spirits came out of their hiding spots. "This is Edvarard of Badlock. He is what we call a Guardian and will be assigned to Josh as his protector. Wherever Josh goes, Edvarard will follow. Guardians like Edvarard here are most powerful and extremely territorial—so do be selective in who comes near Josh. Should an unwelcome spirit—say someone like one of The Others draw near, uninvited—well, Edvarard has permission to ruin their day."

They continued to gasp at the size of the knight. Even Cunningham and Pinkie were speechless, for once.

"How many like him are there?" asked Joe, marveling at the size of the knight. Edvarard towered over them like an unwavering shadowy building.

"Let's just say we have enough Edvarards in our world keep the balance of power in check," said Keryx. He turned to Josh and focused intently upon him. "Joshua, can I trust you to complete your mission?"

To Joe, Keryx either sensed his reservations of involving Josh in his plan and was just indifferent—or he just ignored his concerns altogether. Either way, Joe did not approve, nor did he like how he was being minimized. It made no difference as he watched Keryx gain confirmation from his grandson and put his trust in Josh before saying his goodbyes and reentering the energy field. It seemed the fate of thirty thousand spirit soldiers was now in Josh's hands. His only hope was that his grandson was not in harm's way.

"I'm a big guy, but look at the size of that monster!" bellowed Cunningham as Edvarard followed them home, his triangle-shaped shield clasped to his back.

"I think I can take him!" said Pinkie, cowering behind Cunningham.

"I wish we had this guy back when we was fightin' with O'Banion's cronies," said Cunningham.

"Ya got that right!" chuckled Pinkie.

"I'm sure glad he's on our side," added Cunningham.

"I just thought of something! We're heroes! We're pallin' around with a Templar Knight," exclaimed Pinkie. "Boy, my mom would be so proud of me. She always said I'd amount to nothin'! Look at us now, Cunningham!"

Joe didn't feel the same sentiment—his duties as Josh's guardian being replaced. "Guys! Let's focus! We need a plan," he said.

"*Sheesh*. What's gotten into *him*?" Pinkie's attempt at whispering didn't amuse Joe. "Okay, okay, let's get a plan together."

PLAN IN MOTION

EDVARARD STAYING WITH JOSH AS he slept, allowed the three heroes to devise a plan. They spent many tormented nights in the Morton's attic debating, pacing, pondering deep in thought on how they could get Josh to Gettysburg.

"I got it!" Pinkie finally exclaimed. His shrill screech would've been enough to rustle any curious spirit listening within a few block radius.

"Quiet down, ya nitwit!" yelled Cunningham. "We don't need to draw the attention of any stragglers."

"What ya got, Pink?" asked Joe.

"Josh's dad—what's his name again?" said Pinkie.

"You mean my son?" Joe asked.

"Bill!" snapped Cunningham.

"Yeah! Bill! He's a baseball fan, right?"

"He loves baseball," said Joe.

"Well, me and the big fella were over at the Wagner's place watching their TV the other day and we saw the Cubs are playing the Pirates in Pittsburgh this road stand," said Pinkie.

"My word, I think you figured it out!" Joe proclaimed. "Wait . . . Cunningham, what are you doing?"

Cunningham moved with the grace of a bull oxen—lumbering his husky body back and forth. He even ended up outside the house when he attempted a spin move and barreled through the walls.

"What do you call that—a *dance*?" asked Pinkie.

Joe and Josh immediately saw how beautiful a plan it was. Bill was not only a baseball fan, but he was equally interested in history. Specifically milestone battles of the American Civil War. They decided Josh would ask Bill if they could take a short weekend getaway—starting with a stopover in Pittsburgh for a Pirates game vs. the Cubs. Then they could drive over to see Gettysburg the next day before flying back to Chicago.

"Genius!" Joe exclaimed.

They verified the schedule and the Pirates played the Cubs in Pittsburgh in two weeks—plenty of time to plan, assuming they could get Bill onboard.

They laboriously worked with Josh over the next couple days—Edvarard in tow, his dark brown cloak swaying gracefully with his every movement—coaching Josh on how to approach Bill. They went through every possible scenario.

"So . . . what are you gonna say if your dad asks you why you want to go to Gettysburg all of a sudden?" quizzed Pinkie.

"I have to write a paper for my history class and it would be easier to write if I saw Gettysburg firsthand," Josh replied.

The trio cheered in celebration—once again, Cunningham's antics landed him outside. They laughed at his yelp as he discovered his folly and clamored back to the safety of the attic.

It was time to present the idea to Bill.

"You'll do great, Josh. Go on ahead. We'll be right here," said Joe.

They stood watch—gently cheering him on as Josh presented his plan.

"That's a great idea, son!" Bill yelled before Josh could even finish asking.

"That was easy. All that rehearsing for nothin'," Pinkie sighed.

"*Shhh* . . . We aren't out of the woods yet," exclaimed Joe.

"Do you mind if Melissa comes?" asked Josh apprehensively. He kept glancing over their way for reassurance.

"Sit up straight, son! Forget about Edvarard. Look your father in the eyes!" commanded Joe.

The knight with his head gear, metal chain mail, and tunic draped over his chest—not to mention his longsword hanging at his side—clashed with the cherry cabinets and granite countertops of the Morton's kitchen. Joe could only imagine how Josh felt with that presence lurking over him in this crucial moment.

"Concentrate, son. You're doing great." While Joe's coaching seemed to be helping, it was Sarah who ultimately came to his rescue.

"Why don't we make it a family trip? I'll go with and keep Melissa company," she intervened.

"Really?" asked Bill.

"What? Is it bad I'd like to get to know the girl who has my little boy's attention?"

"No! Not the cheeks!" bellowed Cunningham as Sarah leaned in to give her son a kiss.

". . . and she's messing his hair," said Pinkie.

"That's a great idea! Pittsburgh for a ballgame and Gettysburg the next day. We'll leave next Friday and I'll be back home in time for work on Monday morning!" said Bill.

Josh stood up to leave the table.

"Son . . ." said Bill.

"Yeah, Dad?" said Josh.

"You know . . . your grandfather would *love* that we're going on this trip," said Bill.

Joe locked on Josh's eyes. He didn't need to look at his body or his hands to know his aura was starting to flash.

"I know he would, Dad. Something tells me he'll be there with us," said Josh.

Joe watched as Bill paused for a moment—seemingly in deep thought.

"Yeah, you're right. I miss him every day. Thanks for coming up with this idea, son. It will be a nice tribute to your grandfather," said Bill.

And so it was set. They were headed to Gettysburg where a fourteen-year-old boy was supposed to convince thirty thousand bloodthirsty spirits still fighting the Civil War to lay down their weapons and enter the portal to the afterlife . . . and if he didn't succeed, a Great War could break out to end all humanity.

GOODBYES

"WELL, THIS IS REALLY IT," said Joe. His aura began to flash.

"Don't do that! Don't you *dare* do that!" said Pinkie, whose aura also flickered.

"I just want you to know how grateful I am. Josh and I—we couldn't have done it without you."

"I wish you could go with us," said Josh.

"Us too," said Cunningham.

"Yeah! Us too!" said Pinkie.

"You know, something just dawned on me. When I was living, I don't think I had friends like you two. Today, we are no longer friends. We're family," said Joe.

"You two are like the uncles I never had," said Josh. A tear streamed down his cheek.

"That might be the nicest thing anyone has ever said to me," said Pinkie.

Cunningham grunted in confirmation, too choked up to speak. He and Pinkie and began flashing in unison like two fireflies blinking on a hot summer night.

"Awe, don't flash guys," said Josh.

"We'll be all right. We're just worried about you, that's all," said Cunningham.

"We shouldn't be worried—I mean look at that giant tuna can he has protecting him," said Pinkie.

Edvarad took a big, threatening step forward. His helmet eerily steady atop his body, but the chain mail slithered across his body with every movement.

"I'm sorry! I'm sorry! I'm sorry!" Pinkie yelled as he retreated behind Cunningham.

"Don't worry, Joe. We have plenty to do back here. We've been made ambassadors to LADO worldwide," said Cunningham.

"You know—that whole finding a Bridge thing really pumped up our

263

member status. We have big meetings coming up," said Pinkie as he re-emerged from behind Cunningham.

"We'll be back before you know it," said Josh.

"Just remember to be smart, kid. Look out for yourself," said Cunningham. His aura was flashing wildly.

"I'll only be gone a couple days!" said Josh.

"We'll see you when we get back," said Joe.

"Now go save the world, kid!" said Pinkie. "We're counting on ya!"

"We're proud of ya, kid!" Cunningham bellowed as they left, his *reason* drifting away along with his friend Joe trailed by their new Guardian.

THE JOURNEY

ASIDE FROM A BIT OF turbulence over Lake Erie, the plane ride from Chicago to Pittsburgh was relatively uneventful. They boarded a plane at the Midway International Airport on Chicago's south side. Bill spent several minutes of the drive there—with much eye rolling and scoffing from Sarah—explaining to Melissa how Midway was superior to O'Hare in terms of both cost and convenience.

Joe and Edvarard were on the lookout for spirits, but saw very few at the airport. Only one spirit family—the dad dressed in cargo shorts, a bright Hawaiian shirt, and white tennis shoes—came too close for Edvarard's liking. They tried to get a photo with the large knight, and it didn't end well for the dad. Joe didn't think he would attempt such a foolhardy move again. Josh did an amazing job ignoring them completely.

As they flew to Pittsburgh, Joe wondered why more spirits didn't fly. Spirits could travel via orb, but flying just made him feel more human.

It was a rough landing coming into Pittsburgh International Airport. People shouted and cursed as they were lurched about, and overhead compartments popped open and spilled backpacks and stuffed animals into the aisle.

"Pilot must be former Navy," Bill announced to anyone who would listen. "Naval pilots are trained to land on short runways of aircraft carriers, so they take a sharper angle when landing—even though there's plenty of runway here."

"Glad you know so much about aviation, honey," Sarah scoffed as she picked up her things.

The Pittsburgh International airport looked like any other airplane terminal, aside from the Tyrannosaurus Rex skeleton that towered over the escalator to baggage claim. Joe was sure glad that thing's spirit wasn't lurking close enough to chase him around. *What if that thing has a spirit?* He didn't want to give Edvarard too much credit, so a quick glance over showing the knight was standing "at ease" with his longsword sheathed helped Joe let his guard down.

Bill rambled on to the group about the history of the Pittsburgh Steelers' steel curtain defenses of the 1970s.

"Mean Joe Greene, Jack Lambert, Jack Ham—sure they were good and all, but I'd put the 1985 Bears defense up against any team," he continued—loud enough to garner a snarling look from each passerby.

"Now you know why people who live in other cities think Chicagoans are offensive," Sarah flashed him an eye roll.

"What did I do?" asked Bill, dropping his bags while holding out his arms as the group sped up to put distance in between them.

Meanwhile, Melissa was talking to Josh about how long she'd been a Cubs fan. Bill caught up and it didn't seem to bother him that no one was listening to him. He just kept on talking.

The trams were crowded with recently arrived travelers headed to baggage claim. Joe looked on as Bill would glance up and make eye contact with a passenger who seemed to be slightly interested in what he had to say, which encouraged him to talk even louder—only to have the passenger immediately regret starting a conversation with him.

Downtown Pittsburgh was much smaller than Chicago, but it had a lot of character. The city was built on the shores of three different rivers converging.

"The City of Bridges!" Bill exclaimed. "Four hundred and forty-six bridges, in fact—the most of any city in the U.S."

"Bill, honey—I think the kids have had enough Pittsburgh trivia for one day," Sarah advised.

The yellow paint on the bridges gave a warm welcome as they came into downtown. Pittsburgh is known for being a blue collar town and had a long history of heavy manufacturing, coal mines, and steel mills. Many of the steel mills along the river had been redeveloped into shopping malls, bars, restaurants, and hotels. A far cry from the days when Andrew Carnegie and Henry Fick ruled the city.

They finally made it to their hotel to check in, which was walking distance to PNC Park—home of the Pittsburgh Pirates. "Let's just drop our bags and go. We don't have much time," said Bill.

Being at a baseball game should've been a fun experience, but it made Joe miss Pinkie and Cunningham. Going to Cubs games at Wrigley Field was their thing back home and it seemed sacrilegious to attend a game without them.

Fans poured into the game and settled into their seats as someone belted the National Anthem.

"Show some respect and take off your hat," barked Joe to his grandson. Josh reluctantly complied.

"Good job, honey," said Sarah. "Bill, looks like your son is finally starting to learn some respect."

Joe shook his head as Josh flashed him a smirk. "I guess having your old grandpa around has its perks after all," he whispered.

The club-level seats offered a tremendous view of the entire city, and they had access to a private area with bars and pool tables inside. Because the first few innings were uneventful, Josh and Melissa excused themselves to the club area to play pool after the fourth inning.

Joe stayed with Bill and Sarah. He wanted to watch the game, and didn't feel he needed to duplicate efforts with Edvarard guarding Josh now. He felt a bit displaced, he could relax and watch the game without needing to guard his grandson.

"Are we just going to let them go off on their own?" asked Sarah.

"They're fine! Take a load off," said Bill.

Joe watched as they settled in and drank a couple stadium beers.

The game remained scoreless, and Joe decided to go see what Josh and Melissa were up to. The stadium club was crowded with revelers drinking beer, eating hotdogs, and shooting pool. It made him wish he could eat one last stadium dog and smell the ballpark once more.

He began flashing wildly when he couldn't locate Josh.

"Where in the world is Edvarard?" he said. "Josh!?" he yelled. Then again. And again. It was no use. His voice was instantly drowned by the sea of fans.

THE PORTALS IN THE SKY

"WHAT ARE YOU SO WORRIED about, Grandpa?" asked Josh.

Joe was livid. "Where were you, young man? Do you understand how dangerous it is to go wandering about alone? You are to have someone with you at *all times*. Either me or Edvarard—do you understand?"

"But we're at a baseball game having fun. What can they do?"

"Don't forget we're on a mission," Joe snapped.

"Why are you so serious, Grandpa? Nobody is going to mess with me with Edvarard around," said Josh.

"And where, exactly, is he?" Joe asked. It finally dawned on Josh that Edvarard wasn't there, and he grew instantly concerned. "C'mon, let's go find the big tin can. He better have a good explanation for leaving you two."

"What's wrong? Where are you going?" asked Melissa. She still had a pool cue in her hand.

Joe watched as Josh turned around to address his girlfriend. She dropped the pool cue on the table. "Something is happening, isn't it?"

Josh nodded.

"Okay. I'm with you. Let's go," she said.

They walked out of the Stadium Club and searched for Edvarard. They noticed a number of spirits moving around the ballpark—Josh using his evasive maneuvers so not to attract attention to himself.

They finally caught up with Edvarard. "There he is!" yelled Josh.

"What's he looking at?" asked Joe.

PNC Park is positioned adjacent to the Allegheny River, and the Stadium Club offered a view over the river and of downtown Pittsburgh. Edvarard must've sensed their presence as he raised his arm and pointed at something out over the river.

Joe moved in to get a closer look over the river, and to his amazement, a portal opened up. Out stepped a spirit who held a large spear. He raised it high in the air where a bolt of lightning came down and struck where he stood. It was a truly awesome display of supernatural power. He stepped back into the portal, which closed behind him.

"A Gatekeeper!" Joe exclaimed. "All this time we've been searching for another portal to the afterlife."

Edvarard was silent.

"Are there others like him?" asked Joe.

Edvarard nodded and pointed out over the river again.

Joe was shocked to see multiple different portals open up.

"There must be fifty or sixty of them!" said Joe.

Each one had a warrior Gatekeeper that stepped out. A couple resembled knights like Edvarard, others resembled Native American braves or African tribal warriors—in short, there were warriors from all regions and times up to the present. Portals were lined up, snaking down the river—hovering over the water as far as the eye could see.

"Something is happening," said Joe.

Edvarard's large barrel helm nodded in acknowledgement.

"These Gatekeepers. Are they following us to Gettysburg?" asked Joe, which prompted another nod from Edvarard.

Joe and Josh stood by marveling at the spirits.

"What are we looking at?" Melissa perked up.

"If you had any idea, you wouldn't be standing here," said Josh.

GETTING JOSH TO GETTYSBURG

"YOU KNOW SHE CAN'T GO with us. It's far too dangerous," said Joe.

Josh sat awake in his hotel room, Bill fast asleep in the other queen bed. "I need Melissa there. She understands me," he whispered.

"No way," said Joe.

Edvarard moved forward and halfway unsheathed his giant sword.

"Fine, I'll tell her she can't come with us," said Josh—prompting Edvarard to sheath his sword and take his usual sentry position.

The next morning Bill and Josh joined Sarah and Melissa for breakfast in the hotel lobby. Joe and Edvarard trailed behind.

"You know, I have never been to Gettysburg before. I'm excited to go," proclaimed Bill.

"Do it," said Joe.

"Fine," whispered Josh loud enough to draw his Sarah's attention.

"Honey, are you okay?" asked Sarah.

Josh straightened up in his chair.

"You know, I was thinking. Would you mind if Dad and I just went to Gettysburg? I thought I'd spend some alone time with him," he said.

Joe watched as Bill quickly shoved a forkful of eggs into his mouth.

"Well, that seems like a good idea," said Sarah. "Me and Melissa here can spend the day in Pittsburgh, maybe catch an art museum or two, while you two go on your history tour. What do you think about that, honey?"

"That sounds like a great idea," said Bill, pieces of scrambled eggs falling from his mouth.

Sarah rolled her eyes at Bill and turned to Melissa. "You know, I hear great things about the Andy Warhol museum."

"Great job, Josh!" said Joe.

After breakfast, they checked out and went their separate ways.

GETTYSBURG

TO THE NAYSAYERS, THE DRIVE to Gettysburg was uneventful, but for Josh, it was anything but. He found himself constantly distracted between the two orbs flying outside the front passenger window—each orb racing the other, apparently jockeying for better position to watch over him—and his father's awkward attempts to bond.

"So, uh . . . This morning at breakfast . . . you said you wanted to spend more time with me, huh?"

"You know, Josh, I've been thinking . . . you're going to be in high school soon. Now's probably a good time to talk about the birds and the bees."

Then he said something that resonated with him: "You know son, you never met your grandpa, but he would be proud of you. Proud that you asked me to go to a baseball game. I'm glad you did that. We should do that more often."

"Sure thing, Dad. Let's go when we get back home to Chicago," he said.

"Deal," said Bill settling into the driver's seat with a proud smile on his face.

They rode silently until they arrived. "Here we are! Gettysburg National Park," Bill announced.

It was a scorching hot day outside. The sun beat down unlike anything Josh had experienced before—the tour guide pointing out that soldiers on both sides had to hike mile after mile on hot days like this one. "I've never seen anything like this place," said Bill admiring the vast battlefield below Seminary Ridge. The heat of the mid-afternoon didn't seem to slow Bill down one bit.

"I'm getting tired," Josh whispered to Joe. "It's hot out here. When are the spirits supposed to show up?"

"I'd guess it will be pretty obvious when they do," Joe replied.

Josh inspected Edvarard for any signal there may be other spirits present. Surely he would know, but there was no real change in his stiff demeanor. He was silently watchful, as usual, which to Joe only seemed to irritate

Josh further. He could tell the boy missed his friends back home, but he couldn't worry about that in the moment—they were on a mission and he needed to focus on the task at hand.

They watched Bill stop and pick something up from the grounds.

"Look at this! A real life musket ball! I look at this and wonder who fired it. Was it some Union soldier firing upon a Confederate charge? Or maybe it came from a Confederate sharp shooter?" pondered Bill.

The guide stopped the tour to address him. "Sir, while you will find artifacts readily available, we ask that you not remove any items from the battlefields."

The rest of the tour attendees murmured to themselves, which Bill assumed to be about him. "Well sooorry!" he shot back. "Can you believe these people?" he said to Josh.

"Dad, you're not talking very quietly. They can all hear you," said Josh.

"Hey, it's getting late in the day, what do ya say we go grab ourselves a burger and head back to the hotel and call your Mom?" said Bill.

"Great idea!" said Josh.

"But we're leaving without seeing a single spirit," said Joe.

Suddenly, Edvarard tensed up. He did something neither Josh nor Joe had seen him do before—he brought his shield up to a defensive position while fully unsheathing his sword.

Joe saw them first. Marching silently in the trees was an entire division of Confederate spirit soldiers. They were close enough to see their tattered uniforms and black beady eyes focused on the valley below. Not one of them broke formation, or even so much as looked their way—their trancelike glares all focused on the valley.

They watched as Bill walked toward the car. Edvarard motioned to follow.

"It mustn't be time just yet," said Joe.

JOSH RETURNS TO THE BATTLEFIELD

WHILE JOSH ENJOYED HIS BURGER and getting out of the hot sun, he couldn't take his mind off those soldiers.

"I'm going to the bathroom," said Bill. "I'll be right back."

Josh waited for Bill to get out of sight before turning to Joe and Edvarard.

"Did you see that? All those soldiers marching? Tell me I wasn't seeing things!" he said.

"No, you saw them alright. Plain as day. There were hundreds of them marching through the trees," said Joe.

Edvarard remained silent, guarding their position.

"We need to go back," said Josh.

"I don't know," said Joe.

Edvarard moved forward, halfway unsheathing his sword.

"Okay, we're going back," said Joe. "But tonight—after your father falls asleep."

The ride back to the hotel was uneventful. Even Bill was quiet after the long hot day, until they arrived.

"The Baldaberry Inn! We can almost see the battlefields from here!" he announced as Josh got his bag from the trunk. "Keep your eyes peeled for ghosts. They say this place is haunted. Supposedly they turned the hotel into some sort of makeshift hospital during the war—the doctors performed amputations in there."

"That's probably true, but Edvarard doesn't seem too worried. If there are any Confederate spirits living at this hotel, they could be in that group we saw marching earlier," said Joe.

Josh hastily crawled into bed, pretending to fall asleep while Bill did his nightly bedtime routine. He came out of the bathroom after he finished brushing his teeth.

"You know, I can't believe that many soldiers fought at Gettysburg! Over 175,000 troops. Can you believe it?" Bill's voice pierced the hotel room until he saw Josh lying in bed.

"Oh, I'm sorry, son. I didn't realize you were asleep," he whispered as he pulled the covers onto Josh. "You know, I probably don't say this very often, but I love you, Josh. I'm very proud of the man you're becoming."

He leaned down and kissed Josh on his forehead before retiring in his bed.

If Bill were able to see Joe, he would have seen his aura flashing wildly as he watched the emotional exchange. It was one of those times where Joe was glad he stayed behind.

Joe gave the signal as soon as he was sure Bill had fallen asleep. Josh flung the covers off and jumped up, fully dressed. They quietly slithered out of the room and headed for the battlefields.

THE BATTLE BEGINS

THE AIR SEEMED CRISP AS they moved swiftly through the brisk evening. It was one of those nights Joe wished he could have the sense of touch back. He missed the cool air causing goosebumps on his skin. It made him think about how good it felt when a shiver would trickle down his spine when he held his wife's hand.

They didn't speak, for he was fearful their voices may rustle up a band of spirit soldiers. Even though Edvarard was there, he felt it was better to be safe than swarmed by some renegade spirit army.

They let Edvarard lead, as he not only knew where to meet the portals, but he also offered a mound of protection they were desperately looking for. It took over an hour for them to get to Cemetery Hill. During the war, Cemetery Hill was a staging area for the Union, which provided a hidden spot for artillery fire to commence the attack. Formerly known as Raffensperger's Hill, after the farmer who owned the land, the name was changed after the battle when a unit of Union troops made an encampment on the hill and were in charge of collecting weapons and keeping looters away from the fallen. The Union troops commissioned the pregnant wife of the Evergreen Cemetery caretaker, and other town's people to dig 105 graves for soldiers who had fallen around Cemetery Hill.

It is said there were so many casualties and the bodies were so rapidly decomposing, that many of the dead were placed in shallow mass graves. The bodies were later exhumed and placed in a proper resting place. There are likely bodies still buried near Cemetery Hill or around other areas of heavy fighting on the Gettysburg battlefield.

Edvarard led them atop of Cemetery Hill overlooking the valley below, pausing frequently to allow Josh to catch up. The valley was over a thousand yards wide and was flat, but it pitched as it met the jagged landscape of the hill. Josh took note of a large monument placed at the hilltop, commemorating the battle. The lonely statue of a General mounted on his horse, but proudly overlooking the battlefield. Josh imagined the stone General destined to stare across the valley night and day for the remainder of its existence.

"What now?" said Joe. "His father is going to worry sick if he wakes up before we get back."

As soon as he muttered the words, they saw a Union regiment snake out of the trees onto the battlefield below. Row after row of infantry moving as if they were one large mass marched into formation. Cavalry riders were positioned on the sides of two different infantry divisions which centered the battlefield. Cannoneers used horses to stage rows of large howitzer cannons behind the cavalry and infantrymen.

None of them moved. Edvarard stood upright, towering over them, and had not unsheathed his sword—decidedly a good sign.

They could cut the anticipation in the air with a dull knife as twenty-thousand union troops formed their lines. Joe noticed bands of bright flashes pulsating through the soldiers' regiment below like bioluminescent algae or plankton gathering in an ocean bay.

Boom!

If Joe was alive, the blast of the Union howitzer would've taken his breath away. It made an ear piercing boom so intense they could see the sound wave created as the cannon sucked the air from the immediate area. He saw Josh grab his chest as he felt the concussion wave hit. Joe could almost remember that feeling.

"Look down below!" said Josh.

Grey lines of Confederate soldiers marched across the valley. "They must be a thousand yards away!" said Joe. Thin bands of rows were strung out over a mile long. Different units carried battle flags representing their states. They could hear snare drums tapping and bugles singing and men roaring as they marched.

Powder smoke billowed from another cannon as it boomed, sending a ball leaping toward the Confederate lines.

Suddenly, men scurried and dove for cover as return fire from Confederate artillery found its aim.

Dirt and flyrock exploded, soaring into the air. Joe saw a dead horse and mangled men as the artillery crashed into the Union lines. The soldiers struggled to return fire as the heavy artillery rained bouncing lead balls. A direct hit on a Union caisson sent soldiers scurrying in all directions. Many shells flew overhead, causing a whistling sound as they cut the air.

"Grandpa!" Josh yelled over the din, "What's going on? Can spirits die?"

"I don't really know, honestly. It sure looks like it, though, and I'm not interested in finding out the hard way. At least only a small number of their cannons are accurate," said Joe. "Otherwise, I don't think we'd make it out of here."

Suddenly, the artillery barrage stopped. *"They're coming!"* a Union soldier on the front yelled, prompting fellow soldiers to sound the alarm.

"Here they come!"

"Get in formation!"

A steady roar off in the distance resembled a train coming—but there was no train. There was only the Confederate army and they were charging. The popping sound of a solitary a rifle fired. Then another. Then hundreds of rifles crackled as the Union infantry reformed their lines behind the cement wall.

"Ceasefire! Save your ammo!" The Union Generals screamed so they could assess the situation. The Rebels had remained just out of range causing the finicky Union soldiers to fire precious ammunition.

Then they heard it: a yell so primal that Josh dove for cover in the fetal position. The scream sent Union soldiers' auras into overdrive.

The Rebel yell.

"The Rebs are gonna charge any second now!"

"We still got the high ground!"

"Look how many of 'em there are!"

The Union soldiers were dug in behind the rock wall. They knew the protection was in their favor, but the Confederates had numbers, were dead-eyes with their aim, and fierce fighters.

"If they breach our wall we're done for!" yelled a soldier, his uniform neat but draping off him.

He's just a boy. Can't be much older than Josh, Joe thought. *What kind of madness is this?*

Joe took cover behind the wall hoping the Union soldiers had enough fight in them to hold off whatever was coming next. His grandson's life depended on it. He looked at Edvarard, standing guard—with his shield on his off arm and his longsword unsheathed. A clash was surely imminent.

ACT III

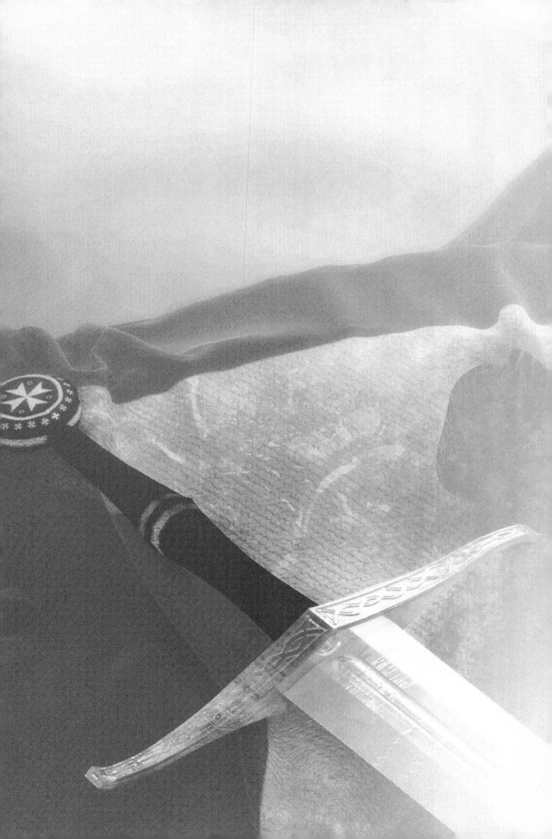

PART FOUR
THE SPIRIT BATTLE
OF GETTYSBURG
THE CONFEDERATE WAVES

THE CONFEDERATES FOUND THEMSELVES IN a precarious position—their army spread over a mile wide. The tree canopy and landscape offered sanctuary from forward observers who may be scouting their positions for artillery fire or to launch an attack, but it caused the soldiers to fan out over a mile with no real ability to form battle formations until they were out in the open.

The valley separating them and the Union forces was over a thousand yards. Pete meandered close enough to hear the General and his advisers arguing about the means and methods of attack.

"The middle is their weakest point."

"Attacking up the middle is suicide! They have the high ground and we have a thousand yards to cover."

"The right is open. We can attack on the right!"

"We can march our army all the way around and avoid them altogether. March all the way to Washington and capture it!"

General Hickman had the final say. "We attack up the center," he said. "We use artillery to hold back their reinforcements and march our army through the middle. Split their army in two. March all the way to Washington."

It was settled. They had their battle plans.

While dissent among the advisers was evident, one thing they all agreed upon was the Union had the high ground, and they weren't moving from that hill. If the Confederates wanted a fight, they could have one—but they would have to attack.

Pete felt a solemn silence come over the Confederate army as they waited their final orders.

Pockets of men sat together, many striking fires and passing a bottle around.

It was just before sunset when regiment leaders on horseback rode through the lines rounding up their soldiers. Grey uniforms lined throughout the trees with their rifles on their shoulders.

Everywhere he looked, men with greasy faces and scraggly beards stood at attention. Rows of dark, beady eyes and gritted teeth centered on the mission at hand—the small blue uniforms hastily moving atop the hill.

Starving men. Tattered uniforms hanging from their bodies. Many shoeless men. Boots broken and worn by the march. The "Confederate Resolve" almost made sense to him.

It would take a man of great courage and determination to fight a war barefoot.

Suddenly, his wandering mind snapped to the General as his voice roared across the valley.

"Forward!" commanded General Hickman.

The defeating sound of a cannon roared sending a lead ball spiraling toward the hilltop. Another cannon fired. Then another.

Pete watched thin lines of Confederate infantry spread across a valley for nearly a mile lurched forward out of the tree line. Music started even though it was largely drowned out by the cannon roars. Soldiers cheered when artillery found its target up on the ridge. Pete could see blue flecks of soldiers' uniforms scurrying for cover as the cannon rounds landed.

"Our artillery is pinning the Federals down while we march through the valley," said Jerald.

"That has to be over a thousand-yard march under heavy fire to reach those Union lines," said Pete.

"We hope our artillery keeps 'em busy long enough to reform the lines and concentrate at the center. If our artillery is accurate, they'll be unable to reinforce the front while our lines approach. The center is their weakest point. We're goin' right up the gut to split their army in two. Then march all the way to Washington," said Jerald.

"If it doesn't?" asked Pete.

Jerald looked off into the distance as if he already knew the outcome.

As quick as the artillery started it fell silent. The sound of Confederate marching songs sprang to life, filling the valley until they were ordered to halt. Bands stopped playing and the Confederates reforming their thin lines into rows in a pinching maneuver toward the center of the battlefield.

That's when Pete heard it—a sound populated with rage, fury, and a core of primordial fear.

"The Rebel yell," said Jerald, proudly taking note of Pete's flashing aura. He shifted in his saddle and tilted his head—scraggly beard hanging straight.

"Don't worry. Your aura ain't flashin' as rapidly as them. Have a look," said Jerald.

All along the ridge, blinking auras of Union soldiers erupted, giving away their positions.

"That Rebel yell got them shakin' in they boots up on that ridge. That's for sure," said Jerald.

A rifle crackled. Then another. Then hundreds, maybe thousands, of Union infantry sent black powder smoke filling the valley. Then the rifles fell silent.

"Scared fire. They can't hit us from that distance. Wastin' all they ammunition," said Jerald.

The Confederate lines remained silent until the smoke whisked through the valley. Not a single soldier had fallen from the eruption of Union fire. The sight of fully intact Confederate lines causing the Union soldiers to flash even more vigorously.

Another Rebel yell. The valley amplified that primal roar as if the echoes themselves had ghosts.

Music flared back up and battle flags blew in the wind.

The charge. Magnificent in nature. Thousands of soldiers fanned out over a mile, coming together for one common cause.

Pete watched them drop. Lines of soldiers sprinting headlong into rifle fire. An entire row of soldiers taken out by Union cannon fire. A soldier down. Another filling the gap in the formation vacated by the dead soldier.

They pressed on. Grey, tattered uniforms. Shoeless. Marching. Being fired upon. Soldiers dropping. Marching forward.

The Rebel yell. Fueled by rage and courage topped off with bewildering fear. Men radicalized by their cause, running into fire, fearing their lives, but these were their orders and they never let their General down.

The Union soldiers did their best to fight off the attacking Confederate army. Reinforcements were slow to arrive due to the earlier cannon fire. The single shot black powder rifles were slow to reload, allowing the grey uniformed infantry to close the gap.

"Our Rebs are approaching the cement wall!" yelled Jerald.

Pete saw a Confederate soldier drop to one knee and shoot. They had specific orders not to stop. Fix bayonets, charge, take one shot, and charge again. Breach the cement wall the Union soldiers were dug in behind. Do not, under any condition, stop. You stop, you die. Charge and you may die, but you have better chances if you keep moving. The attack was designed to capture the momentum. Breach the wall at the center and split the Union army in two.

The soldier Pete watched was a dead aim. He dropped a Union infantryman who peeked over the wall—his arms flailing in the air, dropping his weapon as he fell.

The Confederate soldier knelt among jagged rocks, reloading his musket and recoiling when he was hit in the shoulder. He folded over, still working to reload his weapon. He struggled to raise the heavy rifle when two more minié balls felled him for good.

Pete scoffed as he watched the man fall among the boulders, his twisted body wrapped around jagged rocks.

"That's why we give orders to stay movin'. You drop and shoot—you die. Stay movin' and ya may just have a chance to get your hands on a Federal. Sink a bayonet into 'em," said Jerald unapologetically.

Union canons came to life as new waves of Confederate reinforcements charged into battle. A lead ball bounced across the valley wiping out a column of charging Rebel troops—soliciting a celebratory cry from the Union soldiers up on the ridge.

Horses lay dead, strewn across the battlefield. Confederate soldiers lay among the jagged rocks. Union soldier after soldier fell out of sight behind the cement wall.

Hundreds of Confederate infantry were moving up to the cement wall where the Union soldiers took refuge. "Look! I can't believe it! They might breach the wall!"

THE CHARGE

IF EDVARAD INSPIRED JOE WITH a feeling of safety from the duel unfolding below, just as comforting was the cement wall thirty yards down the ridge behind which rows of Union soldiers rained down bullets on the Confederate army.

The Confederate artillery barrage, while fierce, had been largely inaccurate. Shells flew overhead, landing well behind the Union lines. Had the middle front been reinforced, the shells may have taken out an entire division—but the right and left flanks had been heavily reinforced as General Arlington seemed to anticipate his adversary moving around the army to try and take Washington D.C.

By the looks of how thin the middle part of the army had been reinforced, Joe sensed General Arlington wouldn't have expected an attack straight up the middle—especially with so much open distance between the fronts. But that's exactly where the Confederates attacked. The initial artillery sent blue uniforms running for cover and kept them pinned down long enough for the Rebel army to advance across the valley. Shells whooshed above, crashing into the landscape behind them. A whistle sounded just as a cannon round found its mark sending horse, man, and equipment flying in a jumbled mix of twisted metal, splintered wood, and severed body parts. Shocked soldiers stumbled in no seeming direction, mouths gaping open as they held a severed limb.

"Don't look, son," said Joe, though he himself could hardly look away, fascinated by its gruesomeness but also confused by how any of it could be possible in the spirit world.

It's when the artillery stopped that he really began to panic. He wasn't the only one. Union soldiers began flashing as soon as that horrific sound started.

"The Rebel yell!"

"They gonna charge!"

"Man the wall! Under no condition can they breach that wall!"

A young boy ran past them to the front. Trail-beaten boots. Tattered, sun-bleached uniform hanging from his starving body. Red hair poking out the sides of his blue hat. Buckling with every step under the weight of his pack and rifle. Couldn't have been much older than Josh. A man behind him rushed to the wall carrying the Maine battle flag. Other soldiers hurried to the wall readying their rifles. Trembling. Flashing. Convulsing.

That bloody, screeching yell. Like a freight train was steaming toward them and they were on the tracks.

"Here they come!"

"Fire!"

A shot rang out, sending smoke bursting from the barrel. Then another. Then hundreds of continuous rounds.

A soldier dropped down, sending his blue hat flying. His partner didn't stop reloading and firing to check on him. He didn't have to. He knew his fate. Stop firing and he would likely meet the same.

Soldiers all along the wall dropped. One man—a field commander, likely a Lieutenant, was hit in the hand. He dropped down, his eyes wild in shock, as he surveyed his bloody palm. Joe watched him pull his saber with his other arm, stand up to give an order, and take a minié ball to the head, killing him instantly.

They were closing in—pinching the Union soldiers into the middle. Joe saw a bearded man poke his head over the wall. Grey uniform. Dark, beady eyes. Those radicalized dark eyes. He got a shot off before three Union soldiers fired on him. His beard whipped toward the sky as his head snapped back and he dropped out of sight.

More Confederates approached the wall. Union reinforcements from the flanks converged on the center. It was no use. High ground, double the troops, a wall protecting them—all advantages should have gone to them—but the Union soldiers were giving way to their ferocious opponent.

"Hold the lines!"

"They breached the wall!"

"Fall back!"

Union soldiers fell all around them as grey uniforms poked through the wall. Joe's focus was on protecting Josh should these soldiers find he was a Bridge, but his worries were quickly dispatched when soldiers assembled all around them, mouths gaping, black beady eyes focused on reinforcing the lines in front of them. To the charging soldiers, it seemed as if they were not even there. But one thing was for sure, this many soldiers gathering—it seemed they were at the center of a coming battle.

"Take cover, Josh!" Joe shouted. "They're coming this way!"

Joe looked up at Edvarard—massive broadsword in hand armed with a metal shield in the other—readying himself for a fight.

BLOODLUST

"STAY DOWN!" YELLED JOE. A Union cavalry rider flushed a Confederate sniper from the woods. The sniper howled as he tried desperately to get away. He could see the terror in his eyes and heard the gasp when a rider plunged a sword through his back.

"Grandpa!" Josh cried out as he watched the Confederate soldier lay twitching, holding a gaping wound in his chest.

"Don't look, Josh!" yelled Joe.

Howling sounds pierced the woods as Union cavalry stormed in dispatching the hidden remaining Rebel riflemen. Confederate infantry passed through the cement wall firing single shots and running bayonets through retreating soldiers. Cannons on the right and left flanks erupted, raining fire below onto the still-charging Confederates. A lead ball bounced off the rocky earth and smashed into a line of charging infantry.

All around them battle drums banged, bugles sang, infantry taunted, and horse hooves pounded.

"We have to get out of here!" yelled Joe.

"There's nowhere to go! There are horses all around us!" screamed Josh, hugging a boulder as Edvarard stood guard.

Thousands of spirit soldiers moved across the battlefield like an angry swarm of bees. Union reinforcements emerged from right and left flanks and poured every man, piece of ammunition, and ounce of will into repelling the attack. Confederates piercing the walls were met by crushing blows of Union cavalry swooping in, bringing glancing sabers down on them. Infantry reserves from the right and left flanks converged on the center. What was a neat V-shaped battle formation now a chaotic heap of men.

Few rifles fired. A soldier cracked another in the jaw with the butt of his rifle before swinging the barrel around and plunging the bayonet into another. The stuck soldier sat holding his side, crying out for his ma, as he held his side—his aura rapidly flashing. Red liquid spurted and seeped through his fingers as he held them over his wound. His aura slowed and darkened as he keeled over and hit the ground.

Moaning and gasping sounds of dying infantrymen were drowned out by growling attacking men. Men with dirty, greasy faces and eyes wild with fear, grinding and gritting their teeth. Each fighting while seemingly waiting for a bayonet to be plunged into their back or slashed with a saber. Auras flashing wildly, then dampening as they fell to the ground.

A snarling frothing horse rode limping by—its front leg lost to a cannon shell. Shards of flesh hanging and flapping with every laborious step.

"It's every man for himself!" cried Joe.

Another horse. Screeching. Panting. Hooves pounding the earth. Joe heard it first and turned to see a bearded cavalry rider bearing down. Grey uniform. Eyes—thirsty for blood—rolled in the back of his head. Mouth gaping wide. Sword drawn. Blinded by his thirst for battle. Ready to run his saber through anyone.

"They're all around us! Hide Josh!" yelled Joe. "Find cover!"

He barely uttered the words before a piercing sound zipped overhead, an orb crashing viciously into the jagged ground, unfolding, taking human shape—*Edvarard*. The rivets in his chainmail armor making a clanking sound as he removed the shield strapped to his back, unsheathing his giant broadsword. He held the shield in his off hand, and held the long broadsword—an ornate, double-sided blade which tapered to a sharp point. His cloak draped from his shoulders, making him look even larger than he was.

He seemed to ready himself for the riders to charge. Joe watched as the cavalry soldiers looked at each other in wonder, as if daring the other to charge. One of the riders drew a saber and pointed it at Edvarard. The spirit's horse reared back before pounding its feet into the pebbled soil. The horse spit and bawled as it charged, the rider holding a saber outstretched and ready to plunge through Edvarard if his horse didn't run through him first.

"No!" yelled Josh as he tucked himself behind a boulder trying to get a glimpse of the battle.

"Don't watch, son!" said Joe. "Keep your head down."

Hooves pounded the soil as the rider charged. Joe watched as Edvarard stood his ground, shield held close, sword at the ready. The horse bared its dull teeth as it ran. The mounted soldier leaned forward, mouth agape, readying to run his saber through the knight. Just as the horse was on him, in one motion, Edvarard stepped aside, dodging the horse and the soldier's saber—swinging his giant broadsword through them.

The horse and rider crumbled, pulverized by his sword. Fine dust rained down, blowing in the wind.

Joe watched as Edvarard raised his sword in defiance, daring the second rider to charge. The soldier's horse panted and pounded its front hoof into the ground before the rider steered it away, leaving in a brisk trot.

Joe traveled over to the spot where the rider had been obliterated. A pile of dust, a saddle, and a saber lay in the grass—the only evidence the soldier had ever existed.

"What happened to him? The soldier—he was here just a moment ago, now he's gone. Where did he go?" Joe looked at Edvarard, standing silently over him, his shiny chrome bucket helm and plated armor blocking out the sun.

He knew he would not get his answer—at least not from Edvarard.

THE CONVERGENCE

THE UNION RESERVES ON THE right and left flanks charged in a V-shaped attacking formation, reinforcing the weakened middle where the Confederates had breached. The battle was solely concentrated in the middle. If the Rebel army could break through, they could march all the way to Washington. But breaking through the Union lines was proved difficult with the reinforcements being concentrated to the middle.

"We're losing ground! Send in the reinforcements!" commanded General Hickman.

"Sir, we don't have any more reinforcements," Jerald stated.

"General Ward's troops?" asked the General.

Jerald shook his head in a sobering fashion. "We are *one hundred percent* committed to battle, sir."

Pete watched as the General shot a stoic look toward the ridgetop. He imagined the heaviness that might have weighed on a leader of such a great army—sending so many men and boys to their vicious, bloody deaths.

The remaining commanding Officers drew their swords and spurred their horses forward.

The General looked down at Pete from his great white horse. A cannon roared in the foreground. Men cried out as they fell.

"This is where you have a chance to write your own story," said the General, each wrinkle on his cracked face seeming to tell a tale of war. "The one who can move objects. Your *reason* will soon unfold."

"My *reason* was Jessica," countered Pete. "I can never go back to her."

"Perhaps you have a greater purpose." General Hickman's eyes came to life as he pulled his saber. His horse grunted after spurs dug into its hindquarters.

"Don't go! It's suicide!" yelled Pete.

"Sometimes you have to run into the fire."

Pete heard crinkling leather as the General squeezed the reins bursting forward toward his commanding officers. He looked up at Jerald, General Hickman's portly assistant. Always conniving to gain an edge. Never wavering in the importance of his self-interests.

"Any tricks up your sleeve to get us out of this mess?" Jerald choked.

"I don't think moving objects is going to help us any," said Pete.

"I suppose not," he replied scornfully.

"Don't go, Jerald. You're not a fighter. You'll be killed," he said.

"It's my *reason*, Pete. Like the General said: Yours will be revealed very soon." He pulled his saber and spurred his undersized horse, which strained under the crushing weight atop its back. "Goodbye, Pete Stanton from Philadelphia. I must now join the General."

The horse trotted off toward the General and Pete Stanton was all alone once again.

Jessica.

His loneliness strangely made him think of how he felt when he left her. He began flashing excitedly as he thought of her sitting on their bedroom floor, picking up pieces of the vase he had broken. A feeling of regret came over him as he was ashamed at breaking the vase—a gift he had gotten her. The feelings of shame left, replaced with a strong urge to return to her.

"Jessica!" he yelled just before bursting into an orb and exploding through the woods. He traveled several hundred yards beyond where the main battlefield was located before it struck him. *You can't leave. You have to know what happens to the General.*

Taking human form again, he searched for a vantage point. He heard a commotion in the rocks and prepared himself for a rabid spirit attack.

He moved behind the rocks, just as two figures ran by him. One of them was a spirit wearing khaki pants and a blue polo. He couldn't be quite sure, but the other person looked like a living boy. Both looked out of place—definitely not soldiers.

What was one of the living doing on this battlefield?

Pete stayed hidden behind the boulders as a band of spirit cavalry rode by. *They're going for the boy!* he realized, his aura blinking wildly as he pondered his next move. He was safe here among the boulders; he could turn into an orb and just fly on out of here, be back to his routine with Jessica.

But what about Tim Sampson? She's moved on Pete . . . she's gone . . . and what about the boy? He needs you. Follow him. Maybe he is in danger.

ON THE RUN

"RUN, JOSH!"

They came out of nowhere. Riders emerging from the trees in tattered uniforms, eyes dark as night, converging on them. Edvarard valiantly fought them off, swinging his heavy sword, but there were too many. They split off—running among the jagged boulders of the Devil's Den—the last thing Joe saw was Edvarard bravely swinging a sword, his cloak flapping behind him.

"Keep running, boy!" said Joe. He could almost feel the hot breath of the horses as the cavalry riders trailed them. "Don't look back! Just run!"

Their flight was short lived, as Josh's path became blocked by the twisted, gnarly landscape. They were cornered.

"Try to hide, Josh. I'll distract them." Joe ran back toward the riders and passed through a tree to lead them south and away. But the riders ignored him and barreled toward Josh. With speed he didn't know he was capable of, Joe took an orb shape and darted to his grandson's side.

"Stop! Please! We aren't soldiers!" Joe pleaded as he unfolded, taking human form.

The horses slowed to a brisk walk. The riders approached with gaping mouths and eyes wild in gaze. Patchy, grey uniforms riddled with holes, washed-out pants, and trail-worn boots. The lead rider held his arm up signaling the other riders to stop. A torn sleeve gave way to a nub just above the elbow. He gripped the reins of his spirit horse with his good hand. There was an opening in the horse's chest, a gaping wound where it had been struck by a splintering piece of wood: the cause of its death.

"Please! He's just a boy!" Joe plead.

The lead rider's aura was a sickly black. Deader than dead, it seemed to Joe. Even the rider's sword was etched in battle scars as he raised it preparing to charge.

Joe stood ahead of Josh in an illusion to protect the boy, but he knew he had no powers and the cavalry would mow him down when they charged.

"Grandson—I don't know what's going to happen to me, but don't watch. Remember, they can't hurt you," he said, worried Josh's innocence was being stolen from every terrorizing spirit that moved past, let alone the two horrific spirits atop dead horses. The sight alone seemed to be all Josh could handle and now they were bracing for the charge.

A sudden noise crashed below them through the underbrush. "Sounds like some Rebels on the run!" yelled the lead cavalry rider, spurring his horse giving chase, the other riders following.

From behind a boulder emerged a spirit. He didn't look anything like the spirits on the battlefield. In fact, Joe thought he looked dreadfully out of place—dressed in a sharp-looking business suit, shiny leather shoes. The spirit's aura was bright, like his own—much more full of light and energy than the woeful looking auras the spirit soldiers were carrying around.

"Who are you?" asked Joe.

"My name is Pete Stanton. I'm from Philadelphia. I'm an attorney," he said tossing a rock playfully in his hand.

"You're holding a rock! Carrying it in your hand?" said Joe in disbelief, recalling the difficulty of his own attempts at moving objects before quickly giving up.

"Someone had to bail you guys out. Those spirits looked like they were ready to have their way with you," Pete chuckled.

"That was you? Who made all that noise in the brush? Drawing those riders away from us?" asked Joe.

"Mmhmm," said Pete as he tossed the rock gently to Josh, who caught it.

Joe looked on skeptically as Pete examined his grandson for a moment. "You're alive? One of the living?"

"Yes," said Josh. "I'm alive," after Joe gave him a nod of assurance to speak to the spirit.

"And you can see me? Talk to me?" asked Pete.

"He's a Bridge," said Joe.

"Wow," said Pete, thinking of Jerry—the only Bridge he'd ever met.

They looked up just as Edvarard emerged from the trees, standing at the trailhead with magnificent grandeur. His plated armor and brown tunic with a crimson cross draped across his chest on full display. His sword remained unsheathed—red liquid dripping from it—indicating danger was still near.

"We should move," said Joe. "We should follow Edvarard."

"Who's Edver-er?" said Pete. Then Joe watched him stop, his aura flashing, apparently shocked at the optic of the cloaked knight. "We're following him?"

"You got any better ideas? You could always try and fight these things on your own. Maybe you'll fare better."

Pete took another glance at the grand looking knight. His battle helm glimmered in the sun. "Okay. Yeah. Let's follow him."

DOOMED TO REPEAT ITSELF

THEY MOVED ATOP THE JAGGED boulders, following Edvarard as he guided them safely along a trail. After a short climb, they reached a vantage point where they could observe what was left of the battling spirits below. While they started out behind the Union lines, there were no clear lines anymore. The battle was a singular mass of grey and blue uniforms mixed together, moving through the valley like a roving wave.

Men everywhere—dying. Plunging bayonets. Hand to hand combat. Clawing and fighting to stay alive. A rogue gunshot from a cavalry rider, before foot soldiers pulled him from his horse, to his certain doom.

With so many men committed to battle, it looked to Joe like the battle could be over soon. While they were positioned above the valley, the Southern army was poised to move straight through their position if the few that were left broke through the Union lines.

Joe looked up as Edvarard gave them a silent motion to continue, he thought it best to follow. "Let's move away from here. We need to get to higher ground," said Joe. Travel for him was unwieldy—hovering above the gravel and rocky terrain. For Josh, it was more burdensome.

"Careful, Josh," said Joe. "We don't need you falling and getting injured . . . or worse."

When they climbed an area called Powers Hill, now vacated by the Union command. The landscape offered relative safety, as masses of troops were moving toward Cemetery Hill. They found a secure place behind a boulder that still offered observation of the battlefield and the true scale of death. A wagon blown into splintering pieces by a direct hit from canon. A team of still strapped-in horses lay dead next to it. Mangled bodies twisted among the rocks. Bodies strewn across the valley, so numerous they seemed to cover more ground than the grass.

"Look at all the dead," Joe said aloud but more for himself.

What men were left retreated to Cemetery Hill. Roving pockets of men attacked, fighting to the last man. A sudden flash of movement caught his eye—where he saw a Confederate General atop a white horse and a small group of soldiers surrounded by a band of Union troops with bayonets pointed.

It was General Hickman.

GENERAL'S LAST STAND

PETE WATCHED THE GENERAL, WONDERING if he himself had the courage and strength to lead this many men to their demise.

No, I surely do not.

A great pain went over him as he watched the General attempt to stay atop his horse as the Union soldiers moved in.

The General turned his horse, firing his revolver at charging infantry. The soldiers fell, but there were more. He aimed and fired again. *Click.* He was out of rounds. Jerald—the General's ever trusting, loyal aide—aimed at the infantry and fired.

"He missed!" yelled Pete. He fired again. *He missed again!* Union soldiers stabbed Jerald's horse with their bayonets, flinging him from his saddle. He crashed into the ground with such a thud that his hat flew landing yards away.

"Jerald! No!" yelled Pete. The large soldier attempted to raise himself, but it was no use. His leg was broken. He lifted himself enough to make a feeble attempt to negotiate with his attackers before they plunged a bayonet into his chest. Jerald was dead.

General Hickman crashed his horse into Jerald's attackers, raking his saber across the infantry men—killing them instantly. He had no time to mourn Jerald—charging after other Union soldiers when his horse buckled underneath him. The General and his horse tumbled to the ground where he struck a defensive stance. "They shot my horse! Those sons of bitches shot my horse!"

"No! Not the General!" yelled Pete. He moved to his aid.

"Stop!" yelled Joe. Pete froze. "This is a sacred place. As painful as it is to watch, it is the General's *reason.*"

They looked on as the General clutched his shoulder and staggered to his feet in stubborn defiance.

"The General is the only one left!" said Josh.

"Not the only one," said Pete. "Look there!"

Out of the tree line emerged a lone Union soldier. He melted in and out of the heavy black powder smoke. *General P.F. Arlington.*

"He's walking toward the General!" said Joe.

The Generals met each other and exchanged a handshake. Mutual respect and admiration for old adversaries. General Hickman squirmed in obvious pain as he brought his arm up to a salute. They squared off, standing silently.

"Goodbye, old friend," said General Arlington.

General Hickman became stony-eyed and crazed. With a rapid movement, he ran his saber through General Arlington's abdomen.

Eyes wild in terror, face grimacing behind a perfectly manicured beard, gritting his teeth, General Hickman pulled out the saber and stuck it in the earth beside him. General Arlington took a step back and held his wound with one hand. Reached for his pistol with the other. The shot rang across the quiet valley.

General Hickman fell.

General Arlington went down to one knee. He held himself up with one arm which slowly gave way.

The brave Generals were dead.

A VICIOUS CYCLE

THE VALLEY FELL QUIET. THE black powder smoke dissipated as if the sun were baking off a hazy fog. A gentle breeze the only sound as it brushed against leaves.

"I don't understand," said Josh as he surveyed the battlefield. "Why did Keryx ask us to come here if he knew these spirits would fight each other to the death?"

"Maybe we're too late," said Joe—looking to Edvarard for answers, but none came from the reticent knight.

Pete felt immersed in sorrow as he walked among the dead.

"Why are all the spirit soldiers still glowing if they died?" Pete wondered. "Something doesn't seem right. The fallen shouldn't have an aura, right?"

Edvarard gave another signal that they should move on, prompting Joe to give the order to follow.

"Pete, we should go," said Joe.

Pete ignored the order for a moment, traveling among the dead soldiers when he spotted something oddly familiar.

"I recognize this uniform," he muttered, standing over a body, which was lying face down.

"Pete! Please! We need to leave this place," Joe pleaded.

Crouching down, Pete carefully inspected the patch on the soldier's arm. A familiar insignia—it was a Quartermaster Sergeant's patch. He ran his hand over the soldier's wound. "Shot in the back," he whispered.

The time he and Sergeant Wagner sat sharing empty cups of moonshine, listening to his stories. The Sergeant's voice rang in his head: *"I was shot in the back—by my own men, I might add."*

"I know this man!" yelled Pete.

Joe and Josh moved up to take a closer look.

"This soldier is Sergeant Wagner. He is a great man and the reason I'm here," said Pete.

He continued inspecting the body, running his hand across the back. "But how is he here? I thought he was . . . dead."

"Wait, you said he's the reason you're here?" said Josh.

"Yes!" exclaimed Pete. "We were separated. Spirits on horseback chased us—I thought they killed him."

"Look there—he's still flashing," said Josh, crouching down at Sergeant Wagner's mangled body.

"We must leave here at once!" Joe's aura gave away his excitement as he was trying to pry his uncooperative grandson and Pete from the battlefield. "Josh, we must get you back to your father before he knows you're gone—"

Suddenly, Joe's gaze fell upon Sergeant Wagner. "Wait just a minute, that dead soldier is still *flashing!*" He looked around the valley, and dead soldiers strewn across the battlefield began wildly flashing. "They are *all* flashing."

It was true: thousands of fallen soldiers' auras flashed across the valley like a sky full of fireflies.

Once again, Sergeant Wagner's voice rang in Pete's mind, "*I died in battle from friendly fire. My own men shot me in the back.*"

"Did you die here the same way you died in real life?" Pete spoke softly to the Sergeant's body, his hand floating through the soldier as he tried to gently touch him. "I wish there was some way I could heal him," he added, his aura giving away his sadness.

"Pete, I'm sorry for your friend," said Joe. "I'm afraid we must leave—we must leave this place and get Josh back to his father."

RISE

THEY FLUNG BACKWARDS WHEN IT happened. Had he had a heart, he wondered if it would have been able to withstand such a jolt.

"Did you see that?" said Josh.

"Yeah," said Pete. "I saw it too."

"Impossible," said Joe. "His leg twitched!"

He watched as Pete crouched back down to get another look. *He's much braver than I. A dead spirit soldier who's leg just twitched? No way I'm getting that close,* he thought.

"Maybe it was just a nervous response," said Pete as he moved closer.

Supervising at a safe distance, Joe watched as Pete placed his hand on the back of the body.

"I feel something! It's a strange energy," he said. "Something like a soldier's body, but not really—something strange is at work."

Joe watched cautiously as Pete touched the body again, but this time his hand passed through it—like all the times before.

Suddenly, Sergeant Wagner burst awake and wailed a battle cry, swinging his sword. Joe jumped back and dodged the swinging saber. When he found the courage to look, he saw Josh and Pete standing over the soldier. A moment of shame fell over him for abandoning his grandson, but it did not last long given the strange phenomenon.

Sergeant Wagner sprang to his feet. His gaping mouth and wild eyes poised for a fight.

"Woah!" said Pete. "It's me!"

Joe held his hand up to Edvarard, who was ready to spring and end Sergeant Wagner's very existence. "It's okay Edvarard. Pete knows this soldier."

"Aye, sorry, the Dixiephobia must've got the best of me! The way you's dressed, I thought you was one of them *Yanks*," said Sergeant Wagner.

The trio studied the soldier before Pete stepped forward. "But how are you—"

"—alive?" finished Sergeant Wagner, grinning.

"Yeah, I guess? Something like that?" said Pete.

"Look!" gasped Joe. "There's more of them!"

All through the valley, the dead began rising and surveying the battlefield for their guns, packs, and swords. They were *everywhere*—coming out of the woods, from behind boulders. The soldiers seemingly paid them no attention as they collected their belongings. A horse grunted and brayed as it rose to its feet.

"How is this possible?" asked Pete. "We just saw a gruesome battle. Every spirit on that field died tonight."

"Just like how I *died* when you shot me," the Sergeant clucked. His beard jostling back and forth as he spoke. "I guess you could call it a kind of tradition—a ritual of sorts. We keep coming back to fight the same battles and, mostly, die the same deaths."

"So you got shot in the back," Pete noted.

"Yes, sir. By my own men I might add," said Sergeant Wagner.

"And you all come back here to *die*, the same way you died on the battlefield. Each one of you, like a reenactment of your deaths."

"A remembrance of how we died. Plus, we get to fight the Yanks again, ta'boot!" the Sergeant said cheerfully.

"So the bullets, the smoke billowing from cannons—we saw men plunging each other with sabers," said Pete.

"Here. Take my saber. Run it through my body," said Sergeant Wagner.

"Are you sure?" asked Pete.

"Just do it," said the Sergeant.

They watched as Pete traveled toward the Sergeant, running his saber through him.

"Oh the agony of it all!" the Sergeant playfully chided as Pete's arm passed through him—saber and all.

"Alright, gimme back my saber now before you hurt someone with that thing," said the Sergeant, snatching it from Pete.

"What about the Generals? They didn't really shake hands and kill each other in that manner in the war, did they?" asked Joe.

"No. General Hickman died leading his men into battle. Was shot in the leg. Didn't stop him though. Died from an infection a week later. General Arlington was shot by a sniper."

"Then why did they shake hands and *kill* each other?" asked Joe.

"Sign of respect. They are the last two men to fall every time we fight. Been like that for 150 years," said Sergeant Wagner.

They took a moment to survey the rising spirits collecting their possessions. Packs. Canteens. Rifles. Caps that blew off in the battle.

"Where will you all go?" asked Pete.

"Normally, the spirits would rise—like they are doing now, and the Generals would meet and discuss terms and agree upon the next time we'll get together and fight. They tell us when and where. Sometimes it's here in Gettysburg, other times it's down yonder at Chickamauga, Chancellorsville—we've even fought again at The Wilderness, that blasted place. . . . We usually fight at major battlefields, but Gettysburg is the most common place we come back to. It just holds a special place for us all, I suppose."

". . . and what now?" asked Joe.

"Well, now that you alerted me that the boy here is a Bridge, well. That poses an entirely different set of circumstances. I must take him to see the Generals at once," said Sergeant Wagner.

No sooner did he utter the words through his yellow, tobacco-stained teeth, did Edvarard step forward in all his magnificence unsheathing his sword.

"I think he's losing his patience," said Joe. "I think he wants us to come with him. The meeting with the Generals is going to have to wait."

"How's about you go on ahead with the tin can over there, and I'll alert the Generals of the boy. They'll want to meet him at some point, I'm sure of it," said Sergeant Wagner. With that, he gathered his belongings and traveled away. Joe couldn't help but wonder what changes this would mean for Josh.

"Wait!" yelled Pete. "I'd like to go with you if I can, Sergeant. . . . I was with General Hickman before the battle started, and I'd like to see him off, if that's alright."

The Sergeant watched, Joe taking note of his trail beaten uniform and the holes in his boots.

"That'll be just fine," said Sergeant Wagner. "You come with me, Pete. The rest of y'all better go on with that knight. He seems awfully eager for you to follow. We'll catch up with yas later."

THE PORTALS

AS SOON AS THEY MADE it over the ridge atop Cemetery Hill, it became clear to Joe why Edvarard had been so eager to have them follow. Tucked out of plain sight of the battlefield, bright portals disrupted the landscape—so luminous, he could not look directly into a single portal—a shadowy figure standing at the entrance of each.

"Look past the ridge! There must be several hundred of those things," said Josh.

Their observation didn't last long, as Edvarard motioned them forward. It was slow traveling as Josh slid and slipped in the dewy grass as he ascended the hill. Joe and Edvarard glided up the hill with ease.

The portals seemed much larger as they drew closer, almost as if Joe could walk right inside. His temptation got the best of him as he moved closer. *How amazing! I've been looking for another portal for a long time,* he thought.

"Halt!" a voice rang out behind them. "You cannot enter. I can assure you. You won't be able to enter unless approved."

They whirled around to see a man standing in front of them with a purple tunic and a cloak fluttering in the wind as it draped off his sculpted body. A neatly trimmed beard with short, un-styled hair hanging plainly at the brim of his forehead. *Keryx.*

"I wasn't thinking of entering," said Joe.

"Kathy says hello," replied Keryx, making a point to ignore Joe's comment.

"Kathy? Really? You spoke to her?"

"Of course. She's waiting for you, Joe—but she also understands you have a bit of work to do here yet," said Keryx.

"Work to do?"

"Well, that's why we're here, right?" said Keryx.

"To be honest, I have no idea why we're here. I was hoping you could tell me," scoffed Joe.

"When you look upon the spirits on the battlefield, what do you see?"

Joe glanced at the spirits bunched in the valley below as they rose to collect their belongings. Blue uniforms mixed in with grey uniforms, their dim auras blinking collectively lighting up the valley as they meandered around looking for their belongings that had fallen during battle.

"A bunch of savages," said Joe.

"Well, now. I wasn't expecting that. Anything else?" asked Keryx.

"Their auras . . . they're darker than my grandpa's, like they are fading away," said Josh.

"Smart boy," replied Keryx, unraveling scrolls in his hand that crinkled as he opened them. Joe noticed the paper in the scrolls had a yellowish hue. "This document represents a treaty we signed with The Others many years ago. It outlines the rules of our entire universe. Rules for humanity. Rules for the deceased. This treaty holds together the order of things. When one side violates this treaty, it inches us closer to the Great War. We are closer to conflict with The Others than we've been in centuries. A long time ago, we fought a large and gruesome war. Much damage was done. Species were left extinct. My leadership vowed never again to let that happen and we began anew. The world as you know it—here and now—was born. This treaty was formed as a result. We agreed on a concept of Freewill, that we would not interfere with the living, that the living should be able to use our guidelines set fort—like nature, and karma—and develop their own set of rules and govern themselves. Born from that were rules about the afterlife."

"What do you mean rules of the afterlife?" asked Joe.

"Do you think these portals just exist naturally? We needed somehow to allow spirits to cross over into our world upon their death, only The Others wanted the same thing. Both sides had been collecting spirits, and it turned into a chaotic competition. We agreed, then, that spirits—much like the living—would be able to use Freewill and could choose to enter the afterlife. Should they enter, The Others would be unable to touch them forever. Should a spirit choose to stay, their actions would still be observed. The books would be opened again on Doomsday, where each spirit would be re-judged and considered for reentry. Only we did not account for spirits becoming sick. We didn't have rules for this scenario. The Others had. Their cunning nature prompted them to write in fine print that they would own any spirit that *lost faith*—their words for becoming sick. To this day, they have been collecting every sick spirit and taking them to their lair. That's

why we are here. To prevent The Others from stealing the souls of these soldiers, only we cannot directly intervene, or the consequences will be great.
That's why we need the boy to help. Josh, you mentioned the spirits' auras
are dark. That's correct. There are over thirty thousand spirit soldiers strung
across the valley below. We need to convince them to lay down their weapons
and enter the afterlife before The Others catch on—a rescue mission, of sorts."

"A rescue mission? This sounds dangerous. We did not discuss the terms
of Josh's involvement in such a mission," said Joe.

"Because I knew you would say 'no,'" said Keryx.

"That is manipulation!" cried Joe.

"Perhaps," said Keryx.

"This has nothing to do with my grandson. I forbid him to become
involved," said Joe.

Joe felt like maybe he took it too far as he watched Keryx abruptly close
the scrolls and draw closer. He glanced at Edvarard, who stood at Josh's side,
his massive broadsword sheathed—a good sign.

"You think this has nothing to do with your grandson?" asked Keryx.

"Well, I am failing to understand how," said Joe mildly.

"I could, as you suggest, march down there myself and line up the spirits
and command them into the portal. But you must understand the precedent
that could set. What could unravel from that action. The Others would surely want their take of the spirit soldiers. If we agreed to split them, we would
be forced to draw a new treaty that reads we and The Others would split all
spirits forever going forward instead of giving them Freewill. Do you know
what that means, Joe?"

"I still don't see what that has to do with the boy," said Joe.

"It means one day, when he dies, he has a fifty percent shot at The Others taking him. Your loved ones—Josh's parents? When they die, one would go
with us, one would go with The Others. Josh's children? When they die . . . one
goes with us, one goes with The Others. Do you understand?"

Joe's aura blinked and he sheepishly drooped his shoulders and held his
head low as he weighed the heaviness of the decision. "I had no idea the
importance."

"I must be intentional of my actions, for any decision has a chance to
cause a ripple-effect the likes of which you cannot imagine," said Keryx.
"I know this is a lot to process, but Josh is the last hope these spirits have.
Thirty thousand spirits are about to become sick. Josh is the only one who

can save them while keeping our fragile order intact."

"I'll do it," Josh exclaimed.

Joe looked on with extreme skepticism, but did not dare intervene. The price was too great. The very idea of humanity and afterlife was at risk. While he did not fully embrace Josh being involved, he knew there was something much greater at work that he did not fully understand.

"Okay, son," he said. "But I'm coming with you."

SALUTATIONS

SOLDIERS ON BOTH SIDES SEEMINGLY grew agitated as they awaited the General's decision, causing Pete deliberation on whether another
fight might just break out right here.

"Nothin' to be frightened about. They always bark at each other like that
after a battle," said Sergeant Wagner. "May not seem like it by our tough ex-
terior, but we southerners can be a sensitive bunch and we don't get on very
well with the Union soldiers hemmin' and hawin' at us . . . but we wouldn't
dare attack them again, not without an order from our dear General."

While it reassured Pete, he couldn't help but think all it would take
would be an order from the General for him to be caught in a furious skir-
mish among this haggard-looking lot of battle-hardened spirits.

"Let's just keep moving," he said.

They made their way across the valley, traveling to what was Seminary
Ridge—where the Generals were meeting. A rider approached and stopped
them before they reached the Generals. Pete recognized the soldier—a
large, portly fellow squeezed into a grey uniform so tight it caused gaping
holes showing parts of his hairy belly, where the yarn holding the buttons
stretched beyond the tensile strength. He looked as if he'd topple his small,
grey spotted horse with each belaboring step it took.

"Pete, I'm thankful you made it through the battle."

"Thank you, Jerald," he nodded.

"It may have seemed terrifying but you witnessed something special—
something *ceremonious* today," he said.

"I'm taking it all in," said Pete.

"What's the status of the Generals' meeting? Do they know when we'll
fight next?" asked Sergeant Wagner.

Jerald hung his head, his broad shoulders sinking. "I'm afraid not. The
Generals appear to be discussing a more pressing issue at hand."

"Well, we got a bunch a restless spirits down there ready to go on the offensive if we don't get his settled and go our separate ways very soon," said Sergeant Wagner. "What could be so important that it would take priority over where we's a gonna be fightin' next?"

"We're all getting sick, Sergeant."

"Sick?" gasped the Sergeant. "Come on now, fightin' gives us purpose. It's our *reason.*"

"You're right, but the trauma of reliving our deaths all these years is causing our auras to fade."

"Goldarn dixiephobia," said the Sergeant.

"Plus the cause."

"The *cause?*" stammered Sergeant Wagner.

"Yes, the cause. There's thirty thousand men down there. Staying focused on the cause for all these years has been a miraculous feat . . . being forgotten does something to a man. We ain't got no one living anymore thinkin' about us. Our photos have been taken down off walls. Our uniforms and medals all thrown out, with the exception of a few hangin' in museums around, I suppose."

"I need to talk to the Generals at once. Remind them that our commitment is what emboldens us. Makes us strong again."

"Very well," said Jerald. "I suppose they'd listen to any ideas from their leadership on how to prevent us all from becoming sick."

"I'd like to see the General," said Pete.

"Very well, Sergeant. I'll take you up to meet with the Generals—but Pete, you must wait behind," said Jerald.

"Okay," said Pete watching as the grey-spotted horse buckled when Jerald pulled the reins to turn it. It brayed under stress as it trotted toward the Generals, the wily Sergeant traveling beside.

Pete felt alone again, even though he was among thousands of spirits—but he knew he was not one of them. Very few spirits even acknowledged him as they traveled past. They were focused on their orders: grab their belongings and await the news of when they would fight next. His bright aura, business suit, and shiny black shoes seemed to stick out among a sea of bland-looking auras. While none of the soldiers said it directly, he knew from their stares and sneers that he didn't fit in. He wasn't one of them.

He traveled off a short distance to be alone. He thought of Jessica and questioned why he left her side. He couldn't help but think about Charlie. The twins. None of that would've happened if only he would have stayed with Jessica. He thought about the night she spent with Tim the Lab Technician, and breaking the vase.

It's only natural for Jessica to want to move on with someone. I never should have left her. I miss her so much. When this is all over, I have to find a way back to her. I would do things so differently if I only had a second chance.

"Enjoying the view?"

That accent. A throaty, laborious accent. It was familiar, and sent his aura into a flashing overdrive.

"Better be careful, now. Don't want to see you get *sick*," a second voice jeered.

Pete whirled around and met two sharply dressed men, both wearing black, tailored suits. Matte black button-down shirts. Matching bow ties and tribal tattoos. One's hair was cut short. Spiked. The other's hair longer. Sheeny and slicked back.

The twins. Malitae and Malum.

"You didn't think we'd miss out on all the fun, did you, Pete?" Malitae said.

"What are you doing here?" snapped Pete.

"We are everywhere, Pete," said Malum.

"We couldn't help but overhear your conversation. So sorry to listen in," said Malitae.

"My conversation?" asked Pete.

"Why yesssss." Malum's forked tongue pierced his lips but slid behind his fangs as he grinned. "You'd give anything for a second chance? Don't you remember? You *just* said it!"

Malitae coiled in a mechanical, serpent-like fashion, muttering something to his partner in their throaty dialect. A forked tongue rolled out of his mouth and flickered before retracting. "Pete, what you are doing here is against the rules."

"I'm breaking the rules?" Pete huffed in defiance. "I am standing here all by myself, minding my own business. You know what's against the rules? Collecting a spirit who isn't sick and taking them to Level One!"

Defiant. Courageous against a dangerous adversary.

Pete hardly recognized himself.

"Don't pander us, Peter. We know what's going on here. We've been watching," Malum snarled, his jet black dead eyes staring him down. A flicker of his hideous forked tongue.

"I was captured and brought here," said Pete simply.

"Oh, you were captured. You have nothing to do with this," toyed Malum. "You can turn into your orb and fly right out of here—yet here you remain."

"Pete, there's still time if you want to go back to your wife," said Malitae.

"She says she's lonely without you," said Malum. "The man we sent to make love to her right in front of you told us so. Timothy, wasn't that it?"

"Ah, yes—the lab technician." Malitae smirked.

Pete's silence couldn't hide his thirst to see his wife once more. His dimming aura was a dead giveaway.

"Oh, would you look at that?" toyed Malum. "He's getting angry."

"It can be so easy, Pete. Why are you making it so difficult on yourself? We can see the pain you are going through. You wear it every day. Why don't you take us up on that second chance you deserve?" said Malitae.

Second chance?

Malitae pounced, closing the gap between them in less than a second. "Why, *yes*, Pete—a second chance."

They can hear my thoughts! There's no escaping them!

"Think about it. Back in her arms once more. You could be on a tropical beach together *tomorrow*. Isn't that what you so badly desire? Quality time with Jessica? Think about it, Pete," Malitae charmed. "You could have those children you always wanted."

Malitae retreated. His movement was jerky as he joined his brother. "You know, Pete, they are using illegal tactics—coercion and manipulation to get these spirits into their portals. We have a treaty in place that is centuries old and yet here they are, breaking it once more."

"Do you think that is *okay*, Pete?" asked Malum.

"If they are in violation of a treaty, then no, of course not. They should be held accountable somehow," said Pete.

The twins reveled in the answer.

"Do you hear that, brother? *Accountable*," Malitae snickered with delight. "Pete, you don't know how happy it makes us to hear you say that."

"That's exactly why we came here to see you because we knew you were reasonable," said Malum.

"Help us, Pete—and you can be with Jessica once more. *Your second chance*," said Malitae.

Malum's hand shot up. Suddenly, Pete felt his energy being pulled from him. It was like he was rendered immobile. Like he had entered some sort of trance-like state where he was swayed by their temptation.

"How?" said Pete.

"Pete, you have the ear of the General. These men fight for him. If you can convince the General to enter *our* portal, his men will follow."

"And they don't even need to lay down their weapons to enter our portal. In fact, they should bring them if they want to keep fighting. We encourage it," said Malitae.

"I'll talk to the General."

"Very well. We'll be watching," said Malitae.

"Make us proud," said Malum, snapping his fingers releasing Pete from his trance.

Pete watched their jet-black orbs darting across the battlefield swallowed up by a portal. And it seemed they were gone—for now.

THE BETRAYAL

"WHAT HAVE I DONE?" PETE said to himself. It was as if he had been under some sort of spell in the twins' presence. Looking down, he saw his aura turning darker—it's healthy bright glow dimming.

"Help me!" he shouted in a panic, traveling toward the Generals.

Sergeant Wagner was the first to greet him. "What did you do? Your aura—it's turning black!"

"I think I made a promise to The Others. I don't fully remember," said Pete, frantic, stricken with fear, but a grim feeling of guilt consuming him—for his agreement with The Others meant turning on these spirits. He had seen what happened to Charlie after he had made a deal with them. No, he couldn't go through with it. Not now. Not ever.

"*The Others!? They are here?*"

"They were here a second ago. They . . . uh . . . disappeared."

"We must get you to the General at once. He'll know what to do!"

Before Pete knew it, a stunned crowd of soldiers and officers were encircling he and Sergeant Wagner as they delivered the news.

"His aura!" he heard someone say. "He's becoming sick!" shouted another followed by white noise as the crowd balled and hissed.

"What is the meaning of this?" General Hickman's voice boomed, sending a lot of soldiers standing close by scurrying. "If you had been properly trained by me, this *never* would've happened. This is exactly why I don't like civilians interfering in war-time matters."

The crowd gasped as Pete's aura began flashing. Clearly the General's pontification wasn't helping matters.

"The Others . . . they—"

"The Others! They were *here?*" the General gasped.

"Please—you must help me. They put me under some sort of trance, promised me a second chance at being with my wife," Pete said.

"Under what condition?" demanded the General.

314

"That you and these soldiers enter their portal." Now that he was saying it out loud, it all sounded so stupid, so dangerous. Pete swallowed hard as the General stared back at him, the pair holding the tableau.

"I knew bringing you here was a mistake," said the General, pulling his saber. His horse reared as he prepared to charge.

"Wait! I have something to tell you!"

The General's horse settled as he readied to charge.

"General, I was with Pete before the battle. Might we just listen to hear what he has to say?" suggested Jerald, and Pete felt a *whoosh* of gratitude for the man.

"Very well, make it quick."

"There is a boy who can see spirits. A *Bridge!*" Pete clamored.

"That's nonsense! Bridges don't exist," dismissed the General.

"I was with him just moments ago. He is with his deceased Grandfather... They are with a powerful spirit—a templar knight who is guarding the boy," said Pete.

"It's true," Sergeant Wagner intervened. "I was with them earlier."

"Well, Sergeant . . . why are they here?"

"Don't know. Last we saw 'em, the knight was leadin' 'em over yonder to Seminary Ridge," said Sergeant Wagner.

"Very well, give me a few good men and ride with me to Seminary Ridge. Pete—come with us," ordered the General.

Pete turned to move toward Seminary Ridge with the General when he was stopped by a jolt of terror that pulsed through is aura. There they were. As if they appeared out of thin air. Malitae and Malum standing before them dressed in their perfectly tailored shiny black suits. Malitae with his pushed-up, spiky hair, and Malum with his sheeny, slicked-back hair. Both perfectly groomed, greeting them with narrow, jet black eyes, baring their smooth cuspated fangs.

"We had an agreement, Pete," snarled Malitae.

"I've seen what happens to people who side with you—like poor Charlie. I was never going to help you," said Pete, gaining a sudden confidence. "I don't care what you do to me. I will *never* help you."

"Don't say *never*, Pete. It's such an unflattering word. When you say you'll never do something, and then we make you do the opposite with very little applied influence, it makes you seem so *very* weak," Malum with his enchanted throaty dialect. It was as if Pete was lured to him by his spellbinding voice, but he fought away the bewitching, defiantly facing the twins, scowling.

"*Never.*"

"Brave and stupid is also unflattering, don't you agree, Brother?" Malum added.

The brothers brandished their fangs. Smooth forked tongues rolled, flickering out of their mouths. Their flashy smiles now menacing grimaces. Cold dead eyes, as black as onyx, locked squarely on Pete.

"We offered you a second chance—and *this* is how you repay us?" Malitae growled.

"Second chance? Whatever do you mean?" Soldiers moved to the side as General Arlington's horse trotted to the head of the lines. Pete watched as the twins attention snapped to the General sitting atop his magnificent horse, his proud blue uniform and shiny brass buttons reflecting light from the soldiers' auras.

"Quiet down, you fool!" barked General Hickman. "Can't you see they are manipulating you?"

General Arlington moved past his counterpart, arms slouched to the side, hands dangling—no longer holding onto the reins of his horse, eyes focused on the twins with a trance-like stare, gliding toward them as if he was being drawn helplessly in by their tantalizing allure. Then Pete realized, with abject horror, he must have looked exactly like this just moments ago.

"General, join us and we can make your wildest dreams come true," said Malum, eyeing the General like a hungry lion spying a baby gazelle.

"Tell me, General, what is it you want?" gloated Malitae.

"My wife. I have not seen her since before the war," said General Arlington.

"We can give you your wife back. Put you in her arms again. Alive. Back before the war. It would be like you never even died on the battlefield. All you have to do is join us. . . ."

"This is a sacred place! Why don't the two of you move along and let us leave the battlefield with dignity?" shouted one of General Arlington's officers.

General Arlington held his hand up to silence the officer, but it was too late.

"Step forward, young man!" ordered Malitae. Pete watched as a younger officer with red hair poking from under a weathered cap moved to the front, uniform hanging from his body. The officer looked like he couldn't be older than 16 years, but had of course been dead for over a hundred.

"Such a brave young soldier, you are. You want us to *leave*?" Malitae purred, toying with the boy.

"Yes. We want to be left alone. Whatever quarrel you have with the Confederates doesn't concern us," said the boy.

Malitae suddenly burst into a black orb and, like a bolt of lightning, shot through the officer's body—*disintegrating him,* bursting through him and soaring into the sky—leaving nothing behind but a cloud of fine ashes dissipating in the wind.

Chaos followed. Soldiers taking up arms and firing aimlessly toward the orb, but their small arms were as effective as shooting a bear with a BB gun. It flew over their heads with ease, darting from side to side, taunting them. Rifle stocks bludgeoned shoulders as panic-stricken soldiers fired. Pistols recoiled. A wall of musket balls soared toward the orb. The orb gracefully maneuvered around each projectile, daring them to fire more.

"Cease fire!" commanded General Arlington, his aura dimming more with every passing second as shame seemed to wash over him. Pete felt he *should* be ashamed—ashamed for putting himself before his men, for putting his men's fate in jeopardy, for costing a young boy his spirit life.

His regiment ignored his commands, their auras flashing all along the valley with primal fear. A cannon fired. A ball screamed through a row of soldiers. *Friendly fire.* Nervous cannoneers set up incorrectly. The orb swooped down and darted back and forth across the front lines, plunging into the line of troops taking out the entire first row.

"Do you see what we are capable of, General? All this can be stopped. It's not too late to make a deal. . . ." reiterated Malum.

"My men would *never* follow me if I did. I curse you and your brother!" the General spat, the color in his eyes returning as he escaped their trance. He sat atop his magnificent horse, raising his sword and swinging it through Malum with no effect whatsoever on the demon. The sight terrified Pete. *Could these scoundrel brothers even be killed?*

The twin smiled at the General sympathetically, cocking his head slightly as his eyes became glossy. "I liked you, General. I'm sorry it didn't work out."

Malum exploded into an orb and tore through the General's body. Only a pile of dust remained, sifting away in the wind. Soldiers scattered like ants, grey and blue uniforms mixed together—completely exposed—many running to join General Hickman's regiment on the ridge.

Pete darted for cover as orbs as dark as a moonless night—shiny, like a pressurized volcanic rock—crashed through rows and rows of helpless soldiers.

JOSH'S ROLE

"I'LL DO IT!" JOSH REAFFIRMED, and Joe couldn't help but think it was Josh's gullible youth that had gotten the best of him. But after Keryx explained the importance of Josh's role, he looked upon his grandson with great pride.

Still, he still did not know what Josh's involvement meant for the boy, or what degree of danger he was in. The only consolation he took was that the spirits would not be of physical harm to him; then he recalled the LADO conference and the discussion on Bridges going mad due to harassment. What could happen if the twins—an unstoppable and manipulative duo—gained access to Josh? His aura brightened a slight shade as he glanced at Edvarard, the powerful, loyal knight standing watch over Josh. Until now, he had looked upon Edvarard with a certain disdain. There was an aggravating rigidness about him that he now fond of. An unflappable allegiance. A staunch duty to protect his grandson. *Perhaps he's the one. Perhaps he's the one who can stop them. It makes me feel a whole lot better knowing he's here.*

"What you're agreeing to do will have an impact not just on the spirit world, but on yours as well, Josh. Humanity thanks you," said Keryx.

"Am I helping save the world?" gloated Josh.

"More or less," said Keryx.

"How will we convince the soldiers to disarm and enter these portals?" asked Joe.

"The soldiers are a committed bunch. I don't quite know the answer. We'll have to meet with their Generals," said Keryx.

"You want to involve Josh, and you don't even have a plan?" grumbled Joe.

"Since the dawn of time, soldiers have listened to their superior officers. Infantrymen listen to Sergeants. Sergeants listen to Lieutenants. Lieutenants listen to Captains. Captains listen to Generals. Chain of command. The soldiers listen to their Generals. If we convince the Generals, we convince the entire army," said Keryx.

"Well, there are two Generals and two armies down there. You'll need to convince them both," Joe said, looking down at the valley, something catching his eye. Something stuck out as if it didn't belong. It was General Arlington's radiant white horse beaming among a sea of grey and blue uniforms. Upon closer look, he saw General Hickman next to him, and he smiled as he saw a man dressed in a business suit near the Generals.

"What are you getting yourself into now, Stanton?" he chuckled. Then his aura went into overdrive, filled with whimsical flashing when he saw them. *The twins were here.* They looked stiff, shoulders pulled back, as if they were ready to pounce on the Generals.

"Keryx, you may want to look at this," said Joe.

The sound of Edvarard's sword scraping its sheath as he drew it made Joe cringe to think of what may happen next.

"No, Edvarard. You must stay here with the boy. Keep them safe. That is your duty," said Keryx as they watched an obsidian colored orb gyrating before crashing into General Arlington, pulverizing him from very existence. In a flash, a jet-black orb buzzed over their ridge, circling around before launching toward the battlefield, bursting through a row of soldiers—rifles, packs, and even articles of clothing flung about.

"Edvarard—you must protect the boy at all costs," said Keryx, bursting into a powerful orb—energy radiating and pulsing through it as he shot toward the battlefield.

GUARDIAN WARRIORS

THE EARTH SHOOK AND LEAVES fell from the trees as an object crashed into the rocky battlefield, ejecting plumes of dust and flyrock. Pete looked on as a shadowy figure emerged from the dust plumes, prompting two dark orbs to hover in the area in response.

As the figure drew near, Pete saw a plain-looking man with a sculpted brown beard and hair that hung just above his eyebrows. He had leather sandals, which wrapped around his lower legs and tied together at mid-calf. He wore a white tunic with a purple cloak that draped from his body, reaching to just above his knees.

Pete watched as the two dark orbs hovered and danced in front of the man in a taunting manner before unfolding and taking the shape of the menacing human-like shapes of Malitae and Malum.

"Ah, the mighty Keryx," Malum crowed. "To what do we owe the pleasure?"

"You don't belong here! Leave at once!" hissed Malitae.

"Easy, Brother." Malitae coiled as Malum patted his back.

"You're in violation of the treaty!" snarled Malitae. "You think you can just get away with stealing thousands of battle-ready spirits and go unnoticed?"

"You captured a healthy spirit and took him to Level One. *That* is a direct violation of our treaty!" Keryx responded, unraveling the scrolls and holding them up for display.

"Oh, here he comes now!" said Malitae. The group watched as Pete traveled toward them.

The twins appeared unfazed at their presence. "Pete! My favorite spirit! You don't look so good. What's wrong?" Malum asked, clearly toying with him. "You look the same way you did the day Jessica left you. That had to be *tortuous*. Watching your wife with another man. After you saved her life, no less. You . . . childishly acting out . . . watching them at the restaurant like some kind of voyeur, trying to end their date by spilling plates of food all over her date. But it only drove them closer together, didn't it? It must have been torture having another man using your shower, drying off with your towels—your wife handing him your favorite shirt to change into ..."

"I was never going to help you," Pete's eyes narrowed with hatred, even as his flashing aura gave away his aguish as Malum jolted the vision of Jessica moving on from his memory.

"That's enough! There must be a way we can negotiate," pleaded Keryx.

Malitae approached Keryx with a menacing scowl, bearing pointy fangs, raising his arms in the air.

"We've negotiated for far too long." His eyes no longer black, but red and glowing—like hot, burning coals. Malitae flickered. Vibrating. Shaking vigorously. In a flash, he turned into his authentic form: a reptilian creature. Standing on hind legs. Ferocious yellow fangs. A protective film rolling over his eyes as he blinked. Teeth clanked together as his jaw chomped. Scaly, armored plates. Deadly claws. The fiendish monster swiping at Keryx, snatching the scrolls with razor sharp claws.

He held them in front of Keryx—*and tore them in two.*

It was the first time he saw Keryx even slightly flustered as he looked at the hideous lizard in disbelief. It seemed for at least a second, Keryx would lose his temper and lash out at the wretched beast, but he seemed to regain his composure while sizing up Malum, whose eyes were also red and glowing, but his human form remained unchanged.

Soldiers all around began running for cover, their panicked auras flashing wildly in terror.

Malitae shifted back into his human form, raising his hands to his eyes, which Pete realized were flashing between a red and an almost yellowish hue as he chanted. The air around them popping and fizzing.

"You have broken our treaty," said Malum. "And now you must pay the price."

More fizzing and popping as a dark portal took shape. It was large, dark, hollow—big enough to drive a train through. A chaotic scene erupted as winged creatures burst from the portal. Scaly bodies the size of school buses, with heads like jaguars.

Pete took a step backward, horrified by these hideous, snarling beasts. Black, bony wings protruded from their armor-plated bodies. Elongated, spiked tails trailed from their bodies, ready to inflict devastating blows.

"Our creations," said Malitae. He spoke a word in his hideous tongue. "We call them Catphylon."

"There must be hundreds of those things!" screamed Pete, crouching down as teeth, claws, and leathery wings flapped overhead.

The battlefield erupted as General Ward's unit frantically began firing their weapons. *Fire. Reload. Fire.* Infantry howling in terror as the soaring beasts dove at them. A flip of the spiked tail. A row of soldiers pulverized. Deafening roar as a nearby cannon fired sending a plume of smoke across the general area.

Groups formed lines and fired. Blue and grey uniforms banding together for survival. A lone soldier rushed for the protection of the rocks: grey uniform with shoeless, trail-worn feet. A creature trailing. His unit showered him with encouragement.

"Run, Billy!"

"Don't look back!"

"He's gonna make it!"

Another Catphylon burst from the sky and clutched the running soldier in its claws. The soldier struck the beast, attempting to break free.

"Hit him, Billy!"

"Hit that ugly beast!"

"Stab it, Billy! Pull your blade and stab it!"

Pete heard an increase in sporadic rifle fire, aiming at the creature.

Screeeeech!

Another creature approached. More rifle fire. It flew next to the creature carrying Billy. They squared up. The squawking was deafening. The second creature grabbed Billy with its claws.

More gunfire. Sporadic. A discharged round. Another. Many soldiers hiding. Crippled by fear.

A flapping of leathery wings. A sinister scream filling the air—*and the creatures pulled poor Billy apart.* A hideous scream trailing off until his body burst into a fine dust, blowing in the wind as if he were never there.

Pete looked past the scurrying troops and found General Ward assembling a mixed unit of troops.

"Some of you men fought for the Union during the war! Now fight with me!" The soldiers erupted in cheers as they fixed bayonets. The General's horse reared as he yanked the reins. *"Charge!"*

The frothing, spitting unit lurched forward. Mouths gaping. Ready to plunge bayonets into the first scaly creature that landed. The rebel army, who fought vigorously for their cause, stayed behind in death to fight the war—their *reason*. Now fighting for an entirely new *reason*.

Fighting for humanity.

Pete froze as he watched the creature screech as it dropped, landing nearby among a group of soldiers attempting to form a line. The men quickly circling General Ward in a defensive protecting maneuver.

"Protect the General!" they yelled as the creature, a massive beast, ears pinned back, spit and hissed as soldiers tried to pierce its armored skin with bayonets. It swiped a giant claw, several of the troops guarding the General taking direct hits—*vaporizing into thin air*. A gunshot went off, then another, producing thick powdery smoke while the creature coiled back and let out a vicious scream. It moved alongside the entire formation, rearing back and whipping its ugly, spiked tail—decimating the entire group.

Pete swallowed hard as he realized General Ward—the brave, fearless leader and his loyal troops—were pulverized.

"What happened to them? Where did they go? The soldiers were just there, then they were gone!" he wondered aloud before a squawking creature captured his attention.

Whatever sporadic, unorganized gunfire the soldiers could muster only further irritated the creatures. Outmatched, the remaining troops scattered.

"See what you've made us do?" hissed Malitae with sounds of screeching bat-like creatures diving upon soldier after soldier in the background.

"You don't have to do this," said Keryx.

"Our rules are simple, Keryx. You violated the treaty by manipulating a Bridge and opening portals to capture these spirits without our consent," said Malum.

"Spirits with battle experience, I might add," said Malitae.

"The treaty is not fair to these soldiers. It allows you to collect a spirit when they become sick—and they have no choice in the matter," said Keryx.

"They made their *choice* when they refused to enter their portal after death," said Malum. "By their own *freewill*. We've given in so many times before. We let you establish a Gatekeeper at the portal entry to guide them to the afterlife."

"... and when they refuse to enter because of your precious *freewill*, then they become trapped, and *sick*. That is the fate of a spirit who does not enter the afterlife, and they are ours to collect when they turn sick. No matter their *reason*," said Malitae.

"The spirits don't know their fate when they stay behind. You must allow my Gatekeepers to communicate the consequences. As it stands, we are not allowed to influence spirits—our treaty states we are only allowed to offer passage. Spirits are staying behind en masse because they don't know the rules," said Keryx.

"Ah, *yesssss*, the beauty of our treaty," hissed Malitae, his forked-tongue rolling out of his mouth and flitting before retracting back in.

"It matters not. The treaty is the treaty. Now, because you violated the agreement, we have torn it up. There *is* no treaty any longer, and we can release whatever army of darkness we want on the living humans and spirits alike," said Malum. A terrible grin pierced his lips as the sound of leathery wings flapping and a dark, sinister-looking creature screeched overhead. Slicked, sheeny hair. Forked tongue flickering. "And since our treaty is broken, we can talk to the boy. The Bridge. The one who can see spirits. He will become our greatest asset as we ruin the living. Turn them against each other. Now, Keryx—this will all be a lot easier if you just run along and bring us the boy."

"The Great War is upon us. *Doomsday,*" hissed Malitae.

Doomsday! I must do something! Pete hid out of sight of the twins for fear they would unleash a flying creature on him. He hugged a boulder, but remained in earshot of the twins and Keryx.

All around him, creatures dove, capturing panic-stricken soldiers. Grey uniforms, blue uniforms—it did not matter to the ugly beasts. Dark leathery wings, with heads like a jaguar's—brandishing incisors as long as a man's forearm.

Soldiers scattered like ants.

A rifle crackled. Then another. Black powder smoke filling the valley.

Pete looked for signs of General Hickman, but could not see him as men darted in and out of the haze of smoke and diving creatures. *I must warn the boy, but how? I'd be completely exposed out in the open.*

He peered around the boulder to see if there was a window to escape. Creatures diving, soldiers crying out in terror. Orbs darting every which way. *Why aren't you doing anything, Keryx?* he thought.

"I command you to call back your Catphylon and leave this place at once!" said Keryx.

"Or what? You'll enter the fight?" baited Malitae.

"We've been waiting a long time for a fight," said Malum. "We've had centuries to prepare. This time, we are ready."

"You know my leadership would never allow me to fight," said Keryx "You know the consequences if I enter a war."

"It sounds like we have free reign to take these soldiers then," said Malitae.

". . . and take the boy. The Bridge will now belong to us," said Malum, snapping his fingers and prompting a Catphylon to obediently land beside him. The creature's jaguar-like head rubbed against him in a compliant manner. Its thin, leathery wings folded along its scaly, reptilian-looking body. A tail that could cut a man in two with a simple flip dragged behind it. When it was done brushing against Malum, it looked at Keryx through yellow eyes, baring its fangs and aggressively pawing at the earth.

Pete watched as Keryx stood his ground, looking unimpressed. The creature terrified Pete and he admired Keryx for not folding into an orb and tearing out of there.

"Our beautiful creation," said Malum. "So precious." The creature purred as he scratched its matted fur. "Bring me the boy," he ordered. In a flash the creature screeched, unfolded its wings, and took off flying toward the portals.

"You aren't going to chase it? You're just going to let our creation snatch the boy?" said Malitae.

"The boy is protected," said Keryx.

Pete looked on as Keryx pulled something from inside his tunic. It was a gold chain that dangled around his neck. On the end of the chain looked like some sort of crystal, which he gripped tightly, thrusting his hand in the air. He chanted, looking to the sky as a thin light shot through the clouds. A beacon.

Suddenly, three orbs tore from the sky, crashing into the rocky soil sending plumes of dust into the valley. As they unfolded, he noticed two of the orbs wore garments made of animal skin. They had long black hair so thick he could make out individual strands that whipped in the wind.

One of the beings appeared to be male, as he had a square jawline and thick, dark eyebrows. The skin on his face was so smooth and looked as if no facial hair ever grew there. He carried a spear with a smaller crystal dangling from it—similar to the one Keryx had on his necklace.

"Khoana Chayton," said Keryx. "Thank you for coming."

"Yes, Master," he replied.

A second being stood next to him. She looked similar to Khoana Chayton, and Pete wondered if they were siblings. She wore a garment made of animal skin. A single, thin braid hung to the side of her head, clasped at the end with a shell. She made a fierce scowl toward the twins as she removed the bow that was hanging from her shoulder. A carrier was holding a bundle of arrows strapped to her back.

Pete knew this was not a look of anger, but of one rooted in hatred.

"Toma, thank you for coming," said Keryx bowing.

"Yes, Master," she replied, her scowl returning as she eyed the twins.

The third moved forward, standing next to but slightly behind Toma. "Tanoshi, thank you for coming," said Keryx, bowing.

"Yes, Master," Tanoshi replied, bowing in respect. A warrior, dressed in traditional Samurai armor and headgear. Leather platelets hardened and made shiny by what looked like multiple coats of lacquer, each platelet attached to an iron breastplate. It truly was a magnificent suit of armor in both color and function. Two single-handed katana swords strapped to the back of his armor—each with a leather handle grip—protruded slightly above his shoulder for quick access, should he need to pull one or both in battle.

"Well, this is a welcome surprise," said Malitae. "Toma, Khoana Chayton, Tanoshi . . . You have certainly brought your best, Keryx."

"There's still time to make a truce, redraw our treaty," offered Keryx.

"You have such false hope for the living, Keryx. Look at what they've done. They've killed off scores of species, warmed their planet to the likes where it will be unlivable in less than a half of century. All because of your precious *freewill*," said Malitae, baring his fangs.

"All this talk is making me hungry, Brother. What do you say we go have some fun?" said Malum, bursting into a dark orb and ripping toward the valley, smashing the first soldier he saw.

"Your move," said Malitae before folding into an orb following his brother, smashing through a row of soldiers.

All around them, panic-stricken soldiers screamed with terror and fired aimless shots, while being tormented by divebombing creatures and smashed to pieces by Malum and Malitae.

"What are your orders, Master?" asked Toma.

"Remember Pompeii?" said Keryx.

"Yes, Master. Thousands died that day," said Tanoshi.

"You know the rules," said Keryx. "Under no condition can we engage in battle that will hurt the living. They'll try to draw us into battle over populated areas, where our fighting will cause earthquakes, flooding, and other natural disasters. Remember Pompei."

"The volcano," said Toma.

"Yes," replied Keryx. "We let them draw us into battle. Our indiscretion led to the eruption. Those poor people had no chance to escape. A black mark on our history.

"It would be in our favor if you entered the fight with us," said Toma.

"You know I cannot do that. If I fight, we risk Malum and Malitae opening their portals and unleashing something even more dangerous. We have to contain them here. *Now*."

"Fine," said Toma, bursting into an orb tearing off into battle.

Tanoshi and Khoana followed, their orbs screaming across the valley.

Pete assessed his danger and saw an opportunity to move from his cover, coyly inching closer to Keryx. "Is there any way I can help?" he asked.

"You're the one who can move objects?" said Keryx.

"That's right," said Pete.

"Your destiny will appear shortly. For now, we need to find the General commanding these soldiers and unite these men. Can you help me do that?"

"Yes, Master," said Pete, garnering a slight grin from Keryx. "I know the General."

THE LOYAL GUARDIAN

EDVARARD TOOK UP A PROTECTIVE stance in front of Josh, his double-sided broadsword making a scraping sound as he unsheathed it. The chain mail armor hugging his arms swayed with his every movement as he positioned his shield and crouched over the boy in a protective manner.

Two black orbs screamed across the sky, leaving dark vapor trails in their midst traveling at such a speed they disrupted the air pressure sending what sounded like a crack of thunder over the valley.

Joe's aura flashed with grave concern as he watched as they circled around taking a wide turn before shooting toward the valley, plunging through rows of hapless soldiers.

"Those poor men," he muttered as fluttering creatures appeared squawking their hideous screeches just before diving and snatching their next victims.

He glanced in the direction of the open portals, and sensed tension among the Gatekeepers as they took position. Unprotected, they were completely exposed if the creatures or twins decided to attack. A feeling of uneasiness crept in as he doubted even Edvarard would be much use against so many flying beasts.

A strange shadow crept over them, almost large enough to block out the sun.

"Take cover!" yelled the Gatekeepers as many of them leapt into their portal, closing it completely behind them.

"Josh, run!" yelled Joe as he looked a Catphylon square in the eye. That's what one of the twins had called them: *Catphylon*. He darted toward Josh, staying with him, looking for cover— the only protection a tree line about 100 yards beyond the ridge. "Get to the trees, boy!"

He looked back and stopped in bewilderment as a creature hovering over Edvarard snatching and swiping at him with thick pointy claws. An ear-piercing roar followed as Edvarard knocked its claw away with his shield and plunged his broadsword deep into the creature's leg. Its eyes rolled back as it screeched in pain. It flapped its leathery wings, landing in front of Edvarard. It swiped its claws at him, making a bony, clanking sound as it snapped its ferocious jaws.

"No, not Edvarard. He's our only hope," said Joe.

The beast drew near, testing Edvarard's defenses—looking for any opening to strike when Edvarard thrust his shield into the beast's soft nose, the creature reeled back screeching, snarling, *hissing*. Baring its dagger like teeth.

In a quick movement, it whipped its tail, connecting with Edvarard's chest—sending him crashing into the hard ground.

The creature let out a victorious roar, its black eyes rolling back before setting its sights on Josh, who froze in terror. "Remember, Josh, he can't hurt you!" yelled Joe when suddenly something flew end-over-end, making a *swooshing* sound before piercing the creature's gritty, armored plates.

The beast wriggled, squealing in pain—swiping at something protruding from its side. Turning and thrashing its deadly tail side-to-side its body twisting and torqueing, offering Joe a closer look. *There*, just behind its front shoulder, Edvarard's sword was protruding from its side. Heart and lungs. The creature let out a magnificent bellow as it collapsed—its chin smashing into the earth with a loud thud. Out of the trees came Edvarard, his great helm dented showing no expression as he traveled over to inspect the beast. "We thought you were a goner," said Joe as he watched the knight place an armored boot on the creature's side, two hands gripping his sword and yanking it from his victim. He clasped his shield to his back and motioned them to the trees.

"Keep moving, Josh—get to the woods," barked Joe.

"I'm running as fast as I can!" said Josh.

"*Faster*," ordered Joe as Josh plundered. "We need to move father away. I don't want to be pulled apart by those hideous things!"

"Grandpa, they are scary. I've never seen anything like them before. I'm terrified," said Josh his hands trembling.

"Listen boy, they cannot hurt you. If one comes close to you, just close your eyes. They cannot do anything to you."

"Where's Edvarard?" Josh asked—panting, knelt over, placing his hands on his knees breathing heavily. "We need him!"

Edvarard came trailing behind them, traveling a bit slower than usual. To Joe, he didn't look like himself. His left arm hung low, and he was leaning to the left, as if favoring an injury. His heavy armor looked dented, his chest plate where the creature's tail had struck him was nearly caved. As he approached, Joe saw something that shocked him: red liquid seeped from his underarm.

Blood was running down his arm, dripping from his fingertips. The crimson cross on his tunic filled out with red stains. He removed his heavy chest plate, which made a thumping sound as it struck the ground.

"My goodness, Edvarard. You're badly injured," said Joe.

"Are you okay?" asked Josh.

Edvarard looked upon the boy in silence as he unclasped the plated armor on his forearm. The white garment he wore under his chest plate had splotchy pooling blood. He opened the garment and his hand disappeared, checking his wounds.

Joe was mortified when he pulled his hand out and his leather glove was soaked in blood.

"Edvarard, you're severely injured," Joe said once again. *But, how can a spirit bleed?* He wondered for a moment if Edvarard taking shape to guard Josh actually made him *human?* His attention snapped back as he tried tending to the injured guardian.

No response came from the knight. He bent down—almost mechanically, picking up his chest plate—placing it over his blood-soaked garment, clasping it into place. After reattaching his arm guards, he moved through the trees, motioning them to follow.

Joe looked on, watching his every move with concern as they traveled silently through the forest floor. A sudden snap of a twig caught their attention. They stopped, listening for a few moments before moving on. Another snap.

"What was that noise?" Joe whispered.

Edvarard's good hand went up, motioning them quiet—his injured arm dangling at his side.

Snap! Thud!

Something was following them. Whatever it was, it was heavy. Stomping, but trying hard to be still.

Snap!

"Do you think it could be another one of those creatures?" Joe asked, looking to Josh.

Edvarard using caution not to make a sound, slowly pulled his broadsword with his good arm.

"Well, that can't be a good sign," said Joe.

"No," whispered Josh.

They watched as Edvarard moved silently among the trees, as if he were stalking prey. It wasn't long before he moved out of sight.

"What should we do?" asked Josh.

"I don't know, son. Let's just keep moving for now. He'll catch up," said Joe.

They pushed further into the forest, finding it hard to navigate through overgrowth of thorns and fallen timber. "I can't see a thing," said Josh trying to move through a thicket.

"Duck under this fallen tree," said Joe. "It should keep us out of sight from those things flying above."

Josh started to climb under the fallen tree and froze. Two hooves stood on the other side, hooves *twice* the size of a horse's. Coarse, black hair graced the leg.

"What's wrong boy? Keep moving?" Joe noticed all the color left Josh's face. He'd seen that look of terror before when the creatures first showed up. He slid into position to get a better look at what was troubling the boy when he saw it—*hooves!*

Joe traced the creature's body from its hooved feet to the dark black matted fur on its thick enormous legs. Its body appeared humanoid—but much larger, with a bulging abdomen and pectoral muscles. It had the head of a bull with menacing horns that looked as if they could administer great harm. It stood—moist nostrils flaring, sniffing the air—a long bullwhip dangling in one hand and a spiked club in the other. The eyes. Blood red, glowing eyes.

"Grandpa, be quiet," Josh said. "It's following us."

"What's following us?" He saw Josh trembling in terror, the boy's pale, discolored face.

"It's a Minotaur!" whispered Josh. "I've seen a picture of it in a book."

"A what?" said Joe. His whisper was not as quiet as Josh's.

It was too late. They had been spotted.

Joe saw vapor shoot from the beast's snout as it snorted and roared—its red, glowing eyes fixed on them.

"*Run!*"

They ran toward the battlefield when Josh tripped over a fallen branch.

Joe tried to help him up, but of course, his hands passed right through the boy.

"Grandpa, help me!"

They heard sticks breaking and tree limbs snapping as the Minotaur crashed through the underbrush. The rocky terrain pounded under the heavy weight of the charging beast. Josh watched his grandfather bravely step in front of the horned beast, which reared back in surprise that it was being challenged.

It shook its head back and forth, snorted, and pawed at the ground.

"Josh! It's going to charge! Get out of here!" said Joe.

"My leg is stuck!" he said.

"Josh, go now!" yelled Joe.

The Minotaur brandished a whip at them, banging its club against a tree making a dull, knocking sound. They watched as it snorted and scraped—spittle forming, dripping from its mouth.

"Josh, we gotta go! *Now*," said Joe again, panicked flashes ripping through his aura.

The beast started moving forward with a hollow thud as its hoof came crashing down on the forest floor, only to suddenly stop—it's glowing red eyes narrowed, focusing on something beyond them.

Joe turned to see Edvarard traveling toward them, shield notched and sword drawn, his shoulder still drooping favoring his damaged arm.

The Minotaur snorted and stomped. Frothing at the mouth, spittle flying in every direction. It seemed the beast had switched from rage to excitement—as if Edvarard's presence made it jumpy. Timid. It backed off in the presence of the large knight almost as if it were assessing Edvarard's strength. It seemed like it were turning to flee, until it saw that Edvarard was injured.

"The wind changed," said Joe. "It smells Edvarard's scent. Smells his blood. He knows he's not right. We better go, Josh." It cracked its bullwhip as Edvarard drew nearer, banging its club against a tree, apparently more interested in dealing with the knight than attacking Josh. It split a small tree in half with its horns as an agitated show of strength. Edvarard moved closer—undeterred by his slouched arm. Servant to his uncompromising duty to protect Josh.

The Minotaur roared in annoyance as Edvarard steadily drew near, closing the gap between them. He was now squarely positioning himself between them and the frothing beast, Joe had a sudden moment of relief, and gratitude for the knight. It didn't last long.

"Josh, let's go! We better move from here," said Joe.

"My leg is stuck!"

Joe looking down to see Josh's leg hung up in gnarly tree roots, as if the forest was working for the twins, reaching up and grabbing the boy. "Come on Josh, free your leg!"

The beast roared and cracked its whip, which made a metallic ping as it snapped against Edvarard's shield. Another whip crack. Then another. Joe watched as Edvarard closed the distance, lessening the damage a potential charge might bring.

The beast swung its terrible club, reverberating off Edvarard's shield. A forceful impact, jettisoning Edvarard back, but he recovered and moved forward. Always forward. The beast roared and swung its club, glancing off Edvarard's shield, but grazing his bad arm. Joe saw him buckle, in obvious pain. He saw the beast notice too, for he cracked his whip right at the same spot—striking Edvarard in the same arm. The beast coiled the whip and snapped again. This time Edvarard raised his shield in time to deflect it.

Joe could hear the dull thuds as the Minotaur's hooves pounded the earth. It charged, lowering its large, square head. Edvarard stepped aside, avoiding the charge, swinging his heavy shield just in time to catch the Minotaur under the jaw—snapping its head back.

"That shield strike would've killed most men I know. . . ." Joe cringed at the savageness of the blow, but it didn't daunt the Minotaur. It recovered instantly and retaliated with its heavy club, striking Edvarard's shield over and over, until dropping him to a knee under the force of its blows.

Until eventually, the Minotaur swung its club harder, catching the side of the shield and sending it flying—landing upright against a tree out of reach.

Edvarard is completely exposed! Joe thought as the beast mercilessly snapped his bullwhip against his armor—and each time, Edvarard shuddered in obvious pain. The Minotaur drew nearer, effortlessly knocking his sword away with a swing of its club.

"Get up, Edvarard! Get up!" cried Joe, still struggling to help his grandson off the ground.

A bolt of lightning. A clap of thunder.

And then Edvarard turned into a powerful, gyrating orb, smashing into

THE SPIRIT BATTLE OF GETTYSBURG

the Minotaur's chest, sending them both flying. Edvarard landing near his sword—the Minotaur a giant heap of fur wrapped around a sturdy tree. It wriggled in pain, ribs broken, blood dripping from its snout—signaling probable damage to internal organs, Joe figured, but it wasn't dead. It staggered to its feet, gathering its club. A ferocious charge. The Minotaur had Edvarard dead to rights. Lowering its head, ready to gore him with barbaric horns. Edvarard was still kneeling, his injured arm hanging useless at his side. There was no hope. The beast was on him.

So close that Joe could hear the crinkling sound of leather squeezing as Edvarard gripped his broadsword tightly. A vicious charge by the beast. Head lowered. Horns ready to impale. Edvarard facing the charging bull, rolling away at the last moment. Swinging his sword around. *Connecting.* Sending the Minotaur violently crashing to the ground. Joe watched it thrashing about, attempting again and again to stand, but collapsing with each attempt. Pools of blood blotted fur on its back leg where Edvarard's sword sliced—exposing tendons and rendering the leg immobile. As Edvarard stood over the giant beast, which lunged and thrashed its horns at him, Joe saw hatred in its eyes. It was all the beast could do, as if it knew its fate but refused to give in.

Edvarard dodged the attack, the beast roaring, landing on its belly.

This is it, Joe thought as Edvarard raised his sword and plunged it into the back side of the beast. The Minotaur squealed in pain as Edvarard pulled the sword. He gripped the broadsword firmly and swung it with such might, it made a swooshing sound as it cut through the air. Matted fur and blood dripped from the blade after Edvarard swung through the beast.

All was quiet, except for a crunching of dead leaves and thudding and plopping as the beast's heavy square head rolled down a gulley, coming to rest at the base of a large oak. Its red eyes dimmed to a lifeless grey.

The Minotaur was dead.

"Thank you, Edvarard," said Joe as Josh freed his leg from the tree roots. He turned to thank Edvarard again when he noticed the knight had collapsed.

"He's hurt! What should we do?" cried Josh.

"I'll remove this heavy chest plate off him so he can breathe," said Joe, kneeling, removing clasps, pushing it to the side exposing a white garment soaked in blood. He removed the helmet, hoping to help Edvarard breathe, but the knight's arm shot up in protest, and so he left it.

ROUNDING GENERAL HICKMAN

THE VALLEY WAS IN A panicked disarray—blurs of grey and blue uniforms darting in and out of black powder smoke that settled. A dark creature landed within reach, clutching a soldier in its jaws, and Pete could hear the eerie howl fade as the soldier was dispatched. He ducked under a spiked tail whip. More dark creatures flapped by on bony, leathery wings, tracking targets on the ground.

Overhead, the a clap of thunder sounded as the twins' dark orbs cruised by, dropping down, ripping through rows of infantrymen.

Brave soldiers attempting to form lines and fire their rifles only for the orbs to tear through their entire formation. There was no hiding. Separate, and the flying creatures tracked and tore you. Band together, and the twins bludgeoned your formation.

Through the mess of scrambling soldiers, Pete saw a soldier atop a grey spotted horse trying to gain control as chaos ensued. "There's the General!" said Pete as Keryx followed.

As they approached, Pete noticed the General's aura had virtually been drained of all brightness. The calm, stoic leader now flustered as he watched men become pulverized by the black orbs and snatched from the ground by the hideous creatures.

"We can't fight them, they're killing my men!" said General Hickman.

"General, in order to win this battle, your soldiers *must* fight," said Keryx.

"Our weapons are useless against them," said General Hickman.

A dark creature fluttered over a group of soldiers squawking, ready to dive-bomb them when something tore across the sky. A white orb gyrating and pulsating with energy screamed toward them.

"Tanoshi," said Keryx as they watched the orb draw near.

The creature readied to dive. Squawking, flapping its leathery wings. The orb shot toward it, leaving vapor trails in its wake. The creature let out a primal shriek as the orb struck it, entering its body. It twisted and thrashed

335

in pain, tail swinging wildly before the orb tore out of its body—obliterating the creature.

Scores of soldiers cheered as they watched the orb tear off for another creature.

"The soldiers! They're forming lines!" said General Hickman.

Another orb cruised across the battlefield, unfolding to take human shape as it drew near. Toma.

"Master, their numbers are too great. We need you to enter the fight," she said, panting as if the fight had taken her breath. Her face smeared with blood, her once tan leather garments stained dark red in many places. Upon observation, Pete was relieved to find it wasn't hers. In one hand she firmly gripped a large knotted staff, as if she had cut a sapling and fashioned it herself.

Keryx looked over the battlefield: the black orbs running through spirits; the Catphylon dive-bombing regiments.

"I cannot fight. The consequences would be severe," he said.

"But we need you!" pleaded Toma. "We can end this *now*—if you'll just unleash your power!"

"General, send word to your soldiers they should touch bayonets," said Keryx.

"Yes, sir," said the General as he dispatched aids to ride to the front.

"You know what will happen if I do," said Keryx, looking to Toma, who handed him her staff. "Humanity will pay the price." All across the valley, soldiers began touching bayonets together. Blue uniforms mixed with grey uniforms. "Look. There's the signal. They are ready."

The gnarled wood made the staff seem ordinary as Keryx raised it in the air and spoke in a language which Pete couldn't understand. A clap of thunder roared over the valley as Keryx slammed Toma's staff to the ground, the earth beneath it cracking open as pits of lights formed. Crevices splintering running through the valley toward the soldiers. When the light hit the first soldiers, their weapons illuminated in an incandescent light. A light so bright, Pete raised his hand shielding his eyes before the light flashed and faded away.

"General, if these creatures leave this valley, they *will* harm the living," said Keryx.

"How so?" asked General Hickman. "I thought they could not bring physical harm to the living."

"Physical harm . . . no . . . but they will bring war, famine, poverty wherever they go."

The General's grey horse stirred and panted as he sat atop it silently observing the battlefield as if pondering the great responsibility suddenly bestowed upon him.

"Many men will die here today," he said finally.

"Your soldiers are the last hope of saving humanity," said Keryx. "Its last hope."

FIGHTING BACK

WHEN PETE SAW TOMA'S DETERMINED eyes fall upon an idle cannon, he knew she had a plan. He so desperately wanted to help, but dared not ask. She had a ferocious gaze upon her, one that Pete knew meant trouble if he got in her way. He watched her packing the cannon full of powder, taking aim at a creature fluttering above.

"Fire this cannon," she said to a nearby soldier—the fuse fizzing and sparking as it burned.

The cannon roared a thunderous boom, a heavy lead ball launching from its barrel. They all watched with anticipation as the ball tracked its target—and then, the scaly creature buckling and lurching in pain as the ball smashed into its side. A primal screech before it disintegrated into thin air. Cheers erupted from the soldiers down in the valley below.

"Their weapons work against these creatures now," Toma said with something Pete *swore* could pass as a smirk.

"Form your lines, General. Fight back!" commanded Keryx.

"Aye, sir," saluted the General.

The skies were filled with mischievous dark dots, on what otherwise to Pete would have been a fantastic fall sunset. Shades of yellows, reds, and oranges turned the sky ablaze, almost making the creatures seem more hideous—as if not only were they here wreaking havoc on the soldiers, but bringing fire and fury with them.

It was when the General had formed his lines and began fighting back that Keryx turned to Pete with heavy eyes. The celebratory smile after they had struck a creature had left his face.

"Edvarard. Something terrible has happened to him. I can feel life leaving his body. It means the portals and the boy could be at risk," he said.

"I'll go for him," said Toma, clearly eager to rush to his aid.

"No, I need you here. With me," said Keryx. "As long as Edvarard is alive, he will protect the boy."

"But Master, we must save him if—"

"It is the price we pay. We all know what we are signing up for when we take the oath," said Keryx.

Pete looked over the valley where soldiers were forming lines. Soldiers were firing everywhere. *Reloading. Firing.* Creatures dive-bombing and tearing the scattering soldiers limb from limb. Whipping their spiked tails in columns, pulverizing lines of soldiers. A brave infantryman plunged a bayonet into a creature's hide—a primal shriek. Another stab. Then another, followed by more shrieking. The creature wrangled free.

"Charge!"

The scream that made Union soldiers shake in fear. *The Rebel yell.* A division of soldiers charged toward the Catphylon, plunging bayonet after bayonet. The creature snarled and spit with every bayonet sinking in deep. Finally, the creature burst into dust. Soldiers roared in delight.

The entire valley filled with smoke from sporadic rifle and cannon fire, which seemed to provide cover from the winged beasts above.

"There's so many of them," said Pete. "Even with the soldiers' weapons working—there just seems to be too many!"

A sudden fluttering of wings. A dark shadow on the ground, indicating something circling above them.

"Take cover!" Pete yelled, preparing for an aerial attack.

When he dared to look up, a giant eagle screamed across the sky, circling *above* the dark, leathery wings of the creatures. Silent wings. Talons like daggers. Eyes keen on targets. One of the many Catphylon dove after a cavalry rider, its hind legs and bumpy reptilian-like tail trailing behind it. Khoana shot toward the creature—sinking talons deeply into the scaly backside. The creature shrieked—talons digging further into its organs as it wriggled, trying to free itself, twisting and contorting its body. Its tail flailed wildly as it seemed to try to connect with the feathery eagle, letting out a final, shrill cry before bursting into a cloud of dust.

"How is it the creatures are bursting like that?" said Pete. He wasn't sure he'd get the answer to the question as another Catphylon circled.

Soldiers everywhere screamed in rage, their auras blinking as they took aim, firing upon low-flying creatures. They seemed to concentrate their shots on a single target at a time, pulverizing each flying beast. An orb tore past Pete, circling around, trailing a dive-bombing Catphylon, unfolding to land on the creature's plated back. Tanoshi straddled the beast. The creature lurched back and forth, trying to throw him—only for the Samurai to pull his katana blades, reel back, and sink them deep in between the creature's shoulders.

The Catphylon roared, bearing fangs, eyes rolling back before Tanoshi pulled the blades, turning into an orb blazing toward another target. Soldiers on the ground scattered as the flying beast tumbled end over end, crashing into the ground with such force, clouds of dust formed on either side cascading through the valley.

In all the excitement, Pete almost missed the two obsidian-colored orbs hovering over them. They gyrated back and forth before unfolding into human-like forms: Malitae and Malum.

"Not bad . . . not bad at all," said Malum as the pair approached.

"You really *are* serious about protecting these spirits," snarled Malitae. "We thought once we released our beautiful creations you might tuck tail and run like you always do. I have to admit, I didn't think you had it in you, Keryx. Arming the soldiers so they can fight back? *Nice move.*"

An arrow zipped by Pete. He could almost feel the disruption as it ripped through the air, as if it were physical. The brothers burst into orbs, easily dodging the projectile. Pete expected the orbs to shoot toward him, tear him apart, but they did nothing but hover and gyrate before the twins once again unfolded into their human forms.

A glance behind him revealed the culprit of the arrow. *Toma.* The leather grip on her bow made a creaking sound as she notched another arrow and pulled the bowstring, closing one eye and squinting with the other—aiming at her target. The scowl on her face was one of hatred.

"No! No aggression, Toma!" yelled Keryx, a final attempt to keep the peace.

"Nice shot, Toma," said Malitae, taking his human shape. "You'll have to do better than that."

"That's enough," ordered Keryx. "Toma, we must rise above, not engage in their tactics."

"Oh, Keryx, I *love* it when you show your vulnerability. Your values. Your morals. Your honor. It's *so* endearing. How I wish I could be more like the mighty Keryx," Malum mocked.

The air was littered with the dark bodies of the creatures fluttering in the blazing sunset above the soldiers. Rifles crackled and cannons thundered. A creature flew by with a screaming soldier in its claws. An orb also shot by, *pulverizing* a creature over a formation of scattering soldiers. *Tanoshi.*

If the battle erupting around them wasn't enough to dampen his aura, the twins' presence was.

"Pete, what happened to your nice glowing aura? It was so bright and full of life the last time we saw you," said Malitae.

"You mean when you snatched me from the gas station against my will?" Pete snapped.

A hideous forked tongue rolled out of Malitae's fanged mouth and flickered. "Your friend Charlie says hello. Why don't you come and join him?"

"I said, *enough!*" An energy pulse tore off Keryx, the grass blowing and leaves falling from nearby trees.

"Careful now," said Malum. "It's a good thing none your precious *living* are around. Getting hit with a microburst like that could be pretty destructive."

Pete watched as Keryx cowered, quickly collecting himself—Toma remaining stoic at his side, eyes narrow, hand on her bow. She already had notched an arrow, ready to fire in a split-second. If Pete weren't watching closely, he would have missed Keryx shifting his weight ever so slightly, flashing a subtle glance at the ground. It seemed as though he were ashamed over having let the twins agitate him.

"Hey, Malitae?" teased Malum with a toothy smile. "How about we play a game?"

"Oh, can we? I just *love* games." Malitae chimed in.

"What do you say, Keryx? You want to play?"

"I think your games are about to be over."

Pete cringed as on orb flashed in front of them, smashing into a Catphylon, splitting it in two before it burst into a dust cloud. The orb zipped off, tracking another target. *Tanoshi*. He realized neither the twins nor Keryx and Toma had so much as flinched as they faced off.

"Our games are just beginning," said Malum. "Unless, of course, you agree to our new terms."

"I'm listening," said Keryx.

"We go away. Take our beautiful creations with us," said Malitae.

"What's left of them," Toma snapped.

"*Quiet, you!*" Malitae shook with rage.

Pete could hear the leather on Toma's bow whine as her grip tightened in anger, prompting Keryx to hold a hand out, ordering her to stand down.

"What is your proposal?" asked Keryx.

"The boy—the Bridge. You turn him over and leave him to us," said

Malum.

"In exchange," continued Malitae, "we will take our creations and enter our portals,"

"And what about these soldiers?" asked Keryx.

"Take them. We don't want them anyway," said Malum.

"And the treaty?"

"Your precious treaty. The Order. The Realm which you feel is your duty to protect," hissed Malitae.

"We are prepared to re-establish the treaty," ordered Malum through unblinking, red eyes, which narrowed as he shifted his weight ever so slightly—shoulders back, chest puffed. Pete wondered if he would burst into an orb and tear through them all.

"And if we don't agree . . . If we don't agree to give you the boy?" asked Keryx.

Pete didn't have to be a prior attorney to understand the conundrum they were in. "And what will you do with Josh? Turn him into another Hitler . . . or worse? If we give you Josh, you'll leave and it may be a small victory for us today, but what about tomorrow? The treaty is worthless if you have a Bridge."

"Silence, you weakling," snarled Malitae.

"Or what, Pete? What will you do? Such a frightened, terrified little spirit the last time we met. What will *you* do?" asked Malum.

"*Stop this!* All of you!" Keryx's voice boomed through the valley as he stepped forward. "I shall give myself up. Leave the boy alone for as long as he lives, and I will surrender. Those are the terms. Do you agree?"

"Well now, Brother—what do you think?" said Malum. "I think we can accept those terms, don't you?"

Malitae's tongue rolled out of his gaping mouth—flickering, tasting the air around Keryx. He drew closer. "I think we can agree to those terms," he hissed, producing a pair of bracelets.

"You must order every beast from the battlefield . . . the flying creatures and the Minotaur. . . order them all away from here. Turn the spirit soldiers over to my Guardians, leave the battlefield yourselves, and most of all, you must agree to *never* go near the boy. Not you, or any of your minions, are allowed to go near the boy," Keryx commanded.

"Fine. Put these on," said Malitae tossing the chained bracelets to the ground.

"Master, there must be some other way," said Toma her bow still pointing downward arrow still notched, ready to flip and release upon either twin with a simple twitch of her arm.

"Toma, there is no other way. These are the terms of our new treaty. I appoint you as lead messenger in my absence. You'll need to see to it that these spirit soldiers move through the portals. If they stay any longer, they will become sick and vulnerable."

Tears pooled in her eyes but did not fall as she watched Keryx clasp the first bracelet on his wrist.

"Protect the boy. See to it that he is protected. Will you do that?" said Keryx. As soon as he placed the second bracelet, it was like the connections came to life, like an electric current coursing through his body.

"Master!" Toma yelled as Keryx folded forward, elbows resting on his knees as he writhed in agony.

"Toma, you mustn't—"

His command faded as Toma moved forward. "Do not touch him!" she commanded.

"Toma, move aside. We have a deal," said Malitae, prompting Toma to aim an arrow inches from his neck.

"*Okay*, Toma. You got me," he smirked, raising his hands.

Pete watched as Malum changed into a dangerous obsidian orb. Darker than a moonless night, shiny like a pressurized, volcanic rock.

"Toma! Lookout!" he yelled.

An arrow released, zipping past Malum as he took human shape, dodging it with relative ease. *Bait*. He had baited her—and Malitae had the drop on her, but strangely, he did not attack.

A mischievous smile cracked his pursed lips as he withdrew with his arms in the air. "It seems our new treaty has been broken as quickly as it was established."

Malum snickered at the comment before muttering a throaty, clucky word in their ancient dialect. They both looked to the sky and began a series of chants. "Now you've done it, Toma," he said behind a charming smile.

Just as he said it, the ground began to shake. Pete looked in the foreground, stunned at what he saw. Horns appeared first. Then the terrifying head of a bull came next. Sets of demon eyes bounced up and down as they charged. Coarse, black, matted fur to not one, but *many* bodies. Rushing over the hill was an army of Minotaur rumbling toward the soldiers. Rows of red, glowing eyes and giant hooves.

Terrified soldiers took for the hills. Cavalry riders reared their horses and fled. Lines broke with retreating troops, many turning to orbs and attempting to flee before being snatched up by the claws of flying creatures. The Minotaur army smashed into those who stayed to fight like a freight train mowing over a tin can. Pulverized by horns, clubs, and axes. Sawed in two by powerful whips.

Leathery wings flapped as the dark bodies of the Catphylon dove upon them once again, the soldiers fleeing, only to run into Minotaur swinging axes.

Unless concentrated perfectly, the soldiers' muskets were minimally effective against the Minotaur beasts. Reloading the black powder rifles was slow, and despite some success against the Minotaur, their horns, axes, clubs, and whips were decimating their lines.

Desperate soldiers ditched their rifles and drew sabers, but the wide swings of the Minotaur axes easily overpowered them.

Catphylon dropped from the sky, dive-bombing. Pete was sure he'd never get used to the sight of them: Those jaguar-like heads and fangs like daggers. Their armored plates, a carapace. Powerful tails flipping to decimate entire rows of soldiers.

Thousands of spirit soldiers ran up a hill behind them while the Minotaur army followed, swinging axes and clubs, brandishing whips.

"What are your orders, Master?" Toma obediently asked.

"Stand down," said Keryx fighting for strength.

REFORMING THE LINES

A CATPHYLON DOVE TOWARD GENERAL Hickman. The proud General, vowing to fight the last man, never wavering loyalty to the cause. Only now he had a new cause, a new *reason—defending humanity*. His horse grunted and brayed, racing across the valley. He could hear the fluttering wings and the panting of the flying beast behind him, sending a terrifying screech—delighted to be chasing, closing in.

Ride! Don't look back!

His horse grunted with each vigorous spur.

He could feel the Catphlyon behind him. Its hot breath panting. Leathery wings flapping. So close it blocked out the sun. A dark shadow fell over him, followed by an excited shriek. Screeching. Panting. Fluttering. Drawing near.

Don't look back!

Not this way. I have men to lead and protect.

He pulled his saber. He didn't realize he was yelling.

He looked up just as the beast closed its scaly feet bathed in red liquid. Pieces of torn, grey uniform hanging from the claws.

He crouched low in the saddle, bracing for the beast to grab him when an object streaked overhead. A flash out of the corner of his eye, like a lightning bolt. The beast overhead bellowed: a low, rumbling gurgle. It was a different sound than the shrill screeches of the hideous, dive-bombing creatures.

He ducked just as its claws sailed over his head. He noticed it rearing back. It stopped. Flapping its leathery wings. It let out a low growl before disintegrating. A bright, pulsating orb tore out of the creature's ash, taking shape as a Samurai warrior. *Tanoshi*. He burst from the sky, his katana blades drawn, hitting the ground in a roll—a *rolling* ball with outstretched blades. A line of charging Minotaur snarled, letting out primal squeals as they were severed from their bodies.

"Get to the ridge! Get your men to the ridge! Use the high ground! Fire the cannons!" yelled Tanoshi.

"To the ridge!" General Hickman commanded, pulling his saber and charging up the hill, leading every spirit soldier left—grey uniform, blue uniform, it mattered not. Mortal enemies charging up the hill together to fight for their new *reason*.

Saving humanity.

TOMA

A FIERCE ANGER TORE AT Toma as she looked into two pairs of demonic eyes. Malitae and Malum. Her bow drawn, arrow notched. She was prepared to take at least one of them down with her. Seemingly, they knew it—and neither dared challenge her.

"What do you say, Brother? Shall we leave them and go have some fun?" charmed Malum, emitting a fizzing vibration as he transformed into a dark orb, tearing toward the soldiers. Malitae followed suit, the two orbs dancing through the valley, plunging into any soldier they could find.

"Toma, you must go. You cannot let them win. *Please* do not let them win!" Keryx said through a weak voice, still kneeling—still enslaved by the electrified bracelets.

"Stay with Keryx, Pete!" Toma yelled, folding into an orb. Her orb plowed through a row of Minotaur, giving chase to soldiers up the ridge. She unfolded, transforming into a bear—enraged and charging headlong into another group of Minotaur. Swiping, clawing, mauling any Minotaur she could find—sending terrified monsters running for cover. Another charged and was met with her massive paw. It tumbled to the ground. She stood on its chest, pinning it down while the horned beast roared, neck muscles flexing and torqueing as she ripped and tore its throat until its roar became a wheezing gurgle.

Toma transformed into her human form mid-flight, landing running toward a Minotaur. She pulled a dagger, ducking under a swinging axe—slashing behind the beast's fury leg. The acute sound of tendons popping was quickly drowned out by the great roar that followed, as the beast dropped to one leg. She plunged her dagger into its chest. Quickly pulling the dagger and slashing the beast's neck. Red liquid bursting from its jugular, spurring through the choking beast's fingers as it failed to plug the gash.

Another Minotaur charged. Red, glowing eyes. Spittle flying. Horns lowered, ready to strike. She pulled her bow. Notched an arrow. Her aim was accurate and true. The beast crashed into the rocky earth. She made sure the beast was down for good—firing an arrow into its chest as she ran past.

Another arrow. Sailing. Striking a Minotaur in the chest.

Another arrow. *True. Fast. Accurate.* A direct hit, snapping a Minotaur's lifeless head back before crashing to the ground—an arrow protruding between the eyes.

Running. Toward the Minotaur army.

Toma notched another arrow, raising the bow to find a target, aiming to fire—across the field, she spotted a red glowing eye. *Perfect target.*

A searing pain on the back of her head. Her chin scraped the ground. The gritty taste of dirt. The dewy smell of trampled grass.

A Minotaur stood over her, brandishing a club. She never heard it approach.

She reached for her bow. Tried to notch an arrow. Her equilibrium off. Ears ringing. Red liquid flowed from her head. Her fingers slipped, dropping the arrow.

A sinister snort. Vapor shot from its nose. The Minotaur raised its club, readying to strike again. Rearing back to maximize force. The death blow. She raised her bow to try and deflect it.

The Minotaur swung. The giant club closed in on her. She shut her eyes, bracing for contact, preparing for death.

She had fought well, had given her best. She chanted her death song.

But then there was a strange noise. The fluttering of wings and a high pitched squeal.

She opened her eyes. The Minotaur was gone. She rolled to her stomach and propped herself up from the dirt.

She saw a giant eagle flying with the Minotaur hanging from its talons.

"Thank you, Brother," she whispered.

An outstretched hand. *Tanoshi.*

He helped her up, re-entering the battle. A cannon boomed, sending black smoke lurching across the valley.

"The General! His soldiers made it to the ridge!" Another cannon. Then another. Deadly cannon fire. Beasts pulverizing above them.

Arrow after arrow. Precise. Accurate. Deadly. Dropping Minotaur after Minotaur. Tanoshi swung his katanas, the blades singing in the wind. Minotaur body parts flew. Toma watched in awe as he dissected them with surgical precision.

When Tanoshi was done with the Minotaur, he burst into an orb and shot toward the Catphylon.

He hovered above a winged creature. Unfolding into his human form and landing on its scaly back. He drew his katana blades and plunged them deep into the creature's backside. There was a piercing screech as the Catphylon turned to dust.

His orb burst from the coal-colored dust cloud that was the cat monster and chased down another.

Toma spotted a dark orb dart overhead, leaving vapor trails in its wake.

The tides of war were changing—but the twins were still out there.

THE LOYAL AID

GENERAL HICKMAN'S MEN ASSUMED POSITIONS on the ridge. Pete looked on as they wheeled cannons into position to a clear vantage point of the valley, with a cement wall in front of them. The army clamored as they readied for a fight.

"Fire!" General Hickman yelled.

Muskets clattered. Cannons roared. Revolvers recoiled.

Blue uniforms. Grey uniforms. Fighting together. General Hickman fully in command of the ridge: the high ground behind the cement wall.

"Reload!" Musket rods clanked and clamored as they rammed loads into their rifles. *"Take aim! Fire!"*

Smoke lurched from the rifles and cannons as minié balls surged through the air, raining down on the Minotaur army. They jerked and flopped as they were hit with round after round.

Catphylon took note and dove toward General Hickman's men, disrupting their firing abilities. Pete looked on as the soldiers braced for the dive-bombing creatures.

"Here they come!"

"Hit the deck!"

Pete heard the howling scream of a soldier as he was plucked from the ground and flown away, only to be ripped apart. A tail whip sent a unit of men flying. A cannon fired, sending a ball flying over soldiers' heads, catching a Catphlyon mid-flight.

Minotaur charged up the hill. General Hickman regrouped his men, giving orders. *That sound.* Pete had heard it before. That awful primal scream. *The Rebel Yell.* This time soldiers on both sides screamed in terror, preparing to protect their *reason.*

"Prepare for a charge! Fix bayonets!"

"Fire!"

Muskets recoiled as minié balls shot forward. A Minotaur grunted as it went down. Another ran past it, charging toward the cement wall. Red eyes. Red, hideous, glowing eyes.

"Reload! Faster! Faster!"

"Fire!"

Another Minotaur down. More charging. Frothing. Spittle spraying from their nostrils.

Another cannon roared. The shell flung forward striking the ground in front of a Minotaur. The ball crashed into the rocky earth and ricocheted over the charging beast. Musket fire.

"Here they come!"

Horns popped over the cement wall. They fired a wall of musket balls at the beast—a roar followed as it collapsed, along with a dull crash as it hit the earth. Dust sprung in the air. Loose pieces of rock fell to the ground.

"They're trying to break through the wall!"

"It's not going to hold much longer!"

A lead Minotaur charged, smashing through the cement. Several Minotaur were behind it.

An ear-piercing roar. Hooves pawing at the ground. Snorting.

"Retreat!" commanded General Hickman.

Soldiers scattering as a Minotaur charged, mowing stragglers down with its club. A man on a horse. A large man, seemingly dwarfing his horse.

"No retreat!" he yelled. *Jerald.*

"Charge!"

Soldiers turned, following him to charge the horned beasts. Pairs of red blazing eyes. Glowing. Flaming. Bouncing toward them.

Jerald was separated from General Hickman in the battle. He drew his saber and spurred his horse, which attempted to rear but could not due to the crushing weight of its rider. The horse sprang into action, Jerald charged the lead Minotaur. Retreating soldiers turned around—*charging with him.*

His horse panted and grunted under his weight as it dashed forward, smashing into the lead Minotaur.

Jerald the loyal, ever-conniving aid, was vaporized.

"Charge!"

A bugle sounded. Hundreds of spirit soldiers charged the Minotaur. Mouths gaping. Grey tattered uniforms. Shoeless men. Auras worn from years of fighting. Blue uniforms. Polished brass. Boys, some not old enough to grow facial hair. *All* were charging. Clubs swinging. Axes chopping. Bayonets plunging. The soldiers cheered as the last Minotaur fell. Bugles played. Drums tapped. A cannon roared in celebration.

BRINGING DOWN THE DRAGONS

TOMA'S ARROW PLUNGED THROUGH THE heart of the last Minotaur as it wriggled in pain before it disintegrated.

"What's our plan?" asked General Hickman.

"Our portals are completely exposed!" said Toma.

"We'll never make it to the portals. The Catphylon—" General Hickman looked to the flying beasts that shrieked and squawked overhead.

"Then we bring them down," Toma declared.

Tanoshi, Toma, and Khoana Chayton encircled the ground troops as a defense measure, leaving the only option for an attack—*from straight above*. This concentrated the creatures into a smaller space, making it easier for Toma to target creatures with her arrows.

She fired an arrow, striking a Catphylon in the shoulder. It buckled but stayed adrift.

"I'm running out of arrows," Toma said.

"Can you and Tanoshi hold them off?" asked Khoana Chayton.

"I think so, Brother!"

He burst into an eagle and took flight soaring above the Catphylon. Diving, sinking his talons into a scaly back. The creatures roared and gave chase.

"We need to do something or they are going to catch your brother!" said Tanoshi.

"Perhaps we can be of help," said General Hickman.

"What do you have in mind, General?" asked Toma.

"Signal your brother to fly past our men. We'll fire every cannon we have at those things," he said.

Tanoshi stepped toward the General, firmly gripping his sword. "Toma—you should join the cannons in the rear with your arrows. General, place infantry in the front and cavalry on the sides. I will stay on the front line and help hold the formations together. If any of the Catphylon decide to drop down and fight, I will deal with them."

"That's a good plan. Form the men up. I have another idea to create a diversion and draw those things in closer," said General Hickman.

"Infantry ready?" yelled General Hickman.

"Yes, sir!" roared the infantry.

"Toma, ready?" yelled General Hickman, and Toma let out a fierce battle cry in response.

"Cannoniers, ready?" yelled General Hickman.

"Yes, sir!" yelled the cannoniers.

"Signal Khoana Chayton!" he ordered.

Toma produced a stone from her necklace. It was a shiny, glowing stone the color of a vibrant emerald. She chanted a few words, held up the stone, and a beacon erupted into the sky. She held the stone high, chanting.

"He sees it!" yelled General Hickman.

"He's coming this way!" said Sergeant Wagner.

They watched as the large eagle soared, turning with outstretched wings, now aiming for the beacon. Wings as long as a school bus flapped vigorously, trying desperately to stay ahead of several winged creatures. Dark jaguar heads snarled and squawked, leathery wings flapping, nipping at his tail feathers with dagger-like fangs. He was drawing close to the beacon. A creature drew closer within striking distance.

"Khoana is out of breath! We have to go now!" shouted Toma.

"Take aim!" commanded the General.

Dozens of creatures began tracking behind Khoana Chayton, waiting for their opportunity to assault.

"They are going to catch him!" yelled Toma.

A squeal. An ear-piercing squeal. The beast buckled and reared before crashing to the ground. Its leathery wings mangled and twisted. Its legs twitched before falling still. An arrow protruding from its neck. *Toma's deadly arrow.*

Another flying beast assumed the position of the lead, flying directly above Toma, its claws outstretched. The giant eagle screeched as if knowing its fate. Another screech.

"FIRE! FIRE! FIRE!" yelled General Hickman.

Every arrow, every rifle, every canon round exploded into the air. A wall of projectiles flew. The giant eagle turned, large leathery wings flapping. *Attempted* to turn. Their heavy, leathery wings tangled together. Fighting, clawing, and gnashing teeth to free themselves.

A wall of minié balls, arrows, and cannon rounds closing the distance, smashing into them, disintegrating them as the projectiles pierced their bodies.

Soldiers cheered. That Rebel yell. The Union soldiers lent their own voices. Grey uniforms. Blue uniforms. All fought together, shouting together.

"Well done, soldiers!" said General Hickman.

There was only one Catphylon left circling the battle formation, screaming at the infantry below. Soldiers fired their weapons, but the creature was flying out of range.

The scream of an eagle. That only could mean one thing.

Soldiers cheered and howled in joy as an eagle appeared from the clouds. Its massive wings held it aloft as it circled high above the last remaining creature.

Khoana Chayton shot down from the sky, tearing into the last Catphylon with its large talons. The flying beast wriggled out of the eagle's grip and swung its large reptilian tail around, striking him from the sky. Khoana was broken. He made no attempt to flap his wings. The eagle spiraled into a steep descent, transforming back into his human form.

"NO!" Toma yelled, abandoning all caution rushing to him.

More cannon fire erupted in the background, and Toma turned to see the last Catphylon wings tucked back, tumbling headlong toward the earth. It was dead before even crashing into a nearby hill. Two dark orbs screamed across the battlefield.

EDVARARD

THE VALLEY WAS QUIET. A mild breeze washed over, leaves gently dancing among trees, tall grasses rocking calmly back and forth, sending feathery seeds blowing in the wind and landing among the ripped terrain where, moments ago, a battle raged.

Pete watched the last remnants of the sun retreat for the evening, replaced by a moon so bright it illuminated the battlefield. It would have been a beautiful sight to see on any other night. Perhaps he might've found himself a hillside and admired this moon—thinking of Jessica, and what life might have been, until this bright moon relinquished control back to the sun. On any other night.

For in this moment, he needed to find a way to free a strange and powerful spirit from the bounds and shackles of two demonic beings. In this moment, he needed to protect life as he knew it. Preserve a world around his loving Jessica that he knew she did not understand. Preserve a world around her that he not yet understood.

"I don't know how to remove these bracelets," said Pete as he tugged and pulled on the shackles binding Keryx, so weak he could not even provide Pete with instruction. Though he tried many times, only a weak whisper would come out.

A sudden rustling sound caused Pete to whirl around as he watched Joe and Josh emerge from the trees. Behind them was Edvarard—the loyal Guardian—an injured arm tucked into his body, his chest plate removed, revealing an undergarment soaked in blood. His shield was gone and some heavy armor removed, but he was still wearing his great helm, the blade of his sword dragged in the rocky earth behind him—his hand gripping the sword loosely, barely hanging on. Every step slow, arduous, laborious—but unwavering in his intent to stay and protect Josh.

"Keryx!" yelled Joe as he traveled closer. "My heavens, what's happened to him?"

"The Others . . . They clasped this bracelet onto him. I cannot remove it," said Pete.

They turned to find Edvarard dropping to one knee, but motioning them with vigor, trying to communicate. The more he tried to motion, the weaker he seemingly became, dropping to an elbow.

"Bring me to him." Keryx coughed and choked with what seemed to be his last bit of strength as Pete and Joe helped him to his feet.

Edvarard lay on his back, still, arms at his side. Pete watched as Keryx collapsed to his knees, taking the knight's hand in his. A tear flowed down his cheek, landing on Edvarard's chest.

"I'm sorry, brother. I'm so sorry."

"Is there anything we can do?" asked Pete. "Tell us—tell us what we can do!"

"I'm afraid he's gone," whispered Joe.

Keryx was still. Silent. Tears flowing and pooling, each landing with a patter—thinning the dried, crusty blood on Edvarard's stained garment. The quiet stillness of the valley was broken by sounds of cannon fire.

Pete's eyes rose to meet two black orbs screaming toward them, with two bright orbs following.

CLASH

THE FULL MOON SETTLED, ILLUMINATING the valley. The soldiers' orbs became more pronounced as darkness settled in. All across the ridge, auras blinked and flickered like fireflies in the night. On any other night, Pete would've paused to admire the sight. But with two dark orbs bearing down on them, he readied himself.

Keryx stood with all of his might under the crushing weight of his electrified chains as the twins orbs hovered, gyrating and pulsing in front of him. They opened up, Malitae and Malum unfolding and taking their human-like form—with Tanoshi and Toma's orbs crashing into the earth behind them, unfolding into their human shapes, emerging from plumes of dust.

"Sorry for interrupting," Malum snickered, his eyes fixed on the dead knight lying with blood-soaked undergarments, relishing in Edvarard's death. "Such a touching moment. I see you're leaving his helmet on. Don't want to show the world what we did to him in our last battle? Don't want to reveal his hideous face?"

"Get behind me," Keryx said through a raspy voice, the chains on his wrist clanking, sapping his strength.

The twins surveyed them through red glowing eyes before moving forward. Their movements so jerky, twitchy, not human. "Well now, *this* is a surprise. Keryx and the boy in one place. Hand-delivered for our taking," hissed Malitae.

"You can have me, but you cannot have the boy. That was the deal," Keryx snapped through a scratchy voice with what little energy he could muster.

"Stand back," commanded Toma, traveling toward them, bow drawn, arrow notched. Aiming at the back of Malitae's head. Tanoshi moved in silence—the sound of his katana raking against its sheath as he pulled the blade speaking for him.

"Stand down, Tanoshi. Do *not* engage," Keryx ordered.

"Poor Tanoshi. All he wants to do is fight . . . but so many constraints.

Join our side, and you can fight all you want," said Malitae.

He stood obedient, katana in hand but arms at his side, blade pointed toward the ground.

"Standing there. Powerless. Poor, poor Tanoshi. Wanting so badly to kill me. Remembering what I did to your family. Your wife. What was her name, again? And those little children. Food for my Cerberus. My two-headed dog guarding the gates made short work of them. He still plays with their bones in his lair."

Tanoshi sprang. He raised both katana blades, so sharp they sliced the air as he swung toward Malitae who dodged them with ease.

"You're slowing in your old age, Tanoshi. It's a disgrace what you've become," said Malitae.

Tanoshi spun his blades, raking close to Malitae's neck.

"Close . . . so very close," said Malitae. "The line between success and *failure* can be very thin indeed." He held his hand to his face, touching just below his eye. "Are you trying to give me another scar?"

Tanoshi sprang once again, swords drawn—aimed for Malitae.

"He has the drop on him!" said Pete, as he watched Malitae freeze, likely caught by Tanoshi's quickness. Tanoshi rearing back, ready to plunge the swords deep. Twist the handles. Slice organs. Break ribs. Bring Malitae the utmost pain. Revenge for killing his family. There would be no escaping his lethal blades. Pete saw Malitae's eyes widen in terror. A sudden movement in the corner of his eye caught his attention. It's then when he knew Malitae's eyes weren't widening with terror, but with surprise, as he clearly saw it first . . .

Tanoshi's eyes were fixed on Malitae, his body reared back ready to uncoil, plunging his blades— *and subsequently leaving him completely exposed.*

"Tanoshi! No!" yelled Toma, releasing an arrow that flew past Malum's black orb as it closed the gap, smashing so viciously into Tanoshi that he crashed into the earth, sending rock flying.

"Tanoshi!" yelled Keryx, trying desperately to help Tanoshi to his feet. He was badly injured, motioning to Keryx to leave him there. "Tanoshi. I'm *sorry*, my dear friend. I should've listened"

Pete looked on, Tanoshi desperately gasped for air—lips moving as he tried to find words. Keryx knelt beside Tanoshi, one of his longest friends, and gripped hands. "It's okay, Tanoshi. Just rest," said Keryx.

"Master. The portals," he choked, concerned about guarding the portals until the very end.

"Rest, Tanoshi. Take a breath," Keryx said: a final order.

Tanoshi obeyed. His chest expanded as he took in air. It was the last breathe he would take. Loyal, obedient Tanoshi was dead.

GENERAL HICKMAN
ROUNDS UP THE TROOPS

"THE DARK ORBS ARE HEADED for the portals!" yelled General Hickman.

They were situated in the valley below, their troops still reeling from being attacked from the dark orbs.

"What are your orders, sir?" asked Sergeant Wagner.

General Hickman addressed the men. "You've all fought bravely today against an evil we did not know existed." The soldiers were utterly quiet, still reeling from the battle. "What we've seen here today . . ."

He stopped to collect himself.

"What we've seen here today must be stopped, or your great-great-great-grandchildren alive today, and the next generations after them, will suffer at the hands of these demons!" His voice echoed through the valley below reverberating off the hillsides. "What you've done here today, very few have accomplished in their entire lifetime—and I'm asking you to do it *one more time*."

He raised his sword and the troops erupted in cheers. He lowered his sword deliberately and the soldiers came to a silence. "Be brave just once more!"

The soldiers erupted. Grey uniforms. Bare feet. Starving. Blue uniforms. Brass polished knobs. Bayonets fixed. Savers pulled. Ready to fight. Together.

"*Charge!*"

RETURN

A TEAR POOLED IN KERYX'S eye before it fell to the ground, caking into the dry soil.

The tear formed at the sight of General Hickman and his brave soldiers. Charging toward them. No match for Malitae or Malum. But they charged. Into the fire.

"Well, well, well—what do we have here? It looks like those soldiers still have something left in them," said Malitae as he watched the army rushing across the valley. "Touching, isn't it?"

The Rebel yell. That horrific, primal yell. Men screaming, knowing they are about to die.

"You are not to touch them. That is part of the deal. The remaining soldiers are to enter our portals unharmed in exchange for me!" said Keryx.

"You really believed we would honor that deal?" said Malitae. "Now that you are captured, who will stop us? As soon as we put you in our portal, we will kill these soldiers and make the boy our prisoner. Looks like I get to play a bit more. I'll be right back to deal with you later."

He folded into an orb. Something flashed. Malitae buckled. He let out a hideous, animalistic screech. His serpent tongue dangling from his drooling mouth. Feathers of an arrow protruding from his back. *Toma.*

It wasn't until he turned that Keryx realized just how devastating the injury was. The arrow tip protruded from his abdomen. He held the shaft with two hands.

"Toma!" Malitae snarled. "You've made a big mistake."

His screech was a reptilian hiss as he tore the arrow from his body. Toma notched another arrow as he traveled toward her.

"Brother!" yelled Malum, forming a dark orb and shooting toward Toma. She turned to fire an arrow at Malum, but Keryx knew he was too fast. Even if he could intervene, there was no time. Malum would be on her before he could help. If Malum hit her, it would be devastating. She dropped to one knee and aimed. If she missed, he would have to lay her next to her brother's body. She was their only hope in stopping them.

"Toma, please. Aim true," Pete heard Keryx say.

He watched her drop to one knee, aim, and release an arrow.

The snap of her bow sang as the string lurched forward, releasing an arrow plunging toward the shooting orb. For a split second, Pete thought she missed, then the orb crashed into the earth—bouncing three times before unfolding. He stood, grunting as he defiantly tore her arrow from his chest. The red blood Pete saw flow from both Malum's nostrils was enough to make him cringe, and indicated the vicious demon was badly wounded.

Pete caught Keryx's eye as he traveled toward them. He didn't have telepathy, but he understood the expression on his face, which said: *Pete, get out of here, now! It's too dangerous.*

"You may be right Keryx, but what have I got to lose?" he said.

A rush of helplessness came over him as he watched Malum draw near. He knew Malum would want a fight, yet he knew Keryx—the honorable spirit he was—could not enter the war. Even if he wanted to, the bracelets placed on him by the twins seemed to make it difficult for him to so much as even lift his arms, let alone fight. Keryx was a sitting target, and if Malum wanted to form an orb and burst through him, he knew he could.

"I've waited a long time for this," said Malum as he stalked Keryx, eyeing him like prey. "I was going to take you to my superiors, but I think I'll end you myself. Right here. Now."

"You don't need to do this," said Keryx, his purple cloak snapping in the wind. "There's still time to negotiate. Form a new treaty."

"Treaties. Agreements. Orders of the Realm," hissed Malum, a forked tongue rolling out of his mouth flickering mere inches from Keryx. "I have in my possession the Mighty Keryx. It's over. Can't you see it?"

"The only thing that is over is *you*, if you dare take another step!" Pete heard the string on Toma's bow stretching as she held it pulled back—a deadly arrow notched as she stepped into view.

"*Toma,*" hissed Malum, baring his sharp fangs. "I think I'll have you for lunch when I'm done with your precious *Master.*"

"Leave now, while you still can," commanded Toma.

"Or what? You think I'm afraid of your puny arrows? Don't you see what I just did? I ripped your arrow from my body. Broke it in two. Go ahead. Fire another arrow. Then, I'll show you how it's really done when I twist your head from your body!"

"Toma, lower the bow. Let's just talk this over," said Malitae drawing near.

"Get back!" she aimed the arrow at him, then toward Malum. Then toward Malitae. They were closing on her, slowly. She stepped backward trying to create distance between them.

Pete watched as Keryx snuck behind the twins as they argued. their attention on Toma, Malum didn't see Keryx silently trailing them—and with the last bit of energy he had left, Pete saw Keryx find the strength to wrap his chains around Malum's neck.

"*Now*, Toma!" he yelled spinning Malum around. Her arrow found its mark, bursting through his chest. Keryx let him fall to the ground, writhing in pain.

"You don't know what you've done!" shrieked Malum, writhing, blood seeping between his fingers as he gripped the arrow. "You don't know what you're dealing with! My superiors—they will—" He paused to pick himself off the ground. Blood pouring from his nostrils, splattering in the dusty soil. His knees were wobbly as he found the strength to stand. Choking. Spitting blood. Hovering over Keryx. "I'm no longer going to capture you. I'm going to *decapitate* you. Send pieces of your body parts all over the universe as a warning to all not to go against us."

Claws grew from dark scaly hands. Eyes glowed red. His fancy suit tore away as a large, armored, scaly body emerged with an elongated snout and rows of terrible teeth. A tail drug behind it—enough to terrify Pete as he anxiously looked on, knowing he was no match for Malum.

"The first thing I'm going to do is rip out your heart. Show it to you while it's still beating," said Malum, with Malitae circling, but maintaining his human form—ready to join.

Keryx knelt to the ground, holding his arms in a defensive position. His cloak draping sadly off his body—and for the first time, Pete saw him as vulnerable. He knew the secondary attack would be much worse. Claws would sink deeply into his torso. Fangs would dip into the soft flesh of his neck. A slurping as blood would leave Keryx's body as Malum sucked his veins dry. The hideous lizard creature Malum shifted into would be the last thing he would see, and Pete had no way to stop it.

He locked eyes with Keryx, who motioned to something at his feet. His aura brightened and flashed wildly in excitement when he saw it. It was

Edvarard's broadsword!

Pick it up, Stanton! he thought as he keeled over and swiped at the sword. It was no use. His hand passed through and couldn't grip it.

He heard a scuffle behind him and didn't have to turn to know the attack was beginning. The creature would tear Keryx apart if he didn't do something quick.

He thought of Jessica. The children he always wanted, but never told her about. He thought of the moment just before the car crash when he had told her he loved her, but she did not hear. The vase he pushed off the dresser, Jessica screaming when she found it. He thought of the cook who was trying to kill Jessica for her research—and Jerome who was murdered for it.

If I fail now, I fail them all, he thought, a surge jolted through his body as his hand made contact with the sword, like the handle grip had suddenly become married to his hand.

In one motion, he swung—a sharp whistling sound cut the air, striking Keryx's chains and breaking them in two.

Right in front of the lizard creature who stood before him. The creature pulsated as it shifted. Suddenly, Malum appeared dressed in his sharp suit, hair slicked back—but something was different. His shirt was soaked in blood. He choked and gurgled and spit red blood in disbelief.

"That's *impossible!*" yelled Malum. "No one can pick up Edvarard's sword!"

"Except a spirit who can move objects," said Keryx. "Or maybe you missed that part of the rules."

Pete thrust the sword toward the sky. Keryx raised his fist and a clash of thunder erupted. A lightning bolt exploded into the broadsword, flashing three times before evaporating into the sky.

"Impossible! Keryx, your aura! It's glowing!" Malum hissed.

The familiar whistling sound of the broadsword sang as he swung, swiping through Malum's terrified look—wide-eyed, permanently etched on his face as his head stayed upright for a moment but lopped off. His body remained suspended, as if it were trying to re-grow another head.

"Finish him, Pete!" cried Toma.

He turned into an orb and shot through Malum's body. A *devastating* blow. Blood sprayed through the air. Scraps of Malum's black suit blew in the wind. A metal ring rested in the grass next to his severed head—the only evidence that he had ever existed.

"Brother! No!" yelled Malitae.

Another one of Toma's arrows found its mark, piercing through Malitae's shoulder. Another pierced his thigh.

"Brother!" He continued, charging toward them—ripping out arrow after arrow. Malitae continued walking toward his brother's dust pile. Toma fired another arrow, striking him in the opposite shoulder.

"As long as I am alive, none of you are safe!" screamed Malitae. Tearing the arrow from his body, he charged toward them, eyes reddening with rage.

"FIRE! FIRE! FIRE!"

A voice rang out in the valley below. A bugle sounded. Rifle fire cracked. Thumping roars of cannon fire. General Hickman's army, sent a wall of minié balls and heavy lead balls toward Malitae.

Toma fired another arrow.

Malitae appeared panicked as a wave of projectiles flew. Cannon rounds. Musket balls. Toma's arrows. A wall flying toward him. Every musket round and every cannonball from General Hickman's army.

He quickly made a motion opening up a dark portal.

"None of you are safe!" he said before forming a dark obsidian orb, shooting into the portal, closing just before the wave of projectiles hit him.

The portal closed behind him—and he was gone.

The battlefield was silent for the first time since the battle began between the Union and Confederates.

AFTERMATH

THE VALLEY ONCE AGAIN FELL silent. No one spoke. Not Keryx or Toma, not Pete, not the General and his soldiers. Skeptical of the silence, Pete expected at any moment a portal to open up and release hideous winged creatures or horned beasts.

"It's over . . . for now," assured Keryx, an energy field radiating around him.

Joe and Josh emerged from the safety of the trees once more, but kept a timid distance, making sure all was clear.

"Come on out," said Keryx, prompting a slow saunter from Josh. Pete wondered if the boy would ever be the same as he and Joe strolled up. "It's over."

"We're leaving, I need to get the boy back to his father," Joe barked.

"We need the boy to do one last thing," said Keryx.

The General's grey spotted horse brayed as he approached, Sergeant Wagner riding at his side.

"General Hickman—won't you join us?"

General Hickman sat proudly atop his gleaming white horse, his grey uniform displaying patches and insignia of his status. His neatly trimmed beard and shiny leather boots a far cry from many of his trail-beaten men. He and Sergeant Wagner saluted, chest out, elbows perfectly straight.

"Your men fought well today, General. The Order thanks you," said Keryx.

"Thank you, Master," he replied.

"I have but one more request of you," said Keryx. "Convince your soldiers to lay their weapons down and enter our portals."

"My men . . . What about their *reason?*" the General replied.

"Your *cause* is over. You have a new *reason,*" said Keryx.

"Ah yes, a new *reason* . . . You see, most of these men stayed behind to fight for something they believed in, fighting eternally against those who destroyed our bodies in battle, but these men . . . their true *reason* is their leg-

367

acy. You see, most of their photos have come down off walls. Their uniforms tossed away. Their medals sold. These men are being forgotten."

"Josh, step forward," ordered Keryx.

The grass made a squelching sound as Josh walked across the dewy ground. "Yes, Master?"

"I need your help. You see, these soldiers are at great risk of becoming sick. By now, you've seen what happens when a spirit becomes sick."

"Yes, The Others show up and take them," said Josh.

"I don't see what this has to do with my grandson," Joe barked.

"Allow me to explain?" Keryx said calmly.

"Fine," said Joe.

"Josh, here, is the only one who can help these soldiers be remembered," said Keryx, prompting a gasp from the General.

"He could deliver our memories to our loved ones. My great-great granddaughter would know who I am," said General Hickman.

"That's right, General . . . and the great-great grandchildren of these fine soldiers under your command would hear their stories as well," said Keryx.

"Do you realize what you're asking? There are tens of thousands of soldiers up on that ridge! What you're proposing is Josh send a memory to each one of their surviving families? He's only a boy. That would take him nearly his entire life to accomplish!" said Joe.

"And that is why it's Josh's decision," said Keryx, turning to Josh. "Son, this is a big job, but an important one. The fate of all of these soldiers up on the ridge is in your hands."

"I'll do it!" said Josh.

"Joshua Morton, do you know what you're agreeing to?" snarled Joe.

"I do, Grandpa. I'm saving these men."

"Good boy," said Keryx. "General Hickman. The terms are set. Josh will take one request from each of the men and deliver it to one of the living—in exchange, your men enter the portals."

The sight of Sergeant Wagner's yellow, jagged teeth piercing his scraggly beard reminded Pete of when he had first come across him on that ridge. The world seemed so much simpler then . . .

Suddenly, Pete felt himself accept his fate. He was dead. There was no going back to Jessica. In that moment, he surrendered himself to the unknown. Whatever may come.

"The Sergeant and I agree to the terms. We'll begin collecting the men and march them to the portals," said General Hickman.

A great sense of relief came over Pete. He found the General to be a good man and wanted him to be saved from The Others. He thought it would not be difficult for the General to convince the soldiers, for he had seen both Grey and Blue unite, now mixed together on the ridge—the peace between them firmly holding.

Cheers could be heard across the valley as soldiers rejoiced at the news they'd be giving a last request. A second cheer erupted, a cannon fired. Rifle fire crackled.

"They must've received the news they're getting a portal," said Pete.

"They'll be marching this way—just over this ridge there are hundreds or portals waiting for them," said Keryx. He turned to Josh, Pete noticing a profound admiration as Keryx gazed upon the boy. "Josh, each Gatekeeper will be taking the soldiers' requests, recording them. When the last soldier enters, the requests will be given to you and your work will begin."

"I still don't have a good feeling about this, but I'm proud of you, Josh. What you're doing here . . . you're making an old man proud," said Joe.

"Josh, would you come with me to the ridge? It will make the soldiers more at ease if you're visible," said Keryx.

Josh glanced at Joe as if silently asking for guidance before his grandfather gave a reassuring nod. "Go on, son. I'll be right behind you," he said. Joe's dimming aura showed his contention.

"He'll be okay," said Pete, trying to console him.

"Do you think so? I worry I made the wrong choice bringing him here," said Joe.

Watching Josh move off with Keryx, Joe had a sudden conflict. Had he guided Josh to make the right decision? What if he never introduced Josh to LADO. Maybe they'd never be in this mess, but what if he hadn't? Perhaps The Others would eventually find Josh, and what then?

"What else could you have done? The Others had found him. I've seen firsthand what they are capable of," said Pete.

"Thank you," said Joe.

They watched as the valley lit up with soldiers marching toward the ridge. Their auras turned bright and healthy, illuminating the valley.

"Do you think you would have done anything differently?" asked Joe.

"Pardon? I don't understand," said Pete.

"Back when you were living—if you knew all this was going on all around us—would you have done anything differently?"

Pete thought of Jessica and how badly he had wanted a family. Then an entirely new thought crept into his mind. What if he had children? What then? He still could've gotten in that car accident, or taken a bad fall—one thing he'd learned in all this was fate had a strange way of working. He couldn't shake the thought of having children and dying while they were young.

"No, I wouldn't change a thing," he replied.

"Yeah. I hear you. I wouldn't have changed a thing," said Joe. "But maybe my answer would be different if I hadn't got to spend time with Josh while he grew up."

"There's a lot of us who would give anything for something like that," said Pete. "To spend just another night with my wife, Jessica. What you got to experience with Josh is really special."

"He's doing something good, isn't he?"

"He sure is," said Pete.

"Come on, let's go find them," said Joe.

"You go on ahead. I'll join you in a few," said Pete.

"Are you sure?" asked Joe.

"I don't want to intrude. You should share this special moment with the boy. I'll find you in a little while," said Pete.

"Thank you, Pete," said Joe.

FINDING TOMA

IT WAS EASY TO GET caught in the excitement of the soldiers marching toward their portals. Cheering men—the overall morale elevated to levels Pete had not seen. But he wasn't interested in the soldiers. There was a puff of white smoke raising above the valley, which signaled one thing. *Toma.*

When he caught up to her, she was hovering over three bodies. Her brother Khoana Chayton, Tanoshi, and Edvarard. She had lit a fire, flames shooting as tall as a man, as she performed a ceremony in their honor. He looked on, observing from a distance. He watched her dance around the fire, chanting, spinning, chanting—*when she saw him.*

He began to move away when she motioned him forward.

"I'm sorry, I shouldn't be here," he said, trying respectfully not to look directly at the bodies.

"I may not be alive today had it not been for you. You fought with us. You are one of us," she said.

"I, uh—I'm sorry. I'm just an attorney. I'm not a warrior," he said.

"Sometimes battle brings out your inner warrior. You do not know it's there until you find it within," she said.

"What do you mean?" asked Pete.

"My brother, Khoana Chayton, and I are of the Lakota nation. I was just fourteen when the blue uniforms showed up. I remember the day I became a warrior. I was outside doing chores when my brother and I received word our father had been killed by General Custer's army. After mourning him for three days, we put on war paint. We painted our ponies. We rode together to avenge our father's death. I was one of the only woman to fight next to Crazy Horse in the Battle of Little Bighorn. My brother and I, we were never seen again. Our bodies still lie somewhere in the Montana plains. My entire family killed at the hands of the soldiers."

"I'm sorry," said Pete. "What will you do now?"

"We will take these bodies with us into the portals, and we will mourn them. One day, I will have my revenge," she said.

"Do you mind if I pay my respects?" he said, motioning to the bodies.

"Please do," she said.

He traveled to Tanoshi, the brave Samurai soldier. His armor removed, except for a cloth undergarment. His katana blades lying sheathed at his feet. Khoana Chayton, the brave Lakota warrior, lying still and at peace. His arms folded across his bare chest. Edvarard, the brave and loyal knight lying next to Khoana Chayton, his armor removed except for his great helm covering his head.

"Will you remove his helmet?" asked Pete.

"He asked that we never remove his great helm," a voice commanded. He turned to see Keryx standing behind him. Observing. Watchful. His eyes were heavy, filled with tears that hadn't fully formed yet. "He was hurt badly in the last battle we had with The Others. Wore this protective armor and vowed never to remove it. He, of all of us, knew the cost to face down The Others. Yet here he was, fighting to his last breath to preserve what he believed in."

"What was that exactly?" asked Pete.

"Humanity," said Keryx.

They shared a solemn moment—paying their last respects. A gentle wind blew across their bodies.

"Come now, Pete. Your presence is requested at the portals," said Keryx.

THE LAST MAN THROUGH THE PORTAL

IT WAS AT THE PORTALS where Pete further realized the gravity of Josh's decision, and his pride grew for the boy. Soldiers all across the ridge were lined up, in joyous formations preparing one-by-one to enter the portals. Music flared up, men struck fires while waiting—dancing barefoot, passing around bottles.

Josh was busy helping a Gatekeeper record a request from a soldier, and Pete decided to listen in.

"I, Jeremiah Longfellow, request that the boy find my long lost relatives: the Longfellow clan that now resides in Alpharetta. Tell them I fought bravely on the battlefield. Let them know there are family heirlooms hidden in the floorboards at our old farm house outside of Atlanta. We hid our personables when we learned Sherman's march was coming our way. The old farmhouse is still standing. I had been trying to signal them all these years, let my living relatives know their family history. Now they'll know, and I thank you, Son."

Standing next to Keryx, Pete watched as a Gatekeeper made a few motions, recording the request before the soldier entered the portal, before General Hickman rode up, his white horse coming to a slow trot as he approached. Sergeant Wagner rode at his side. They both saluted Keryx before trotting toward the boy.

"General, I can't think of another way to honor these men," said Josh.

"I hope you still feel that way several years from now when you've still barely made any progress," said General Hickman.

They paused momentarily out of respect, for in the distance they saw soldiers lining up helping transfer the bodies of Khoana Chayton, Tanoshi, and Edvarard to a portal. Soldiers removed their caps, paying their respects. A cannon fired. A band of soldiers fired the twenty-one gun salute in their honor.

"They fought bravely," said Keryx.

Toma nodded. "Thank you, Master."

"Toma?" A light voice. Not a soldier's voice, but Josh's.

"Yes?" she said turning to him.

"I'm sorry about your brother . . . and Edvarard. I'm going to miss Edva-rard being around. Your brother . . . You all saved us," said Josh.

"Thank you, Josh. It was worth it. You are very important to the order of things. You need to be protected at all costs," she said, removing a necklace and handing it to him. "If you ever get in trouble, there is a crystal inside. Remove it and point it toward the sky. It will signal us."

He wrapped the necklace around his wrist. He remained speechless. Awestruck by her beauty. Thick hair whipping in the wind. Sun-kissed skin.

"Goodbye, Josh," she said. Deadly Toma, with such grace and savagery, entered the portal.

"All soldiers are accounted for?" said General Hickman.

"All except for you and I, sir," said Sergeant Wagner.

"You go first," said the General. "I will be the last soldier off."

"Very well," said Sergeant Wagner. He looked around the battlefield, the calm valley below. So peaceful and still. "I'm going to miss this place, and I'm going to miss roaming the hills of Pennsylvania."

"I realized something today, Sergeant Wagner," said General Hickman.

"What's that, sir?" asked the Sergeant.

"All these years—fighting for our *cause*. It wasn't a wholly good cause. I know that," said General Hickman. "Fighting to preserve our way of life—a way of life that bound and shackled other men. We were wrong about that part, Sergeant."

"We saw something so much bigger today, sir," said the Sergeant.

"Well, you'll get a chance to make it right where you're going," said Keryx. The General saluted. "See you on the other side."

Pete waited for the Sergeant to finish with the General before approaching Sergeant Wagner. "I'm glad you found me wandering those hills, Sergeant."

"A pleasure to have met ya," he replied through crooked yellow teeth.

"Any last requests?" asked Josh.

Sergeant Wagner thought for a moment. "Josh, I want you to tell this story. The story that just unfolded on this battlefield."

"Wait just a minute," said Joe. "Demons. Minotaur. Winged creatures that we can't even explain. What were they called? Catphylon? People will think my grandson is *crazy*."

"Maybe they will," said Sergeant Wagner. "But if even only a few believe him, he will have made the world a better place."

Joe replied, "Absolutely not. It's too risky. That Malitae fella is still out there. Edvarard is no longer protecting him. If my grandson goes around telling people, there will be repercussions."

"Grandpa, the Sergeant is right. People deserve to know," said Josh.

Keryx intervened. "What if we assigned Josh a new guardian? Would that make you comfortable?"

"Well, I suppose so," said Joe. "I've done all I could for Joshua. I can no longer protect him in the way that he needs."

"Very well. I now assign Pete as Josh's guardian and protector," said Keryx. "I'll have to get it approved by our Leadership, but I don't think they'd object."

"Wait—me? A Guardian?" asked Pete. "What is a Guardian, exactly?"

"We are angels of course," said Keryx, handing him something. "We are protectors of the realm."

Pete opened his hand to find a metallic-looking pin, with an insignia written in an language he did not understand. "What is this?" he asked.

"Why, those are your wings, of course," said Keryx. "You didn't think we had actual wings, did you? We'll have to go before Leadership soon for your official *winging.*"

"Leadership? Who are they?" asked Pete, puzzled.

"The archangels. The highest in our order," said Keyrx.

"And who commands the archangels?" asked Pete.

"The Almighty, of course."

Pete was still, looking down at his wings, thinking about his new responsibility. So much about this spirit world he didn't know about. "You really think I'm cut out to be an . . . *angel?*"

"I'm sure I'm not the only one who saw what you did to Malum. He's one of the strongest I've ever faced," said Keryx.

"He was injured," said Pete.

"Even an injured Malum is most formidable. Besides, if Malitae decides to appear, then Josh can use Toma's crystal to summon us." Keryx paused, looking to Josh. "Why don't we see what the boy thinks. Josh?"

"What about my grandpa?" asked Josh.

"I'm afraid your Grandfather is no longer able to protect you. It's time for him to move on," said Keryx.

JOE CROSSES OVER

"MOVE ON?" ASKED JOE. HE saw her as soon as he uttered the words. Black-and-white polka dot dress. Hair tied with a ribbon. Red lipstick. "Kathy!" He barely recognized her. The dress. He remembered the dress. She wore it on their first date. "Kathy! It's really you!"

"Are you ready to join her?" asked Keryx.

"Will my grandson be okay?"

Keryx nodded in assurance.

"Josh . . . it's time for me to go," he said, his aura dimming, giving away his sadness to be leaving him behind.

"I know, Grandpa. Thank you for staying with me all these years," said Josh, a tear pooling and streaming down his face before hitting the ground.

"Hey, buddy. Don't cry," said Joe.

"It's just that I'll miss you, Grandpa! I don't know if I'll be able to do this without you."

"I'll always be with you, son. In *here*." He pointed to Josh's heart.

"Okay," said Josh, but he didn't seem convinced.

"Say goodbye to Pinkie and Cunningham."

"I will," he said.

"Goodbye, Grandson. You've made an old man proud. I'll always love you."

They watched as Joe entered the portal. He turned to wave, fading into a shadowy figure.

And just like that, he was gone.

GENERAL HICKMAN'S TURN

"GENERAL HICKMAN?" THUNDERED KERYX.

"Yes, sir!"

"It's time for us to enter," he said.

He was staring out across the valley.

"We haven't seen the last of them have we?" said the General solemnly.

"I don't suppose we have," said Keryx. "But our treaty is reestablished for now."

"I'm here to serve you, Master," said General Hickman, bowing to Keryx.

"Thank you for your service, General. We'll need help guarding the universe and we can talk about how you can help on the other side," he said.

Keryx took one last look at the empty valley before stopping at the portal entrance. The wind gently blew against the trees. Long grasses bobbed back and forth in the breeze. It was a tranquil quiet valley, as if they had never been there.

"You've done a great thing here, Josh. It will always be remembered. If you need me, just use the crystal," said Keryx. In a blink they were gone. The portals closed.

Just Pete and Josh remained at the battlefield.

TIME TO GO HOME

"HEY! WHAT ARE YOU DOING out there?" Two security guards came up to Josh.

Pete turned into a sphere, readying to spring, but Josh motioned him to stand down.

"The park is closed," said a guard.

"Josh!?" It was Bill. He was with the security guards. "Is that you?"

"Yeah, Dad," he said as a security guard shined a blinding light into his face.

"What are you doing out here all by yourself?" barked Bill.

Josh looked up at Pete, and he glanced back at the security guards. "If I told you, you wouldn't believe me."

"Son, didn't you feel that earthquake?" asked a guard. "Come on. We'll get you back to the hotel. You shouldn't be out here by yourself like this."

"It's a long story, Dad," said Josh riding in the backseat of the car, twenty minutes later.

"Are you okay?" said Bill.

"Yes, I'm okay."

"You're mother hears not a *word* about this, you understand? If she found out I let you out of the hotel room in the middle of the night—"

"Dad, I promise. It stays between us," said Josh.

"Is he with you?" asked Bill as they pulled up to the hotel.

Josh shook his head.

"He's gone, Dad. He left us and went to a better place," said Josh.

"And you saw this happen?" said Bill.

Josh nodded his head. Bill gave Josh a hug but failed to hide the tear that was forming in his eyes. He wiped it away with his sleeve.

"Let's never tell your mother about this, okay?" said Bill.

"Sure thing, Dad. Our secret," said Josh.

"Let's get back to Pittsburgh. We need to meet your mother and Melissa

378

so we can fly home. Hope they enjoyed their time together. If not, Melissa's probably going to dump you when you get back home," Bill snickered.

"Probably not, Dad," said Josh under his breath. "Not after what we've seen together."

The drive to the Pittsburgh airport was a couple hours, and Bill fumbled the radio before finding a local news station. The announcer read: "An earthquake registering 5.7 magnitude hit Gettysburg yesterday. It knocked out windows and activated car alarms in Harrisburg and was felt as far away as Philadelphia. One of the aftershocks registered a whopping 4.8 on the Richter scale."

"That was some earthquake last night, huh?" said Bill. "We don't get those back in Chicago."

Josh paused for a moment. If only his father knew what he'd seen.

Soon enough, he would—he made a promise to Sergeant Wagner that he had to tell the story.

Josh slept as Pete rode in the backseat. The airport was abuzz with weekend travelers. Josh and Bill took their seats about midway in the back of the plane. Josh looked out the window and saw they were sitting next to the wing. Pete's orb flew just outside the plane.

"What are you waving at, son?" asked Bill.

"Oh, nothing" said Josh before settling in and falling asleep.

In the very back row sat a man. An awkward-looking man, with glasses and long brown hair spilling out the sides of his baseball cap, a hard slant to his mouth. There was nothing truly peculiar about him, until a forked tongue rolled out of his mouth and flickered.

THE END

AFTERWORD

"We're gonna miss your grandpa. He was a good man," boomed Cunning-ham.

"Thanks," said Josh. "He was the best."

"Who's this?" chirped Pinkie.

"His name is Pete," said Josh.

"Pete! *Pete*. Why don't ya tell Pete here that he looks like a stiff?" said Pinkie.

"Come on, Pink. Leave the man alone. You don't even know him," said Cunningham.

"You're right! We don't know him! I mean, look at him. Dressed in a suit. Shiny leather shoes. Hair perfectly in place. I knew guys like him. You know what we called them? *Feds*. Cuz Feds dressed like that back in my day."

"Pinkie, he's not law enforcement—he's a *lawyer*," said Cunningham.

"Even worse!" screamed Pinkie.

"Hey, uh, Josh—I didn't wanna say nothin' but where's the big guy?" asked Cunningham.

"Yeah! Edvarard! That big tuna can. Built like a brick firehouse. Where is the big lug? I was just starting to like him!" said Pinkie.

Josh looked at the ground. A tear formed in his eye. A wet spot formed on the carpet.

Pete put his hand on Josh's shoulder and simply shook his head.

"Awe, rats!" said Pinkie. He removed his bowler hat and held it to his chest. "I'm sorry, I didn't mean nothin', kid."

They held a short ceremony for Edvarard. Cunningham said a eulogy that caused them all to have tear-filled eyes. He about popped a suspender when he blew his nose. It didn't take Pinkie long to start quizzing again.

"Say, Josh. Keryx gave you a crystal to contact him whenever?" asked Pinkie.

"Yes," said Josh. "Well, one of his warriors gave it to me. Toma."

"Listen, Keryx promised us portals and we want to talk to him. We thought since things settled down and all we could get a meetin' with him," said Cunningham.

ACKNOWLEDGEMENTS

Writing a book is one of the most challenging, yet truly rewarding things I've ever done. I couldn't have done it without the help of my closest family and friends who listened to me carry on about the story for the past seven years.

To Mom: You are missed. If I had not had the dreams about the afterlife around the time of your passing, Crossing Over would not exist. This book is for you.

To my siblings: Tim, Billy, and Kelly. You know I was always the older protective brother growing up. I'm proud of you and Mom would be too.

To my oldest friends: Dan, Paul, Vic, Brian, Luke, Joe, CJ, Jason, Brad, Megan. Thank you all for supporting me all these years.

To Jill, who spent many an early morning listening to me pontificate on my latest plot hole fix, often at an hour she was not yet awake. I'm convinced we'd still be together if only I would've let you sleep a little longer.

To Clarke and Tripp, who greet me with wonderful curious eyes. The world and it's infinite possibilities is yours for the taking. Always remember you are part of the solution that preserves the world for generations behind you. Either do something memorable, or write something worth remembering. Thanks for allowing me to be your hero.

A VERY SPECIAL THANKS...

To Brad Fruhaff, I came to you after finishing my first draft thinking I was ready to publish. That was at least 7-8 edits ago. There's not a word in the story that hasn't been re-written. Thanks for teaching me your ways. More importantly, thank you for believing in the story.

To Anna Vera, I approached you with a half finished manuscript. You charged me up to power through and finish the project in six months. It is your fantastic creative mind and colossal energy that helped me re-discover my *reason*, and I cherish our new friendship.

TWO MORE...

To Laura, thanks for always believing in me and emphasizing doing the right thing even when no one is watching.

To Trey, Mike, Paige, and Jon: I wrote Crossing Over largely with Ghost - 11/17/97 on repeat. Thanks for making the donuts.

Luke 1:37: "For nothing will be impossible with God."

ABOUT THE AUTHOR

DANIEL FRANK currently lives in Oak Park, IL a sleepy village on the west side of Chicago. When he is not writing, he can be found helping others in his insurance consulting profession, playing with his two children, or hanging out at his local CrossFit gym.